P9-CCZ-781

DANGEROUS AFFAIRS

DANGEROUS AFFAIRS

DIANA MILLER

Montlake
Romance

The characters and events portrayed in this book are fictitious. Any similarity to real persons, living or dead, is coincidental and not intended by the author.

Text copyright © 2012 Diana Miller
All rights reserved.

Printed in the United States of America.

No part of this book may be reproduced, or stored in a retrieval system, or transmitted in any form or by any means, electronic, mechanical, photocopying, recording, or otherwise, without express written permission of the publisher.

Published by Montlake Romance
P.O. Box 400818
Las Vegas, NV 89140

ISBN-13: 9781612186016
ISBN-10: 1612186017

CHAPTER 1

The knife had obviously been there a long time, nestled in the dust bunnies and wood shavings between the walls, in the space one of the two mahogany doors that separated the Victorian-style living room from the *Brady Bunch* decor of the family room usually slid back into. And it was covered with blood.

Abby Langford leaned the broom she'd used to fish out the knife against the wall, then picked the knife off the floor and studied it. Despite the day's warmth and the sunlight streaming through the picture window, a gloomy chill engulfed the room. She could almost feel the steel blade scraping down her spine, raising goose bumps on her shoulders and arms.

This knife had killed someone.

Then she shook herself, dispelling most of the prickly cold. As usual, she was letting her imagination run wild. This wasn't some menacing murder weapon, but an ordinary kitchen knife, with a nine-inch steel blade and a wood handle that looked parched enough to absorb a cup of mineral oil. The blood consisted of a few reddish-brown splotches on the blade, splotches that to her looked too smeared to be rust. It could be old food, though, something like dehydrated ketchup or oxidized chocolate. Or even blood, but from a rare steak, not a human.

Another shiver slithered across Abby's shoulder blades. Because if this were an innocuous kitchen knife, why had someone hidden it so carefully?

"Mommy, what happened to the door?" Maddie asked as she and her black curls bounced across the Persian carpet that covered the living room floor. Her vivid blue eyes were focused on the door, which had slid past its stop and nearly to the other side of the space, exposing the two-inch-wide opening between the walls.

Damn. Abby tried to conceal the knife behind her leg. "I was closing it and pulled too hard." She raised her empty hand and flexed her arm. "I don't know my own strength."

"Where'd you find the knife?"

So much for her hope Maddie hadn't noticed it. Abby pointed to the space the door slid back into. "When the carpenters were installing the doors, someone must have accidentally kicked it in there."

Maddie wasn't looking at the space, but at the knife now dangling at Abby's side. "It's got blood on it."

"It's just rust," Abby said firmly. Mothers of impressionable nine-year-olds weren't allowed to have wild imaginations.

"It could be blood," Maddie persisted. "Should you call the police?"

"Because I found a rusty kitchen knife?" Abby raised the knife to eye level and examined it with exaggerated interest. "You think somebody reported losing it? Maybe there's even a reward."

Maddie rolled her eyes. "Because somebody might have used it for a murder."

"I think you watch too much TV."

"There's no such thing as too much TV."

"You sound like your father. How are the Sims doing?" Computer games were the only things keeping Maddie from turning into a TV addict this summer, not that they were much better.

Maddie wrinkled her upturned nose, the sole feature she'd inherited from her mother. "Not too good. Their kids are causing lots of problems."

"That's what you get for raising them in Hollywood."

"I think they might be moving. OK if I get some lemonade?"

When Abby nodded, Maddie skipped across the brown shag-carpeted family room to the kitchen, the knife apparently forgotten. Which was good, since it was probably nothing, but it was the kind of nothing that could trigger nightmares.

Fortunately Maddie never had nightmares. She always slept soundly, just like her father. Abby's lips compressed into a line so thin her jaw locked. Colin never had any trouble sleeping, which showed how unfair life was. When you considered—

The phone rang before Abby could get going on a really good rant about Colin. She ran into the family room and grabbed the receiver.

"I'm so glad you called," she told Laura Stuart, plopping onto an avocado-colored recliner that no longer reclined. "I was vacuuming out the space behind the doors separating the living and family rooms, and I found a knife."

"You what?" From Laura's shocked tone, her eyes were as wide as Maddie's had been when she'd spotted the knife.

"I found a knife," Abby repeated, setting it onto a walnut coffee table with more bumps and dents than a relief map of Asia.

"Not that," Laura said. "I was talking about the vacuuming part."

Abby made a face. "Scary, isn't it?" She propped her bare feet on the coffee table, beside the knife. "I was using that pointy-nozzle

3

thing to clean the edges of the floor and the tops of the baseboards."

"The woman who considers even the most basic housework cruel and unusual punishment was vacuuming edges and baseboards?"

"Anyway, I was closing the doors and pulled one past its stop. I thought before I pushed it back, I should vacuum the dust between the walls."

"The dust between the walls?" Laura emphasized each word. "You've clearly gone over the edge. I'm on my way."

Abby's lips curved. Laura knew her well.

"I assume the writing's going badly," Laura continued. "Since nothing else would make you so desperate for a diversion you'd be vacuuming edges and baseboards, let alone between walls."

"Going badly would be an improvement, since at least it would be going somewhere."

"Maybe you should have Marissa come to Minnesota to do something more interesting than sell her dead aunt's house," Laura said. "Make her a soap opera star who quits her show and moves back to her hometown to face painful memories from her past. They always say you should write what you know."

Abby's rueful smile held a touch of pain. "I think I'd better wait to find out how that works out in real life before I write about it." To be honest, she wasn't sure she'd ever be ready to open that particular vein for the sake of her art.

"You'll be fine," Laura said firmly. "You already are."

"I hope so," Abby said, then shifted her feet from the table onto the carpet. "I could use some advice about the knife. What should I do with it?"

"What kind of knife is it?"

"An old kitchen knife." Abby picked it up again, this time holding the edges with her shirttail and fingertips. If the knife were important, she'd hate to smear more valuable fingerprints than she already had. "It's got several dark splotches on the blade that could be blood. But I've never heard of anything violent happening in this house."

"I haven't, either," Laura said. "The blood's probably from a cooking injury."

"Then why was the knife stuck between the walls?"

"You wouldn't believe the places things end up in my house." Laura had three energetic kids, two of them boys.

Abby set the knife back on the coffee table. "I don't feel right throwing it away if it could be important. But I hate to call the cops and risk having them label me a hysterical female."

"And risk reading about it in next week's *National Enquirer*," Laura said. "Every time I think about those articles and what Colin got away with—"

"He doesn't get to see his daughter much," Abby interrupted. Laura could rant about Colin even longer than she could.

"Like he cares. Has he called since you moved to Minnesota?"

"I'm sure he's been busy," Abby said, picking at the edge of a strip of duct tape patching one arm of the recliner.

Laura sniffed. "Boffing his TV daughter, no doubt."

"I assume she's gotten too old for him. She must be twenty-one, even though she's always played five years younger on the show." Abby pulled up the tape, exposing yellowed foam. "The last I heard, he'd moved on to an eighteen-year-old who's on *Search for Love*." Talking about Colin's infidelities didn't even sting anymore, thank God. "About the knife…"

"Call Harvey Hancock."

Abby smoothed the tape back over the rip. "Is he still a cop?"

"Going on forty-two years, as he brags every time I see him. He finally took a desk job, so I'll bet he's at the station. He'd never think you're being hysterical."

"Or alert the *Enquirer*." Abby remembered Harvey. When she'd worked at Ruby's Diner, he'd been one of the friendlier regulars, coming in every afternoon for a piece of pie and a cup of coffee. He'd been equally friendly on those frequent occasions when he'd brought her dad home from whatever bar he'd gotten kicked out of.

She'd planned to talk to the Harrington police at some point about her writing—being a lifelong mystery fan didn't make her an authority on police procedure. Harvey would be a terrific resource, and this would be a way to break the ice. And she'd get rid of the knife.

"That's a great idea," Abby said. "I'll talk to Harvey, and then I'll never have to think about it again."

– – –

Josh Kincaid massaged the bridge of his nose with one hand, deleting the e-mail from a so-called "friend" with the other. So his ex-wife and his ex–best friend were now the proud parents of a baby boy. How nice Jennifer had found a man who made enough money to be father material.

He jerked open his desk drawer, dug out a bottle of Tylenol, and washed down a couple of tablets with lukewarm coffee. Then he glared at an in-box twice as full as when he'd left last night. Where was it written that the size of a police department should be inversely proportional to the amount of paperwork it generated? He'd bet no one in Chicago had nearly this much.

He'd just started skimming a four-page memo from the mayor lecturing against wasting office supplies when Harvey Hancock knocked on his door frame.

"Abby Langford found an old kitchen knife hidden in the house she bought," Harvey said, stepping into Josh's office. "With what could be blood on the blade. I said we'd send someone over to get it. You want to handle it?"

"Why would I want to handle something like that?" Josh asked. He was the police chief, after all. He spent his time doing important things, like paperwork.

"Because she's famous."

"She was just on a soap opera."

"She played Samantha Cartwright for seventeen years. Won nine Emmys." Harvey crossed his arms over his small paunch. "Before her daughter Maddie was born, she did guest spots on prime-time shows all the time."

Despite Harvey's obvious heroine worship, Josh had no desire to meet Ms. Langford. He certainly wasn't about to interrupt his day for her nonemergency summons.

"She's also been Laura Stuart's best friend since grade school," Harvey said. "Laura's parents are Bill and Mary Tate, and they were pretty much surrogate parents to Abby while she was growing up. Good thing, since her real parents were the wrong side of worthless, God rest their souls."

He might not take the most direct route, but Harvey eventually hit the guts of the matter. Harvey had been a Harrington, Minnesota, cop for as long as Josh had been alive and knew nearly everyone in town. That had proven a godsend, since in the eight months Josh had lived there, he'd discovered that even with only forty-two thousand residents, protocol and politics in Harrington were as important as in Chicago. "So the real reason I should handle it is so I won't offend the former senator and his philan-thropic wife," Josh couldn't resist saying. He should suck it up and shut up, but sucking up annoyed him.

"Up to you," Harvey said. "I'd be happy to take care of it. Abby always was a nice girl."

"Nice girl?" From what Josh had read about Abby Langford, nothing was further from the truth.

But Harvey nodded his bald head. "When she was in high school, she worked at Ruby's. Waited on me nearly every day, and she was the sweetest thing. Not a bit like Samantha Cartwright, let me tell you."

"You said Ms. Langford found a knife in her house," Josh said, returning to the matter at hand. "The big Victorian on Maplewood, right?"

"Yep."

"Has there ever been an incident there?"

"Not far as I know. Far as I know, everybody who's lived there was respectable."

If anything remotely suspicious had happened there, Harvey would know—his memory for things like that rivaled any com-puter's. That meant this was nothing, but if Josh didn't deal with Ms. Langford personally, he'd no doubt end up fielding an irate call from Bill Tate and maybe another from the mayor. He was in a lousy enough mood without that.

"You're right," he said, accepting the inevitable. "She's famous enough that I should handle this. Besides, my sister would never forgive me if I passed up a chance to meet her. Kim's a major fan."

He grabbed his car keys and briefcase, then strode to the door. His ex-wife had been a major fan, too, taping *Private Affairs* every damn day and talking incessantly about all its screwed-up characters. She'd idolized Samantha Cartwright, a woman who'd lied, cheated, and manipulated her way to a glamorous lifestyle filled with designer clothes, expensive houses, and a series of rich, successful husbands and lovers. Hell, Jennifer had probably used Samantha as a role model.

Josh's official Crown Victoria was parked in his reserved spot in front of the station. He opened the door and got into a vinyl-scented sauna, the seat nearly hot enough to raise blisters through his dark-blue uniform pants. He started the car, then rolled down the windows and turned on the air conditioner.

Although he was far too familiar with Samantha, he'd had no idea who portrayed her until his sister had told him about Abby Langford moving back to Harrington. After that, he'd seemed to see articles about Abby everywhere, ones he'd skimmed while waiting in line at Erickson's Market or Target.

If even a tiny fraction of the tabloid claims were true—claims Abby had never denied—she wasn't much different from Samantha now, no matter what she'd been like growing up. Her husband had gotten fed up with her cheating and other mistreatment of him, plus shopaholic habits that had them on the verge of bankruptcy, and he'd divorced her. Abby had left her show and California and was now capitalizing on her celebrity by writing a book.

A mystery.

Josh shut the windows, then pulled away from the curb, suspicion flickering through his brain. Granted, she might be genuinely concerned about a knife a former occupant had forgotten in some basement corner or under a radiator. But this could also be part of a plan to increase interest in her book. A sophisticated actress from LA was bound to assume cops around here would be too backward, bumbling, and awestruck to question anything she said.

His hands tightened around the steering wheel. If that was her game, it was too bad for her she'd gotten a former Chicago detective who ran an efficient, professional police department.

And one who'd had more than his fill of manipulative women.

– – –

Abby looked out the living room window just as a white car bearing the gold, blue, and black Harrington Police Department logo eased up to the curb in front of the house. If she could beat the doorbell, maybe Maddie wouldn't realize she'd been concerned enough about the knife to call the police. She raced to the door and yanked it open, expecting to see a balder but still kindly Harvey.

Instead, an enormous, fierce-looking man stepped up onto the curved front porch. Actually, enormous was an exaggeration— he was about a foot taller than she was, which put him at around six feet four, and while his shoulders blocked out the sunlight, his muscular body was nicely proportioned. But she'd gotten the fierce part right. With eyes as dark and fathomless as the night ocean, straight black hair nearly long enough for a ponytail, and a definite five o'clock shadow darkening his square jaw, he resembled a pirate, and not one with a buried heart of gold.

She resisted the urge to slam the door and call 911. Since he was wearing a police uniform, he presumably wasn't out to harm her, no matter how intimidating his expression. He was no doubt annoyed at having been delegated to handle her nuisance call, and she didn't blame him. Her problem must rank even lower in importance than rescuing poor Fluffy from an oak tree.

"Is Ms. Langford in?" he asked in a deep voice that fit his appearance.

"I'm Abby Langford."

He studied her silently.

"I know, I don't look at all like Samantha Cartwright," she said, smiling faintly. Barefoot, dressed in khaki shorts and an oversize blue work shirt, with her blonde hair in a high ponytail and most of the blush and lipstick she'd applied that morning faded away, she must look more like the cleaning lady than the glamorous Samantha. "My stylist and makeup artist deserved even more awards than they've won. Did Harvey send you?"

"He told me you'd called. I'm Chief Kincaid."

"Chief?" Abby focused on the badge confirming his claim, her stomach clenching. The knife must be important for the police chief to be concerned.

"Don't I look like a police chief, either?" he asked.

"I expected Harvey to handle this. Or a patrolman."

He raised one eyebrow. "You have a problem with me?"

"Not at all. But you must have more important things to do."

"Why don't you explain so I can get back to doing them, Ms. Langford?"

"Please call me Abby."

In response, Chief Kincaid smiled, and Abby's stomach somersaulted. While he still wasn't conventionally handsome, he now radiated a combination of warmth and sexiness that had her pulse accelerating and body heating.

"You must be Maddie."

Abby abruptly realized Chief Kincaid wasn't smiling at her, but at Maddie. Maddie was sitting at the bottom of the stairs smiling at him, a smile identical to the one that had convinced Abby to forgive Maddie's father more times than she could count.

"This is Chief Kincaid, Maddie. He's here about the knife." Abby waved her hand with more nonchalance than she felt. "I thought I should give it to the police because otherwise I'll worry, even though it's nothing."

Maddie approached the chief and extended her hand, her nails painted the same turquoise as her T-shirt. "It's nice to meet you, Chief Kincaid."

He set down his black leather briefcase, squatted at Maddie's level, and shook her hand. "I'm happy to meet you, too, Maddie. How old are you?"

"Nine. I'm going into fourth grade."

"I thought you looked the same age as one of my nieces. How do you like Harrington?"

She frowned. "The town's very nice. I can't wait until school starts so I can meet some kids my age."

"By the time we moved here, it was too late to sign up for any summer activities," Abby said.

"Moving in the summer is tough," Josh told Maddie. "I guarantee a lot of nice kids live in Harrington—including my niece."

Abby rested a hand on Maddie's shoulder. "I need to talk to Chief Kincaid, sweetheart. Are the Sims doing better?"

Maddie's solemn expression brightened. "Lots better. I moved them to Utah, and their parents are so strict now they can't even watch your soap." She turned to go back to her bedroom.

"She seems like a good kid," Chief Kincaid said as Maddie ran upstairs.

"She's the best. Do you have kids?"

He shook his head. "But I've got seven nieces and nephews. Where's the knife?"

"I'll get it."

Instead of waiting for her to retrieve it, he picked up his briefcase and followed her into the family room.

"Most of the furniture came with the house. I haven't had time to replace it," Abby said, since the two duct-taped vinyl recliners and war-torn coffee table looked even less Samantha-like than she did.

When they reached the coffee table, Chief Kincaid slipped on a pair of latex gloves, then picked up the knife.

"I touched it. Sorry," she said as he examined it. "The dark spots on the blade could be blood someone didn't completely wash off."

"Possibly." He turned the knife over and studied the other side.

"You can test it and find out, can't you?"

He removed a bag from his briefcase and dropped the knife into it. "Where did you find it?"

"Stuffed inside the wall, back behind one of the pocket doors, as Harvey called them," Abby said, pointing into the opening. "The stop gave out, and I pulled the door out too far, so I decided to vacuum between the walls. That's when I found the knife."

Chief Kincaid glanced at the vacuum cleaner, then at Abby. "You were vacuuming between the walls?"

She didn't mind his skeptical tone. "I thought I might as well take advantage of my only chance to do it. Like when you get a new refrigerator and clean the floor under the old one for the first time in fifteen years."

He put the bag into his briefcase, followed by the gloves. "To be honest, it would never occur to me to clean anywhere people won't see."

She was starting to like him. Anyone who shared her aversion for housework and was nice to Maddie had to be a good guy. "Ordinarily it wouldn't have occurred to me, either, but I was using it as a delaying tactic. I'm writing a book, and some days I'll do anything to avoid sitting at my computer."

Chief Kincaid crossed his arms, accentuating tanned biceps resembling Popeye's after an infusion of spinach. "I heard you're writing a mystery. Is there a knife in it?"

"Not so far, but I'm only halfway through the first draft. That could change."

"Although I guess this would do the job regardless."

"What job?"

He looked grim enough to be contemplating sending her on a stroll down a long plank. "Ms. Langford, we might not be as overworked as the cops in LA, but we still don't have time to do publicity work for you."

Abby wrinkled her forehead. "What are you talking about?"

"An actress who's writing a mystery coincidentally discovers a real-life mystery in her own house?" He looked around the family room. "Where are the photographers?"

Now she got it—a month surrounded by nice midwesterners had obviously dulled her reflexes, since she'd never been that slow on the uptake before. And she took back everything she'd thought about liking him. Her hands clenched into fists, and she raised her chin. "You think I staged this?"

"Nothing violent has ever happened in this house. Yet you still found a knife when you were"—he paused—"vacuuming between walls? Add in that you're writing a mystery and currently unemployed and it's not real hard to connect the dots."

Abby's nails were etching crescents into her palms. "Look, I found a knife hidden in the wall and was concerned it might be important, maybe even a missing murder weapon," she said, struggling to keep her tone level. "That's why I called the police instead of throwing it away. If you think I should toss it, I'll be happy to." She reached toward his open briefcase.

He snapped it shut. "Don't expect to read about it in tomorrow's *Herald* or any other paper. Unless you call them yourself."

Abby gave him the look a television critic had claimed would wither a cactus. "Calling the press is nowhere on my to-do list. I moved out here to escape the press."

"Right."

"Just take the damn knife," Abby said. "Thank you for your time," she made herself add.

He picked up his briefcase and nodded curtly. "I'll see myself out."

As he strode toward the front door, Abby stood perfectly still, grinding her teeth and pressing her lips together to keep herself quiet. She'd learned long ago there were three groups of people it never paid to piss off: directors, female costars, and cops. She'd become expert at suppressing even the most suitably sarcastic comment, no matter how well deserved.

"Bastard," she muttered the instant the door slammed behind him. Sometimes, even after all those years of practice, taking the no-comment route was easier thought than done.

– – –

Josh got into his car, so hot under the collar the stifling interior barely registered. God, she was good. She'd nearly had him.

She hadn't been at all what he'd expected. With those wide violet-blue eyes and wearing a ponytail, shorts, and big shirt, she'd looked almost wholesome, although still hot enough to melt a diamond. The knife had been as understated as she was. A nice touch—he'd expected it to be bigger and bloodier if she'd been trying to stage something. He'd almost been ready to believe her.

Until she'd pushed it too far. Claiming she'd just happened to pull out a door and just happened to decide to vacuum between the walls and just happened to find the knife stuck back there. Like hell she had. He could imagine what Merry Maids would say if he asked to have someone vacuum between his walls next week. She must think he was an idiot to expect him to fall for that.

He jabbed the key into the ignition and started the car, pushing the accelerator a couple of times to rev the engine. God, he was sick of people looking down on cops, considering them either Neanderthals who loved violence or frustrated lawyers too dumb to get into even the most unaccredited law school. He'd gotten enough of that in Chicago and not only from Jennifer. Being chief might be a big deal around here, but to a woman like Abby Langford, the police chief in a town like Harrington was probably as impressive as being fire marshal at a kiddie water park.

Maybe he'd been a little harsh, but he'd wanted to make clear he knew what she was trying to pull. He was running a police department, not an aid society for unemployed soap opera divas, and he didn't have time to waste helping Ms. Abby Langford with her new career. Shoving the gearshift into drive, he roared away from the curb.

– – –

After hours of fuming, Abby finally found the antidote for her anger at Chief Kincaid—an evening trip to Dairy Queen.

If she hadn't been concerned about setting a bad example for Maddie, she'd have licked every last drop of chocolate and ice cream from her Styrofoam sundae bowl. It was such a relief not having to worry about squeezing into one of Samantha's form-fitting outfits. Life was too short to avoid something as heavenly as chocolate.

Especially since it was also clearly a wonder drug—Abby was feeling downright mellow by the time she pulled her car into the former carriage house-turned-garage. She and Maddie walked through the backyard to the house in a quiet unknown in LA, undisturbed by the voices, car engine rumbles, and swimming pool splashes. Overhead, stars sparkled in the smog-free sky, and the full moon had the cracked sidewalk between the garage and back steps glowing like the yellow brick road.

"It's bedtime," Abby said when they'd stepped into the equally peaceful house. "Although with all that sugar in your system, you'll probably never get to sleep."

"I'll probably just have really sweet dreams." Maddie grinned. "Maybe I should eat a Blizzard every night before bed."

"Only in your really sweet dreams."

Maddie hopefully was right about the sweet dreams, Abby thought as she walked downstairs after tucking her in. She could use a few herself tonight.

On her way to the living room, she stopped to pick up the mail the carrier had stuffed through the front door slot. She'd been so busy being mad she'd forgotten about it. After dropping a half dozen catalogs destined for immediate recycling back onto the floor, she flipped through the letters.

Mixed in with the credit card offers and charitable donation requests was a plain white envelope with her name and address typed in capital letters, no return address, and a Harrington postmark. Abby ripped it open, then pulled out and unfolded a single sheet of paper, its message printed in bold, oversize capitals:

EVIL WOMEN LIKE YOU AREN'T WELCOME HERE.
LEAVE OR ELSE.

It was signed, "YOUR BIGGEST FAN."

CHAPTER 2

Abby shook her head as she refolded the letter. She'd long ago accepted hate mail as the price of playing a TV bitch, and she certainly wasn't surprised to be getting it now. Samantha was still on the show and behaving especially outrageously to give plenty of characters motives to kill her, as the plot and last shoots dictated. In the last month, she'd bet the studio had collected a carton of similar letters.

As hate mail went, this was nothing, so tame and vague she wouldn't have bothered forwarding it to studio security. That it had come to her house only meant it was from a local Samantha hater, since everyone in Harrington no doubt knew where she lived. Still, Maddie might worry if she saw it. So Abby carried the letter and envelope outside to the trash, ripped both into a dozen pieces, and dropped them into the metal can beside the garage. By the time Maddie got up tomorrow morning, this letter should be on its way to join the same writer's two previous missives in the local landfill.

And after Samantha was killed off next week, this letter writer would have to get another hobby.

– – –

The knife was in the air, pointing downward at an angle. Fresh blood stained the tip, halfway up the steel blade. A fisted hand clenched the brown walnut handle—a man's hand, she could tell that even though she could only see his hand and wrist.

The man thrust the knife down through the air and out of view, raised it, thrust again. More and more blood coated the blade, dripping into the air below and sending rivulets toward the handle, as the knife rose and plunged, over and over.

Then the knife disappeared. Instead she saw a window, built-in bookshelves, a light wood floor. Narrow planks with an oval pool of bright-red blood seeping onto some pale-blue fabric beside it. A pool that was getting bigger...

Abby bolted up in bed, her heart hammering, her body and T-shirt drenched in sweat.

She grabbed her pillow and hugged it as she forced herself to breathe slowly. It was only a dream. A dream about that damn knife.

She recognized the location, too—the window and bookshelf molding were distinctive. It was the spare bedroom she used as her office, where she spent countless stressful hours writing. No wonder the dream had been set there.

Abby glanced at the clock. Just after five, too early to get up now that she didn't have those awful early makeup calls. She replaced the pillow, plopped down on it, and closed her eyes.

The knife plunged through the air.

She opened her eyes and stared at the ceiling. What she needed to do was think about something else, like that jerk Chief Kincaid. How could he imagine she'd plant a knife for publicity? She'd come out here in part to escape publicity after having every breath she took—and even more she hadn't—written up. For a while, if she'd smiled at a man anywhere, he'd be cast as her newest lover. If she didn't smile, she'd be depressed and considering suicide.

Abby closed her eyes again, but the blasted knife reappeared, and unfortunately it wasn't skewering Chief Kincaid. She gave up and got out of bed, slipped a white terry-cloth robe over her damp T-shirt, then headed downstairs. Through the round window at the curve of the staircase, she could see the sun rising, the sky the impressionistic mosaic of pinks, corals, and tangerines that was the only pleasant thing about being up at this ungodly hour.

Yawning, she trudged into the kitchen. The room was a vision in gold, from the harvest-gold refrigerator, stained gold linoleum, and gold-flecked white Formica countertops to the glittery, gold kitchen table and chairs left by a previous owner. Abby filled a mug with water and stuck it into the microwave, then opened the cupboard and stared at her selection of decaffeinated teas. Eleven varieties and none looked appealing. Divorce-induced stress had convinced her to give up caffeine, and with the stress of the move, she hadn't dared go back to it. Some mornings, though, she'd have killed for a double espresso.

Even several minutes sipping an herbal tea called "Tension Tamer" and inhaling chamomile-scented steam couldn't banish the dream's images from Abby's mind. The blood had looked so real, coating the knife, dripping through the air, pooling on the floor. It had all looked so real...

But it wasn't real. She'd never been in this house before she'd bought it, so she certainly hadn't witnessed anything like that. For it to be real, she'd have to be psychic, and she didn't believe in psychics. She was going to drink her tea and forget the dream like the rational grown-up she was.

A moment later, Abby set down her mug. She knew herself, and in addition to being imaginative, she was a little neurotic.

That much blood would likely leave at least a faint stain, right? Which meant that rational or not, this was going to bug her until she looked under the carpet and saw that it covered nothing but unblemished wood. She went over to the kitchen drawer that housed her growing collection of tools, dug out her second-largest screwdriver, and took it upstairs.

She had no idea when the room she'd designated as her office had been decorated since she couldn't imagine it ever being fashionable. The brown and forest-green shag carpet looked like grass caught in a mudslide; the green, cream, pink, and brown paisley wallpaper—on the ceiling as well as the walls—gave the sensation of being engulfed by a swarm of bizarre insects. With windows on two sides and built-in bookshelves, however, this room would make a beautiful office after she repainted and recarpeted.

She walked over and stared down at the carpet to the left of the bookshelves, where the blood in her dream had been. This was really stupid, she scolded herself. But she knelt down beside the baseboard anyway, then used the screwdriver to pull up the carpet staples along the walls on either side.

After about ten minutes, she'd loosened enough for her purposes. Holding her breath and starting at the corner, she rolled the carpet back until the section of wood that had been blood-soaked was exposed.

The floor was constructed of narrow, light wood planks, just like in the dream. It had a few scratches, but nothing that could conceivably be even a shadow of a bloodstain.

Abby let out a long, relieved breath. She wasn't psychic or crazy or who knows what else. Dropping the carpet, she sat down on the floor and surveyed the room. Actually, this exercise hadn't been a complete waste of time. She'd planned to put in new carpet, but the wood looked like it was maple and in decent shape.

If the rest of the floor wasn't plywood or too beat-up, she should have it refinished. With yellow or peach walls and a light wood floor, this room would look cheery and warm instead of dark and angry. That would have to help her writing.

Since she'd done this much, she might as well check the rest of the floor. Abby used the screwdriver to remove the staples from the walls she'd already started on. Then she rolled back the loosened carpet.

And froze, her blood turning to slush.

On the wood floor to the right of the bookshelves was a rusty stain, oval shaped and nearly half a foot wide, with a few drops like squished flies around it. The stain was no longer bright red, but otherwise it was identical to the bloody pool she'd seen in her dream.

– – –

Josh walked into the police station at just after seven, sipping the large French roast he'd needed despite the half pot of coffee he'd drunk at home. What made bands think they should start playing at eleven on weeknights? Didn't they realize most of their audience worked day jobs?

He nodded to Tiffany Williams, the department's receptionist, who was talking on the phone. Tiffany always looked perky, even though she came in at six thirty, and he knew her nights were usually as late as his had been. Of course, she got off at three in the afternoon, so maybe she took a nap. Or maybe being twenty-something instead of fortysomething was the secret. He had to face it—he was getting old.

He was just stepping into his office when Tiffany spoke to him. "Abby Langford's on line one. You know, the actress."

The reverence in Tiffany's voice annoyed him—for God's sake, from all reports Abby had been basically playing herself, which took as much talent as a reality show. "What does she want?"

"To talk to someone, but it isn't an emergency."

"I'll take it." He went into his office and picked up the phone. "This is Chief Kincaid. What's the problem, Ms. Langford?"

Silence met his ear. "I was tearing up the carpet in the bedroom I use as my office, and I found what could be blood on the floor," she finally said. "After finding the knife, I thought I should have it checked."

"*You* were tearing up carpet? At seven in the morning?" That was even more fantastic than her claim to have been vacuuming between walls.

"It came up pretty easily. The carpet's hideous, and I wanted to see what shape the floor was in so I could decide whether to refinish the wood or recarpet."

"You just happened to find blood," he said, not bothering to hide his skepticism. "A few drops?"

"No, an oval six or seven inches across."

"How do you know it's blood?"

"I don't. Look, I thought I should call and report it. If you don't want to have anyone check it out, fine."

He'd sent the knife in for analysis on the off chance he was misjudging her, but now he knew he needn't have bothered. Ms. Abby Langford had to understand that she would not be using his department to promote her damn book. "I'll be right over."

– – –

Abby stabbed the off button of her phone, then sat glaring at the receiver. Just what she needed, another run-in with the chief.

Although between the dream and finding the blood, the morning was already pretty much shot.

She sipped her tea, noting with satisfaction that her hand had finally stopped shaking. It had taken three cups of chamomile and nearly an hour of agonizing before she'd calmed down enough to call the police. At only a few minutes after seven, she'd assumed she'd explain things to some nice patrolman. What was Chief Kincaid doing there this early? As far as she could tell, Harrington's only crime consisted of speeding, DWIs, and an occasional bar fight.

Not only had he taken her call, but he was now on his way. *Terrific.* Especially since she was starting to think she'd overreacted. The stuff could very well be paint she'd just happened to uncover. Every carpeted floor in the house probably had similar spots; painters could be sloppy when they knew their spills and drips would be covered. Her dream was like a horoscope—if you tried hard enough, you could always find some truth in it.

Chief Kincaid arrived within fifteen minutes, looking even more irritated than he had the previous day. "Where is it?" he asked as he stepped into the house.

"Upstairs," Abby said.

"Is Maddie still asleep?"

"Uh-huh."

He followed Abby up the curved staircase and into her office, closing the door behind him. "I can see why you're replacing this carpet," he said.

Abby rolled back the carpet, exposing the stain. "What do you think? Is this blood or just paint?"

He squatted beside the stain and studied it for several seconds, scratching it with his fingernail. Then he rolled the carpet back over the stain and stood. "Have you ripped up the carpet in the rest of the bedrooms?"

"I started here. This carpet's the ugliest," Abby said. "I also spend a lot of time writing in here." None of that was a lie.

He nodded slowly. "So yesterday you pulled out a door, vacuumed behind it, and found a knife flecked with what could be blood. Then this morning you decide to rip up the carpet in one bedroom and coincidentally find more blood?"

It did sound a little fantastic, but Abby certainly wasn't telling him about the dream. "You think I dumped it there myself?"

"Makes it seem more like you've got a mystery in your own house, doesn't it? It looks like paint to me, but I guess it could be real blood. I'm sure it's easy to buy the stuff in LA."

She threw up her hands. "Do you honestly think I brought blood out here with me? Just stuck it in a carton with my dishes and had the movers load it up?"

"Or you could have ordered it on the Internet."

"Or stolen it from the Red Cross. Look, I didn't pretend to find the knife for publicity, and I didn't plant this stain for publicity. I told you, I don't want any more publicity."

When he didn't respond, Abby massaged her temples and concentrated on taking calming breaths. If she'd been able to hold her tongue the entire six weeks Vanessa Mason had guest starred on *Private Affairs*, she could do it now. "I was simply trying to do my civic duty by reporting it."

"Next time don't bother." Josh turned to leave.

"Don't you think you should take a sample on the off chance it's something important? Like blood that's been there for years?"

Josh turned back toward her. "Are you implying I'm a bad cop, Ms. Langford?" he asked, his voice ominously quiet. "I spent a lot of years in Chicago, including seven as a detective. I'll bet making detective there is nearly as hard as winning a daytime Emmy."

"I'm sure it is," she said, waving one hand. "I'm sure you've got a wall full of commendations, too. I'm just suggesting you might be missing something important."

He glanced at his watch. "You're right. I'm missing prep time for a meeting scheduled to start in fifteen minutes." He opened the door and left the room.

Abby had just followed him into the hallway when Maddie stepped out of her bedroom, her Harry Potter nightgown nearly as rumpled as her hair. "What are you doing here, Chief Kincaid?" she asked.

"Call me Josh," he said. "If you call me Chief Kincaid, people will think you're talking to someone important."

He'd never told *her* to call him Josh, Abby noted. "He had a few more questions about the knife, sweetie. No big deal, but cops like to be thorough."

Maddie nodded. "Otherwise you'll get in trouble from the press, right, Josh? Even if you don't deserve it."

"Right," Abby said, answering for Josh. In Maddie's mind, the press functioned primarily as an evil and not necessarily truthful avenger—yet another reason for getting her away from LA and tabloid land. "Did we wake you?"

"My dream woke me."

Abby's stomach tightened. "What kind of dream?"

"About some kids from my old school," Maddie said. "We were at Monroe Park. First we ate ice-cream cones from the stand, then we went swimming. We had so much fun."

That might be preferable to dreaming about blood and knives, but Maddie's wistful tone still spread the tightness in Abby's stomach to her chest.

"You like to swim?" Josh asked.

"I love to swim," Maddie said almost reverently.

"Would Maddie like to meet my niece?" Josh asked, shifting his attention to Abby. "My sister, Kim, is having a barbecue tonight, and I'm sure she'd love to have you both come. Rachel is Maddie's age, and they have a swimming pool."

Maddie clasped her hands together. "My best friend in California is named Rachel."

"With a coincidence like that, you have to meet my niece," Josh told Maddie. "Tonight, if that works for your mother." He looked back at Abby. "It isn't a party, just Kim, her family, and me. She always makes way too much food, and she's a big fan of yours."

The last thing she wanted to do was socialize with the police chief, but Maddie seemed so excited Abby forced herself to smile. "We'd love to go, if you're sure your sister won't mind. What's her address?"

"I'll pick you up."

"I can certainly drive."

"They live in Ridgeview, so your place is on my way," Josh said. "I'll be here at a quarter to seven. Bye, Maddie."

"Good-bye, Josh," Maddie said.

Without another word, Josh turned and walked down the stairs.

– – –

Josh barely resisted slamming Abby's front door, clenching his jaw and his fists as he strode to his car. What the hell had he been thinking, volunteering to spend the evening with Abby Langford? She was trying to manipulate him, for God's sake. No matter what he'd said about blood, the stain had honestly looked like paint to him. She'd probably prepared it as part two of her publicity campaign, or maybe uncovering the paint stain had given her the idea to plant the knife in the first place. Then she'd assumed her sex appeal would turn him into some nodding bobblehead, willing to believe everything she said. That was not happening. He'd stopped thinking with his hormones years ago.

The trouble was, Maddie had looked so sad when she'd talked about her old friends, and it had reminded him of what she'd said yesterday about being anxious to start school so she could make new ones. She was clearly lonely, and he hated seeing kids unhappy. He'd always liked kids—had it been his call, he and Jennifer would have had at least two. Even if Maddie and Rachel didn't hit it off, Kim would make sure Rachel's other friends met Maddie.

Inviting Maddie to meet Rachel was the right thing to do. Besides, Kim was such a big fan that she'd monopolize Abby. He wouldn't have to say a word to her all evening.

He was feeling better by the time he got back to the station and called Kim. "Is it OK if I bring someone tonight?"

"Heather?"

His sister's tone spoke volumes. Josh scowled at the phone. "Lay off Heather. You admitted she's nice."

"She's a kid, Josh."

"She isn't a kid. She's almost twenty-three."

"Compared to you that's a kid. There's got to be another way to build yourself back up after Jennifer. You're too old to be playing with Barbie dolls."

Josh's hand tightened on the receiver. "My personal life is my business, Kimberly."

Kim sighed. "I know, and I'm sorry. But I worry about you. You've always been my favorite brother."

His hand relaxed. Kim really did love him, even though she could be a pain in the ass about some things. "I appreciate your concern, but it's unnecessary," he said, his tone warmer. "Actually I want to bring Abby Langford and her daughter."

"My God, you're dating Abby Langford now, too? I'm dying to meet her."

"Calm down—I'm not dating her." Josh swiveled his chair so he could look through the one-way glass in the bulletproof window behind his desk. "I don't even like her. But she's got a daughter Rachel's age who seems like a sweet kid and is having trouble making friends since school's out. I thought she and Rachel might get along."

"That's nice of you, but I'd be happier if you were dating Abby."

"After everything she did? She's worse than Jennifer." At least Jennifer had only cheated with one man, and she'd married him.

"I hate to disillusion you, but the tabloids exaggerate and sometimes even make things up."

"No, really?" Josh asked. "Abby never denied a single thing. Doesn't that tell you something?"

"Only that she was sick of the press. People who knew Abby growing up swear she'd never have done any of the things the tabloids claim."

"People change." A car sped through the four-way stop at the corner. Josh grabbed a pen and wrote down the license-plate number. Anyone who'd run a stop sign by the police station deserved a ticket, or at least watching.

"I'll have to decide for myself after I meet her tonight," Kim said. "How do you know her?"

"I met her on police business." He ripped off the page and stuck it on top of his overflowing in-box.

"That knife she found. I didn't realize you handled it."

Josh's grip on the phone tightened again. "How did you know about the knife?" Although he could guess.

"From what I heard, Tiffany spread the news," Kim said. "She's not especially discreet. But then, she's young."

"That's enough, Kimberly." He'd actually met Heather because of her frequent visits to the police station to see her best friend Tiffany. "It wasn't a secret." That didn't mean Abby hadn't also publicized it.

"Whatever you say. See you at seven."

Josh hung up the phone. Kim was wrong about Heather. She was exactly what he needed right now—a lot of fun and young enough that she was only out for a good time. She was always telling him how smart and successful and great in bed he was, and after Jennifer, who could fault him for enjoying that? And she thought cops were a lot sexier than lawyers.

He raised his hand and stifled a yawn. He only wished Heather's idea of a good time started a few hours earlier.

CHAPTER 3

Abby cut it too close and scraped the tire of her black Volvo against the curb in front of the Alma County Courthouse. She backed up, repositioned the car, then jammed the gearshift into park and shut off the ignition. This was all Chief Kincaid's fault. She should be writing, but how could she concentrate on a made-up story when she had possible evidence of a real live crime in her own house? Evidence the idiot police chief had chosen to ignore.

Just because finding the stain after her dream had been a co-incidence didn't make it nothing. The least Chief Kincaid could have done was taken a sample, since blood matching the type on the knife could be evidence of a murder. But no, he'd completely discounted it, assuming everything was part of a publicity campaign that existed only in his warped mind.

When Abby entered the red granite building, the scents of dust, must, and furniture polish resurrected memories of grade-school field trips, probably the last time she'd been in here. She crossed the marble-floored lobby and opened a door with PROPERTY RECORDS printed in chipped black letters on its frosted window, smiling when she spotted the petite woman with a helmet of silver curls who stood behind the counter. She'd lucked out. If they awarded Emmys for gossiping, Eleanor Blake would have a mantel full. Her extensive knowledge could save hours of research time.

"It's wonderful to see you, Miss Blake," Abby said. "I wasn't sure you still worked here."

The woman returned her smile. "Call me Eleanor, now that we're both grown-ups, Abby, although I'm substantially more grown up than you are. I'll never retire. How else would I keep up with what's going on?" She closed an oversize, cloth-covered volume that had been lying open on the counter. "I heard you bought the Stanford house."

Abby nodded. "That's why I'm here. I'm interested in the prior occupants."

"Checking to see who might have owned that knife you found?"

So Chief Kincaid hadn't kept his mouth shut. He'd probably also mentioned her crude attempt to use his department for PR, not that Eleanor would repeat that part of the story to her. "The police don't think it's anything."

"I don't know about that. Seems odd, a knife between the walls." Eleanor reached up and straightened her thick bifocals. "And something about that house gives me the willies."

"What do you mean?"

"I'm not sure. I've always been sensitive, and whenever I pass by, I get goose bumps and a feeling something real bad happened there. Look, just talking about that did it." She held out her arm, pulling her navy polyester sleeve up to her elbow. Sure enough, the skin was pimpled. "Have you noticed anything?"

"Nothing like that," Abby said, not wanting to give Eleanor additional fodder for gossip. "I know Gerald Castleton built it in 1893, so it's over a hundred years old. I thought it might have an interesting history."

"Not that interesting," Eleanor said, pulling her sleeve back down. "The Castletons only lived there a few years before they built that huge place on Crosby Hill."

She shook her head. "Don't know why they needed such a big place. It was just him and the Mrs., and by then they'd have known they'd never have any kids. Of course, their mausoleum could hold dozens of bodies even though only the two of them are in it. I guess rich people just have to have the biggest of everything, whether they need it or not."

The wrinkles lining Eleanor's forehead deepened. "I don't know who owned it between them and when George and Mildred Henson moved in, but Mildred lived there close to fifty years, until cancer got her. George died ten years earlier of a heart attack. Only suspicious thing about his death was how he managed to make it to ninety when he smoked like a plugged-up chimney.

"Dr. Jim and Helen Stanford bought it after Mildred died. Shocked the entire town, cheap as they are, but they must have gotten a good deal. When the doctor retired a few years ago, they moved to Arizona and rented out the place while they tried to sell it. Furnished it from Goodwill, I heard. They wanted some exorbitant price, and it took a while to find anybody foolish enough to pay it. Not that it wasn't worth it," Eleanor added, apparently recalling that she was talking to the fool who'd paid the exorbitant price.

Abby smiled faintly. "I know I paid a lot, but compared to houses in California, it was a steal. Even with all I'm spending fixing it up."

"I'll go get you the records," Eleanor said. "We haven't got the old stuff on computer yet."

Abby had known that Mildred Henson had owned her house before the Stanfords, but she hadn't realized she'd lived there so long. Mrs. Henson had belonged to First Presbyterian, the church Abby had attended with Laura's family, although Abby had never talked to her—it was a big congregation. Abby had never met Dr. Stanford, but his wife had come into the diner a few times and Ruby had pointed her out as the new owner of the house Abby liked so much. Built like a German opera singer, Mrs. Stanford had favored brightly colored polyester pantsuits, worn her brassy gold hair in an updo reminiscent of a tuba, and, according to Ruby, never tipped more than a nickel.

"Here you are." Eleanor returned after a minute with a large volume she set down in front of Abby. She paged through it. "This is your property." She glanced toward the door as another woman entered. "Soon as I help Sally Gardner, I'll come answer any questions you've got. And tell you about the renters."

Abby carried the heavy volume to a table and sat down. Before coming here today she'd tried to narrow down the time frame the knife could be from, with no luck. Nothing on the knife indicated who'd manufactured it, and a couple of hours on the Internet established that the knife's design was too generic to be helpful. Stainless steel hadn't been invented until 1913, but she wasn't positive the blade was stainless steel, so she couldn't rule out any previous owner.

According to the records, Abby had been in junior high when Mrs. Henson had died, and the Stanfords had bought the place five months after her death. Abby wrote down the owners prior to the Hensons—she didn't recognize any names, but they'd lived there long before she was born, so that wasn't surprising. Maybe Eleanor would know more about them.

When she left the property records office nearly two hours later, however, all Abby had learned was that although her house gave Eleanor Blake goose bumps, nobody remotely suspicious had ever lived there. And the origin of the horrible furniture that had come with the house—maybe Goodwill would be willing to take it back.

At least her research had distracted her from thinking about how much she did not want to spend the evening with Chief Kincaid. Josh, that is; she'd be darned if she'd call him chief anything on a social occasion, except for maybe a few words Maddie wasn't allowed to say.

On the other hand, she'd put up with Colin and his little girlfriends for years for Maddie's sake. She could certainly handle one evening with Josh Kincaid.

– – –

"Maddie, Josh is here," Abby called as she went to answer the front doorbell.

She opened the door to find him wearing a polo shirt that accentuated his muscular torso and blue jeans that hugged his tight butt and thighs. Just looking at him made her body heat, which annoyed her. She'd obviously been celibate far too long if she was reacting to such an ass. She turned away to call Maddie again.

"I'm coming," Maddie said as she hopped down the stairs, her red sundress and primary-color beach bag both flying. "I'm so excited to meet Rachel."

Josh smiled. "I'll bet she's excited to meet you, too."

Even though he'd directed his smile at Maddie, Abby's stomach backflipped, which annoyed her even more. "We'd better go," she said, picking her purse off the foyer table.

"We don't want to be late."

"Mommy's neurotically prompt," Maddie said as they walked to Josh's car. "At least that's what Daddy says."

"Do you know what that means?" Josh asked.

Maddie gave him a disdainful look. "Of course I do. It means she really, really, really hates to be late," she said. "Daddy always says the same thing on his TV show about Catherine. That's his wife on *Heavenly Days*. Do you watch it?"

"Sorry, no," Josh said. "I don't watch much TV. I've never seen your mother's show, either."

No surprise there. As Josh opened the back door of his black Prius for Maddie, Abby got into the front passenger seat.

"On *Heavenly Days* Daddy has five kids," Maddie said when she was belted in and Josh was sitting behind the wheel. "I'm glad he doesn't have that many in real life."

"I don't think Josh is interested in your dad's show, honey," Abby said.

Josh started the car, then pulled away from the curb. "Actually, my parents have five kids in real life. Four boys and one girl. Things got pretty wild around our house sometimes."

"Do they live here?" Maddie asked.

"Just my sister, Kim. Almost everyone else lives in Chicago. And Rachel only has one brother. He's five."

Maddie continued talking the entire drive, asking questions about Rachel, her house, her family, her swimming pool, and related topics, questions Josh answered with more good humor than Abby would have thought he possessed. She really hoped Maddie and Rachel got along—she hadn't seen Maddie this animated since they'd left California.

Kim and Eric Anderson's house was a two-story stucco with enormous windows and a four-car garage located only a few blocks from where Laura lived. Tall and dark haired like Josh, Kim had softer features and, unlike her brother, warm brown eyes and an even warmer smile. "I'm so glad you could come," she said after Josh introduced them. "I've watched you since you started on *Private Affairs*. I couldn't believe it when Eric took a job at the Masters Clinic and we moved to your hometown. You're such an amazing actress. Even when Samantha did the most horrendous things, you managed to make her impossible to totally hate…" Kim broke off, pressing three fingers over her lips. "I'm sorry. I'm babbling like an awestruck fan, which I guess I am."

"Don't apologize. I appreciate it." Abby glanced at Maddie, who was looking around and shifting her feet. "Maddie's very anxious to meet Rachel."

"She's in the pool," Kim said. "Let's go."

Within minutes, Maddie and Rachel were splashing themselves and a half dozen pool toys around the water with Rachel's brother, Nathan. The adults sat at a wrought-iron table with a red-and-black umbrella that matched the chair cushions, sipping an excellent chardonnay and, in Josh's case, a Heineken. A half dozen black pots filled with lush red-and-white flowers decorated the cement patio.

"I want to thank you again for inviting us," Abby said. "I moved in the summer so it wouldn't disrupt Maddie's schooling, but the trade-off's that she hasn't met any girls her age yet."

"I should have called you," Kim said, pushing her straight, shoulder-length hair back behind her ears. "Nathan plays soccer with Laura Stuart's son, and Laura mentioned you had a daughter Rachel's age who was also going to Harrington Academy this fall. To be honest, I was a little intimidated. A couple of my friends with daughters the same age said the same thing. We didn't want to bother you."

Abby shook her head. "That's what I like about the Midwest. People are concerned about bothering you, instead of assuming you live your entire life for their entertainment. I hope everyone will feel free to bother me in the future. I moved here in part so Maddie can experience midwestern friendliness." Her lips twisted. "And because I wanted her away from parents who spend more on sixth-birthday parties than most people spend on weddings and grade-school girls who consider bulimia a group activity."

"Are people really friendlier in the Midwest than elsewhere?" Kim asked. "I've always assumed that was a rumor started by midwesterners to make us feel better about our horrible winters."

"Overall they seem to be, although there are a lot of wonderful people in LA. And some nasty ones here," Abby added before she thought to stop herself.

Kim looked pointedly at Josh, who was engrossed in conversation with Eric. "Like my brother?"

Kim had obviously noticed Josh had ignored her since they'd arrived, but Abby wasn't about to offend her by insulting her brother. "Of course not. I was talking about the person who's been sending me letters telling me I'm evil and should go back to California or else."

"What are you talking about?" Josh asked.

Abby glanced toward the pool, but Maddie was giggling safely out of earshot. "Nothing important. I've gotten some hate mail here. Three letters, all from the same person."

"Threatening, you said. Why didn't you report them?"

"To the police?" Abby asked. "I've received thousands of threatening letters during my career. That's the price of playing a TV bitch. These are mild compared with most I've gotten."

Josh rested his hands on the table and leaned toward her. "When I take you home I want to see them."

"I threw them away."

"You threw threatening letters away?" He looked as if she'd announced she'd discarded Marlon Brando's annotated script from *The Godfather*.

"I didn't want Maddie to find them. She might worry."

"Were they addressed to you or to your character?"

Abby really wished she'd admitted to Kim that Josh was the nasty person she'd been referring to instead of mentioning the letters. After the way he'd discounted the knife and bloodstain, she couldn't believe he was getting worked up over them. "They were addressed to me, but that's probably to guarantee the mail carrier would deliver them," she said. "I'm sure they're directed at Samantha—she's been horrid lately. People who are upset with me personally always mention my ex-husband or Pastor Jim, and this writer never has."

"Who's Pastor Jim?"

"You'll have to forgive Josh," Kim told Abby. "His TV viewing is limited to the news and sports." She turned to her brother. "Pastor Jim is TV's most perfect dad, on the show *Heavenly Days*. Abby's ex-husband has played him for the past six years."

"I knew he was on that show, just not his character's name," Josh said. "What did the letters say?"

"Variations on the theme that I'm an evil woman and should leave, like I said. I mean, that Samantha's evil. I'd rather discuss them later, if at all," Abby said.

"How's your house?" Kim asked, clearly picking up on her discomfort.

Abby gave her a grateful smile as Josh responded to a similarly tactful question from Eric. "I love it, even though it needs a lot of work. Finding out the house was for sale is what convinced me to move back here."

"Why's that?" Kim asked.

"I grew up in a trailer in Windsor Court, and I passed that house every day on my way to school." Abby picked up her wineglass and twirled it, watching the golden chardonnay swirl as she continued, "I thought it was the most beautiful place I'd ever seen and used to fantasize about living there someday. When I was considering moving to Harrington, a Realtor mentioned the place was on the market. It seemed a sign I should come back and buy the house, even though I'd never been inside it in my life. I had Laura and her dad check it out. Bill warned me the place would be a money pit and tried to talk me out of buying it, but I was a little irrational about it."

She sipped her wine before continuing. "Unfortunately, Bill was right. I've only lived there a little over a month, and so far I've installed a new roof and air-conditioning, replaced all the pipes, and bought a new water heater. I've gotten so tired of having workers around that I've declared a temporary moratorium on home repairs."

"I can sympathize," Kim said. "Our previous house was built in 1923."

"I still don't regret buying it." Abby traced the rim of her wineglass with her index finger. "Something about that house—I can't explain it, but I need to live there. I think it has to do with proving to myself that I've overcome my childhood, which wasn't exactly idyllic. And maybe also proving to the world that I'm not at all like my parents, who could never have afforded that place." She looked down at the table, her cheeks heating. She hadn't meant to say so much, but Kim was proving easy to talk to. "Sorry about the psychobabble. I obviously lived in California too long."

"It makes perfect sense to me." Kim picked up the chardonnay bottle and refilled Abby's glass. "I have to admit I was delighted to hear you were the person Josh wanted to bring tonight, and not just because I've been dying to meet you." She topped off her own wineglass. "I thought he might be bringing Heather Casey. Do you know her?"

Abby shook her head. "I remember a Steve Casey who was a high school football star when I was in junior high, though."

"That's her dad." Kim set the bottle on the table. "As an unbiased observer, don't you think it's pathetic a guy like Josh is dating a girl young enough to be his daughter?"

"I think we should check on dinner, Kimberly," Eric interrupted, getting to his feet. He gave Abby a wry smile. "They've had this discussion before, and it isn't pretty."

Josh looked at Abby. "Do you think it's pathetic that a guy dates a woman technically young enough to be his daughter? Who's almost twenty-three, by the way."

He had a much younger girlfriend. She should have known. Abby tamped down her knee-jerk response, determined to be nice. "I think I'll stay out of it."

Josh glanced at Kim, who'd stood but hadn't followed Eric to the house. "Because you think it's fine, but don't want to disagree with my sister since she's the hostess, right?"

Josh's self-satisfied tone torpedoed Abby's vow of niceness. "No, because I've found that most men pursue much younger women because they're feeling old or inadequate and figure making it with a young babe proves they're still hot." *And because they're shallow jerks*, but she managed to stop herself before adding that.

"Is that why you dated a younger man?"

"Josh. That was uncalled for." Kim's appalled tone matched her expression. "You also know you can't believe what you read in the tabloids."

Abby had forgotten the tabloid lies about her and Matt Turner, who'd played her daughter's boyfriend on *Private Affairs*. She held up a placating hand. "You're right that the tabloids lie, but my comment was out of line." Even if she disliked Josh, she had no business insulting him because he'd unintentionally tapped a raw nerve about Colin. "I don't know anything about your relationship with Heather. I'm sorry."

Josh rocked back in his chair, his fingers laced together on what looked like six-pack abs. "Not that I need to explain myself, but I was divorced a couple of years ago, and I'm not in the market for a serious relationship. You don't have to worry about younger women wanting to get serious."

"You mean unlike women my age who are all desperate to nail down a man before we lose the minimal sex appeal we've still got left?"

"A woman in her early twenties doesn't hear her biological clock ticking."

Abby rested her elbows on the table and her chin on her hands, Josh's failure to dispute her minimal sex appeal comment striking a couple more nerves. "I think I'd be more worried about peer pressure and the influence of *Brides* magazine than biological clocks in a town this size. Unless she's into her career."

Kim snorted. "Not hardly. Heather works part-time as a receptionist at State Farm."

"At least she graduated from college," Josh said, rocking back again.

Abby sat up. "It took ten years of night classes, but so did I," she said, resenting his implication she was dumb, not that a college degree proved anything in that regard. "From UCLA, magna cum laude, with a double major in literature and international politics."

"Heather's degree is from Metro U in fashion merchandising. I'm not sure how she managed even that, since I've never seen any evidence of a brain." Kim gave her brother a look. "I have no idea what you find to talk to her about."

Josh righted his chair and picked up his Heineken. "It's not like I'm looking for a woman who's rocket scientist material."

He could have at least given Heather's intelligence a perfunctory defense. She'd gotten the shallow jerk part right. Abby raised an eyebrow. "The first rocket scientist was actually a woman. Did you know that?"

Josh set down his bottle. "I suppose you minored in rocket science."

"No, but I've always liked to read. Her name was Ella Wheeler Wilcox, and she developed the theory of trajectory matter."

"What the hell is the theory of trajectory matter?"

"The reason rockets can escape the earth's gravity. C plus mc squared minus the square root of T."

"You're lying."

Abby narrowed her eyes at him. "What do you know about trajectory matter?"

"Not a thing."

"Yet you assume I must be lying." She took a sip of wine, then set the crystal glass carefully back on the iron tabletop and met his eyes. "I'll bet I know exactly what you and Heather talk about." She might not have met her, but from tonight's conversation she could predict the type of woman Josh would go for. "She spends all her time discussing fat grams, nail polish shades, and what clothes she's buying with her next paycheck, right? And whatever was in *People*, *Cosmo*, the tabloids, and the fashion and beauty rags, which are the only things she reads. She probably refuses to go to any movie with subtitles and finds politics too dull for words, so those topics are out. The only news she cares about is entertainment news."

Abby shook her head. "I'll bet if you ask her about trajectory matter or rocket science or even Darfur or the Taliban, she'll have no idea what you're talking about. Then again, you aren't dating a twenty-two-year-old for intellectual stimulation."

Kim was laughing, but Josh was glaring, appearing every bit the fierce pirate Abby had originally cast him as. "It's really none of your business, is it?"

Abby looked down, embarrassed at a tirade aimed more at Colin than Josh. She'd better lay off the wine for a while. "You're right, it isn't. You hit a sensitive subject."

"Because actresses are considered over-the-hill once they hit their midthirties?" Josh asked.

She gave him a tight smile. "Thanks for pointing that out."

"Believe it or not, I didn't mean it as a slam," Josh said, his expression less hostile. "I think Hollywood's emphasis on youth when it comes to women is sexist and stupid. Most actresses improve with age."

"Kim, can you please help me set things out?" Eric yelled from the doorway of the house.

"I'll be right there."

"I'll help, too," Abby said, getting to her feet and following Kim to the house. Because despite one nice comment about aging actresses, she had a feeling that without Kim as a buffer, any conversation with Josh would soon resemble a misfiring rocket.

– – –

"I wonder where Josh is?" Kim asked after dinner. She, Abby, and Eric were all drinking coffee on the deck—the screened one, out of deference to the mosquitoes that had appeared en masse at dusk. Rachel was showing Maddie her bedroom. They'd apparently bonded, which had Abby in a terrific mood.

"There is no such thing as the theory of trajectory matter," Josh said, striding from the kitchen onto the deck. The screen door slammed behind him. "Ella Wheeler Wilcox wasn't even a scientist. She was a poet and not a particularly good one."

"Why would you think that?" Abby asked with mock innocence.

He towered over her. "I Googled it. Although you're an actress, so no wonder I half believed you."

"Good thing I don't lie, isn't it?" she said. "Other than about rocket science."

Josh didn't answer, instead turning to Kim. "I hate to break up the party, but I need to get going. I've had a long day."

"So have I," Abby said. A day that had started with a nightmare and included far too much contact with Josh Kincaid. "I'll get Maddie."

CHAPTER 4

Abby had braced herself for a replay of the nightmare, but she didn't open her eyes until nine the next morning. Her subconscious had apparently concluded that if neither her research nor Eleanor Blake could identify anything suspicious connected to her house, then nothing had happened there.

Her relief about Maddie also had a lot to do with her restful night. Abby hadn't anticipated the social difficulties moving in the summer would create. Laura had enough trouble juggling her own three kids' summer schedules without asking her to arrange playdates for Maddie.

Maddie had been so excited and happy on the ride home last night, talking nonstop about Rachel and how much fun she'd had. Rachel had invited her over this afternoon, and Kim had promised to introduce her to more girls her age. Thanks to Rachel and Kim, Maddie was going to be fine.

Thanks to Josh, too, Abby grudgingly conceded. He might be an ass, but she was grateful for what he'd done for Maddie. He'd also apparently accepted her assessment of the threatening letters she'd received since he hadn't brought them up on the drive home. And now that she knew the knife and stain were nothing, she'd never have to see him again.

On that positive note, Abby threw off her teal duvet and got out of bed.

– – –

Abby's good mood continued through the weekend. She moved her office to the other empty bedroom, which had screaming-orange shag carpet and brown-and-orange plaid walls but at least didn't trigger disturbing memories of her dream. Then she spent hours both Saturday and Sunday writing and was unusually productive, especially once she realized the police chief would make a perfect—and unexpected—second murder victim. Now it was Sunday night, and she and Maddie were navigating their way through the basil-, pepperoni-, and tomato-laced air and darting kids that filled Pizzaville, the combination amusement center and pizza place Laura's youngest son, Brandon, had selected to celebrate his fifth birthday.

This was what Abby loved most about living in Harrington—being able to spend a casual evening with her family, which is what Bill, Mary, and Laura were, much more than any biological relative had ever been. She still thanked God every day that her kindergarten teacher had made sure she got into the gifted and talented magnet school for first grade, where she and Laura had become best friends. Because without Mary and Bill in her life, who knows what might have become of her?

"Did you get any writing done this weekend?" Laura asked after sending Maddie to play miniature golf with her two younger kids and husband, Greg. "Or did you come up with more ways to avoid it?"

Abby set a wrapped gift on the red vinyl tablecloth, then sat down on a coordinating vinyl-and-chrome chair. "I didn't go to the courthouse Friday to avoid writing. I actually got a great idea for my book while I was there. Eleanor Blake reminded me about the Castleton mausoleum, and I realized a mausoleum would be a perfect place to store the smuggled items until they can be shipped to purchasers."

"You'll be able to write a creepy cemetery scene, too," Laura said.

Abby nodded. "I was thinking Marissa could find something there—a piece of jewelry or something else that she'd think was nothing but later realize was a vital clue to what's going on."

"But you didn't go to the courthouse for inspiration. You went because you're neurotic," Laura said, getting to her feet. "That's why I told Dad about your dream and asked him to look into having the stain on the floor analyzed. He can tell you about it while I check on Jeremy in the video arcade. He thinks he's too old to have his parents around, but I don't completely trust him."

When Laura walked away, Abby turned her attention to the older man sitting across from her. "I'll have a friend in Minneapolis FedEx me a kit so I can take a sample of the stain and have it analyzed," Bill Tate said. At sixty-one, he was still fit and handsome, his thick silver hair glowing under the restaurant's bright lights.

Then again, Bill had to keep up with his wife, who with her short auburn hair and trim figure could pass for at least a decade younger than she was. As Laura frequently noted, good genes and old family money could keep any woman looking young. Although so far Mary had only resorted to a little Botox, and Abby hoped she never decided to get a full face-lift. The laugh lines at the corners of her green eyes and generous mouth added character and warmth it would be a pity to erase.

"Don't bother," Abby told Bill. "I've concluded I overreacted. According to Eleanor, no one suspicious ever lived in the house."

"She'd know," Mary said, her tone a combination of disapproval and admiration.

"The nightmare obviously resulted from the combination of finding the knife and eating a hot fudge sundae too close to bedtime. The stain has to be paint, and some kid probably planted the knife as a joke or it ended up there by accident."

"You knew where to find the stain because of your dream," Mary pointed out.

"It was in a different place on the floor," Abby said. "I'll bet if you removed the carpet in any room, you'd find paint stains."

"It could be blood," Mary said. "I think you should check it out to be sure. Maybe you're psychic."

Bill snorted. "Mary and I have agreed to disagree on the existence of psychics. That doesn't mean you didn't stumble on blood. Say the word and I'll check it out, if only for your peace of mind."

God, she loved these people. "I appreciate it, but I'd rather forget it. How was Minneapolis? Laura said you got home yesterday afternoon."

"Bill had to work, so ask me," Mary said. "I spent all day Friday at a spa." She sighed loudly. "Talk about heaven. Sometimes I can't believe you moved away from a place where people consider massages a necessity."

"I did get a little time off," Bill said. "We went to the Guthrie. They did *A Midsummer Night's Dream*, and for once it wasn't one of their modern interpretations."

Mary waved her hand, her nails a subtle pink. "Bill can't stand anyone updating Shakespeare. He's such an old fuddy-duddy sometimes."

Bill chuckled, shaking his head. "A *fuddy-duddy*?" Then he turned to Abby, his expression again serious. "I'm sorry we were gone when you found both the knife and stain. Otherwise we could have helped you with the police. Laura said you had a few problems with Chief Kincaid."

"I can't believe he accused you of staging both those things for publicity." Mary raised her chin and voice. "He doesn't even know you, and the way he treated you was out of line. Right after Laura told me about it, I called Bobby."

"You didn't have to do that," Abby said, suppressing a frown. Actually, she wished Mary hadn't. Bobby was Mayor Robert Sinclair, Mary's close personal friend, partly because of her charm, but also because of her substantial contributions to his pet projects. After a lecture from the mayor, Josh would be even more unpleasant if she encountered him again.

Mary planted her hands on the red tablecloth. "I most certainly did. No one gets away with treating you like that."

"In his favor, Josh noticed Maddie was lonely and invited us to his sister's on Friday night so she could meet his niece. Rachel and Maddie really hit it off," Abby said. "He also reportedly knows his job and is no doubt right about the knife and stain being nothing."

"Perhaps," Bill said. "But Laura told me something that concerns me more. You got another one of those letters."

"I told you before they're no big deal. It's been well documented that anonymous letter writers rarely do more, especially when the threats are as nonspecific as these are." Abby smiled faintly. "Although I mentioned them when we were at Kim's, and Josh took them seriously. I wondered why, but now I realize he was probably terrified if he didn't, I'd sic Mary on him."

"Chief Kincaid took them seriously because they're serious," Mary said. "Bill and I agree on that."

"I told Jeremy I'd pay him ten bucks to go help his dad with the other kids," Laura said as she approached the table. "That arcade music was driving me nuts." She sat down in an empty chair beside Abby. "What's serious?"

"These letters Abby's been getting," Mary said.

"She really does get them all the time," Laura said, then tilted her head at Abby, her auburn hair skimming one shoulder. "Remember when Samantha seduced that priest? You sent me copies of some of those. They were awful."

"Because that whole story line was awful, and I don't care if he did turn out to be a mob hit man only pretending to be a priest." Memories of that particular story line always made Abby feel as if she'd bit into an apple, then spotted half a worm. "Naturally people are going to object when you seduce a priest, especially when you do it to win a bet."

Laura nodded. "My point is that Abby's gotten lots of them before, way worse than these."

"And security sent anything that looked potentially dangerous to the LAPD," Abby said. "Out of hundreds, maybe even thousands of letters they reviewed, the cops only thought a half dozen warranted investigating, and those all turned out to be nothing."

"This time you got three letters from the same person," Bill said. "They also came to your house, not to *Private Affairs*."

"That just means it was easier to find my address than the station's."

"And that the sender knows where you live," Bill said.

"I already got a lecture from the police chief." Abby raised her right hand. "I solemnly swear from now on I'll give any anonymous letters I receive to the police." She should never have mentioned those blasted letters to anyone. She should have realized most people without her experience wouldn't dismiss innocuous letters like these the way she could. "Are you still willing to watch Maddie on Tuesday, Laura?"

"Nicole would be crushed if she didn't come over. Maddie's her idol." Nicole was six.

"Olivia Hayes has an appearance at the Mall of America on Tuesday afternoon," Abby explained to Mary and Bill.

"I'll bet she tries to convince you to go back to the show," Laura said.

"It would be a little anticlimactic if I returned after the terrific send-off they're giving me."

"We can't wait to see it," Mary said.

"Be prepared." Abby's cheeks heated. "It gets a little racy."

Laura grinned. "Because Evan comes back."

"Evan? Patrick Dane's still playing him, I hope." Mary pressed her hand over her heart. "I've had a crush on him since he started on the show."

"Patrick signed a two-year contract," Abby said. "I loved working with him again, even if only for a few scenes."

"Is he single?" Mary asked.

"You aren't," Bill said firmly.

"But Abby is."

"Patrick and I are just good friends," Abby said. "Platonic friends."

"You'll have to continue your matchmaking later, Mom." Laura's gaze was on her husband and the four kids he was shepherding toward their table. "Adult conversation time has apparently ended."

– – –

Josh was in a crappy mood, and it was all Abby Langford's fault. He'd been dating Heather for nearly three months and had enjoyed his time with her. Maybe they hadn't had any deep discussions, but he hadn't cared because they'd had a lot of fun.

Until tonight. Before tonight he'd never realized just how much Heather talked. And that nearly all of her conversations concerned exercise, diets, fat grams, and clothes she'd tried on or bought in either size two or size zero, whatever the hell size zero was. She'd also rhapsodized over the dress some actress he'd never heard of had worn to some awards ceremony he'd also never heard of, then spent forever on a story about her quest for the perfect red nail polish. He never would have noticed if it hadn't been for Abby's comments.

That didn't necessarily make Heather uninformed. So he'd tried asking her about the presidential election. Heather had flipped her long dark hair over one shoulder and told him she considered politics so boring she'd never even voted, except for *American Idol* and *People's Choice*, of course. He'd asked her a question about Darfur. She'd flipped her hair over the other shoulder and said she hadn't heard of him, but then she wasn't a big fan of rap music.

He didn't bother asking her opinion of foreign films, not that it mattered since the film they were seeing tonight was definitely all-American. As in *American Pie Forever*, which Heather had been dying to see since its release last week. Josh normally wouldn't have rented it as a last resort, but he could handle it. At least during the movie he wouldn't have to listen to Heather talk.

Something he'd always enjoyed until Abby Langford had butted into his personal life.

– – –

Abby sat back in the family room recliner that still reclined, picked the remote off the coffee table, and turned on the TV. When they'd gotten home from Pizzaville, Maddie had willingly gone straight to bed, but Abby felt as a grown-up, she should make it until at least ten.

She yawned. On the other hand, one of the good things about being a grown-up was you didn't have to prove you were one. She released the footrest, turned off the TV, and headed upstairs.

After checking on Maddie, Abby went to her own bedroom. The tan walls and mint-green shag carpet weren't her style, but far less atrocious than the other bedrooms' decor. She'd furnished the room with mission-style furniture—her first priority when she'd moved in was going to Minneapolis to buy bedroom furnishings. With all the sleepless nights Colin had given her, she took being able to sleep seriously.

She yawned again as she pulled an oversize Bruce Springsteen T-shirt off a hook in the closet. Colin had insisted she wear fancy nightgowns, but she really wasn't comfortable in those. Samantha Cartwright wore silk and lace, but Abby Langford liked soft, faded cotton. No wonder she'd ended up back in the Midwest. She carried the T-shirt into the bathroom adjoining her bedroom, then flipped on the light.

And started shaking.

– – –

"Aren't we going to your place first?" Heather asked as Josh turned off Castleton Street onto Lincoln Avenue.

He hadn't realized he'd started driving Heather home after the movie. He'd obviously let Abby's comments make him too critical, but he wasn't about to let her ruin the entire evening for him. "I was thinking about something else. I'd love to have you come over if you want to."

She ran her tongue over her full lips and squeezed his thigh. "I definitely want to. I've got big plans for tonight." She brushed her fingers over his crotch. "Really big."

Josh turned his attention back to the road before she saw his grimace. Jesus, that sounded like something from *Cosmo*, "Trash Talk That'll Turn Him On."

So what if Heather read *Cosmo*? Even if he sometimes felt she was experimenting with something she'd read about instead of caught up in passion, he still enjoyed it. Occasionally he wished he felt a little more connected to her, but anything that made sex more than recreation also might make a woman get serious, which he didn't want. Heather liked sex as recreation, especially with him. She'd told him often enough she'd never realized how much she liked it until she'd met him.

Although *Cosmo* probably told you to say that, too.

When his phone rang and he saw the number, Josh was actually relieved. He pulled over to the curb. "I need to take this. It's work."

"I thought you were off tonight," Heather said, pushing out her bottom lip.

"Sometimes I still have to check in." As she knew. This had happened before, and every time she'd pouted.

"What is it?" Heather asked after he'd called the dispatcher back.

"I need to take you home," he said, the dispatcher's message worsening his foul mood. "I have to handle this personally."

Abby Langford strikes again.

CHAPTER 5

The doorbell rang, shooting a fresh blast of cold panic through Abby. She opened her mouth, but swallowed her scream—it had to be the police. Bad guys didn't use doorbells. She unlocked and opened the front door with frozen fingers.

Josh was standing on the front porch, dressed in black jeans and a burgundy polo shirt, his hand on the doorjamb and his eyes narrowed. "What's such a damn emergency?"

"I got another message. From the person who hates me."

Josh expelled a clearly exasperated breath, running his fingers through his dark hair. "Look, I know I told you to take the letters seriously, but since the mail carrier delivered it hours ago, this isn't exactly an emergency. Bring it to the station tomorrow. I'd like to get back to my date."

"It didn't come in the mail this time." Abby's voice rose an octave, her words tripping over each other. "It's on my bathroom mirror, written in lipstick. Someone got into my house, and they could get in again." She sounded half-hysterical, but she couldn't help it. This was in a different category from her normal hate mail.

Josh stepped into the house, closing the door behind him. "You were gone tonight?"

She slumped against one wall of the foyer, hugging herself and struggling to regain her control. "Maddie and I were at a birthday party for Laura's youngest son. At Pizzaville. We got home around nine thirty, and I put Maddie to bed. I read in the family room for a while, then went back upstairs. And found it."

"Show me." Josh grabbed her forearm and directed her up the stairs.

The message was short and to the point, capital letters written in red lipstick on the wall-size mirror:

LEAVE OR DIE BITCH. YOUR BIGGEST FAN

Abby looked away, unable to face those screaming letters. "I think he used my lipstick. My Lancôme Hot Nights is missing, and it's that color. So I could have staged this, but I didn't. I promise I didn't..." To her disgust, her voice shook, then faded. She was an actor—why couldn't she act calm?

"Let's go downstairs so we won't wake Maddie," Josh said after he'd taken a photo of the message with his phone. He used a hand towel to shut the door, then took Abby's arm again and led her down to the living room. "Were all your doors locked?"

"The windows, too."

"Wait here. I'll be back in a few minutes."

Abby lowered herself stiffly onto the couch. She sat shivering with her arms wrapped around herself, staring at the closed venetian blinds and listening to Josh walk around the house and basement, opening and closing doors.

After several minutes he returned to the living room. "I can't see any evidence of a break-in, but the lock on the back door would be easy to pop." He sat down beside her. "You said you've had a lot of workers around. Did you give any of them a key?"

She shook her head. "My friend Laura Stuart's the only one with a key." Her lips were so frosty she wouldn't have been surprised to see her breath.

"I'll need their names anyway. We'll also need to check for prints."

She hesitated before she spoke. "I don't want Maddie to know about this."

"She's going to Kim's tomorrow, right?"

"At ten."

"I'll wait to do it until after she leaves. Assuming you can stay out of that bathroom until then."

Abby nodded mechanically. She wasn't entering that bathroom until the lipstick was erased, if ever.

"You need new locks," Josh continued. "Yours are crap. I'll arrange for a locksmith to come while Maddie's gone. I'll also give you the names of a couple of Minneapolis companies to call about security systems."

Abby nodded once more, her eyes again fixed on the dingy cream slats across the room. This couldn't be real. She had to be on the *Private Affairs* set, playing a scene. No one could hate her enough to break into her house and write a threat on her mirror.

Except she felt too cold to be acting.

"I'm sure nothing more will happen tonight," Josh said. "To be safe, I'll have a squad car make frequent trips by your place, and I'll give you my cell phone number. If anything comes up, call me, even in the middle of the night."

"I'd hate to interrupt your date again," Abby said.

He shot her a wry look. "I'd rather have that happen than lose my job, so call. The mayor ordered me to handle your calls personally."

Abby lowered her chin and closed her eyes for a moment. She truly wished Mary hadn't interfered. "I didn't request that."

"He said you didn't. Get your cell phone and you can enter the number."

"Just tell it to me. I have a good memory."

Josh recited the number, then got to his feet. "I'll send someone over tomorrow at ten thirty."

"Does this mean you believe I didn't do this myself?" Abby asked. "Or are you following orders to humor me?"

He studied her for a moment, then shrugged. "Damned if I know."

– – –

Which was the truth, Josh acknowledged as he pulled away from the curb and onto the deserted, well-lit street. Although he'd told the dispatcher to notify him if Abby called, he'd never intended to handle her calls himself, to hell with the mayor. He'd only done it tonight because, thanks to Abby, he hadn't been in the mood to be with Heather. When he'd headed over, he'd assumed he'd encounter yet another part of a publicity campaign.

But Abby had honestly seemed scared. She was an actress, but her arm felt cool and shaky, she was so pale even her lips were white, and her eyes looked like blue-violet marbles. He wasn't positive she could have faked all those physical reactions, so he'd decided to take the threat seriously. Instead of exhibiting even a hint of triumph at convincing him, she'd appeared more scared, as if his taking it seriously meant it was worse than she'd feared.

Even if she hadn't staged it, she should be safe tonight. Assuming the writer intended to do more than threaten, he clearly wanted to savor her fear for a while first. Otherwise once he'd broken in, he'd have stuck around.

On the other hand, there was something decidedly deranged about breaking into a house and threatening an actress because you hated her character. If the problem instead was with Abby's personal life, he could be dealing with a certifiable religious fanatic who'd confused the minister her husband played on TV with reality. How could you predict someone that crazy wouldn't decide to return in a couple of hours to finish the job?

Josh pulled into the driveway of a brick Colonial, backed out, and turned his car around.

— — —

Abby opened the door an instant after Josh knocked—he hadn't wanted to risk waking Maddie by ringing the bell.

He glared down at her. "You should never just open your door like that. Who knows who might be out here?" Jesus, he'd come back because he was worried, and she was acting like a five-year-old with negligent parents.

"I saw your car pull up." She planted her hands on her hips. She was still pale, but at least her skin had a pink tinge and her eyes weren't so wide and glassy. "Did you conclude I wrote the message myself and return to deliver another lecture about not using the police department for PR purposes?"

"I told you I'm not sure whether you did it or not," he said, stepping around her and into the foyer. "On the off chance you didn't, I realized that whoever's responsible could be crazy enough to come back tonight." He closed the door. "So I'm staying."

Her jaw dropped. "You are not spending the night here."

"If I don't, and you end up dead, I'll be in major trouble with the mayor," he said, locking the sorry excuse for a dead bolt. "Even worse, Rachel will never forgive me if something happens to Maddie."

Josh strode into the living room with Abby trailing behind him. "The couch looks long enough. If you'll get me a pillow and blanket, I'll sleep there."

"You don't have to do this," she said. "I'll admit I was scared when you showed up earlier, but I'm better now. I'm sure you're right, that nothing more will happen tonight. I'll even call the mayor and tell him I refused your protection."

"Don't bother. I'm staying." He sat down on the couch and untied his shoes.

"I hate ruining your date," Abby said.

He met her eyes. "It was already ruined."

"I'm sorry."

"We saw *American Pie Forever*." She looked so contrite, he had to admit that.

"From the reviews, it makes my soap look like a best picture contender."

His gave her a rueful half smile. "The reviewers were too kind."

She nodded with a slight smile. "I'll get you some bedding." She turned and went upstairs.

Josh slipped his shoes off and sat down on the couch. Maybe he'd imagined it, but she'd looked relieved when he'd told her he was staying. Maybe some crazy really had left the lipstick message.

And maybe he was the crazy one, spending the night on this couch instead of getting a good night's sleep in his own bed. He stood as Abby returned carrying sheets, a blanket, and a pillow.

"I'll make it up for you," she said.

"I'll do it." He took the bedding from her and set it on the couch.

"There's a bathroom just off the kitchen. I'll put a new toothbrush and some toothpaste by the sink."

"Thanks. I'll be gone by six. I wouldn't want Maddie to wake up and wonder why I'm here."

"I appreciate it." She cleared her throat. "I also appreciate your staying. I know it isn't in your job description."

"As I said, my niece would never forgive me if anything happened to Maddie." Josh picked up a blue, flowered sheet. "Go get some sleep."

- - -

The knife was in the air, pointing downward at an angle. Fresh blood stained the tip, halfway up the steel blade. A fisted hand clenched the brown walnut handle—a man's hand, she could tell that even though she could only see his hand and wrist.

The man thrust the knife down through the air and out of view, raised it, thrust again. More and more blood coated the blade, dripping into the air below and sending rivulets toward the handle, as the knife rose and plunged, over and over.

Then the knife disappeared. Instead she saw a window, built-in bookshelves, a light wood floor. Narrow planks with an oval pool of bright-red blood seeping onto some pale-blue fabric beside it. A pool that was getting bigger...

"No," she murmured, shaking her head vehemently on her pillow. The blood. There was so much, so much blood.

"Abby, I'm coming in."

Abby bolted up and opened her eyes, blinking against the overhead light as Josh crossed the room in three steps, gun in hand.

"From the noise, I was afraid someone had broken in." He towered over her, shirtless, his jeans zipped but unsnapped. "Are you OK?"

She tried to slow her breathing. "I had a nightmare. I'm fine now." She was outside the covers and so cold her bones felt like icicles. She wrapped her arms around her sweat-drenched T-shirt.

"You don't look fine. Do you want to talk about it?" He set his gun on the nightstand and sat down beside her.

She shook her head again, trying to dislodge the images. She didn't want to think about it, let alone talk about it.

He rubbed his darkly stubbled chin. "It must have been a bad one, the way you were moaning and thrashing around. I'm surprised you didn't wake Maddie."

"Maddie sleeps through everything." Abby closed her eyes and tried to picture Maddie. Instead she saw the knife stabbing up and down, the blood. She shivered.

Suddenly, warm hands closed on her shoulders. Then even warmer lips touched hers, tasting of mint with a hint of espresso. Abby instinctively circled her arms around Josh's neck and pressed her breasts against his chest, his heat penetrating her damp T-shirt. He felt so warm, so solid, so safe.

His whiskers rasped her skin and his teeth grazed her lip, the friction generating more heat, heat that every accelerated heartbeat pumped through her body. Abby opened her mouth, letting his tongue stroke its way inside. Her breasts were steaming, her nipples straining beneath her T-shirt. She arched her back, pressing hard against his chest, enjoying the wonderful warmth coursing through her.

Just as suddenly, Josh released her. Without another word, he retrieved his gun and left the room, switching off the light and closing the door behind him.

Abby stared at the door, her hand fisting around the duvet. Her blood was boiling, but no longer from passion. What the hell had just happened?

She didn't have a clue why Josh had kissed her. She was annoyed that he had and then just walked out. But to be honest, she was more annoyed with herself. What had she been doing, responding that passionately to a man she disliked? So what if Josh was a world-class kisser? So what if outside of work, she hadn't been kissed in far too long? Was she really that desperate?

Then it hit her. It was because of the nightmare and the lipstick message. She'd read that stress triggered the urge for sex, and those two things had her so stressed-out she'd probably have reacted to any man.

She released the duvet, nodding. That's all that had happened tonight. She'd simply had a normal, physiological reaction to stress.

With that thought, she plopped back down on her pillow, closed her eyes, and slept.

CHAPTER 6

"I cleaned the mirror after I finished printing and photographing the bathroom," Officer Ben Alton said, walking into Abby's family room late the next morning. "I didn't think you'd mind."

Abby looked up from the book she was unsuccessfully trying to read. With his smooth complexion, sun-streaked brown hair, and wide hazel eyes, Ben barely looked old enough to shave, let alone be a police officer. However, his professional manner had confirmed what Abby had assumed, that he was one of the best. Josh wouldn't dare send anyone incompetent to handle her.

He hadn't shown up himself today, and it was lucky for him. Because the instant Abby had opened her eyes, she'd realized exactly why he'd kissed her, and she was even more furious than she'd been last night. Josh had the warped idea she was trying to manipulate him. So he'd taken advantage of her agitation to prove he could manipulate her and with sex, no less. That she was also pissed at herself for falling for it only made her madder.

"I appreciate it," she said, giving Ben a warm smile. It wasn't his fault that his boss was an ass.

He set a black canvas bag on the carpet. "The chief had me drive my own car here, so no one will realize you had a cop stop by. He doesn't want this to end up reported in the *Herald*. He's afraid getting publicity might encourage the guy to act again."

Josh was no doubt more concerned about her getting publicity, but Abby let it pass. "I certainly don't want that. As I said, I appreciate your taking care of this."

"No problem." Ben stuffed his hands into his pockets. "I used to watch you all the time when I was in college." He grinned. "To be honest, I only started to get in good with my girlfriend, but I kept watching even after we broke up. I still watch sometimes when I'm off weekdays. You're terrific." His cheeks had reddened slightly, making him look even younger.

"Thanks. I'm hoping when Samantha's finally killed off my message writer will be satisfied."

"I guess someone could have gotten you confused with Samantha. You're so good at playing her, and there are a lot of kooks around." Ben picked up his bag. "If you're sure you're OK, I'd better get back to the station. If anything comes up, even if you just get nervous being here alone, call Chief Kincaid. He said you have his number."

No way was she calling Josh for anything, not even if she dug up a dead body in the backyard. But Abby simply nodded, keeping a pleasant expression on her face as she walked Ben to the door. Then she headed upstairs.

Half an hour later she was staring at the cursor on her computer screen, indented and ready for a new paragraph if she could figure out what the heck to write. And she needed to write. She was counting on it to help her escape reality the way acting always had.

To help her forget that someone hated her or Samantha enough to risk breaking into her house to leave that horrible message.

Unfortunately, she had a major case of writer's block. She stood and stretched, then crossed the orange carpet to the window. Maplewood Avenue was empty, even the birds and squirrels taking a break in the midday heat. No inspiration there.

She returned to her computer and opened her e-mail account. Nothing new had arrived in the five minutes since she'd last checked it, so she returned to staring at the blank monitor page.

Maybe the problem was that damn kiss. Even knowing Josh's despicable motivation, her creative subconscious probably couldn't plot the murder of a character inspired by the man who'd given her the hottest kiss she could remember. Her hand tightened on the mouse. Now Josh was not only annoying; he was also interfering with her writing.

She wasn't about to eliminate the police chief victim, but she'd focus on something else today. Like revising the earlier chapters about the first victim, the eighteen-year-old actress.

She clicked the mouse and scrolled backward.

– – –

Thank God Kim had invited him for lunch, Josh thought as he pulled into her driveway. She'd distract him from what a morning of meetings hadn't managed to—obsessing about last night. What had he been thinking kissing Abby Langford? Although the answer was painfully obvious. He'd done it because he hadn't been thinking, and because even pale, sweaty, and tangled, she'd looked so damn sexy he hadn't been able to resist.

He got out of his car and headed to the house, striding through the front door without knocking. "I had to bust my ass to get here before noon, like you insisted," he said as he stepped over a flute case and music book on his way to the kitchen. "Whatever you made had better be worth it." He didn't doubt it would be— Kim had taken their mother's excellent cooking to an even higher level.

"I got sandwiches from Baldridge's," Kim called from the family room. "Get your food from the kitchen and bring it in here."

"Why?" Josh asked, detouring to the family room.

Kim was clearing several magazines off the cherry-and-black-steel coffee table. "Because we're watching *Private Affairs.*" She set the magazines on the tile floor beside the deep, ruby sofa. "This is Abby's last week, so she's got a lot of airtime."

"No way in hell."

Kim crossed her arms and got that look, something besides her cooking skills she'd picked up from their mother. "If you see what a terrific actress she is, you might have more respect for her. She did quite a bit of prime-time work, but stopped when Maddie was born. And she turned down lots of movie offers because she didn't want to haul Maddie around on location."

"How damn noble of her."

"See, you're totally biased against her."

"I'm not—"

"Are you two done eating?" Kim asked, looking over Josh's shoulder. He swiveled his head to see Maddie and Rachel coming out of the kitchen.

"Kim said you're watching Mommy's show today," Maddie told Josh. "That's awesome." She was wearing her hair in a thick braid, making her blue eyes look enormous.

Even on the off chance Kim would let him skip out, how could he disappoint such a cute kid? Josh stifled a sigh. "I guess I am. Are you watching with us?"

Maddie shook her head. "Mommy won't let me. I get to watch sometimes, but most of the time she says the show's too old for me. She didn't want me to see her get killed this week, even though she just gets hit on the head, falls into the water, and disappears."

She covered her mouth with her fingers, looking guilty. "I shouldn't have told you that. Now I've ruined the suspense."

"Your mom already told me." Kim started toward the kitchen. "We'd better get our food if we don't want to miss anything, Josh. Today should be really good because Samantha's daughter just found out her mother slept with her boyfriend."

Josh selected a muffuletta sandwich, then grabbed a bag of jalapeño potato chips. He'd better eat fast, and not just because this wouldn't get his mind off Abby. He also had a feeling two minutes of watching that crap would kill his appetite.

Except it didn't. Some of the lines were hokey, but much as he hated to admit it, Abby was good. She seemed more sad than cocky about having slept with Blade, claiming it had been his idea and she'd gone along to prove he was slime. Her daughter, Jessica, said she didn't believe her, that she'd obviously seduced Blade to hurt her and was no longer her mother, then ran out of the room. And Samantha broke down and cried, so pitifully Josh started feeling sorry for the bitch who'd slept with her daughter's boy-friend. No wonder Abby had won all those Emmys.

Kim muted the TV when they broke for a commercial. "Isn't she terrific?"

"Doesn't this show have any other characters?" Josh asked, annoyed he agreed with Kim's assessment.

"Of course it does. They're concentrating on Samantha so lots of people will have motives to kill her."

"OK." Josh stood up. "I've watched the show, and I'll admit Abby's got talent. Now can I go?"

"Not until you have dessert. I made a fruit tart."

Josh sat back down. "I knew there was a reason you're my favorite sister."

A moment later Kim returned to the family room, carrying two plates. "Oh my God."

"What's wrong?" Josh dropped the *Sports Illustrated* he'd been paging through and accepted the larger piece of fruit tart.

"Evan's back. Abby didn't tell me that part." Kim unmuted the TV.

Sure enough, the show was on again, and some dark-haired guy in a suit was talking to Samantha's secretary. "Who's Evan?"

"He and Samantha were in love, but they had a big fight, and he left town a couple of years ago. She married Max on the rebound, and they got divorced after three months because she hasn't gotten over Evan."

"I can see why you're so excited," Josh said sarcastically. But he couldn't take his eyes off the TV when Evan stormed into Abby's office, hauled her out of her chair, and kissed her passionately. Then Abby was kissing Evan back, just like she'd kissed him last night.

"Abby told me love scenes are weird to do," Kim said. "Every movement has to be choreographed because acting natural doesn't always look good on film, and you also can't risk offending the TV censors. She said you usually don't even open your mouth when you kiss."

OK, maybe Abby wasn't kissing Evan *exactly* like she'd kissed him, but God, it was bringing back memories that were making Josh hard. Especially when Evan started kissing Abby's neck and unbuttoning her blouse. Then her blouse was off, and he was kissing the impossibly creamy skin just above her lacy black bra. Abby—no, Samantha—pulled her shirt together and told him to stop. He said he'd locked the door, and he'd never stop. She said good and let her shirt fall open. Then they cut to commercial.

"I can't believe how terrific Abby looks," Kim said. "She's almost as old as me, but she makes me feel like a frump."

Josh took a big bite of his tart, hoping the fruit and cream would moisten his dry mouth enough that he'd be able to answer. "You look great, and you know it," he got out once he'd swallowed. "Looking good is her business. She probably spends a fortune on it."

"She had a personal trainer, but not a bit of plastic surgery, not ever. Even her boobs are real."

This discussion was not increasing Josh's comfort level. "You certainly learned a lot about her in one evening."

"I also talked to her when she dropped Maddie off today," Kim said, waving her cream-coated fork. "She's easy to talk to. Although I didn't mention I was going to make you watch *Private Affairs* since I was afraid you'd refuse."

Abby apparently hadn't told Kim he'd spent the night on her couch. Good, because he didn't want his sister to get the wrong idea. "She probably would have told you not to bother, that she didn't want a fan like me."

"She'd figure you'd only have eyes for her TV daughter anyway—knowing your fondness for ingénue types."

Josh opened his mouth to respond, but Kim shushed him because the show was back on. Jessica was talking to a man Josh didn't recognize. Maybe Abby and Evan had finished for the day.

No such luck. In just over a minute, the show switched back to them. Now Evan had Abby on the desk and was telling her how beautiful she was and that he loved her and had been a fool. He took off his own shirt, then Abby's skirt, exposing more black lace, plus a black garter belt with black stockings. Josh shifted uncomfortably in his chair. She looked so blasted hot, writhing on the desk as Evan kissed and touched her.

Josh tried to make himself close his eyes, but he couldn't, even though he felt like a voyeur. He didn't want to be watching, he wanted to be on that desk with her, and she wouldn't be wearing that bra anymore. Then she told Evan she'd always love him and kissed him, arching her back so her beautiful, bra-covered breasts pressed against Evan's bare chest, the same way she'd been pushing her T-shirted ones against his bare chest last night. And then the scene stopped and the closing credits came on.

"Well, that was fascinating," Josh said, managing to sound normal despite his pounding heart and a hard-on threatening to rip through his trousers.

Kim set her empty dessert plate on the coffee table. "It's difficult to believe she's the same woman we know, isn't it? Though that wasn't Abby. It was Samantha Cartwright."

"Mommy, Nathan's bothering us," Rachel yelled from upstairs.

Kim got to her feet. "I'd better go referee."

"I'll let myself out," Josh said. "Thanks for lunch."

"Thanks for being a good sport about watching."

"Mommy!"

"I'm on my way," Kim said, running up the stairs two at a time.

Josh hurried to the door. The instant he got into his car, he was calling Heather. God willing, she'd be free tonight, because he needed to see her, bad. Heather would be able to exorcise this ridiculous crush his hormones appeared to have on a woman he didn't even like.

– – –

"Josh watched the whole show," Maddie said as Abby drove her home later that afternoon. "Kim said he liked it."

"Uh-huh," Abby said noncommittally. Kim certainly wouldn't have told Maddie Josh's real opinion of the show. She pulled up to the four-way stop two blocks from their house. Then inspiration struck.

"Where are we going?" Maddie asked when Abby turned right, heading in the opposite direction from their house.

"I want to show you where Laura and I went to grade school and junior high," Abby said. "I can't believe I haven't done that yet."

"You should show me the house where you grew up, too," Maddie said.

"Not today." Actually, not ever, if Abby could avoid it. She'd forced herself to go see it a few days after she'd moved back to Harrington, but not for sentimental reasons. She'd been hoping that seeing it again after all these years would trigger any memories she still might be blocking out.

The trailer was on the same lot in Windsor Court, a little shabbier and rustier than when she'd lived there, although the current owners had spruced it up by planting flowers along one side. Abby had pulled up to the curb and viewed it from inside her idling car, not bothering to get out. She hadn't remembered anything new, but the memories she'd already faced apparently haunted the trailer. They'd rushed into her brain like a DVR on fast-forward, making her heart pound so hard and fast it felt about to burst through her chest and acid swirl in her churning stomach. She'd shifted the car into drive and raced away, needing to leave before she threw up, maybe even had a heart attack. She was not planning a return trip.

Abby drove into the nearly empty, blacktopped parking lot in front of what was now Burrows Neighborhood School. Other than the name change, the place looked the same as when she'd gone to school there, a sprawling single-story brick building with far too few windows, probably as much to minimize distractions for bored kids as to save on energy costs. The windows of the lower-grade classrooms had always been covered with student art—cutouts of birds, flowers, leaves, or snowflakes, depending on the season. The glass was bare now, either because the classrooms were unused in the summer or because, even in Harrington, teachers no longer considered cutting with scissors a valuable life skill.

Abby shut off the car. "Let's go inside." As she and Maddie walked along the sidewalk to the front door, she could hear kids' voices in the distance, playing at the playground behind the school.

Abby opened the front door of the school, and she and Maddie stepped inside. She couldn't describe the school's smell, but it was so familiar it produced a barrage of memories, good ones this time. She'd loved school. She'd been a top student, and it had been nice to get praise from her teachers after all the crap she'd gotten at home. More important, school had been a safe place, somewhere she didn't have to worry about her parents abusing her verbally or her dad hitting her or her mom—the kind of abuse she'd managed to make herself forget until recently.

The principal's office door was open, so Abby walked inside. She didn't recognize the woman behind the counter, but with her graying brown hair, plump, pleasantly middle-aged face, and warm smile, she was the stereotype of a school secretary. A nameplate on the counter identified her as Mrs. Hoover.

"I went to school here years ago and wanted to show it to my daughter," Abby said. "Is it OK if we look around?"

"Of course, Ms. Langford," Mrs. Hoover said. "I imagine it was a magnet school back when you were here. We shifted to a neighborhood school five years ago."

"Call me Abby, and it was." Thank God it had been, since otherwise she'd never have gotten to go to school here. Although her parents' trailer had only been eight blocks away, it and the school for her neighborhood were both across the railroad tracks—which had definitely been the wrong side of the tracks.

"Everyone should be gone except the custodians," Mrs. Hoover said. "Even the principal, who took advantage of the beautiful day to play golf." She made a face. "Wish I could do that, but I'm here for another hour. Feel free to look around."

Abby and Maddie walked down cool, dimly lit hallways, occasionally stopping to open a classroom door. Abby smiled when she recognized a teacher's name, memory warming her. Coming here had been one of her better ideas.

"I had Mrs. Murphy for fourth grade," Abby said. "She was great. I remember we had to memorize the poem 'Daffodils.' She let us go outside to recite it since it was a nice day, even though the daffodils hadn't started blooming yet."

"Did you have to memorize a poem because you wanted to be an actor?" Maddie asked.

"No, everyone in class had to do it."

"Why?"

"Because teachers thought some poems were important to know, I guess."

Maddie's forehead furrowed. "Couldn't you just look it up on the Internet if you ever needed to know it?"

"This was before the Internet had been invented, and yes, I'm that old," Abby said. "That reminds me of something. Come on." She grabbed Maddie's hand and led her around a corner, then to the end of the hallway. "This was my favorite place in the world. The school theater." Abby reached for the door, but it wouldn't open. "Too bad it's locked."

"Mommy, is this you?" Maddie asked. She was standing in front of an illuminated glass case, pointing at one of the many photos inside.

Abby walked over and looked into the case, then smiled. "That's when I played Cinderella. I was in eighth grade." She searched the photos, and her smile grew. "Believe it or not, that's me, too," she said, pointing to another photo. "With the red braids. That was the first play I ever had the lead in. *Pippi Longstocking.*"

Maddie giggled. "You look funny with red hair."

Suddenly Abby's breath caught, then goose bumps sprouted on her arms and shoulders. Something was wrong; she could sense it. Someone else was here. She took a couple of steps so she could check the dark hallway around the corner, then looked down the hallway they'd come from. Nothing but empty silence.

Maddie grabbed Abby's arm. "I was asking if this was Laura," she said. "What are you looking at?"

Abby forced her attention back to the first photo Maddie had asked about. "You're right, that's Laura. She played one of the ugly stepsisters." She managed to keep her voice level, but her pulse was racing and she felt cold, fear like icy fingers scraping down her spine.

Stop it. She was being ridiculous, getting freaked out because of that lipstick message, maybe having some kind of post-traumatic stress incident. She was in a public school, for God's sake, one of the places she'd loved growing up. Mrs. Hoover was guarding the front door, kids were outside, and custodians were doing their rounds. Otherwise no one was around, certainly no one who'd want to hurt her.

Abby looked around again, saw no one. But her brain was spinning, and she couldn't think, couldn't be reasonable. All she knew was that she couldn't stay here; she had to leave now. Her heart was hammering so hard she was surprised Maddie didn't hear it.

"Let's go," she said, taking Maddie's hand.

"I want to look at more pictures."

"We'll do it another time." She was nearly dragging Maddie down the hallway.

"Why are you in such a hurry?"

Because your mother's gotten so paranoid she's seeing monsters everywhere, like some overimaginative kid who's scared of the dark. "Because I got so interested in my writing today that I forgot to buy groceries," Abby said instead. "I need to go home and make a list, then we'll go to Erickson's. Otherwise we won't have anything for dinner."

As they walked down the hallway, the only sounds Abby heard were the thud and click of her and Maddie's sandals over the tile floor and the blood throbbing in her ears. But the chill and uneasy feeling didn't disappear, not even when they stepped out of the school and back into the day's sunny heat. Abby didn't start warming up until she was in the car and driving away.

– – –

Erickson's Market was located at the edge of Harrington's still-thriving downtown. As the carryout boy loaded her seven bags into the trunk of her Volvo, Abby looked around. Although Erickson's had been updated inside and out since she'd left Harrington, and most other downtown businesses had been replaced or refaced, the block across the street hadn't changed a bit. Granny's still had a hand-painted sign advertising A MILLION CALORIES' WORTH OF CANDY AND ICE CREAM, refusing to recognize this was a more health-conscious time. The Ben Franklin store was a little faded but otherwise looked the same. Yarn World was next door, with its bright-yellow storefront and windows displaying what could very well be the colorful knitted and crocheted garments that had been there nearly twenty years ago. Then there was Carmelo's Restaurant. It had appeared stuck in the sixties when Abby had been a kid, and it still did, with the same red, black, and silver facade, the same red awning over the door, and the same flashing neon sign in one window announcing it served Italian-American food. They probably still played Frank Sinatra's greatest hits non-stop. From the customers streaming in and out the front door, it was as popular as ever.

A car door slammed down the block. Abby glanced toward it and spotted Josh standing beside his Prius. His eyes met hers. Then he broke eye contact and wrapped a possessive arm around an attractive brunette who'd just exited the car, kissing her hair. Heather, no doubt.

Abby forced her attention back to the carryout boy, giving him a smile along with his tip, even though she was inwardly seething. Josh had to rub it in that his kiss last night had been nothing personal since he—like most males on the planet—preferred much younger women. When he'd watched *Private Affairs* today, he'd probably spent the entire time lusting after Jessica and wishing she'd been the one with Evan in that black getup.

"Don't get into the car yet," Abby told Maddie. "I forgot something."

"What?" Maddie asked as they headed back to the supermarket.

"Frozen Dove bars."

Personally, she'd take chocolate and ice cream over any male. Especially Josh Kincaid.

– – –

Heather had wanted to go to Carmelo's, her favorite restaurant, and Josh had agreed, although he'd taken her there before and found the food inauthentic and uninspired. During dinner he went out of his way to be attentive to her, letting her talk about whatever she wanted to and doing his best to act interested. Which was an act, since he kept remembering all the same things that had bugged him about her last night. He needed to concentrate on the things he liked about Heather—she was fun, didn't want to get serious, and had an incredible body, much better than a thirty-five-year-old woman who'd had a baby, at least once it was no longer enhanced by black lace.

After dinner, Josh drove Heather to his place. She grabbed him the minute they stepped into the kitchen, kissing him as she pressed her amazing body against his.

Josh put all he could into kissing her back, slipping his hands under her T-shirt so he could caress her bare breasts and rub his thumbs over her hard nipples.

"Jesus, you're in a hurry tonight," Heather said. "We may have to do it on the kitchen table."

He blinked at her voice, realizing he hadn't been thinking about her when he'd kissed her, hadn't been kissing her at all. He moved his hands away. "We need to talk."

"Later." She pulled her T-shirt up, displaying breasts that were definitely those of a twenty-two-year-old.

Josh pulled her shirt back down. "No, we need to talk now. Heather, this isn't working."

"What do you mean? It's always the best with you."

He leaned against the granite-topped counter. "I don't think we should see each other anymore."

Her dark eyes widened. "Are you telling me there's someone else?"

His desire for Abby wasn't the reason, since he'd never attempt to satisfy it. However, that and Abby's comments had provided an unwelcome—and necessary—wake-up call. "There's no one else. I've realized that much as I like you, we're too different." Josh's lips twisted ruefully. "To be honest, I'm too damn old for you."

Heather grabbed his arms, her long red nails biting into his skin. "You're not too old. You're perfect."

"It'll be a lot more perfect with a guy closer to your own age. You have so much to offer, and it's unfair of me to take up so much of your time. You might lose your chance to find the guy you're meant to be with."

Her grip on his arms tightened. "You're the guy I'm meant to be with." Her voice quivered.

"Heather, I'm not," he said, gently removing her hands. "Once you've calmed down and thought it through, you'll realize this is for the best."

"Tell me what I need to change. I'll do whatever you want. Just don't dump me." Her eyes were wet, a few tears overflowing to streak her cheeks.

Josh felt like a heel, but he had to do this. "It's not you, it's me. Like I said, I'm too old."

"But I love you."

"You can't love me." Love hadn't been part of their deal.

"Of course I love you." Tears were streaming down her face now, nearly as many as Abby had shed on TV. "I was waiting for you to say it first. I'll always love you, Josh. I thought you loved me, too. Don't you at all?"

"I'm sorry," he said, feeling even lower. And dumb. "I'll take you home now, Heather."

She cried the entire trip.

When he got back to his house, Josh sat in the dark living room staring at the blank television. He hadn't handled that well. The problem was he hadn't broken things off with anyone in so long that he'd forgotten how to do it compassionately. He also honestly hadn't thought Heather cared that much about him. He should call her and try to explain.

No, he shouldn't. He'd either make things worse or she'd start hoping they had a future, no matter what he said. Too bad he didn't have a male friend to commiserate with, but he hadn't made any close ones here, and his best friend since junior high had lost that designation when he'd started sleeping with Jennifer. He could call Kim, but he wasn't up to hearing her try not to gloat.

Actually, he should call Abby and tell her what the preliminary investigation into the message writer had turned up.

It had turned up exactly nothing, which showed how pathetic he was. He had to stop obsessing about Abby, and since Heather wasn't going to help tonight, he'd have to find an alternative. He headed to the kitchen for a beer, then returned to the black leather couch and picked up the remote. When all else failed, beer and sports were always there for you. Thank God for ESPN.

CHAPTER 7

Abby's stomach was doing figure eights by the time she strode into the police station the next morning. Being summoned there ASAP without explanation was like waking to a ringing phone at three a.m. It jump-started your heart and was inevitably bad.

She approached a young blonde receptionist seated behind a gray metal desk flanked by the Minnesota and United States flags. "Chief Kincaid wanted to see me. I'm Abby Langford."

The receptionist—Tiffany, according to her name tag—nodded. "I know, and I'm so psyched to meet you. I absolutely love *Private Affairs*. It's the best."

"Thanks."

"I wanted to go to the Mall of America today to see Olivia Hayes, but I couldn't get off work. Instead I get to meet you at work." She shifted in her chair, grinning. "I can't believe how cool this is."

Despite her eagerness to learn what Josh wanted, Abby couldn't be curt to a fan. She smiled. "I'm going to the mall to see Olivia myself."

Tiffany's eyes—a brilliant turquoise that had to be courtesy of contacts—widened. "Don't you hate her?"

"In real life, she's one of my best friends."

"That's so funny, since Samantha and Blair are enemies on the show."

"Olivia's nothing like Blair," Abby said. "And I hope I'm not much like Samantha."

"Olivia looks a lot like Heather Casey," Tiffany said, flipping her long hair over one shoulder. "She's Chief Kincaid's girlfriend and my BFF. Except Heather isn't part Hispanic, and Olivia's way older. But they're both tall and dark haired and beautiful."

Abby really wasn't up to hearing about Heather's youthful virtues this morning. She rested her hand on the desk. "Could you please let Chief Kincaid know I'm here?"

Tiffany lifted the receiver and called. "He said you can go right back." She cocked her head to indicate a door behind the reception area. "He's the first office on the right."

Josh was sitting behind a mahogany desk reviewing typed pages, concentrating so hard he didn't look up when Abby walked through his open doorway. As a kid she'd visited this office several times with Mary and Laura. She remembered the desk, credenza, and Persian carpet, all of which Mary had donated to the previous chief. However, the landscapes that had graced the walls back then had been replaced with a couple of decidedly modern paintings.

"Did you learn something about my message writer?" Abby asked after a moment, too anxious to wait politely for Josh to finish what he was doing.

He looked up from his papers. "No. Sit down."

Abby lowered herself into one of the cream-colored tweed and mahogany chairs in front of Josh's desk, his grim expression increasing her nervousness.

He took a sip from a Starbucks disposable coffee cup, then rocked back in his chair. "Kim made me watch your show yesterday. I have to admit, I'd never seen it. You're an excellent actress."

"Thank you." That was the last thing she'd expected him to say. Then she remembered which episode had broadcast yesterday, and her cheeks heated. "Why did you want to talk to me?"

Josh righted his chair. "Maybe you don't restrict your acting to television."

His voice had a sharp edge that made Abby's hands tighten around the mahogany chair arms. "What's that supposed to mean?"

"You can't get my attention with a knife and blood on the floor, so you happen to mention some threatening letters you've received. Letters you conveniently threw away."

"Ask Laura. I told her about them when I got them."

He waved his coffee cup. "I'm a little more receptive to those, so a couple of days later you get an even more menacing message, this one written on the mirror. Although there's no evidence anyone broke into your house, the writer used your lipstick, and the only fingerprints we found were yours and smaller ones we assume are Maddie's."

Abby was gripping the wooden arms so tightly her knuckles matched the chair's fabric. "You think I staged the lipstick incident?"

"In my experience, the most logical explanation is usually the right one." He set down his coffee, then picked up the *Herald* and held it out to her, pointing. "I assume you saw this."

"I haven't had time to read today's paper yet." She took it and skimmed the front-page article he'd indicated. It was all about the threatening message on her mirror, including the exact wording and that it had been written using her own lipstick. *Damn.* "How did they find out about it?"

"No one around here would have told them," Josh said. "That leaves only one possible source."

"It wasn't me." She tossed the paper back onto his desk. "I didn't want Maddie to know about it. Why would I have leaked it to the press?"

"That was very good, Abby," he said, applauding quietly. "Exactly the right amount of maternal concern. As I said, you really are an excellent actress."

"I wasn't acting."

He raised an eyebrow. "What about when you pretended to have a nightmare, knowing I'd come into your bedroom to find out what was wrong?"

"I didn't pretend. I really had a nightmare."

"Then what about when I kissed you?" He rested his hands on his desk and leaned toward her, his eyes narrowing. "Why would you have kissed me back, someone you clearly don't like, if you weren't acting? Obviously you thought it would make me easier to manipulate."

She could not believe this. Abby got to her feet, pressing her arms against her sides to keep herself from dumping his coffee over his asinine head. "Funny, but I assumed that's why you kissed me in the first place." She grabbed her purse off the floor. "If that's all you wanted, I need to be going."

– – –

Josh jabbed the *Herald* with his pencil as Abby stormed out of his office. So she was angry that he'd called her on her scheme. Tough. He was even angrier that she'd thought she could get away with it.

She'd seemed so frightened about the lipstick that he'd ignored his strong suspicion she'd already staged two other incidents for publicity. Until he'd seen the story in today's paper, that is. She was the article's only possible source—after Kim's disclosure about the knife, he'd given Tiffany a lecture about leaking information, and no one else would have considered doing that. That meant Abby must have written the lipstick message herself. Otherwise she'd never have risked giving her message writer publicity that could encourage him to act again, something Ben confirmed he'd warned her about.

His hand tightened on the pencil. He'd sworn no woman was going to make a fool out of him again, but he'd nearly blown it. He should have known better than to fall for Abby's act. He'd seen on TV yesterday just how good an actress she was. Hell, he'd seen her acting ability firsthand when she'd responded to his kiss.

The pencil snapped. He'd been a fool to kiss her and even more foolish to consider believing her, let alone waste the night sleeping on her couch. But no more.

"Here are the copies you asked me to make," Tiffany said, walking into his office. That Heather apparently hadn't told Tiffany about their breakup yet was the only good thing about today. He didn't need a pissed-off receptionist on top of everything else.

She set the copies on the corner of his desk. "Did you get everything straightened out with Abby Langford?"

He dropped the pencil halves onto the newspaper. "I damn well better have."

– – –

The Mall of America was one of the largest enclosed shopping areas in the world and a top Minnesota tourist attraction, with four floors housing more than four hundred stores, as well as an amusement park, a multiplex theater, an aquarium, and a variety of restaurants. Abby arrived to find its rotunda packed, hundreds of people in everything from cutoffs, T-shirts, and sandals to business suits and heels making up the snaking line that led to the stage where Olivia sat at a table, signing autographs. Abby tried to hide in back beside a kiosk selling watches, hoping to avoid notice until Olivia finished and they could go to dinner. However, that proved impossible in a crowd of rabid *Private Affairs* fans—especially after Olivia pointed her out and called her to the front to join in signing autographs.

Three hours later, Abby and Olivia had left the mall and were relaxing at a corner table at Vincent's Grill. The restaurant's quiet elegance, low lighting, widely spaced tables, and exceptional food made it a romantic dining favorite in every local poll.

"I miss you already. When are you going to swim to shore and wander back to Oak City?" Olivia asked after they'd ordered. Samantha was scheduled to presumably drown when someone knocked her out and pushed her off the pier into the ocean. In true soap opera fashion, however, the police would find her blood on the pier and her purse in the water, but no trace of her body.

"I'm not planning on coming back. You know I've wanted to write." Abby selected a piece of bread from the basket the waitress had delivered with the menus, dipped it into the pool of olive oil on her plate, and took a bite. Not having to obsess about calories was heaven.

"You can write and do *Private Affairs*," Olivia said. "You found time for all those college courses."

"I wasn't a single parent then. I can afford to take a few years off, and it seemed a good time to leave LA."

Olivia took a sip of the chardonnay she'd ordered the instant they'd sat down. "Speaking of reasons for leaving LA, I assume you heard that Colin's involved with Melinda Maris."

Abby set her bread on the edge of the plate, skirting the olive oil. "From *Search for Love*. She's just his type."

"Because she's blonde and beautiful like you?" Olivia asked.

"Well, she's also only eighteen. Colin's forty-five, isn't he?"

"Forty-six." Her age made her even more Colin's type, although Olivia didn't know that. She might have suspected Colin had cheated, but Abby had confided the whole story to only her therapist and Laura.

"Despite that she's barely legal, the press is giving him a free ride on it, claiming it's an understandable reaction to the devastating breakup of his marriage."

"Colin has an exceptional publicist." An understatement, considering David had managed to convince the tabloid press Colin had been at home alone eating his heart out over their split, while Abby had been going through men like M&M's. Of course, Abby had helped by agreeing not to deny any tabloid article involving men or money issues, subjects of previous articles that hadn't hurt her career. Her agent had been appalled by her refusal to comment, but it had been Abby's decision, and what she'd gotten in return had been worth it.

"Colin needs a great publicist to make up for his lack of talent," Olivia said. "Was your therapist right that moving back would trigger more of those awful memories?"

Abby shrugged. "I had a couple the first week, but none since. Which must mean I've finally faced them all."

"I hope so."

"So do I." Abby stared at a candle flickering in a ruby glass holder in the center of the table. "It's not like I thought my mom and dad were good parents who loved me. But remembering specific incidents has been hard. As you know."

Olivia had been there for the first recalled memory, when in the middle of rehearsing a scene, Abby had abruptly zoned out as Blair proclaimed Samantha would never control Matrix Corporation. Instead she'd been fifteen again, walking into her trailer house to find her dad swearing at her mom as he beat her with his fists, pounding her head and upper body over and over. Her mom was slumped against the wall beside the TV set, her hands half covering her face, blood and tears dripping onto her chin, onto her misbuttoned pink shirt.

A combination of horror, fear, and helplessness had engulfed Abby, and she yelled at her dad to stop it. When he ignored her, she ran to the kitchen and called 911, screaming at the dispatcher to stop her dad from killing her mom. While the dispatcher's soothing voice was telling her the police were on the way, her dad's hands had closed like vises on her upper arms. Pain loosened her fingers, and Abby dropped the phone, leaving it dangling on the cord. Her dad shook her so hard her teeth chattered as he spit alcohol fumes at her, telling her he should kill her, that she was as worthless as her mother.

Using all the strength she could muster, Abby raised her knee and rammed it into his groin. Her dad dropped her arms and doubled over, his angry words reduced to moans. She raced to her bedroom, locked the door, and shoved her dresser against it. Then she sat down on the fake wood floor with her back against the dresser and began reciting her lines for Emily in *Our Town*.

Unsurprisingly, her dad was at her bedroom door, pounding so hard the dresser vibrated against her back, but she ignored him. Instead she focused on her lines, even when the police arrived and hauled her dad to jail.

Her mother refused to go to the ER. She also refused to press charges or let the police talk to Abby, so Abby's dad was back the next day, but on his best behavior. By then Abby had forgotten the entire incident, had even convinced herself she'd bruised her arms during play rehearsal and that her mother's claim that she'd gotten her black eye running into a door was true.

The incident had remained forgotten until that *Private Affairs* rehearsal, when out of the blue the horrible memory had slammed Abby with the force of a punching bag filled with boulders. She'd felt like she was reliving it, and the pain was so intense she could barely breathe, as if her ribs had splintered into shards of bone that were stabbing her gut and chest.

Abby picked up a piece of bread, forcing her mind back to the more pleasant present. "I'm glad that between gossip Bill and Mary had heard and a few things I'd told them but then made myself forget, they could confirm enough that I knew my recalled memories were real." Since that had only been the first of many similar episodes. "Otherwise I'd have thought the divorce was making me lose it." Her lips twisted. "Of course, discovering I developed the ability to block out a large part of my childhood doesn't exactly make me the picture of mental health."

"You did that to help yourself get through a hard time *without* losing it, which is a good thing," Olivia said.

Abby nodded. Those incidents were also part of the reason she'd gotten into acting, yet another good thing. Acting had allowed her to escape and become someone else for a while. It had also given her lines that she'd used like a meditation mantra, reciting them over and over again to clear her mind after an unpleasant incident until it had completely disappeared from her conscious memory.

She looked down at her plate, surprised to see she'd been picking her bread apart. She dropped the rest of the piece on top of the fragments. "Although I clearly shouldn't have waited until my divorce to get therapy."

Olivia reached across the table and rested her hand on Abby's arm. "You've had a rough couple of years, with the divorce and the memories. And all those tabloid lies. I still think you should have sued over them. You still can, I bet."

Abby smiled faintly. Her parents may not have cared much about her, but between the Tate family and Olivia, she'd gotten more than her share of protectors. "I appreciate your support, but I want to go forward. Especially since I've finally faced all the memories I repressed. That's why my therapist thought I felt so strongly about moving back to Harrington, because subconsciously I wanted to force myself to do that, and I have. So here's to me." Abby raised her glass in a mock toast, then took a sip of water.

"That might be part of it, but you know the primary reason you moved back is to give Maddie the perfect childhood you wish you'd had."

"You're right."

"Of course I'm right. You're the world's best mother." Olivia waved her hand. "I'm seriously considering nominating you for Mother of the Year."

Abby raised her eyebrows. "Samantha Cartwright as Mother of the Year?"

"You've got a point. Sleeping with your daughter's boyfriend is probably an automatic disqualification. And that's one of the less atrocious things you've done lately." Olivia picked up her wine. "You should be flattered that the studio's received a record number of irate e-mails and letters."

"Someone in Harrington is so upset with Samantha that he broke into my house and wrote a message in lipstick on my bathroom mirror."

Olivia froze, her wineglass at her lips. "Someone got into your house? Please tell me you called the police."

"It happened the night before last, and yes, I called the police. I've also gotten new locks, and I've arranged to have a security system installed next week." Abby had visited one of the Minneapolis companies Josh had recommended and signed a contract before heading to the mall.

"I'm relieved you haven't become so publicity-phobic you'd try to handle it yourself."

Abby waited until the waitress had delivered the works of art that were their salads before continuing. "The police promised to keep it quiet, but it somehow leaked out anyway. Ended up on the front page of the local paper." She picked up her fork and stabbed a tomato.

"Terrific. Although I guess that's better than most of the recent stories about you." Then Olivia grinned. "I don't suppose you met a hot, single policeman. That's always been one of my fantasies."

Abby swallowed, grimacing despite the exquisite flavors of garlic, basil, ripe tomato, and aged balsamic vinegar. Being in the Twin Cities and seeing Olivia had diverted her attention, but Olivia's words reignited her fury at Josh. "The police chief himself handled it. He's divorced, and I guess some women would consider him hot." Herself included, before she'd gotten to know him. "But he's a jerk. He thinks I wrote the message on my mirror myself to get publicity for my book."

"He's obviously also incompetent since he's confused you with Samantha," Olivia said, spearing a piece of fennel. "If you can't avoid publicity and asshole males in Harrington, you might as well come back to *Private Affairs*." She waved her fennel-laden fork. "I mean, how long can you possibly stay there anyway? It's not only dull and has five months of winter, but there probably isn't a single man you could stand to have dinner with, let alone take to bed."

Abby held up her hand. "I've sworn off men, remember?"

"Because you claim Maddie would be upset you're dating. Which is bull, since the Maddie I know would more likely be thrilled. I think the real reason is you're afraid to get hurt again."

"Well, since there isn't a decent single man in Harrington, it's not an issue." Abby raised a forkful of baby lettuce to her mouth. "Now tell me about *your* love life."

– – –

Abby reluctantly dropped Olivia off at the airport, then started back to Harrington. As the sky turned from orange and pink to gray and then onyx, she thought about her decision to leave *Private Affairs*, about her life in LA, about what she was doing now. She missed a lot of things about her former life—her friends, acting, doing something she knew she was good at as opposed to starting a new career writing. She might not need the income, but after years of accolades, rejection would be hard to take. On the other hand, she'd had the desire to write mysteries for years and had never had time to give it a serious shot. Maddie was finally making friends in Harrington, and it was a better place for her to grow up in, especially with Laura, Bill, and Mary to love and spoil her.

When Abby exited the interstate onto the two-lane highway that led to Harrington, she stopped thinking and flipped on the radio, enjoying the tranquil night, the world dark except for the moon and stars glittering overhead and the dim glow of headlights far behind her. After a couple of minutes, however, the headlights in Abby's rearview mirror had gotten annoying close. Undoubtedly some male salivating for a chance to pass her—testosterone made men turn even the stupidest things into a competition. To her mind, getting rid of those blinding headlights was more important than keeping the lead. Abby slowed down.

So did the other car, although it was safe to pass. She was going sixty, but maybe the speed limit here was only fifty-five. Her tail probably figured if she was in front, she'd get the ticket. Abby slowed to fifty-five.

The other car still didn't pass.

The radio announcer reported the temperature tomorrow would be over ninety and shifted to a commercial for Wedding Day Jewelers. Abby punched the button for Minnesota Public Radio, then checked the mirrors.

The car was still on her tail, its headlights filling her rearview mirror. Time to induce passing behavior. Abby slowed to fifty.

So did her pursuer.

Her heartbeat kicked up a few notches, and she accelerated. The car behind increased its speed, staying the same short distance from her.

She slowed down again. The other car did the same.

Abby's heart was pounding now, the blood throbbing so loudly in her ears that it drowned out the Brandenburg concerto on the radio. That car was definitely following her.

And the driver could be the person who'd left a lipstick threat on her mirror, ready to finish the job.

CHAPTER 8

Abby's breath was coming in sharp gasps that scraped her lungs. She had to calm down. So what if someone was tailgating her? It was probably a teenage boy being funny or even a fan who wanted to keep her in sight and get an autograph when she stopped. Besides, she wasn't a defenseless woman alone in the country. She had a cell phone and could call the highway patrol.

And tell them what? That a car seemed to be following her, although otherwise it hadn't done anything threatening? Any patrolman would assume she was being overimaginative, if not neurotic, which she probably was.

Abby glanced in the mirror again. The car was still there, still close behind, still making her nervous. Talking to Laura would help. Although she usually didn't use the phone while driving, she wasn't about to pull over. Forcing herself to breathe slower, she flipped off the radio and picked up her phone. Then she reconsidered; Maddie was at Laura's and might overhear. Laura was probably busy putting the kids to bed now anyway. Bill and Mary would worry, so she couldn't call them, either.

She knew one more number she could call, someone she could guarantee wouldn't take this seriously, let alone worry. She could also guarantee he'd say something infuriating enough to distract her from worrying. If she interrupted a date, tough—he'd told her to call him anytime.

Josh answered on the first ring.

"It's Abby Langford," she said through the phone's speaker, already regretting her impulsive call.

"What now?"

This was definitely one of her dumber ideas, but it was too late to hang up. "I'm on my way back from the Twin Cities, probably five miles outside Harrington. The car behind me seems to be following me. It's making me nervous, even though I know it's nothing. I remembered your number and thought talking to you would stop me from being paranoid."

"Why do you think the car's following you?" Josh asked.

"Because it's stayed on my tail, even when I've slowed down and sped up."

"How long has it been behind you?"

His questions were making her more nervous. She'd expected him to accuse her of staging another publicity stunt or at least tell her she was being ridiculous. "I didn't notice it until I left the interstate, but it might have been there before that."

"You're on Highway 17?"

"Yes. But I'm sure it's just a kid. Or maybe a fan. My fan sites state I drive a Volvo, and there aren't a lot of those around here."

"Better safe than sorry, my mom always said," Josh said. "I'm on my way. Keep driving until you see my car."

Abby felt her cheeks heating. He probably didn't think it was serious at all and was humoring her to placate the mayor and Mary. "Please don't bother. I don't want to interrupt another date."

"I don't have a date tonight. I was just leaving Kim's, so I'm already halfway there."

She looked in the mirror at the now-blinding light. Her stomach clenched, fear displacing every iota of embarrassment. "It's gotten closer."

"Speed up."

She pressed the gas, then glanced in the mirror again. "The driver sped up, too. And I'm going nearly eighty."

The peaceful night seemed to have morphed into black ice, as if the pursuing vehicle were chasing her into a cold, unpredictable evil. The clenching in Abby's stomach spread to her lungs, squeezing out her breath.

"I'll call for backup," Josh said.

"Don't hang up on me." Abby gripped the steering wheel painfully with her left hand, the phone with her right. Her slamming heartbeats made her voice quiver.

"I won't. Can you tell what kind of car it is?"

"I can't see it real well. I'm bad with cars, anyway." She checked both outside mirrors, then glanced over her shoulder. "I think it's an American sedan. A light color."

"Can you see the driver?"

"No." She jerked as she heard a sharp ping. "Something hit the fender."

"What?"

Another ping, then another. Too many direct hits to be pebbles thrown up by tires.

"I think he's shooting at me!" she choked out, catching the phone between her ear and shoulder and clutching the steering wheel with both hands.

"Slump down as far as you can and still see. What did he hit?"

"The fender again." Her voice sounded higher than shrill. She scrunched down in the seat, heard another ping. "Another one, still on the fender." Her sweaty palms made it hard to keep hold of the steering wheel.

"He's probably trying to hit a tire. If he does, it might blow, and you're going to have to work to control the car. You need to have both hands on the wheel."

Abby's heart was pounding hard enough to burst through her chest. "I do," she said, Josh's calm voice the only thing keeping her from hysterics.

"Good. Have you ever had a blowout?"

She jerked at another ping, nearly losing the phone. "No, never."

"If it happens, let up on the gas, but don't push on the brake. And hang on to the steering wheel."

"How will I know if—"

Abby's car lurched, then bucked wildly along the blacktop. She lifted her foot off the gas. The car bumped and jerked as it flew over the road, jarring her hands on the steering wheel. She needed to slow down.

Josh had said not to brake. She anchored her foot on the carpet to stop from instinctively doing that and gripped the wheel, using all her strength to keep the vehicle from careening off the road. The phone slipped, bouncing off the passenger seat and onto the floor.

"Abby, are you OK?" She could still hear Josh's voice. "Hang on. I'm almost there. Abby?"

She couldn't keep her car in her lane anymore, couldn't even keep it on the blacktop. Her nose bashed hard against the steering wheel as the car plunged into a deep ditch on the left side of the road, nearly flipping. Abby muscled the steering wheel as far right as she could. The car turned, tilted, drove forward. Then it stopped, angled up one side of the ditch with both the front wheels on the level ground above it.

Abby unclasped her cramping fingers from the steering wheel and took a long, shaky breath as she pulled the emergency brake. She hadn't crashed; the air bag hadn't even inflated. She was still alive and the only thing hurting was her nose.

"Abby?"

Josh's voice was coming from the phone on the floor. She leaned down and reached for it. It slipped from her fingers. She grabbed it again. "I'm OK. I'm in the ditch."

"Where's the other car?"

The world was dark except for her headlights. "Gone, I think."

"He may have doused his headlights. Hunch way down and stay inside the car. Lock your doors."

His words gripped her stomach. He was right—the absence of headlights didn't guarantee the other car was gone. "Do you think the driver's coming to get me?"

"I'll get there first," Josh said. "What side of the road are you on?"

"The west."

"I see you. I'll be there in a second."

Abby unhooked her seat belt and curled in a fetal position around the gearshift, hugging her knees to her chest. After a moment she saw the glow of headlights approaching her car, and she held her breath, praying it was Josh. She didn't breathe again until she saw his face peering through the front windshield. Then she sat up and unlocked the door.

"Are you OK?" he asked, yanking open the door.

She managed to nod and step out of the car. The second her feet landed on the ditch's uneven grass, her knees buckled. She grabbed for the door. Josh caught her, pulling her out of the ditch and close against him.

"I'm sorry, I shouldn't have bothered you, but I was so scared." Her voice wobbled.

His arms tightened around her. He smelled like pine soap, coffee, and garlic, reassuringly normal smells. Abby leaned into him for several minutes, his warm strength an antidote to the cold terror of the last few minutes. Then she remembered who she was leaning on. She straightened. "I'm fine now."

Josh released her and took a backward step. He was holding a gun, his eyes scanning the area. "Why were you in Minneapolis?"

Away from his warmth, she felt cold again, or maybe it was seeing that gun. She wrapped her arms around herself. "A good friend from *Private Affairs* had an appearance at the Mall of America, so I met her there. Olivia and I had dinner at a restaurant near the mall, then I dropped her off at the airport and drove home."

"Did you notice anyone following you earlier in the day?" he asked.

"No, but I wasn't paying close attention."

"Did anyone notice you at your friend's appearance?"

"Olivia announced I was there. I ended up signing autographs with her."

A siren wailed in the distance. "I called for reinforcements," Josh said. "When they get here, I'll brief them, then take you home. Where's Maddie?"

"At Laura's."

"Do you want her to stay overnight there?"

"I want her with me," Abby said, hugging herself tighter. Another siren, lower toned, had joined the first. "I don't want her to know what happened."

"The press will find out about this," he said. "You should give Maddie your version before she hears about it from someone else."

"I have to tell her about the lipstick, too." She swallowed, trying to dislodge the lump in her throat. "The same person who left that message did this, didn't he?"

"Possibly," Josh said. "He could have followed you to the Minneapolis event or else was at the mall, either hoping you'd show or because he's obsessed with *Private Affairs*."

She nodded stiffly. "I need to hire someone to guard my house." She should have done that after the lipstick incident. "Someone discreet so Maddie won't know how worried I am."

"I can recommend a good agency in Minneapolis. It'll be expensive."

"I'm having a security system installed next week, so it may only be until then," she said. The siren duet was getting louder as two sets of red lights approached at top speed—on the assumption she was seriously injured, if not dead. She shivered.

"Let's go to my car," Josh said. "You can wait there."

He walked Abby to his car and opened the passenger side door. "Let me grab my flashlight before you get in," he said, reaching in, flipping open the glove compartment, and pulling out the flashlight. "I'll be back soon."

As he headed back to Abby's car, Josh couldn't shut down the skeptical part of his brain. She'd seemed genuinely upset, even terrified. Then again, she was a hell of an actress. She hadn't been injured, either, and the air bag hadn't even inflated. She'd claimed a car had been pursuing her, but he hadn't encountered another car on his way out here or spotted any distant headlights or taillights. He hadn't heard any shooting or even engine noise in the background while he'd been on the phone with her, so he couldn't swear Abby had been driving her car when she'd been talking to him. Maybe she'd had a blowout and decided to take advantage of the situation.

The biggest sticking point was that she'd called him. If she'd been genuinely scared, wouldn't she have called 911? If she'd wanted someone to keep her from being paranoid, why not call a friend? He certainly wasn't her buddy, especially not after this morning. On the other hand, what better way to convince him she really had a stalker than to make him an audio witness? What better way to motivate him to keep investigating and keep her name in the news?

Josh flipped on the flashlight and illuminated the blacktop for several yards behind where Abby's car had gone off the road. No skid marks, although there might not be any if she'd followed his advice about not braking. He shone the light on the back window, then made a quick check of the other windows. No cracks or chips. If someone had wanted to kill her, why not shoot out a window and hope it hit her or at least disorient her enough that she'd crash? Why just try to blow a tire?

He flashed the light on the back tire, the one on the driver's side. It was definitely blown, but that didn't mean it had been shot. Tires blew out every day just from natural use.

Then he saw it, embedded in the back fender. A slug from a handgun. Abby could conceivably have shot the fender and also the tire to deflate it, but he couldn't believe she'd take any ruse that far.

Shit.

"Is Abby OK?" Ben Alton asked as he approached. Josh should have guessed he'd be the first one here.

"She's shook up but otherwise fine," Josh said. Guilt had his gut churning. "She's in my car."

"Someone shot at her?"

Josh nodded. "Blew out her tire. She was coming from the north. See whether you can find any more slugs along the highway."

"Will do. She's damn lucky she didn't get hurt."

"Yeah, she was," Josh said. "When the highway patrol shows, tell them we'll handle this since it's related to the lipstick message. I doubt they'll object, but if they do, have Steve call me." The local highway patrol was overworked enough that so far they'd always been happy to have the police take over, a welcome change from Chicago, where turf wars were as common as mosquitoes. "I'll give Abby a ride home, then come back here."

"You need a security system tomorrow," Josh told Abby the instant he got into the car. "If the company says they can't install it that fast, let me know and I'll talk to them. I'll also sleep on your couch again tonight."

She'd been staring straight ahead at the darkness outside the window, but now she looked at him. "That's unnecessary."

"You could have been killed, by someone who may have stalked you all the way to Minneapolis and back. This is serious."

"I know, but I have new locks, and I'll keep my cell phone beside my bed. You don't need to sleep on my couch."

Josh couldn't believe she could be so blasted nonchalant—or stubborn—about this. "Look, if you won't let me use the couch, I'll sleep in my car outside your house." His voice vibrated with frustration. "I'd prefer the couch."

Abby stared at him for a moment. Then she nodded.

Josh had retrieved her phone from her car. He handed it to her. "Call Laura and tell her what happened so you won't have to explain in front of Maddie," he said as he started the car.

Laura was standing on the front steps when Josh pulled into her driveway. She ran to the car and hugged Abby the instant she got out. "Are you all right?"

"I'm fine. Where's Maddie?"

"Sleeping with Nicole. Are you sure you both don't want to stay here tonight?"

"Thanks, but no."

"I'm sleeping on her couch tonight," Josh said. "She'll have a guard by tomorrow."

"Good. I'll get Maddie," Laura said when they reached the house's brightly lit foyer.

"I'll go." Abby hurried toward the staircase, then ran upstairs.

"Are you finally convinced Abby was telling the truth about the knife?"

Josh shifted his attention to Laura. "I don't think this has anything to do with the knife. The guy who left the lipstick message is more likely, assuming she didn't simply end up in front of a lunatic."

"Whoever it is, you should know that Abby doesn't lie," Laura said. "She's the most honest person I know."

"If you consider cheating on your husband honest," Josh said, then mentally kicked himself. The comment was inappropriate, reflexive.

"You can't judge her. You don't have any idea what went on in Abby's marriage." Laura's sharp tone made it clear that in her case the fiery redhead stereotype was accurate.

And after the way he'd fucked up, her anger at him was justified.

"Abby's a truly decent person," Laura added.

Even if she wasn't, it didn't matter, didn't excuse his comment or his conduct. "If she is, I've heard it was because of everything your family did for her while she was growing up."

Laura's features softened. "The primary reason Abby turned out so well was Abby. My parents helped, but she's always been determined to be different from her parents, even to make up for what they were."

"What were they?" Josh asked.

"To be blunt, they sucked, both as parents and as human beings," Laura said. "Neither even pretended to care about Abby. Her dad was too busy hanging out in bars and screwing any woman who'd have him. Abby's mom did her drinking at home and passed out in front of the TV most nights, but every so often, she'd wake up enough to fight with her husband when he finally got home. She usually ended up in the ER, and he spent the night in jail, though she'd never press charges."

Josh looked up as Abby appeared on the top landing, her arms around a nightgowned Maddie. She started down the stairs with Maddie sleepwalking beside her.

When she'd reached the bottom step, Josh came toward her, holding out his arms. "I'll carry her to the car."

Abby shook her head, hugging Maddie closer. "Thanks for everything, Laura. I'll call you in the morning."

– – –

During the drive home, Abby stared out the passenger side window, her mind racing. She couldn't believe anyone hated her—or even Samantha—enough to kill her. But after the lipstick message, any hope this was a random act of violence was wishful thinking.

"I had a unit drive by and check things out," Josh said as he pulled up in front of her house. "It appeared quiet, but I'll look around inside and make sure no one's left any rude surprises. I'll get Maddie."

This time Abby let him carry her; the adrenaline rush she'd experienced was wearing off, leaving her exhausted. At her request, Josh carried Maddie to Abby's bed, then went to check out the house while Abby tucked her in.

When Abby came downstairs with Josh's bedding, he was in the kitchen, talking quietly on his cell phone. She sat down on the couch, hugging the pillows and folded sheets, totally drained.

He strode into the living room a few minutes later, stopping directly in front of her. "We'll get whoever's behind this, Abby. Until we do, I'll make sure you and Maddie are safe. I promise." His features were set in stone, his eyes warm velvet and fixed on hers.

The intensity in his look pulled Abby to her feet. "Because Rachel would never forgive you if anything happened to Maddie, right?" She couldn't tear her eyes from his.

"Right." His gaze slipped to her lips for an instant, returned to her eyes. He reached out and touched her hair, pushing a strand that had escaped her twist back behind her ear. "Sleep well, Abby." He lowered his hand and took the bedding from her.

"You, too." Then she turned and headed upstairs.

CHAPTER 9

Josh felt like crap. He hadn't slept more than an hour, but not because the couch was uncomfortable or because Abby had another nightmare, since if she had, he hadn't heard it. It was because of the terrified look on Abby's face when he'd reached her car in the ditch, the way she'd trembled in his arms and later clung to Maddie, who could very well have lost her mother last night. The shooter could have hit Abby instead of a fender or the car could have crashed into a tree or flipped over instead of driving into one of the few ditches deep and wide enough to slow it down. Abby could have been killed.

And it would have been at least partly his fault. He should have done more to find out who was responsible for her threatening letters, especially after the lipstick message. He should have interviewed her neighbors, checked into possible grudges against her, looked into mental cases and religious fanatics living in the area. All things he'd normally have done if he hadn't been convinced Abby was a gifted actress who was trying to use both him and his department to further her new writing career. Hell, even last night he'd still thought she was lying. He knew better now, especially since Ben had found another bullet on the highway a hundred yards north of where Abby had gone into the ditch.

Josh took a sip of overheated station coffee that tasted as lousy as he felt, but drinking it instead of Starbucks this morning was part of his penance. What had he been thinking? He'd always prided himself on being a good cop. This time, however, he'd let his past and prejudices lead him to assume the victim was lying, even though from what people had uniformly told him—and he'd uniformly disregarded—Abby Langford wasn't a liar. She was a nice, honest, decent woman, pretty much the opposite of the character she played so well.

She was probably totally unlike Jennifer, too, except for the cheating, but Laura was right. He didn't know what had gone on in Abby's marriage. In any event, it didn't justify the unprofessional way he'd treated her.

Josh took another sip of coffee and grimaced. His parents hadn't expected him to be perfect, but they had raised him to admit his mistakes and try to rectify the situation. He was going to do everything in his power to find out who was behind the threats and harassment. But first he was going to apologize. He took a deep breath and grabbed the phone.

"How did you sleep?" he asked when Abby answered.

"Surprisingly well. Thanks for staying."

He didn't deserve to have her sound so friendly. "I talked to a friend in Minneapolis about a guard," he said. "Sam used to be a cop, but now owns a private security company. I'd trust anyone who works for him with my life." He'd called Sam at six thirty this morning and asked him to send out his best men, as well as cut Abby a deal.

"He already called me," Abby said. "I've arranged to have a guard from ten at night until seven in the morning. After I calmed down, I realized having one during the day would be overkill and too easy for Maddie or the neighbors to notice. I'm also getting my security system tomorrow."

"Good. Did you talk to Maddie?"

"I told her about last night and about the lipstick message," Abby said. "Then we read the paper together. You were right about the coverage."

Josh glanced at the *Herald* on his desk. This front-page story was even bigger than the lipstick one, complete with a picture of Abby's car in the ditch. "How did she take it?"

"She said she thought all the crazies lived in California. Then she called Rachel about a birthday party they're both invited to, so I guess she took it OK. I have to admit I downplayed it and took advantage of Maddie's belief that the press usually exaggerates. I don't want her worrying."

"That's understandable," Josh said. "I checked with the *Herald*'s editor." Yet another thing he should have done before. "He got an anonymous call about the lipstick message. The voice was so muffled he couldn't tell whether it was a man or a woman, and the call couldn't be traced. After the story about your knife leaked out, I lectured our receptionist about not leaking information. However, she apparently didn't realize she was doing that when she confirmed information the paper already had, which is why they ran the story." Josh picked up his pen. "Do you know anyone who hates you?"

"I'm sure numerous people dislike me, but not enough to do something like this," Abby said. "I assume it's someone who hates Samantha since it happened after a *Private Affairs* event. He should leave me alone after she's killed off."

"That happens on Friday?"

"She's shoved into the ocean at the end of Friday's show. On Monday the police determine she's been murdered."

"If he's such a big fan he must already know she's being killed off," Josh said. Which meant, of course, the person actually hated Abby.

"Only if he reads fan magazines," Abby said. "I imagine a lot of people who watch the show don't."

That sounded like wishful thinking to him, but if it made her feel better, fine. She'd still hired a guard. It certainly didn't change his course of action since next Monday was five days away. "I'd like to talk to someone at *Private Affairs* about whether they've gotten similar letters."

"I'll give you the number for the head of security."

"I'd also like to talk to Laura and the Tates about possible enemies you might not have thought of. Just in case the target isn't Samantha."

"I hate to even think that, but go ahead. You should also talk to Eleanor Blake at the courthouse. She's worked in property records forever and hears more gossip than anyone."

"I'll let you know what I find out." Josh finished writing down the names, then paused, clearing his throat. "I want to apologize for thinking you lied about the letters and wrote the lipstick message yourself, then leaked it to the press. And for assuming you lied about the knife and stain."

"I didn't think cops ever apologized."

"They do if they grew up in my house," Josh said. "Knowing my parents, they'd insist I do it in person. Would you have dinner with me?" The words came out before he'd consciously thought them.

Silence greeted his impulsive invitation. "Would this be business?" Abby finally asked.

He drew a star below his notes. "The mayor didn't order me to do it, if that's what you're asking."

"Sorry, no."

He traced the star again. "Of course not." What had he been thinking, asking a woman so far out of his league to dinner?

"What's that supposed to mean?"

"A woman like you would never have dinner with a cop." He shaded the star's center. "Forget I asked."

"For God's sake, it's not because you're a cop," she said. "It's because you have a girlfriend who might misunderstand."

"Not that Heather and I had an exclusive relationship, but I broke things off with her a couple of nights ago." He dropped his pen onto the paper. "To be honest, I realized dating her was a pathetic attempt to prove I'm not old and inadequate."

Abby's laugh encouraged him to try again. "So how about dinner at Giorgio's?"

"I wouldn't want Maddie to think it's a date," she said, although her tone was noticeably warmer. "She's gone through a lot with the divorce and now moving. I'd hate to upset her more."

Josh raked his fingers through his hair. "Look, I've got to do this apology properly, or Kim will have me barred from all future family celebrations. Tell Maddie we're having dinner as friends. Since she likes Rachel, she shouldn't be upset if you have dinner with Rachel's Uncle Josh."

Abby was quiet for a moment. "OK, when?"

His smile and desire to high-five the world were entirely inappropriate considering this was supposed to be a penance. "How about tonight?"

– – –

Once again Josh had managed to confuse her, Abby thought as she hung up the phone. She had no idea why he'd really asked her to dinner. Unlike the kiss, she couldn't believe it had anything to do with manipulating her—he'd sounded genuinely sorry for doubting her. But he could have apologized in person without including dinner.

One thing she did know was that he hadn't asked her because he enjoyed her company. He might believe her now, but that didn't mean he liked her.

Which was fine since she didn't like him, either. She'd agreed to go because his invitation had caught her off guard, and she'd resented his implication that she'd never have dinner with a cop. She also was grateful for the way he'd helped her last night, and not just by coming to her rescue. Sleeping on her couch and calling to arrange for security went way beyond his job description.

On the other hand, Josh's motivation was only a minor concern. Abby stood and crossed the kitchen to the window over the sink, hoping that gazing at her sunlit, summery backyard would calm nerves that even today were still twitching. The lipstick message had scared her, but last night had been far worse than a break-in and threatening message. Someone had tried to kill her. God willing, what she'd told Josh was right, that it was a *Private Affairs* fan who hated Samantha. Someone who'd leave her alone once Samantha was killed off.

Because the alternative was too terrifying to even consider.

– – –

Josh finally made it to the courthouse at just after three. The property records office was deserted except for a petite woman with enormous glasses, steely hair, and hot-pink lipstick standing behind the counter. "Miss Blake?" he asked.

"Call me Eleanor," she said. "It's not often I get a visit from the police chief. Actually I never have before today."

"I'm trying to identify Abby Langford's stalker. She mentioned you might know whether anyone hates her."

"You mean because of those awful things the tabloids printed about her?" Eleanor asked. "I think most people are like me and don't believe them. Even if they do, well, that's how things are in Hollywood. As long as she's nice to us, most people don't give those stories no never mind."

"I'm more concerned with when Abby was growing up," Josh said. "Maybe something has festered for years, and when she moved back the person snapped."

Eleanor rested both hands on the counter and furrowed her forehead. "To be honest, I can't think of anyone. Abby didn't make many enemies. Some girls might have been jealous of her being so pretty, but she never had time to date so it wasn't like she was stealing boyfriends. She was always so nice and unassuming that she won over even people who had reason to dislike her. Look at Mary Tate."

Josh blinked. "What about Mary Tate?"

"Mary's daughter, Laura, and Abby have been best friends since first grade. Laura's pretty, but not in the same category as Abby. Laura also was into acting, same as Abby, but Abby was the one who got the leads. To be blunt, Abby overshadowed Laura. You'd have thought that would be hard for Mary, being from one of those rich New England families and always used to being on top."

"From what I've heard, the Tates treated Abby like a daughter. Are you telling me that isn't true?"

Eleanor held up one hand. "Nope, it's the God's truth, and that's my point. I mean both Mary and Bill are wonderful folks, helping out people who need it and giving to causes. But they weren't nice to Abby just because she needed help, but because they couldn't help loving her. Abby was that kind of girl. That's why I can't see her having any enemies who'd have done something like this."

"I've heard her dad was a different matter."

Eleanor snorted. "I can think of a lot of husbands who hated Dan Langford, and quite a few women. Although in case you're wondering, there wasn't any talk about his death being murder. He died driving drunk, plain and simple. The only thing surprising about it was that the woman in the car with him when it happened was his wife."

"Can you think of anyone who might have a vendetta against Abby because of her dad?"

She chewed her lip for a moment. "I can't believe anyone held what he did against Abby. If anything, people felt sorry for her having a dad like that." A few flecks of pink lipstick were now on her teeth.

"Even so, could you give me the names of any women you can remember who slept with Dan Langford and live in the area? Especially if the woman's husband is still alive."

Eleanor gave him a wry look. "Might be quicker if I gave you a list of the women he didn't sleep with."

– – –

Abby spent a lot of time getting ready for her dinner with Josh, agonizing over her hair, trying on and rejecting four different dresses before deciding on her favorite black silk. That was just because she could easily run into a fan who'd expect her to look like Samantha at the fancy restaurant Giorgio's reportedly was.

She was glad she'd dressed up when Josh arrived wearing a gray tweed sport coat over a black shirt and pants. Despite her ambivalence toward him, she had to admit he looked good. He might still resemble a pirate, but tonight it was the hot Hollywood type, as skilled at handling women in bed as enemies on board. If this had been a date, her accelerated heartbeat would have been from anticipation, as opposed to concern over what he'd learned about her stalker.

Unfortunately he hadn't learned much, as he told her during the fifteen-minute drive to Giorgio's. *Private Affairs* had received more than a thousand disapproving letters and e-mails, some even threatening, but nothing from her "biggest fan." No one in Harrington had any idea who could hate her enough to hurt her. They were questioning anyone who might hold a grudge against her dad and be taking it out on her, although that was a long shot. He hadn't unearthed any known religious fanatics or any felons or mental cases with similar MOs residing in the area. The bullets were the only tangible evidence, and they weren't much help without a suspect or weapon. On the plus side, they'd gotten several calls with possible leads. They'd find him, Josh promised, and between her guard, security system, and the squad cars he'd instructed to pass her house at least four times every hour, she'd be safe until they did.

He finished his update just as he pulled into the parking lot, which he called perfect timing because he was through talking business for the evening. So he hadn't invited her to dinner for more questioning.

They walked into the restaurant, then followed the hostess through a dining room that resembled an idealized Tuscan villa. The light stucco walls were decorated with painted landscapes of the Italian countryside, the appetizing aromas similarly Italian. When they were seated and the hostess had left, Abby decided it was time for the direct approach. "Why did you really invite me to dinner?"

"I told you," Josh said. "Because I'm sorry I didn't believe you."

"You were just doing your job. You didn't know me, and I could have been staging everything." After the way he'd helped her, she was ready to give him the benefit of the doubt. "If you're worried I'll complain and Mary will get the mayor on your case again, I won't. You don't have to take me to dinner." Abby wrinkled her nose. "I probably should have told you that before we got here, but I just thought of it. If you want to leave now..."

He covered her hand with his, his touch sending a sizzle up her arm. "I know you won't complain. I honestly do want to apologize. Since our first encounter, I've been unfair to you, and it wasn't because I was being a careful cop. It was because of my ex-wife."

She hadn't seen that one coming. Abby tilted her head, her forehead creasing. "Do I look like her?"

"That's not it." He removed his hand from hers. "I was a cop when we were married, had made detective by then. I did a year of law school at the University of Chicago right after college, but dropped out when I realized I wanted to be a cop. Jennifer seemed fine with it at first, but after a few years she started ragging on me about making more of myself, going back to law school or getting an MBA." He picked up his salad fork, turned it idly in his fingers. "She'd gotten a job as a sales rep for a drug company and had become obsessed with how much money people made, what kind of cars they drove, where they lived, that kind of thing. She spent her entire paycheck on clothes and always wanted to do whatever her friends did, see shows and eat at fancy restaurants. Things we couldn't afford."

"Is that why you got divorced?"

His fork clinked down on his bread plate. "We got divorced because Jennifer found a more promising husband and had an affair. He's a successful lawyer, a partner at Chicago's biggest firm.

She's now married to the guy and from all reports is blissfully happy with him and their new baby."

"I'm sorry," Abby said, the rawness in his voice scraping an unhealed nerve of her own. Dealing with a spouse's affair was difficult on so many levels.

Josh's expression was pained, as if someone had kicked him in the stomach. "Yeah, it was shit." He picked up his water glass and took a long drink before he continued, "Jennifer taped your show every day. She was always going on about Samantha's clothes, career, and whole glamorous lifestyle. And her rich, successful husbands and lovers, who were all the opposite of what she considered me to be. I'd never even seen *Private Affairs*, but I hated everything about it. Hell, maybe I subconsciously blamed it for Jennifer's dissatisfaction with our life.

"The tabloids portrayed you as being a lot like Samantha, and I was so bitter I believed them. Before I'd even met you, I'd concluded you were a lying, cheating, manipulative bitch."

He took another drink of water, then met Abby's eyes. "Thanks to Jennifer's constant put-downs of cops, I also have a chip on my shoulder. I know some of Chicago's upper-class citizens view cops as ignorant thugs, barely better than the criminals we arrest." He shrugged. "I assumed that as an actress from LA, you'd have even less respect for cops, especially ones in smaller towns. Because I'd already decided you were manipulative, I was half convinced you'd faked the knife for publicity before I even got to your house. Then when you told me you'd found it vacuuming between walls—"

"Writer's block can make you do scary things," Abby said. "I can certainly understand your skepticism."

He slammed his fist on the tablecloth. "But damn it, I shouldn't have put the letters and lipstick message in the same category!" His voice was harsh, the rawness gone. "The way I acted and things I assumed about you weren't only unprofessional, but juvenile, if not irrational."

His obvious anger at himself dissipated any remnants of anger Abby might have still felt toward him. "From my experience, divorce leads to a lot of juvenile and irrational behavior," she said quietly.

"That doesn't excuse mine. I've been unfair to you and rude. Worse yet, I let my feelings make me discount what happened to you. I apologize."

It wasn't just cops who didn't apologize—in Abby's experience, no man did, at least not without some ulterior motive or qualification. Both her dad and Colin had always claimed that their failings were partly and even primarily her fault. But Josh looked sincere. More important, the emotion in his voice rang true, his words more dragged out than rehearsed. Unless he was a better actor than she'd ever encountered, he'd meant every word.

"Apology accepted," she said.

Josh studied her face for a moment, his scrutiny so intense Abby almost looked away. Then he smiled, and her stomach flipped over just as it had the first time she'd seen that sensuous smile. "Now that we've gotten that out of the way, let's order," he said, picking up a menu. "I'm starving."

The food was excellent, the conversation even better. They talked almost nonstop through appetizers, salads, and entrées. Abby found herself discussing all sorts of things she'd never thought a man like Josh would be interested in—politics, movies, literature, and even art—he'd bought the modern paintings she'd seen in his office.

"Do you want anything?" he asked after the waitress had recited the evening's dessert menu.

"Just coffee. Decaf."

"I'll take the tiramisu. And bring two forks."

"I've always had a weakness for tiramisu," Abby admitted after the waitress had left.

"So have I. I spent a college semester in London, and with travel so cheap in Europe, we took several trips to Italy." He flashed a grin. "Mostly because we thought Italian women were hot, but the tiramisu was good, too."

She'd never even considered that Josh would have traveled abroad, let alone lived several months there. She was rapidly realizing she'd misjudged him as much as he'd misjudged her.

The waitress set the tiramisu in front of Josh. He tasted it. "Excellent." He scooped up another forkful, this time holding it toward Abby's mouth. "Try this."

She took a bite from his fork, then swallowed the cream and sponge cake, her eyes on his. "It's wonderful."

"You've got mascarpone above your lip. To the left."

She flicked her tongue over her top lip. "Did I get it?"

"Not quite." He reached out his finger and wiped the corner of her mouth. "There." He moved his finger to his own mouth and licked off the speck. "Feel free to eat more."

She nodded but didn't pick up her fork. She couldn't move, couldn't tear her eyes from his. She felt as if they'd turned off the air-conditioning, the warm air almost too thick to breathe.

"I—damn," Josh said, breaking eye contact. He removed his phone from the case clipped to his belt. "I'm sorry, but I've got to take this. They'd never bother me unless it was important."

The interruption broke the spell and loosened Abby's lungs. "At least you know it isn't a call from me."

As soon as Abby could tell the call wasn't about her stalker, she stopped paying attention and started picking at his tiramisu.

When Josh finished his call, he signaled to the waitress for the check. "I'm sorry, but I have to go," he told Abby. "There was a fatal car crash. We don't get a lot of those, so I'd better supervise."

"Do you want me to take a cab home?"

He shook his head. "It's not a rush. As soon as I get our bill, and you finish your dessert, I'll give you a ride."

She set her fork on the nearly empty plate, looking sheepish. "I have eaten most of it, haven't I? Sorry."

He waved his hand. "Finish it. Fatal car accidents ruin my appetite."

"I'm done, thanks," Abby said. "Do you ever get used to it?"

"I haven't seen all that many car crashes, but I've seen far too many dead bodies," he said. "You never get used to it, but you figure out ways to deal with it, both during and after."

She hesitated, cleared her throat. "Do you ever dream about it?"

"Sometimes. Not nearly as much as at first."

"Have you ever dreamed something that turned out to be right?" Abby's voice was barely above a whisper. "Like seeing the murderer actually kill or stash the weapon?"

"You mean before I'd tracked down the evidence, like a psychic?" A corner of Josh's mouth quirked. "I think that stuff only happens in writers' imaginations."

– – –

Josh was silent on the drive home, mentally preparing himself to deal with the accident scene, no doubt. Something they had in common, although comparing his job to mentally preparing to play a *Private Affairs* scene was like comparing a fireman to a barbecue chef.

When he pulled up in front of Abby's house and shut off the ignition, she rested a hand on his arm. "Don't bother walking me to the door. I know you've got things to do."

"They can wait a few minutes." He circled the car and opened the passenger side door. "I'm sorry work ruined our evening."

"That's what happens when you have a demanding job," she said as she exited the car. "Or kids—they always come down with strep throat at the worst possible moment."

The night was quiet as they walked through the floral-scented warmth to the house, the sidewalk shimmering under the nearly full moon and a couple of streetlamps. "I can't even see the guard," Abby said. It was almost ten thirty. "I hope that means he's being discreet, not playing pool at some bar."

"He's here. As I said, I know a lot about the company."

They stepped up onto the circular front porch. "I appreciate your recommendation," Abby said. "I also appreciate the dinner. A simple apology would have sufficed, but I really enjoyed myself."

"Me, too." Then Josh's arms were around her.

Memories of his earlier kiss triggered an immediate response to this one, a charge that sizzled from Abby's lips through her entire body. She shivered, then circled her arms around his neck and clung to him. Her body heated at the feel of his tongue teasing hers, at the rasp of his whiskers like fine sandpaper against her chin, at the same focus and intensity that had overwhelmed her senses the other night.

Far too soon, he removed his mouth from hers. "Maybe that's the real reason I asked you to dinner," he murmured, his lips still so close to hers she could feel his hot breath. "Because I wanted to see if kissing you was as good as it was the other night." He brushed her lips with his. "It was even better." Then he took the key from her shaky fingers and unlocked and opened the door. "I'll call you."

"Are you OK, Ms. Langford?" Bethany, a college student Laura promised was substantially more intelligent than the ditzy blonde she pretended to be, walked into the foyer. She had a floral bustier purse over her shoulder and a jean jacket on her arm.

Abby shook herself out of her stupor, realizing she was gripping the doorjamb to hold herself upright as she watched Josh walk to his car. It was just a kiss, for heaven's sake—a really good kiss, but she was far from being a naive teenager. "Sorry, I was lost in thought. I told you to call me Abby."

"I know, but it feels weird to do that. Since you're so famous."

"Not that famous," Abby said, closing the door.

"You are to me and my friends," Bethany said. "They're going to freak out when they hear I got to babysit for you. We record *Private Affairs* every day, and you're the best. Are you ever going back?"

"I don't plan to, but you never know." Abby pulled her billfold from her purse, extracted several bills, and held them out to Bethany.

"You don't have to give me that much."

"That's what Laura pays you."

Bethany rolled her eyes. "Laura has three kids. Two boys."

"You still had to give up your evening and on short notice, so take it. Would you be willing to babysit again?"

Bethany stuffed the money into her purse. "Anytime. Are you dating Josh Kincaid?"

"We had some things to discuss about what happened last night and decided to do it over dinner. We're friends because Maddie and his niece Rachel are friends." If Bethany did babysit again, Abby didn't want her to contradict the story she'd given Maddie to explain tonight's dinner.

"Maddie talked about Rachel," Bethany said, slipping on her jean jacket. "I figured it wasn't a date, since Josh is going with Heather Casey, and Tiffany would have told me if they'd broken up. Tiffany is Heather's best friend, and she's also one of my housemates this summer. That must have been wild last night, having someone shoot at you. Do they know who did it?"

Abby managed to carry on her side of the conversation, but the instant Bethany was out the door, she slumped against the wall, her chest feeling as hollow as the Tin Man's. So Josh had lied about giving up his younger girlfriend. Although she shouldn't be surprised. She knew from painful experience that the old joke about being able to tell when a man was lying was based on fact.

The only question was why Josh had bothered lying. Her best guess was he'd wanted to make a grand gesture apology to placate Mary and the mayor and realized she wouldn't accept a dinner invitation if he were still involved with Heather.

Abby plodded up the stairs, trailing her hand along the smooth railing. Why Josh had done it really didn't matter, since she'd never see him again, other than professionally. Any disappointment she felt was simply because she'd thought he was honest and actually liked him. Then he'd turned out to be just like Colin, proving once again that her instincts were shot to hell.

It was a good thing she'd sworn off men.

CHAPTER 10

Josh waited until nine the next morning before he called Abby. "Now I have to apologize for rushing away last night," he said, smiling faintly. One benefit of having to cut their date short was that it gave him a good excuse to ask her out again. "There's a French film at the Cinema 8 with a title I'm not going to even try to pronounce, but as long as it has subtitles, I can handle it. Do you want to go?"

"I don't think that's a good idea," Abby said.

"You don't like French films? Is there something else you want to see?"

"I love French films."

His smile faded. "I thought you enjoyed last night. I certainly did."

"I'm sure you know why it won't be repeated." Her tone was nearly cold enough to give his eardrums frostbite.

"I don't have any idea what you're talking about," he said.

"I'll bet you can figure it out if you think for half a second. Please let me know if you learn any more about my case."

Josh set down his phone, then massaged the bridge of his nose, as confused as if he'd walked into the middle of a Fellini movie. He'd been up until three about that damn car crash, then gotten home to find four tearful messages from Heather on his machine. When he'd arrived at work, he'd discovered Heather had told Tiffany about their breakup, so Tiffany now considered him the devil incarnate. And in five minutes he had to go to a city council meeting to defend his proposed budget. The only part of today he'd been looking forward to was talking to Abby and, hopefully, seeing her again tonight.

What was she so upset about? Maybe she'd been offended he'd kissed her, although she hadn't seemed to be. Or maybe it was because she was famous and he was a nobody whose ex-wife had left him for a more successful man, which made him a loser, too. If so, he was also an idiot because he'd read her way wrong, but as Jennifer and Heather had proved, reading women wasn't his forte.

But he didn't have time to agonize over that now. He needed a dozen copies of his proposal, and he didn't have to be a genius about women to know he'd better not ask Tiffany to make them. He grabbed the proposal off his desk and headed for the copy machine.

– – –

While Honeywell installed her new security system, Abby spent the morning shopping with Maddie at the Spring Place Mall, a two-story center housing a couple of dozen stores and an equal number of kiosks. It had only been built fifteen years ago, and Abby was still amazed whenever she drove through the part of town it was in. When she'd been growing up, the area had been cornfields and wheat fields. Now it sported not only the busy mall, but a Target, a Fleet Farm, and a dozen fast-food and other chain restaurants—and had presumably made some former farmers very wealthy men.

Maddie's top priority was buying a birthday gift for Hannah, a friend of Rachel's she'd met once and whose birthday party she was thrilled to be attending that evening. Abby had called Kim for gift recommendations, since she'd had a feeling the appropriate price range here would be lower than in Beverly Hills, and she was right. She couldn't believe she could get away with buying a nail art kit and some glitter makeup at Bath & Body Works.

After spending nearly as much at Hallmark on the perfect card, paper, and bow, Abby and Maddie headed to the Macy's store that served as the mall's anchor tenant. As usual, Maddie needed clothes—she seemed to be growing an inch a month.

"You really don't have to help me," Maddie said as they walked past the glass counters and colorful displays of the store's cosmetic department. "I'm old enough to pick out my own clothes."

"And pay for them?" Abby asked, steering Maddie out of spritzing range of a perfume demonstrator waving a bottle that smelled like a mixture of cut grass and oranges.

"I could if you'd give me a credit card."

"You're too young for a credit card."

Maddie tilted her head at her mother, her dark curls covering one shoulder of her pink shirt. "Natasha Alton had one in first grade."

"And your point is?" Natasha Alton gave new meaning to the word *spoiled*. She'd probably receive a sports car for her fourteenth birthday, after one of her parents convinced the governor to issue an official proclamation authorizing Natasha to get a driver's license two years early.

"I'll bet Daddy will let me have one."

"No, he won't." Not if he had to pay the bills.

Maddie no doubt knew that, because she didn't pursue it. "It's just that I'm not a little kid anymore," she said in a plaintive tone. "You don't need to pick out my clothes for me."

They'd reached the preteen section now—Maddie insisted she was too old for the kids' department. The cropped tops on the first rack were more appropriate for a nineteen-year-old than a nine-year-old—Exhibit A as to why Abby wasn't about to give Maddie free rein. "You can pick things out, but as long as I've got the Visa card, I've also got veto power," she said firmly.

Maddie let out a pained sigh. "Can you at least go to a different department until I decide what I like?"

Maddie was growing up so fast, Abby thought as she wandered over to the dress department. She hadn't expected these kinds of battles for at least a couple of years. Although leaving LA would hopefully slow the maturation process a little.

Abby flipped through a rack of dresses, primarily sundresses and strapless numbers. Apparently this was the younger area of the dress department, since virtually everything required pre-breast-feeding pectorals. But she didn't want to get too far away from Maddie, and she didn't need anything herself, anyway.

"I thought that was you. I'm Heather Casey, Josh Kincaid's girlfriend."

Abby turned from the rack and toward the brunette who'd been with Josh the other night. Heather was even more attractive up close, with a figure that could have graced a Victoria's Secret ad, displayed to perfection in a skin-hugging red T-shirt and black miniskirt.

"I heard you were at Giorgio's with Josh last night," she said accusingly.

"We're just friends. His niece and my daughter are friends." Although Abby had no idea why she was giving Josh an out. She should be telling Heather the truth, that Josh Kincaid was a typical two-timing male she'd be well rid of.

"When Josh broke up with me, I never thought he meant it," Heather said, flipping wavy hair that reached her mid-back over her left shoulder. "I mean, I didn't even bother telling any of my friends because I figured we'd get back together the next day. When he didn't answer my phone calls last night, and Felicia saw him at Giorgio's with you, though, I figured it out."

"Josh broke up with you?" Abby asked, focusing on the important part of Heather's statement.

"Only because he wants to sleep with you because you're famous." Heather waved her darkly tanned hand, displaying inch-long nails the exact shade of her T-shirt. "You know, like girls always want to sleep with rock stars even if they're ugly. For notches on their bedposts."

Abby's forehead creased. "Notches on their bedposts?"

"That's just a saying." Heather waved her hand again. "Josh doesn't have real notches or anything. You're not ugly, but you're not exactly young. Men like younger women, you know."

"I know." She couldn't argue that one.

"I forgot about your husband having a younger girlfriend now. Sorry," Heather said, not sounding at all contrite. "But that proves Josh would never look twice at you if you weren't famous. I mean, you couldn't wear a dress like this, could you?" She reached into the rack and selected a tube of strapless Lycra not much bigger than a hand towel in a lurid combination of pinks and oranges.

"No, I couldn't." To be honest, Abby would never have been caught dead in even a distant cousin of that thing.

Heather leaned toward her, lowering her voice. "And Josh loves sex. Lots of it. He's like a sex machine. A woman your age could never keep up with him."

"Why are you telling me this?" Abby asked, not bothering to hide her impatience. The age cracks were getting old. Heather apparently believed those bitchy confrontations on reality shows were not only unscripted, but socially acceptable.

"I don't want you to think you can take Josh away from me." Heather clasped her hands together. "We love each other. He just needs to prove he can sleep with someone famous first, to get it out of his system before we get married. Like with my sister Brittany. When she was engaged to Shawn, he slept with one of the Timberwolves cheerleaders. Brittany was going to break up with him over it, but then he explained he only did it because it was his last chance. It wasn't like she was some ordinary woman he met in a bar, she was a real-live, professional basketball cheerleader. So Brittany forgave him, and now she and Shawn are married and have a baby and are perfectly happy."

"You and Josh are getting married?" Abby asked to clarify.

Heather waved her hand again, so expansively her nails barely missed snagging a couple of crystal necklaces hanging from a display rack. "He hasn't exactly proposed yet, but he will. I mean, he's older, and he's already been married, so he'll want to settle down soon and have kids. Josh loves kids. He's not like those guys my age who won't get married until they're at least thirty." She flipped her hair onto her back, so it covered her right shoulder. "That's why I decided he was the one for me."

Abby widened her eyes in mock innocence, starting to enjoy herself. "Does that mean you want me to sleep with Josh? So he'll get me out of his system and be ready to settle down with you?"

In contrast, Heather's brown eyes narrowed. "No, I want you to leave him alone. He'll come back to me no matter what you do."

"You're worried I'll be hurt." Abby patted Heather's arm. "That's sweet, but you don't need to be. Since I'm older, I'm sure I can handle whatever Josh decides to do."

"That's not exactly what I meant…"

Abby glanced across the store and spotted Maddie, hauling an oversize armload of clothes toward a dressing room. "I'd better go find my daughter. It's been very nice meeting you, Heather."

‒ ‒ ‒

Abby had ended up agreeing to let Maddie buy more than she probably should have, primarily because she'd been anxious to finish their shopping expedition, go home, and call Josh. Not because she wanted to see him again, she told herself. It was because she was going to enjoy showing him that he didn't know as much about women as he thought.

"Is your invitation for a movie still open?" she asked the instant he answered. OK, so maybe she was anxious to see him again.

"Abby?"

"Did you issue multiple invitations this morning?"

"Of course not," he said. "I'm just surprised to hear from you. I thought I got a definite no."

Abby sat down in the beige, nonreclining recliner, setting her bare feet on the coffee table. "I was under the misconception you hadn't really broken up with Heather."

"I said I did."

"Men frequently lie."

"I don't."

She was starting to believe that. "Can I change my mind about the movie?"

"Absolutely. I'll pick you up at seven."

"I'll be ready." Abby held out one hand and examined her short, unpainted nails. Maybe she should get a manicure before tonight. She'd never had one outside the studio, but she was competing with a fashion-conscious twenty-two-year-old now. "Although to be honest, I'd never have pegged you for a groupie."

"Because I want to take you to a French film?" Josh asked. "I don't even know who's in it."

"No, because you only asked me out because I'm on TV."

"What the hell are you talking about?"

Screw the manicure; even fake nails and bright polish wouldn't make her look any closer to twenty-two. "I ran into Heather at Macy's today. We had an interesting conversation."

"What did Heather say?" Josh asked, sounding wary despite Abby's deliberately casual tone. Or maybe because of it.

"She confirmed you broke things off with her," Abby said. "She told me it's only because like most men, you have this thing about sleeping with famous women, even if they're old and ugly. Notches on your bedpost, she called it."

"Oh, God."

"She doesn't think I'm ugly. But at my age, I could never keep up with a sex machine like you."

He made a strangled sound.

"She was sweet to warn me," Abby said. "She didn't want me to be devastated when you dropped me and went back to her since you two are getting married."

"We're what?"

Abby smiled at his horrified tone. "You haven't proposed yet, but you're the marrying type, since you're divorced, older, and like kids. That's why she chose you instead of some guy her own age who doesn't want to get married until he's thirty."

"She thinks I want to marry her?" he asked incredulously. "I dated her because I thought she wasn't interested in marriage."

Abby's smile widened. "So much for your brilliant theory about young women and biological clocks. Unlike mine, which also contrary to your theory, stopped ticking years ago."

"Does that mean you're inviting me to sleep with you?" Josh asked.

Abby snorted. "Wrong. Trust a man to read between the lines and get that."

"Too bad, since sleeping with a TV star would be a major notch on my bedpost."

She rolled her eyes but didn't answer.

Josh's tone turned serious. "I'm sorry you had to deal with Heather. I'd better talk to her."

Abby moved her feet onto the shag carpet. "I wouldn't," she said equally serious. "I think she's still in the phase that no matter what you say, she'll take a call from you as evidence you'll eventually come back to her." She could still remember being young, romantic, and heartbroken. The best remedy was a clean break, then quick cauterization of the wound by the attentions of a new man.

"I handled things badly."

"There's no painless way to break things off." Abby paused for a moment as inspiration struck. "Instead of going to a movie, why don't you come over here for dinner? Maddie will be at a birthday party."

"You cook?"

"I love to cook." That cooking was one area where she'd bet she far surpassed Heather had nothing to do with her offer. "Can you make it by six thirty?"

"I'll be there."

Abby hung up the phone, then headed to the kitchen and got a mineral water out of the harvest-gold refrigerator. To be honest, she'd kind of enjoyed her encounter with Heather, and not just because she'd been able to needle Josh about it. Growing up she'd felt she had to be especially nice so people wouldn't think she was like her parents. That feeling had continued after she'd moved to LA, at first because she was terrified that otherwise *Private Affairs* would fire her and later because she'd gotten a reputation for being nice and people expected it. She was basically nice. That didn't mean she never got the occasional urge to be a little bitchy. Since Heather had started it, she'd been able to indulge without feeling guilty.

Abby opened the bottle and took a long drink of water. She'd never really thought about it, but that was probably why she'd enjoyed playing Samantha, because she could get that urge out of her system. Sort of like sleeping with someone famous.

Speaking of Josh—who she was not going to be sleeping with—she had promised to cook, which meant she'd better get over to Erickson's. But first she needed to make a quick revision to her manuscript. She set the water on the counter, then headed to the spiral staircase and raced upstairs, two steps at a time. She'd suddenly realized the eighteen-year-old blonde first victim would work much better as a twenty-two-year-old brunette.

CHAPTER 11

After feasting on chili-rubbed steaks, roasted poblano mashed potatoes, and salad, plus a tart made from the fresh raspberries Abby hadn't been able to resist buying, she and Josh brought their glasses and the remainder of a bottle of cabernet into the living room.

Josh plopped down onto the couch. "That was terrific. You really can cook."

Abby raised an eyebrow as she sat down beside him. "You thought I lied about that, too?"

"I've concluded you haven't lied about anything—except rocket science." He looked around. "This rug is beautiful," he said, referring to the Persian carpet that covered most of the hardwood floor. He stretched his arm along the back of the cobalt couch. "I assume it didn't come with the house."

"Good guess. The rug was one of the two furnishings I brought from California. The other was this couch. Everything else was too modern to look good in this house." And more Colin's taste than hers, even though she'd paid for all of it.

"Why did you decide to move back to Harrington? Because of your divorce?"

Abby swirled her wineglass, watching the ruby liquid lap the crystal. "Partly. After I got divorced, I wanted Maddie to still feel like part of a family, and that's how I think of Bill, Mary, and

Laura. Mary also needed angioplasty last year. She's fine now, but I realized none of us are going to live forever." She swirled the wine higher, like a connoisseur trying to impress. "I've also wanted to write for years. It seemed a good time to make a major change. Why did you leave Chicago?"

"I needed a change after my divorce, too." Josh's snort sounded constricted. "I told you my wife left me for a more successful man. The man had been my best friend since fifth grade. On top of that, Jennifer told me the real reason she'd claimed she wasn't ready to have kids was because I didn't make enough money to be a good dad."

He took a long drink of wine before continuing. "I stuck around Chicago for a year, but Kim knew I was in bad shape. When the chief's job here opened up, she convinced me to apply." He met Abby's eyes. "You were right that I was dating Heather to prop up my ego."

"That was my own bias talking," Abby said, his intense gaze making her look away, down at the Persian carpet. "My ex-husband has an eighteen-year-old girlfriend." Yet again.

"Your criticism was on the money in my case." Josh drained his wine and set the glass on the floor. "After my marriage fell apart, I felt like a loser. So I had far too many one-night stands to prove I wasn't, then I moved here and dated an easily impressed twenty-two-year-old." He massaged the back of his neck with his hand. "But none of that made me happy. It was just a bunch of Band-Aids, not a cure."

"Is this job a Band-Aid, too?"

"I don't know," he said, stretching his arm along the back of the couch again. "I miss things about my old job and Chicago, but I also love being near Kim and her family. I'm not real anxious to return to Chicago and those bad memories, either."

"That's the way I feel about California," Abby said. "Divorce sucks, doesn't it?"

"No argument here." After a couple of minutes of commiserating silence, Josh moved his arm from the couch down around Abby's shoulders. "Although getting a soap opera star into bed would do wonders for my battered ego," he said, a hint of laughter in his voice.

"I'm not having sex with you."

"Why not?" He fingered her loose hair. "I'm healthy."

"Two days ago, I didn't even like you."

"You didn't really know me then." Josh's fingers slipped beneath her hair and stroked her neck, raising goose bumps. "And I was acting like an ass."

"I don't really know you now."

"Yes, you do, and I hope you like me." He'd leaned toward her, and his lips were against her ear, his voice low and sensual, sending titillating shivers across her shoulders and neck. "I definitely like you." He slipped his finger under her shirt and caressed her collarbone.

Not a good idea, since the sensations were tempting her to ignore her brain. Abby jerked away from his hand, then turned and faced him, her arms folded. "I'm still not having sex with you. I haven't known you long enough."

"That's legitimate. We've known each other long enough to make out, haven't we?" Josh wrapped his arm around her and pulled her against his side again. "We can pretend we're back in high school."

"I never made out in high school," Abby admitted. "I was too busy with acting and working to even date."

Josh lowered his head, his lips so close to hers she could feel their radiating warmth. "That's OK, because I'm really good at it." Then he kissed her, a kiss that went on and on, his lips and tongue tasting and caressing hers until the blood pumping from her wildly pounding heart had her entire body simmering.

"You are really good at this," Abby said when he finally moved his lips away. She unwound her arms, which had somehow ended up around his neck.

"I'm just getting started," he said, deftly unbuttoning her shirt as his lips moved down her neck. He kissed the slope of one breast, then put his mouth over one lace-covered nipple, sucking and licking until the lace was wet.

She didn't even think of stopping him, instead she braced her hands on his shoulders, her nails biting into his shirt. Her breast wasn't the only part of her getting wet.

"I wouldn't want the other one to feel neglected," he said after a moment, then he repeated the process with her other breast.

When the lace was soaked, he lifted his head and removed Abby's hands from his shoulders. Then he pulled her shirt down, sliding it just far enough that the sleeves secured her arms at her sides. "At the risk of sounding like a groupie, I've been fantasizing about doing this ever since I watched your show," he said, his voice a rumble that sent her temperature even higher.

"The day Evan came back?"

"You looked so damn hot in that black underwear that I couldn't resist recording the rest of the week. The bathtub scene nearly drove me crazy." Josh unhooked the front clasp of her bra and separated the cups, exposing her breasts. "God, you're more beautiful than my fantasy." He circled one crest with his tongue.

Abby shuddered. "Now you're driving me crazy."

"That's the general idea. We called this getting to second base. Do you like it?" He sucked her nipple deep into his mouth.

She moaned.

"I'll take that as a yes," he said, sliding his hand down her stomach. He undid the front button and zipper of her denim skirt and slipped his hand inside her panties.

"What are you doing?" Abby asked, stiffening. As good as it felt, her brain wasn't ready to go too fast. "I thought we were just making out."

"We are. This is getting to third base." He stroked her gently, still sucking hard on her breast.

"You did that in high school?" Abby got out; the sensations he was triggering were so arousing she could barely breathe, let alone speak.

He chuckled deep in his throat as he pulled her silk panties down with his free hand. "Back then I didn't realize the girl was supposed to enjoy it, too." He slipped a finger inside her, then another as he intensified his massage with his thumb.

Abby moved against his fingers, her eyes closed, her core winding tighter, tighter, tighter. Without warning she exploded, crying out as hot sparks shot through her brain and body, shocking every nerve. She slumped against the couch, her breath coming in gasps, as Josh removed his fingers but continued stroking her gently with his thumb.

When she could think again, she realized she wanted to take control, to make him feel as good as he'd made her feel. She shrugged off her shirt and moved his hand away. Then she slipped her panties onto the floor and straddled his lap wearing only her unzipped skirt. "My turn," she said as she pulled his polo shirt over his head. She stroked the sculpted muscles of his shoulders and chest. "How much do you work out?"

"A lot more since my divorce," he said. "Stress relief."

"It had other benefits." She licked one nipple, her fingers playing with his rough chest hair. His palms cupped her buttocks, pushing her skirt up even higher. His erection felt like hot iron even through his jeans.

As she kissed and licked her way down his six-pack abs, she slid slowly along his thigh. The slight roughness of the denim had her close to coming again before she finally moved off his leg and onto her knees on the carpet in front of him. She set her half-full wineglass far out of the way, then undid his jeans. The rasp of the zipper was the only sound besides his labored breathing.

Josh rose up to help her pull down his jeans, easing them over thighs as impressively muscular as his chest, then down around his ankles.

"I think third base is my favorite," she said, massaging his solid erection through his briefs. She pulled them down just enough to release him, then circled him with her tongue.

"I think that's beyond making out," Josh said, his voice a little unsteady.

She took him into her mouth, moving down and back up his length before she lifted her head. "You don't like my version?"

"I love your version."

She used her hands and mouth on him, his taste making her hot, his groans as she sucked him making her even hotter. Then he abruptly grabbed the sides of her head and moved her mouth away. "I think it's time to stop," he said thickly.

"Do you really want to stop?"

"What do you think?"

She stroked her finger down his length. He was rock hard and so hot and damp she was surprised not to see steam. "Neither do I," she said.

"Are you sure?"

Despite how quickly things were progressing, Abby suddenly was, and not just because he made her so hot she could barely stand it. There was more to it than simple lust. She nodded. "Can we take it slow? It's been a while for me." Nearly three years, since she'd discovered Colin was having yet another affair and developed a chronic headache that appeared on those rare occasions he'd tried to initiate sex. "Unless that's too much pressure for you," she added, managing a light tone.

His slow smile heated her blood to a rolling boil. "I think I'm up to it," he said, kicking off his jeans and briefs. As he reached to pull a condom from his jeans pocket, she studied him. He was muscular everywhere—no wonder she felt so safe with him.

His erection was as well developed as the rest of his body. She closed her hand around it and massaged him. "You're beautiful, too." OK, maybe lust had a lot to do with this.

He moved her hand away. "I'm going to be embarrassed if you don't stop playing with me and let me get inside you," he said, donning the condom. Then he moved her onto her back on the carpet, pulled off her skirt, and slowly pushed into her, an inch at a time. "Jesus, you're tight. Tell me if I'm going too fast."

She could feel his veins throbbing as she took him in, but she was so wet her celibacy and his size didn't present any problems. "It's perfect. That feels incredible."

"It's more than incredible." He pushed once more until he was all the way inside her. "This is way better than my fantasies, too."

Abby wrapped her legs around his back, but Josh took hold of her ankles and pulled them higher, nearly to his neck. He started thrusting, every stroke adding more flames to the inferno inside her. She exploded again, her cry this time closer to a scream. Seconds later, he jerked, then collapsed on top of her.

She had no idea how long they lay glued together by sweat, their hearts pounding and breaths coming in nearly the same triple-time rhythm. Josh broke finally the connection. "I'll be right back. Don't move."

Abby rolled onto her side into an almost fetal position, her arm covering her abdomen, post-sex euphoria replaced by reality. She hadn't been with a man besides Colin since long before Maddie's birth, and the few insecurities she'd had about her body back then paled in comparison to what she had now. Especially compared to the twenty-two-year-old Josh was used to.

He was back in a minute, carrying a handwoven throw he'd gotten off one of the recliners. He lay down beside Abby, covering them both with it. "You moved. I wasn't finished yet." He pushed her onto her back, then reached down and fingered her clitoris.

"Don't. I can't."

He continued a light massage. "You don't think so?"

Her breath was coming faster. "Do you get three notches if you make a soap opera actress come three times?"

"I forgot all about the notches. I'd better give this my best shot." He pulled the throw off her and slid down her body.

"No." She covered her abdomen with her hand, trying to move back onto her side.

"Why not?"

Her face heated, and she looked away, but she couldn't think of any logical reason except the truth. "I've got stretch marks." She concealed them with makeup when necessary on *Private Affairs*, but she wasn't wearing makeup now. "I should have them lasered."

"Why?" Josh muscled her arm away and traced the offending marks with his fingertip. "Don't you think Maddie was worth every one of those?" She could feel his hot breath on her abdomen.

"Of course, but men don't think like that."

"I do." He kissed each mark, then moved his mouth lower. She would have sworn she couldn't. She was wrong.

– – –

"I got the information you wanted," Nick Walton said when Josh answered his office phone the next morning. He and Nick had gotten to be friends when they both were Chicago cops, and although Nick returned to his hometown of Minneapolis years ago, they'd kept in touch. Josh had called Nick for help about Abby's stalker.

"Three Mall of America guards worked the event," Nick continued. "None of them noticed anyone following Abby and Olivia."

"Was the event videotaped?" Josh asked, making a note.

"No. I'm sure a lot of people who attended took pictures and video, but you'd have to track them down."

"I doubt we'd find anything useful since most of the photos would be of Olivia and Abby."

"Probably," Nick said. "The good news is security cameras record everything that goes on in the mall's parking ramps. Abby parked in the west ramp and went east on 494. The next ten cars to leave that ramp went west. Number eleven went east, but it was a minivan, a woman and at least two kids. The next six after it also went west."

"Are there usually that many more cars going west than east?" Josh asked.

"During weekdays, since most mall traffic then either goes to one of the 35W exits or the western suburbs, especially people parked in the west ramp. We're lucky Abby went east, since it made checking easier."

"So no one followed her out of the ramp," Josh said. "How about at the restaurant?"

"They don't have cameras in their lot, but they reviewed their receipts for me," Nick said. "One couple paid seven minutes before Abby did. According to the manager, they're regulars, in their eighties, and always take a cab. After Abby paid, there wasn't another payment for twenty-one minutes. So it's unlikely her stalker ate there. The airport came up empty, too."

"I owe you," Josh said. "Especially considering the Mall of America isn't even in Minneapolis." It was in Bloomington, a next-door suburb.

"Lucky for me my girlfriend's a Bloomington cop."

"Anything serious?"

"I don't know yet," Nick said. "Melissa and I just started dating." He chuckled. "Which is why she was more than happy to do me the favor of checking through the surveillance tapes. After a few more months with me, she might not have been so accommodating."

"I saw Brooke on *News Break* a couple of nights ago," Josh said. "Her career has really taken off."

"What's Abby like?"

Josh accepted Nick's abrupt change of subject. Some topics were destined to stay off-limits forever. "Not at all like the tabloids. She's actually a very nice person. A wonderful mother."

"Who's got a stalker."

"Yeah," Josh said. "She's convinced he hates her because he's got her confused with Samantha, the character Abby plays on *Private Affairs*. Abby's convinced that once Samantha is killed off, her stalker will be satisfied and leave her alone."

"Do you agree?"

Josh frowned. "I think in real life things are never that clear-cut. But if it makes her feel better to think that, it doesn't hurt anything."

"When are you moving back to Chicago?" Nick asked.

"Why would I do that?"

"Because you're a detective like I am, not a damn administrator."

"Right now I'm where I need to be," Josh said. "I couldn't stick around Chicago. Not after my divorce."

"You don't have to explain it to me," Nick said. Leaving Chicago after a painful divorce was yet another thing Josh had in common with him. "If you ever want to go back to real police work but can't face Chicago, give me a call. We can always use good cops in Minneapolis."

"I'll do that. Thanks for the help."

"It was nice to do something that didn't involve a dead body," Nick said. "Although from what I read and what you told me, you were lucky you didn't have one."

Josh's hand tightened on the phone. "You've got that right."

Josh's next call was to Abby. "Maddie's busy tonight, right?"

"Why do you think that?" she asked.

"Because I asked Kim to invite her overnight," he said. "I told Kim I needed time to get those notches Heather accused me of wanting."

"You're kidding."

He smiled at Abby's appalled tone—who'd have suspected she'd be so easily embarrassed? "I am about the notches part. Come to my place for dinner around six thirty."

"How do you know I don't have other plans?" Abby asked.

"Cancel them."

"You're pretty cocky, aren't you?"

He chuckled at the double entendre. "I'll take that as a compliment."

"That's not what I meant." He could almost hear her cheeks heating.

He chuckled again, then cleared his throat. "Since the Neanderthal approach doesn't seem to be working, let me try another. Will you please come to my place for dinner?"

"Just for dinner?"

"That's up to you." His tone lowered and roughened. "But I'm planning something special for dessert."

– – –

Abby stopped running when she reached the sidewalk in front of her house and bent forward, panting. With Maddie at Kim's, she'd taken the opportunity to do her daily four-mile run outside instead of on the treadmill in the family room.

She swiped her hand over her forehead to stop sweat from dripping into her eyes. Running was nowhere on her list of favorite things, but she'd made it a habit years ago when she'd realized otherwise she'd have to live on roots and berries to fit into the designer clothes Samantha favored. For a change, she'd actually enjoyed today's run. The weather was warm but without a hint of oppressive humidity, the sky a breathtaking shade of blue that LA's ever-present smog made unobtainable. The blacktopped running path near her house followed the Willow River, which today's crystal sunlight had gleaming like polished sterling.

Abby smiled faintly, wiping her sweaty forehead again. Or maybe she'd enjoyed the run because she was in such a good mood. Last night had been a major breakthrough. She hadn't even dated since her divorce, and she'd honestly worried that she'd never have sex again, never meet a man she liked and trusted enough to have sex with. Now she had one less thing to worry about.

Her smile broadened. She was definitely looking forward to tonight—especially to dessert.

When she was no longer breathing like an overheated Saint Bernard, Abby shut off her iPod and crossed the grass to the back steps, stopping to pull a few weeds from the flower-filled garden that stretched along one side of the house. When she was a kid, the garden had been as beautiful and majestic as the house. The previous owners had neglected it, but she'd hired a gardening service to design, plant, and maintain it until she'd moved here. All she had to do this year was a little weeding and watering, and the service had promised they'd planted enough different varieties that the garden would be filled with blooms through fall.

After tossing the weeds out of sight behind the bushes by the back steps, Abby went into the kitchen and got a mineral water. She'd downed half the bottle when the phone on the counter rang. A private caller, no number listed. She picked up the phone. "Hello?"

"This is your biggest fan. You deserve to die for what you did to your daughter. And you will."

CHAPTER 12

The temperature seemed to plummet fifty degrees, freezing Abby's sweat into an icy sheen. The voice sounded cartoonish, but the words had been deadly serious. "Who is this?"

"By the way, you look good in blue." Then the line went dead.

Terror was squeezing Abby's lungs, making it hard for her to breathe. She ran to the window over the sink, not bothering to look out before she shut the blinds. Then she grabbed the phone and called Josh.

"I got a phone call. From my stalker." The words catapulted out the instant he answered, high and shrill.

"What did he say?" In contrast, Josh's voice was low, soothing.

"'This is your biggest fan. You deserve to die for what you did to your daughter. And you will.'" The horrible words were branded on her brain. "Then he told me I look good in blue. I was out running, and I'm wearing a blue T-shirt. He was watching me."

"Not necessarily," Josh said. "You wear a lot of blue, don't you? Maybe it was a general comment or a lucky guess." His voice was still calm, but Abby could feel tension underlying it. He didn't believe that.

"To be safe, I'll have a unit make several passes through your neighborhood. If he's around, that should scare him away. I assume the number didn't show up on caller ID."

"Just as an unidentified caller."

"We'll check the phone company records, although if the guy was smart, he used a burn phone. Did the call come to your home or cell phone?"

"My home."

"Is it unlisted?"

Abby willed herself to calm down, to focus. She was safe inside her house. Her guard wasn't here yet, but she'd armed the security system when she'd gone running, so no one could have gotten in. The police would be by any minute, and Josh was on the other line. "My cell is unlisted, but my landline number is published."

"So anyone could have gotten it. Are you sure the caller was a man?"

"Actually I couldn't tell," Abby said thoughtfully. "It sounded like a cartoon voice. Computer generated maybe. He called himself my biggest fan, so it must be the same person who wrote the lipstick message. And he knows about Maddie." The hysteria was back in her voice. "She's at Kim's. I need to go get her."

"No," Josh said. "He hasn't threatened Maddie, just you. I'm sure he's gone, but stay in the house. I'll pick you up at six."

Josh hadn't needed to warn her to stay inside. If the caller was the person who'd written on her mirror, he was also the person who'd shot at her car and could very well have been watching her run today.

And he could still be watching.

– – –

"Could you trace the number?" Abby asked the minute Josh arrived. She'd been waiting anxiously for him, but not because she was still terrified. A long hot shower and time had calmed her down and made her realize something she wanted to run by him.

"The call was from a prepaid cell phone that's been shut off," he said. "We can tell the call came from within a two-mile radius of the downtown tower on Sixth Street, but that covers a lot of buildings."

"Including my house," Abby said. "The good news is that we know for sure he's upset with Samantha, not me."

"Why do you think that?"

"He said I deserve to die for what I did to my daughter. On the show Samantha just slept with her daughter's boyfriend. If I hadn't gotten so freaked out by the call, I'd have realized right away that's what he's talking about. I've never done anything to hurt Maddie. That means once Samantha's dead, he'll leave me alone."

"We don't know that," Josh said. "Even if you're right about Samantha being the target, he's apparently confusing you with her. If he sees you in Harrington or even talks to you on the phone, he could view that as evidence Samantha's still alive."

"I'm not sure he was really *threatening* me," Abby said. "Samantha was wearing blue in today's episode when she was shoved into the ocean. The previews for Monday make it clear she's dead. Maybe he was just calling to gloat that Samantha got what she deserved."

"I hope you're right," Josh said. "In case you aren't, promise you won't go running outside until this is over. You should also consider having the guard full-time. If people notice him, tough. It will have a deterrent effect."

Her theory had to be right. Her stalker had to hate Samantha, not her personally, if only because otherwise she'd never be safe, not until she was dead. She couldn't bear to even consider that.

But Abby wasn't about to bet her life on it—or Maddie's. She nodded. "I'll call the company tomorrow."

"I'll call Sam and arrange it right now," Josh said, pulling out his phone. "Another guy will come out at seven tomorrow morning," he said after he'd hung up. "Now it's time to start our date. Let's go."

After collecting two large bags of food from Taste of Thailand, Josh drove to one of a half dozen new-looking town houses, situated in a neighborhood of two-story houses, mature trees, and well-tended lawns and gardens. He and Abby walked from the attached garage into the kitchen.

"This is nice," she said, taking in the cherry cabinets, maple floor, dark granite countertops, and gleaming appliances. She'd been determined that the threat wouldn't ruin tonight, and that wasn't proving difficult. Being with Josh and at his place made it easy to forget about the call, to feel safe.

"You lucked out—my cleaning lady was here today." Josh set the bags of food on the counter. "I need to change. If you want something to drink, check the refrigerator."

Abby was sitting at the kitchen table drinking a mineral water when Josh returned, dressed in jeans and a navy T-shirt that accentuated his muscular physique and had Abby ready to suggest skipping dinner and going directly to dessert. Before she could work up the nerve, he started removing white containers from the bags. "Everything still feels warm. If you'll set the table, I'll get the wine. Dishes are up there, flatware's in the top drawer," he said, gesturing with his head.

They made a sizable dent in food that tasted as good as it smelled, then went into the living room.

"When did you move to LA?" Josh asked, setting the wine bottle and his glass on the coffee table.

Abby set her own wineglass beside his, then sat down on the black leather couch. "The day after my high school graduation. Between what I'd managed to save and what Mary Tate loaned me, I had enough money to buy a cheap car, drive out there, and rent an apartment. I got a waitressing job right away, and three weeks later lucked into the part of Samantha."

"Lucked into?" Josh sat down beside her. "I think your talent had a lot to do with it."

"A lot of talented actors don't get the breaks they deserve. I just happened to have what the producers were looking for, although I'll admit I'd have been happy waitressing for years." She grimaced. "Anything to get away from Harrington."

"You didn't like it here?"

"The town was fine. My parents weren't. They were so bad I actually developed the ability to block out painful encounters with them, things I've only recently remembered."

The instant the words were out, Abby clamped her mouth shut, wishing this were a *Private Affairs* shoot she could redo because she'd definitely blown her lines. Her recalled memories weren't exactly secret—she'd mentioned them in an interview. However, *Soap Opera Digest* readers had known her much longer than Josh had and were less likely to think she was psychotic or even lying, given some people's skepticism that such memories were real.

"I imagine acting helped you block things out, since you could pretend to be someone else," Josh said. "When did you start remembering?"

Relief he'd not only accepted what she said but understood encouraged Abby to elaborate. "While I was getting divorced, I saw a therapist for the first time in my life. The memories started after a few sessions, even though my parents hadn't been the focus of my therapy. I guess when I finally slowed down enough to deal with my feelings, those were the ones that most needed dealing with."

"Physical abuse?"

"Some, although that stopped when I was in third grade and admitted to Laura that my dad had given me my black eye. The Tates tried to have me removed from my home. But my parents managed to convince social services that I'd gotten hurt when I'd sneaked out to ride my bike and fallen, and that I was lying to get back at them for grounding me for sneaking out. So then Bill went to see Dad and told him he'd personally make sure he rotted in prison if he touched me again." She rested her head on the back of the sofa. "After that my parents either ignored me or verbally abused me, telling me how worthless and stupid I was, things like that. They never came to any of my plays. When I left Harrington, my dad told me the only acting jobs I'd ever get would be in adult films."

"No wonder you blocked that out."

"That's all in the past. I haven't had a single memory since the first week I was back, which means I've remembered everything, thank God."

"What's your ex-husband like?"

Abby raised her head off the sofa back. From his cocktail-party expression, Josh appeared to be asking either out of curiosity since Colin was fairly famous or simply to keep conversation flowing, but she was still tempted to answer in truthful detail. "Not a whole lot like Pastor Jim," she said instead.

"I assume that was a blessing, from what I've heard about his show."

"Pastor Jim is a little too insufferably good," Abby agreed. "Although maybe our marriage would have worked if Colin had more of Pastor Jim in him." She couldn't imagine the good reverend ever cheating on his perfect wife, Catherine.

"You mean if he'd been more forgiving. That's hard sometimes."

She hadn't considered Josh might interpret her comment that way. It was fortunate he had, since she shouldn't have made it. On the other hand, she wasn't willing to let it stand at that. "Colin and I both made mistakes in our marriage."

Josh reached for his wineglass. "I didn't mean to imply you were the only one at fault. Much as I blame Jennifer, I know I did a lot of things wrong, too."

Between the wine and her mellow mood, Abby was in grave danger of disclosing all sorts of things she couldn't. She reached out and trailed her fingers down Josh's bare arm, below the short sleeve of his T-shirt. "Do you realize I've been here nearly three hours, and you haven't shown me your bedpost? In fact, you haven't even kissed me."

He met her eyes, a corner of his mouth quirking. "I didn't want you to think I only invited you here for sex. I was trying to be the perfect host first."

"The perfect host would have jumped me hours ago."

"I apologize." Then he moved his lips to hers, pushing her back onto the buttery black leather.

Warmth. That was the overriding sensation when Josh's lips touched hers, when his arms wrapped around her, when he pressed his body against hers. He radiated heat, even smelled warm. Abby felt as if she were wrapped in a heated cocoon, relieving all the tensions stemming from the stalker and the dreams, even from her divorce. She somehow knew Josh would never hurt her, would never let anyone hurt her. She relaxed into his kiss as he threaded his fingers through her hair, caressing it, massaging her scalp.

Then his tongue pushed its way inside her mouth and the resulting spark transformed the warmth to a torrid blaze. Abby couldn't stop her hands from running through his thick hair and over his soft cotton shirt, pulling it out of his jeans so she could stroke his damp back. He unbuttoned her shirt and moved his lips to her neck, into the valley between her breasts, his moist mouth and the slight rasp of his chin impossibly erotic. Then her bra was loose and her breasts were free, and his mouth was devouring them, licking, sucking, making the nipples so tight and hot they felt about to erupt. She needed his skin against hers, needed it more than she'd ever needed anything. She slid her hands from his back to the bottom of his T-shirt and pulled it up.

He raised his head to help her remove the shirt, and she rubbed her breasts against his chest, surprised her nipples didn't ignite his chest hairs. He pulled off her skirt, then half carried her off the couch and onto the floor, out of the way of the coffee table, discarding his shoes and jeans as she shed her panties. She reached inside his briefs and her fingers closed around him. He was so hard, so hot. She wanted to taste his salty moisture, to suck on him, to hear him groan. But she couldn't take the time. She needed him inside her so desperately she couldn't think of anything else, could only yank down his briefs with one hand as she held on to him with the other, positioning him against her.

Josh abruptly pulled away. "Oh, shit." Abby could feel the gravel in his tone. "I don't have a condom. I thought we'd make it to bed." He bent a knee and pushed himself up. "I'll be right back."

She grabbed his arm, stopping him. "I'm healthy and on the Pill."

"Thank you, God." He thrust into her. Then the world fell away, leaving nothing but him, his body attached to hers, moving against hers. When they both exploded, she felt closer to him than ever, their juices and sweat combining, his heat encompassing her, his pounding heart an echo of hers.

"I haven't had sex without a condom since I was married," Josh said when he finally moved off her. He rose up on one elbow, lifted Abby's chin, and kissed her gently on the lips. "I've also never spent an entire night with a woman since Jennifer left. But I'd like to wake up with you beside me." He kissed her again, a lot less gently. "Will you stay tonight?"

After the promise of that kiss, no way could Abby turn him down.

– – –

The knife was in the air, pointing downward at an angle. Fresh blood stained the tip, halfway up the steel blade. A fisted hand clenched the brown walnut handle—a man's hand, she could tell that even though she could only see his hand and wrist.

The man thrust the knife down through the air and out of view, raised it, thrust again. More and more blood coated the blade, dripping into the air below and sending rivulets toward the handle, as the knife rose and plunged, over and over. The knife disappeared. Instead she saw a window, built-in bookshelves, a light wood floor. Narrow planks with an oval pool of bright-red blood seeping onto some pale-blue fabric beside it. A pool that was getting bigger...

Then she saw the victim. A woman, lying on her side and facing away, her peroxide-blonde big hair obscuring her face. She was wearing only a blue bra and matching panties. The pale-blue lump Abby had seen before, the one beside the pool of blood.

"Abby? Are you having a nightmare?"

She opened her eyes, blinking a couple of times to orient herself. The murder and blood had been a dream. Josh was holding her, and she was safe. It was only a dream.

She nodded against his chest. "I'm fine now. Go back to sleep."

"The way you're still shaking, you aren't that fine," Josh said.

"Tell me about it. Talking usually helps."

It probably would help, but for so many reasons she couldn't tell him. "I don't need to talk about it. It was one of those confused nightmares that when you wake up you know it scared you but can't remember why. I really am fine now." Her voice might have been steady, but if Samantha had sounded that tentative, their director would have ordered a retake.

Fortunately it was enough to fool Josh. "If you're sure."

"I'm positive," she said. "Go back to sleep."

She closed her eyes and snuggled close to him. Within a couple of minutes, his even breathing indicated that he was asleep.

Sleep eluded Abby. She rolled over onto her back and lay staring through the dark at the ceiling, her brain spinning. Because she was afraid if she went back to sleep, she'd have the dream again. And this time she'd see the victim's face.

CHAPTER 13

Considering she hadn't done a first morning-after in nearly twelve years, Abby was surprised how comfortable she felt sitting at the maple kitchen table with Josh the next morning, reading the paper and sipping a cup of Constant Comment tea from the decaffeinated variety pack he'd considerately bought for her. She was wearing one of his shirts, faded blue denim that came down below her knees, the cuffs folded up a half dozen times. Even though it smelled more like detergent than Josh, it still made her feel as warm and secure as she did in his arms.

Josh was sitting on the chair to her right. He'd thrown on a pair of gym shorts, but his chest was bare, his face darkly stubbled, and his black hair tousled with a couple of spikes. He looked so blasted sexy she had the urge to do a few creative things with the squeeze bottle of honey she'd noticed on the same shelf as the tea.

"Tell me about your nightmare," he said. "Was it the same one you had the night I slept on your couch?"

OK, the honey would have to wait. She should have known he wouldn't let it go. He was a cop, used to getting complete information and knowing when people were evading.

"Mostly the same," Abby said. "Like I told you last night, it isn't a big deal."

"If you've had it twice and reacted strongly both times, it's a big enough deal you need to talk about it." When she didn't respond, he covered her hand with his. "Was it about the stalker? Or more memories of your parents?"

"No, nothing like that."

"Tell me."

She raised her cup to her lips with her free hand, stalling while she thought. She should get the honey after all. But the warm concern in his eyes, combined with the weariness of her sleepless night, overruled her reservations. She set down her cup. "The night I found the knife, I dreamed I saw it being used to commit a bloody murder in my house. I've had the dream two more times since then. It's always the same, except last night I also saw the victim. A woman."

"Did you recognize her?"

"I could only see her back, but I'm positive I've never seen her before."

"Where in your house was the murder committed? Where you found the knife?"

"In the bedroom I first used as my office. Which is a logical place to set it, considering how much I stress about my writing and that I'm writing a mystery there." Or had been, before the dream had motivated her to move. "Except..." She broke off, chewing her lower lip. So far Josh seemed to believe her, but continuing could very well change that.

"Except what?"

"Except that's how I knew where to find the stain under the carpet, because of my dream." The words came out before she'd consciously decided to tell him. "Although the stain in my dream was on the opposite side of the window, and there are probably stains under the carpeting in every room," she added, then gripped the edge of the table, bracing herself for an angry accusation.

"I'm not telling you this for publicity," she said when Josh studied her with hooded eyes. "All I want is to stop having that dream."

He reached for her hands, peeling them off the table edge. "I know you're not doing it for publicity. Do you think you're psychic?"

"I don't believe in psychics." At least she didn't think she did.

"Neither do I." He was holding her hands, gently rubbing the backs with his thumbs. "I'm no psychiatrist, but I'll bet the dream's the combination of stress and the vivid imagination you claim you have. Especially since you had the first dream right after you found the knife and the second right after the lipstick message." He was holding her hands, gently rubbing the backs with his thumbs.

"That makes sense," Abby said. "I frequently had nightmares after filming disturbing scenes on *Private Affairs*, which was still stressful even though it wasn't real."

"To be sure, I'll take a sample of the stuff on the floor," Josh said. "The lab found human blood on the knife, but also traces of food, so the blood was likely from a cooking injury. I assume the knife ended up between the walls by accident when they installed or replaced a door or after someone pulled it out too far the way you did. Or maybe a kid put it there thinking it would be funny if a future owner found it and worried it had been used in a murder."

Abby's eyes widened. "You checked the knife for blood? Even though you thought I'd planted it?"

He shrugged, his thumbs halting. "I like to cover my bases. I probably should have checked the floor, too, but to be honest, the stain looked like paint to me. The blood on the knife is O positive, which is too common to narrow things down, and they couldn't

DNA type it. But if the stuff on the floor isn't O-positive blood, you'll know you're not dreaming about anything that really happened."

Abby's hands tightened on his. "You don't have to tell anyone about my dreams, do you? The only people who know are Laura and her parents. Anyone else might think I'm crazy and report that to some tabloid."

"I won't tell a soul," he said. "I'll take a sample from the floor myself this morning, before you pick up Maddie." He drained his coffee, then stood up. "We should get going."

– – –

"I'll send it in, but I still think it looks more like paint someone wiped up than blood," Josh said when he came downstairs after taking the sample. "I'm not just saying that to make you feel better."

"That you're checking it out makes me feel better," Abby said. She'd waited in the living room while he'd worked, not wanting to face the stain when her nerves were already so on edge from last night's dream. "Bill offered to arrange to have it checked out, and I turned him down, but I think that was a mistake."

Josh glanced at his watch. "I'd better go. I've got a stack of paperwork to get through."

They walked to the front door in silence. Abby unlocked it, then reached for the door handle.

"Before I go, I need to say something," Josh said.

She gripped the door handle, a hollow ache in her chest. She knew exactly what was coming. With minor variations, she'd played this same scene many times on *Private Affairs*. It's the "it's been fun, but so long" scene.

"I've realized admitting you were the first woman I've spent the night with since my divorce might have caused your nightmare last night," Josh said. "Especially since we went out three nights in a row."

She stared at him, releasing the door handle.

"I mean, it was probably because of the phone call. But if it was because of what I said, all I meant was that it's been long enough since my divorce that I was ready to have a woman spend the entire night. It didn't mean I want a serious relationship, so you don't have to stress out about that."

"I wasn't at all concerned about that," she said honestly. "I'm sure it had nothing to do with my nightmare."

He let out an audible breath. "Good. Then would you like to have dinner Tuesday night? Or is that too soon for another date in a casual relationship?"

Abby met his eyes. "It's definitely not too soon."

"I'll pick you up at six thirty."

His smile sent her stomach tumbling and loosened her kneecaps. Abby grabbed the door handle again. "Should I see if Laura or Kim will keep Maddie overnight? Or is that too soon for a casual relationship?"

Josh lowered his head and kissed her, one of his soul-searing specialties. Then he rested his forehead on hers. He was breathing fast, his voice a little husky. "It's definitely not too soon."

– – –

"I thought the dream was like the ones I've had before after filming stressful scenes or fighting with Colin," Abby said. "I was sure if I ever saw the murderer, he'd be Blade and Samantha would be the victim, since I'm convinced Blade killed her. Or maybe the victim would be one of Colin's girlfriends." Her hand tightened on the phone, and she swallowed the hysteria that was threatening her voice. "I haven't seen the murderer, but I'm sure I don't recognize the victim, and that freaked me out. What do you think?"

Without Josh to distract her, the horror of seeing the victim had returned, the scene running over and over through Abby's mind, like a video clip on auto replay. She'd made a futile attempt to meditate, then tried a stress-relief yoga DVD, but her body was too tense to do the postures, let alone relax into them. So she'd muted the TV and called Teresa Wallace, her former therapist. She'd hated to bother her on a Saturday, but she'd been desperate. It was either Teresa or the Psychic Friends Network.

Teresa had listened without comment while Abby told her about the knife, the stain, and her dreams. "You're sure you were never in that house before you bought it?" she finally asked, her voice as low and soothing as the DVD instructor's. "Not for a party or to pick up a donation or anything? Something you may have forgotten?"

Abby shook her head vehemently. "I'm positive, and I would have remembered since I thought the house was so beautiful. I knew who the former owners were, but we weren't friends. I'd actually never even talked to them. I did walk by the house almost every school day, and sometimes the blinds were open so I could see into the living room, but never upstairs."

"So we can rule out another recalled memory."

"It's nothing like that." Abby had expected that to be Teresa's initial focus. "I've always been awake when I recalled memories, and they've only involved my parents. Once I remembered the incident, I always knew it had really happened. This dream is completely different."

"What do *you* think it is?" Teresa asked. "You're obviously worried about something specific. Otherwise you wouldn't have called me."

Abby was silent for a moment, watching the TV. The participants, dressed in coral-colored yoga wear, were posed in forward bends with the Hawaiian ocean lapping behind them, but the serene scene did nothing to calm her—or make the words easier to say. "I'm worried I'm psychic and dreaming about something that happened in this house."

"Being psychic would upset you?"

"Of course it would upset me," Abby said, annoyance sharpening her tone. Granted, therapists were supposed to ask questions, but this answer seemed obvious. "It's bad enough remembering things that happened to me. But a murder that happened to someone I don't even know?"

"I assume nothing violent ever occurred in that house?"

"Not that anyone ever reported. Although a woman mentioned she gets goose bumps whenever she passes by here."

"Do you trust her judgment?"

Abby considered that, her eyes on the TV. The participants were doing a downward-facing dog pose now. "Knowing Eleanor, it's very possible that hearing I'd found the knife influenced her memory of her reaction to my house."

"You found the stain on the floor because of your dream, but it wasn't located where you saw it in your dream, right?"

"It was on the other side of the windows," Abby said.

"Does the stain look exactly like the blood in your dream?"

Abby chewed her lip, considering that. "They're both oval shaped. But I think the stain was bigger than the blood in my dream." Or maybe wishful thinking was influencing her own memory—she hadn't looked at the stain since the first day.

"Oval is hardly a unique shape, and you don't know for sure what's on the floor is blood," Teresa said. "You said the police think it's probably paint. What about the timing of the dreams? Did they occur after especially stressful situations?"

Thanks to her earlier discussion with Josh, Abby could answer immediately. "Every one of them did." Including last night's—even if she wasn't concerned Josh wanted a serious relationship, spending the night with a man for the first time since her divorce had undoubtedly been more stressful than she'd consciously realized.

"Like you said, when you were on *Private Affairs* and dealing with Colin, your nightmares after stressful incidents always featured people connected with *Private Affairs* or Colin. Now you're a writer. Is it possible you're subconsciously imagining characters you might use in a future book and they're showing up in your dreams?"

Abby hadn't thought of that. "Maybe. I have ideas for a lot more mysteries, including a couple set in Minnesota, and Minnesota's full of blondes. So you think I'm just having more stress-related nightmares? And finding the stain really was coincidental?"

"Based on what you've told me, that's a logical explanation," Teresa said. "Although if you discover the murderer and victim are real, that's a game changer. That could mean you're psychic. Or more likely, it's another repressed memory that somehow involves your parents and for some reason you've set it in your current home."

Abby hung up the phone, feeling much better. Then she shut off the TV, got a screwdriver, and headed upstairs. Time to put a stake through her last bit of concern over the dream.

She opened the door of her former office and stepped onto the mud-and-grass-colored shag carpet. Her nerves were twitching and buzzing as if she'd gotten a double espresso jolt—back before she'd given up caffeine—but she needed to do this. She took a deep breath, then crossed the room and rolled up the carpet until the stain was exposed.

Josh had removed a shallow chunk of the floor on the side of the stain where it was darkest. Abby studied the brownish-red blob for a minute, then closed her eyes and forced herself to visualize the dream. She looked at the stain again, and her nerves slowed to a quiet hum. She'd been right. Both stains were oval, but this one was several inches bigger than in the dream. Actually, other than both being ovals, the stain wasn't much like the blood in the dream and definitely on the wrong side of the bookshelves.

She rolled back the carpet, then headed to the bedroom she now used as her office. She loosened both sides of one corner of the orange shag carpet and rolled it back, baring several triangular feet of wood floor. Five smeared paint splatters decorated the narrow wood planks, three sage green and two gold. The largest was only a couple of inches across, but if she pulled up the entire carpet, she could very well find a paint blob at least as big as the one in the other room.

That proved it. She wasn't sensing a real murder. Her dream was just that—a dream.

She replaced the carpet, then headed back downstairs and re-started the yoga DVD.

– – –

"Did you have that horrible dream again?" That was the first thing Laura asked when she called Sunday night, home after spending several days with her husband and kids at their cabin on Gull Lake.

Abby set the mystery she'd been reading on the couch beside her. "Unfortunately, yes. This time I saw the victim. Just her back, but I swear I've never seen her before. She had big platinum hair that's pretty distinctive."

"So you might be psychic after all?"

"I doubt it," Abby said. "I've concluded the dream's just a reaction to the stress I've been under and finding the knife. I called my therapist, and she agreed."

"That makes sense," Laura said. "Although Mom will be disappointed if you don't turn out to be psychic. What about the stalker?"

"Don't you want to hear my big news?" Abby asked. She didn't want to think about the stalker. After tomorrow's show, he'd be done with her anyway. She had to believe that. "I've gone on a date. Three dates, to be exact."

Laura actually squealed. "It's about time. Someone from LA?"

Abby walked over to the picture window and gazed out between the open blinds. The sun was beginning to set, turning the sky a hot, rosy orange. "No, from Harrington."

"Craig Tucker?"

"God, no," Abby said, remembering their high school classmate, who she'd heard had just divorced wife number three. "Craig's a nerd."

"He's a multimillionaire software nerd now. Who?"

"Josh Kincaid."

She could almost hear Laura's jaw drop. "You hate him. Besides, he has a girlfriend."

"He broke up with Heather, and I've had a change of heart," Abby said with a satisfied smile. She rarely surprised Laura.

"How long has this been going on?"

"Since the day after my car was shot at. He asked me out to apologize for thinking I was lying, and we hit it off."

"And you haven't mentioned it to me?" Laura asked in an offended tone.

"You've been out of town," Abby said, closing the blinds. "You're the only person besides his sister who knows we've been dating. Maddie thinks Josh and I are friends because she's friends with Rachel."

"Maddie would be thrilled."

"Anyway, we're keeping it quiet," Abby said. She wasn't in the mood to revisit the issue of Maddie's feelings with Laura any more than she'd been with Olivia. What did Laura and Olivia know? They'd both had happy childhoods with intact families. "You can tell your parents, but no one else."

"It's your call," Laura said. "Have you gone all the way?"

"What kind of a question is that?" Abby could feel her cheeks heating, probably turning the color of the sky.

"The kind your best friend's allowed to ask," Laura said. "Since you're being evasive, the answer must be yes. How is he?"

Memory spread the warmth in Abby's face through her body. "I can't believe you even asked me that," she said, adopting Samantha's her-majesty-is-not-amused tone.

Laura chuckled. "You're evading again, which must mean he's terrific. This sounds really serious."

"It isn't serious at all."

"Of course it is. I've known you forever, and you never sleep with a guy unless you're serious, except right after you got to California. The only question is whether it's *really* serious."

"Good-bye, Laura."

"Are you in love with him?"

"I'm hanging up now, Laura," Abby said, flipping off the phone.

It was because Josh made her feel safe and because she liked him, that's why she was sleeping with him. And because of the sex itself—she couldn't remember experiencing such intense sensations with any other man. That was because it had been a long time for her, and Josh put more effort into it than other men had, either because he was that way with every woman or because he viewed her as a particular challenge.

No way was she falling in love with Josh Kincaid.

Abby went into the kitchen and removed a mug from the cupboard. Maddie wasn't ready for her to date, let alone fall in love. She wasn't ready to fall in love. She'd only known Josh for a couple of weeks, had only been able to tolerate him for a few days. She wasn't falling in love; she'd just fallen in lust.

Josh certainly wasn't falling in love with her. She turned on the water and filled the mug. He was only with her because she wasn't a twentysomething romantic but a sophisticated divorcée who wouldn't read a relationship into a casual affair.

She shut off the water but stood staring out the window over the sink. The creeping Charlie that dominated her backyard glowed in the orange dusk. Unfortunately, Laura was right—she always took romance and sex seriously. But it was time to change. After her years with Colin, she deserved some fun. Josh was definitely fun, which was all she wanted from him.

She had to keep thinking that way because she had enough problems already. She didn't need to add the heartbreak of loving another man who didn't love her.

– – –

Although she wasn't falling in love with Josh, she was definitely looking forward to tonight's date, Abby acknowledged Tuesday afternoon. To be honest, she couldn't remember being this excited about a man, not even when she first met Colin. Being older and wiser about life's fickleness must make you experience all its emotions more intensely.

She took a long bath in her most expensive oil, did her nails, then agonized so much over what to wear that she changed four times before settling on the first outfit. She glanced at the clock. She was completely ready, and Josh wouldn't be here for two hours. Even allowing a generous twenty minutes to drop Maddie off at Kim's, she had more than an hour and a half to fill. So what was she going to do?

Write. She suddenly knew exactly who needed to see the earring Marissa had found in the cemetery and why. Abby went into her office, flipped on her computer, and started typing.

– – –

"Mommy, someone's ringing the doorbell," Maddie yelled from her bedroom. "I can't see who from my window."

Abby had been so engrossed in complicating Marissa's life that she hadn't even noticed the doorbell's persistent ringing, and Maddie wasn't allowed to answer the door. She glanced at the clock. Just before five. Maybe Josh was early. "I'm coming," she yelled. She headed downstairs, then opened the door, smiling.

Her smiled faded. "Colin. What the hell are you doing here?"

CHAPTER 14

"Is that any way to greet your husband?" Colin asked, flashing the trademark grin that had turned Abby to melting Jell-O back before she'd known better. In his olive silk trousers and black linen short-sleeved shirt—both presumably Italian and expensive—he looked ready for a *GQ* photo shoot.

"Ex-husband," Abby said. "I repeat, what the hell are you doing here?"

Colin waltzed through the open door, then leaned against the gold-and-brown paisley wallpaper. "I've missed you, Abby. You and Maddie. Is she here?"

"Are you planning on staying longer than to say hello?"

"That's unfair, Abby." He raked his fingers through his dark curls, a move he'd practiced so he looked appealingly boyish rather than disheveled. "Especially after I came all the way to this godforsaken place."

Abby closed the front door. "Maddie's upstairs."

"Maddie? Maddie, come down, sweetheart," he yelled. "It's Daddy."

"Daddy!" In seconds, Maddie had rocketed down the stairs and launched herself at Colin. "What are you doing here?"

Her expression spoke volumes. Colin was Maddie's father, and she loved him, in no small part thanks to Abby's determination she'd never know the kind of man he truly was. She couldn't puncture Colin's facade now.

"I came to see you, of course," Colin said, wrapping his arms around his daughter and lifting her off the floor. "You and your mother."

"How long are you staying?" Maddie asked.

"A couple of days, if that's OK."

Maddie nodded so enthusiastically her curls continued bouncing after her head stopped. "I've missed you, Daddy." She kissed Colin's cheek.

"Well, I'm here now." He set her down on the stained tan carpet. "Do you still like pizza?"

"I love pizza."

"Good, since that's what we're having for dinner tonight. Where should we go?"

Maddie's eyes were sparkling like twin Hope Diamonds. "You, me, and Mommy? Like a family?"

"Exactly like a family."

"Green Mill has the best pizza."

"Green Mill it is," Colin proclaimed. "Right now I need to talk to your mother in private. After I'm done, I want to see your room, so you'd better go clean it." He winked. "Since you take after you mother when it comes to housekeeping."

Maddie lifted her chin. "That's because there are a lot of things in life more important than cleaning."

Colin waved a perfectly manicured hand. "Then go upstairs and do something more important."

"Why are you here, Colin?" Abby asked when Maddie was out of earshot. "Don't give me that spiel about missing Maddie. You never showed much interest in her while we were in California, let alone since we moved here."

"You're the one who hauled my daughter to the middle of nowhere."

She gave him a tight smile. "We have telephone service, believe it or not. You also didn't care when we negotiated all this."

Abby tensed when Colin's blue eyes widened. That innocent look always preceded some outrageous statement—like he was in bed with Tara because they'd gotten so tired rehearsing they'd decided to take a nap.

He didn't disappoint. "That was before I realized moving here would endanger my daughter," he said, pressing one hand over his heart. "I've heard about your problems with that crazy fan, Abby. Pam Wilson at the *National Enquirer* called and asked me for a comment. It would have been nice if I'd known what she was talking about."

Abby suppressed a sigh. She should have expected the tabloids to find out about it. "I've gotten crates of hate mail throughout my career, as you well know," she said. "Samantha was so horrible at the end, I was tempted to send her a letter myself."

He gave her a wry look. "I can't recall anyone ever writing on your mirror or shooting at you."

"One of his messages made it clear he was upset with Samantha, and she's been killed off," Abby explained. "Nothing has happened since then, so he's obviously satisfied." She had to keep believing that.

"Not necessarily," Colin said. "You know, I agreed to let you take my daughter to Minnesota because I thought it would be good for her to be raised in a smaller town and with midwestern values."

"So you told the press."

Colin folded his arms. "It's true. But a stalker changes everything. My primary concern is for Maddie's safety."

And a *Playboy* subscriber's primary concern was for the articles. Colin was wearing his most sincere Pastor Jim face. He was up to something, and she'd bet it wasn't protecting his daughter. Abby's eyes narrowed. "Cut the crap, Colin. What do you really want?"

He studied her face for a moment, then obviously decided she wasn't buying his concerned act, because his expression switched to calculating. "Simple. I want you back. You and Maddie in our house in California."

Abby gaped at him. She'd been ready for a request for another cash payout to get him out of a financial bind. She'd been prepared to promise she wouldn't deny some new story he'd planted about her misdeeds, something aimed at increasing public sympathy for him before he dropped his current girlfriend for an even younger one. But Abby had never contemplated this scenario. "Why would you possibly want Maddie and me back?"

"We're a family, Abby." A sensuous smile played at his lips as he slowly raked his eyes over her. "You look good. You must have sensed I was coming."

"Actually, I had other plans, which I'd better cancel."

She hurried into the kitchen, closing the door behind her. First she called Kim, telling her that Maddie wouldn't be coming over because something had come up and hanging up before she could ask questions. Then she called Josh—at home where she could leave a message, since she couldn't explain with Colin in eavesdropping vicinity.

"Who did you have plans with?" Colin asked, coming into the kitchen just as Abby finished her message to Josh.

Abby set the phone on the counter. "Laura."

"I thought maybe it was that policeman you've been dating."

"Why do you think I'm dating a policeman?" So much for her plan to keep that quiet.

"The same way I heard about the stalker. My friend at the *Enquirer*." Colin walked around the kitchen, opening and closing the dark-wood cabinet doors and drawers. "From what I've seen of this house, it could be nice, if you're a fan of old-fashioned places. It would take a lot of work."

"It's my money, Colin."

"I don't care what you do with your money. But this town." He turned and gestured expansively. "My God, Abby, how can you stand being buried here? Not only is it small, it's so provincial. I couldn't rent a foreign car or even a Cadillac. I'm driving a fucking Buick, can you believe it?"

Despite herself, Abby smiled. "I admit I never expected to see that."

Colin clearly perceived her smile as an opening, because he moved in front of her, taking her hand. "It's worth it to see you."

She freed her hand. "Let's cut to the bottom line, Colin. What is this about? And don't try to sell me that you've missed me or Maddie or are worried about us. You're not that good an actor."

Colin looked at her for a long moment. "I need you back, Abby," he finally said. "You and Maddie. *Heavenly Days* is talking about not renewing my contract. Ratings are down a little, and they think killing me off could give them a boost."

"Killing you off?"

He grimaced. "Then they'd have all those touchy-feely episodes with poor Catherine having to console the kids and live without me. And trying to love again, men with cheaper per-episode costs. That can't happen. I need the big contract they were considering until some idiot suggested getting rid of me."

"So you want me back because a real-life reconciliation would energize your fan base and net you another two-year, big-bucks contract."

Colin smiled broadly. "Exactly. Will you do it?"

Abby was stunned. Given their history, she couldn't believe even Colin was arrogant enough to think that she'd lift one finger to help him, let alone do something like this. He was obviously confusing her with one of his adoring young girlfriends. "You've got to be kidding," she said.

"I wouldn't be quite so hasty." Colin leaned back against the counter, resting his elbows on the gold-flecked Formica. "You got sole custody of Maddie because I agreed to it."

"Of course you agreed," Abby said, suddenly wary. She didn't trust the look in Colin's eyes. "We had a deal."

"I agreed to what I thought was best for my daughter, but living here while her mother's being stalked is not what I anticipated. I've talked to my lawyer, Abby, and that's enough for a court to revise our custody arrangements."

"You are not getting Maddie." Abby's tone was lined with steel. She met his eyes, her own narrowed. "I'll tell the truth, that I didn't have affairs, but you sure did. If you're not honoring our agreement, I won't, either."

"Who's going to believe you?" He raised his hands as if pronouncing a benediction. "Who will people believe? That bitch Samantha Cartwright or the sainted Pastor Jim?"

"I'll take my chances." No way would Colin let word of his infidelity get out, especially not now when his primary concern was enhancing his popularity with his fan base. Not everyone was stupid enough to confuse her with Samantha, and he knew it.

He lowered his hands. "Who's going to believe you had that information and didn't use it in our divorce? That instead you let your cheating husband be deified while you had your reputation trashed? Everyone will think you made it all up now to keep me from my daughter, who I'm only trying to protect."

Abby opened her mouth to deny it, but the words wouldn't come. When you put it that way, he unfortunately had a point.

"And speaking of Maddie, you know she'll be upset if we end up fighting over her in court," Colin continued. "You won't be able to shield her from it since she'll most likely have to testify."

Abby flinched, his words like painful punches. Damn him, but he might be able to do it, and she had to think of Maddie. "What do you want?"

He smiled his patented Pastor Jim smile, but with a sinister edge. A smile that said he knew he'd won. "Another deal. You come back to me for six months, and I'll let you keep Maddie."

"And you'll pull this type of extortion again the next time you want something."

He shook his head and raised one hand. "I solemnly swear to put everything in writing this time. I'll also agree to terminate my parental rights."

She wouldn't have trusted his sworn promise even if his other hand had been resting on a Bible, but a written contract was different. "We can leave after six months?"

"More or less. Think of your daughter, Abby."

"That's the only reason I haven't thrown you out."

Colin draped an arm around her shoulders and herded her out of the kitchen and toward the front door. "Our public beckons, darling. Follow my lead. If you don't, you've lost your daughter."

Abby walked with him, feeling as shell-shocked as an extra in *Saving Private Ryan*. Colin opened the front door to nerve-jarring camera clicks and excruciatingly bright spotlights.

"You wanted to know why I'm here," he said to the crowd of reporters and camera operators gathered on the front lawn. "The truth is, I'm miserable without my wife and daughter and want them back. I'm willing to forgive and forget and make a fresh start. I need my family."

"Are you remarrying, Ms. Langford?"

"Give her a little time to catch her breath. As you all know, I've been in town less than an hour." Colin squeezed Abby's shoulder in a gesture the reporters no doubt found affectionate, but she recognized as threatening.

In response, she managed a faint smile.

"Where are you staying?" someone asked.

Colin loosened his grip on her shoulder. "Here, of course." He nuzzled Abby's neck, then grinned rakishly. "Abby and I have a lot of catching up to do."

– – –

An hour later, Abby was sitting in the Green Mill, sipping a glass of Chianti and watching Maddie and Colin talk. Colin's attention had Maddie glowing like her bright-yellow sundress. She looked so happy, it was almost worth putting up with him. *Almost,* Abby reiterated as she watched Colin shift his attention from his daughter long enough to give a leisurely once-over to the college-age waitress falling over herself serving their beverages.

After Colin had finished with the press and let Abby return to the house, she'd headed to the privacy of her bathroom, locked the door, and placed an emergency call to her divorce lawyer. Fortunately, Jeannie had been in the office. Unfortunately, she'd informed Abby that under the circumstances, Colin had a good chance of convincing a California judge to change Maddie's custody arrangements, especially since in front of an audience, Colin excelled at playing the concerned father. Moving herself and Maddie back to California probably wouldn't help; while it might eliminate the stalker issue, it also could make a judge decide joint custody was now the best option if Colin pushed it.

Jeannie had more bad news, namely, that if Colin called Maddie as a witness, she'd have to testify. In addition to the stress of having her parents fighting over her, Abby also needed to consider the effect the inevitable publicity would have on Maddie. Even if they could get a gag order, it probably wouldn't work given the tenacity of the press and Colin's love of publicity. Colin lived for publicity, as did most actors. No wonder Josh hadn't believed her claim to hate it.

Josh. Abby set her wineglass down and massaged temples that ached nearly as much as her heart. Things were over between them, of course. For Maddie's sake, she couldn't see any option besides going along with Colin. She wouldn't be able to tell anyone the truth, not even Josh. That would be part of the deal, just like before.

Abby glanced at Maddie. But when the choice was between her daughter's happiness and her own, it was a no-brainer. She grabbed her wineglass and drained it.

– – –

Josh angled his car into a space in front of Corner Drug, then got out and walked the half block to Ruby's Diner. He opened the glass front door; the appetizing odors of burgers and fries made his stomach growl. Between its mirrored soda fountain and red vinyl, beige Formica, and chrome decor, it looked exactly the same as it had when Abby had worked there, according to

Harvey. Actually, Harvey said the red polyester zip-front dresses the waitresses wore were also the same. Josh grinned. He'd have loved to have seen Abby in one of those.

"Nice to see you," Ruby said when he walked in. "I'll check on your burger."

Josh leaned his elbows on the beige countertop as he waited for the food he'd called to order. Since Abby had canceled, he certainly wasn't about to make his grandmother's Bolognese sauce just for himself.

"It's so romantic. I mean, the way he's forgiving her for everything." A dark-haired waitress wearing a red uniform was talking to another girl sitting at the counter a couple of stools away. Both looked high school age, which was probably why they considered forgiveness romantic.

"It's got to be true or it wouldn't have been on the news," the other girl said, exhibiting even greater naïveté, to Josh's mind. "Besides, they looked so happy, don't you think?"

"It'll be done in a jiffy, Josh," Ruby said, then she turned to the waitress. "Who looked happy, Meagan?"

"Didn't you hear?" Meagan asked. "Abby Langford's husband is in town—Colin Walsh, who plays Pastor Jim on *Heavenly Days*. He's missed Abby and their daughter so much that he's forgiving her, and they're getting back together. He must be as wonderful in real life as Pastor Jim is."

Josh felt like some lowlife had landed a sucker punch in his gut. "How do you know that?" Ruby asked.

"It was on the news." Meagan sighed, hugging herself. "It's so romantic. Abby's just gorgeous, and he's so handsome. With their adorable daughter, they're this ideal family." She looked toward the twelve-inch TV perched on a stand near one end of the mirrored wall behind the counter. "Turn up the volume. It's going to be on *Entertainment Tonight*."

Ruby turned up the TV just as the local news signed off and *ET* began. Sure enough, Colin's visit to Harrington was the lead story. Josh watched in a daze as Colin and Abby stood outside her house. Colin had his arm around Abby as he announced their reconciliation. Abby stood close to Colin and smiled at the camera.

"Here's your order," Ruby said, setting a white paper bag on the counter in front of Josh. "I hope you're hungry. Tammy saw it was for you and gave you a double helping of fries."

Josh tore his eyes from the television, pulled some money out of his wallet, and handed it to Ruby. "Thanks," he said, taking the bag. The smell made his stomach heave. "Keep the change."

When he got home, Josh threw the burger and fries in the kitchen trash, then played back the four messages on his machine. He foolishly hoped one would be from Abby telling him things weren't as they seemed or at least explaining what was happening. All the messages were from Heather, who'd seen the news and offered to come over.

He grabbed a beer and took it into the living room, not bothering to open the blinds or turn on a light. He plopped into the black leather chair in the corner, rested his feet on the matching ottoman, and flipped on the TV. To a sports channel.

The doorbell rang when he was midway into his second beer. He jumped to his feet, then chastised himself. Abby was with her husband tonight. She certainly wouldn't stop by.

He opened the door to find his sister standing on his front stoop. "What are you doing here?"

"Checking on you," Kim said. "Are you OK?"

"I'm fine."

She walked through the door and headed directly to the living room. "No, you're not." She pointed at the blaring TV. "You're watching professional wrestling. You hate professional wrestling."

"I watched it in college."

"You did a lot of stupid things in college. Do you have a mineral water?"

Kim had turned the TV off and a table lamp on and was sitting on the black leather couch when Josh returned with a bottle of water. "Have you talked to Abby?" she asked.

Josh handed her the water, then moved a stack of magazines from the couch to the floor so he could sit beside her. "She left me a message she couldn't get together tonight. If you're asking whether I've heard she's reconciling with her ex-husband, the answer is yes."

"Did she tell you they're reconciling?" Kim asked. At Josh's silence, she continued, "She told me Maddie couldn't come over because something had come up, then hung up. She obviously didn't want to talk about it."

"Her message didn't say a damn thing. But of course they are." Josh took a long drink of his beer. "I don't know why you're acting like this is a big deal. We've only had a couple of dates, and it would never have been anything serious. She's famous, for God's sake. And I'm not even good enough for Jennifer." He took another swig of beer.

Kim turned on him. "Don't you dare go there, comparing Abby to Jennifer or blaming yourself for the fact Jennifer left you. She's a snob and a shallow bitch, but Abby's nothing like that."

"Those articles sure say otherwise."

"I don't believe them, and now that you know Abby, you shouldn't, either," Kim said, waving her bottle for emphasis. "She wasn't using you the way Jennifer did. If she's going back to Colin, it's probably for Maddie's sake. Or maybe she does still love him but thought it was over and was going on with her life. She wouldn't have been with you if she didn't like and respect you, which isn't surprising because you're terrific. You should call her and ask her to explain."

"Like I said, it isn't a big deal."

Kim opened her mouth, then shut it without saying anything. Instead she took a sip of water. "What are you planning to do tonight?"

"I don't know." He shrugged. "Maybe I'll call Heather. She's left four messages."

Kim's eyes narrowed. "Don't you dare call Heather. It won't help, not really."

"At least she doesn't have an ex-husband."

Kim set down her half-empty bottle of water and got to her feet. "Eric's on call and expecting to have to go in, so I need to get back home. Do you want to come over for a while? We'll watch whatever you want. Even wrestling."

"I'd rather stay here." He stood. "I'm OK. Really."

"I hope so," Kim said. "You had such a hard time with Jennifer and Mark, and now this."

"This is nothing like that. You don't have to worry about me."

She hugged him hard. "I can't help it. You can be a real jerk, but I love you."

"I love you, too, Kim. Thanks for stopping by."

After Kim left, Josh sat back down on his chair. He should call Heather. But why? He certainly didn't want her company, and to be honest, he didn't even want to have sex with her. The only person he wanted to be with was Abby, a realization that would have worried him if it hadn't been so damn depressing.

At least he had beer, which wouldn't really help, either, but wasn't nearly as counterproductive as calling Heather. And he had his good buddies from the WWE to keep him company. He turned the TV back on, then got up and headed to the refrigerator.

CHAPTER 15

The only benefit of having Colin sleeping in her house was that she could leave Maddie, Abby thought as she slipped out the back door at six the next morning. The world was tranquil, wisps of pink and peach streaking the pale-blue sky, only a few early bird cardinals awake enough to break the silence. No reporters, but then Colin had informed them last night that he wouldn't have a statement until eleven, since—he'd added with a smirk—he and Abby would be busy until then. She probably had a couple of hours before the first vultures arrived.

Despite the peaceful morning, Abby felt uneasy. She'd promised Josh she wouldn't run outside, but she didn't dare drive. She looked around, searching for anyone who might be watching, as she made her way across the backyard and slipped through the arborvitae to Maplewood Avenue.

Then she shook herself. The guard would have noticed anyone lurking around her house, not that anyone would risk trying to hurt her in broad daylight. Besides, even if Samantha's death hadn't been enough, her stalker had to be satisfied she was leaving after hearing Colin's announcement they were getting back together, an announcement that had been reported on every damn local and Twin Cities news show last night, in addition to being featured on *Entertainment Tonight*.

Abby jogged down Maplewood Avenue away from the river, her shoes pounding a steady pace she hoped would calm her. The slight possibility a stalker could be watching wasn't the only potentially bad part of this scenario. Visiting Josh this early was almost certainly a mistake, starting with the fact he probably wasn't alone. She'd bet he'd called Heather and this time let her stay until morning. Maybe this was an even worse idea than it had seemed when she'd come up with it during her sleepless night.

She had to do it, although not because she and Josh had a future. Any hope he'd be conveniently available and want to see her when she finally escaped Colin was fairy-tale thinking. But she couldn't let him think she'd been using him to make Colin jealous or until someone richer, more famous, or otherwise arguably more successful came along, the way his ex-wife had. That could propel him back to one-night stands or women like Heather who would never make him happy. It would also make him hate her, and she couldn't bear that—because she'd stupidly gone and fallen in love with him. The excruciating emptiness she felt knowing she'd never be with him again made that painfully clear.

Not that Josh would necessarily believe a thing she said. Worse yet, he might assume she was lying to manipulate him and be so angry he'd call the tabloids. Except she couldn't see Josh doing that. In the middle of the night she'd finally realized she was letting her past influence her common sense. Josh wasn't like Colin or her dad, selfish men who thought only of themselves. Josh was a decent man who'd never do anything that would hurt Maddie. She could trust him to keep what she said confidential whether he believed it or not. And he just might believe it.

Abby walked around to the back of Josh's town house, taking deep breaths as she tried to compose herself. The red and purple petunias Kim had planted along both sides of the door were drooping, probably because it hadn't rained for over a week, but she preferred to think they were being sympathetic. Taking one last deep breath, Abby knocked on the door.

She immediately reconsidered. This was a bad idea on so many levels. She was turning to leave when the door opened.

Josh was standing there, dressed in his uniform and holding a mug of steaming coffee that smelled almost as delicious as he looked.

"This will only take a few minutes. Can I come in?" Abby checked over her shoulder. "I think I've ditched the press, but you never know."

"I was about to head to work," he said, but he stepped away from the door. "You ran over here when you know someone's trying to kill you? What the hell were you thinking?"

Much as she'd like to believe his agitated concern was personal, she'd bet it was professional, since Mary and the mayor had made him responsible for her safety. "I didn't dare drive and risk having the press report I was visiting you."

"You certainly didn't have to risk your life to come here to explain," he said, closing the door behind her. "I know what's going on."

"Can I please have some coffee?" she asked.

"It's caffeinated."

"That's fine." With all the stress she was under today, caffeine couldn't make things worse. She strode across the room and helped herself to a mug. "Is Heather here?"

"Not that it's any of your business under the circumstances, but no, she isn't."

"Good, because I don't trust her to keep this to herself." Abby took a couple of bracing sips of real coffee. She'd forgotten how wonderful it tasted.

"Look, as I said, I know what's going on," Josh said. "I need to get to work."

"You don't have a clue what's really going on."

Josh looked at her expectantly, but for some reason she couldn't start. If he went to the press with this, Colin would make her life even more hellish than it was already destined to be. And Maddie would be devastated.

"Abby, why are you here?" Josh asked after a moment.

Abby took another sip of coffee, then set her mug on the counter. She had to trust Josh, believe she was right about him. "I want to tell you the truth about my marriage."

"Which is?" Josh asked.

She hesitated again. But she'd made her decision. "I never cheated on Colin. Never," she said, plunging into the guts of the matter. "That was a fantasy cooked up by the press, based on hints from Colin and his publicist."

"Really." Josh didn't look like he believed her. He didn't look like he cared, either, but she forced herself to continue.

"Colin was the one who cheated. He did so several times, with much younger women." She grimaced. "Hence my strong feelings about men who date younger women." She carried her mug to the butcher-block table and sat down.

"Colin started cheating when Maddie was two. At least when I confronted him, he swore it was the first time. He was about to turn forty and claimed it was a midlife crisis thing he'd never do again. Unfortunately, he did, but I always made myself get over it. After my lousy childhood, I was determined Maddie's would be perfect. Divorce and a cheating father weren't part of my scenario."

Abby's fingers tightened around the handle of her mug. "I also was afraid if I sued for divorce, Colin would demand joint custody, since his *Heavenly Days* fans would expect it. He would have gotten it, too. The caring father act is his specialty, although in reality he usually ignores that he has a daughter. I always made excuses for him to Maddie, but if she ever lived with him when I wasn't around, she'd discover how low she fell on his list of priorities. So like I said, I kept ignoring his affairs. Until the last time."

Josh sat down across the table from her. "What was different about the last time?"

Abby's lips twisted. "I found out he was sleeping with the actress who plays his oldest daughter on *Heavenly Days*. That one pushed me over my limit." For many reasons, but she was taking a big enough risk without getting into specifics.

"I didn't see a thing about any of his affairs," Josh said. "All I read about were yours."

"That's because Colin and I made a deal. The Christian conservatives who adore Colin's show would have a fit if they found out a married man who plays the perfect minister dad was having a fling with the girl who plays his sweet, innocent, fourteen-year-old daughter. Although Tara plays younger than her age, so at least she was really eighteen and legal." Abby was gripping her mug handle so tightly she was surprised it didn't snap off. "I agreed to keep quiet about Colin's affairs and refuse to comment on anything related to our divorce, which he intended to blame on me to protect his fan base. In return, I'd get sole custody of Maddie."

"You agreed to let the tabloids print lies about you?"

Josh's face was unreadable, but he sounded incredulous. To someone like him, agreeing to have your reputation trashed must be as incomprehensible as killing in cold blood. She clenched her hands together on her lap and tried to explain. "In seventeen years, I've put up with so many tabloid lies that I'm immune. They can print anything they want, and unless you're willing to sue, there's nothing you can do. Denying things only gives the false rumors another week or two of press."

"Didn't you worry Maddie would hear about your affairs?" He sounded as if he were interrogating her.

Abby sat up straighter before continuing. "I told her I didn't have any, and she knows I don't lie. She also knows the tabloids stay in business by lying."

"Lots of people did believe everything the tabloids printed about you," Josh said. "You were forced to leave your show, for God's sake."

"I wasn't forced to leave my show, no matter what a couple of tabloids said—everyone begged me to stay. When you play someone like Samantha, not much hurts your image. I've also always been easy to work with, and you'll notice none of the stories hurt my professional reputation, just my personal one. That was part of our deal."

Abby abruptly realized her hands hurt and looked down at them. She was wringing them so vigorously they were chafed and bloodless. She pressed them onto the tabletop to keep them still. "To be honest, I also didn't want Colin to lose his job because I was afraid I'd get stuck paying him alimony. I was already going to end up giving him a lot of cash in addition to the house and furnishings I'd bought, thanks to California's wonderful community property laws and my romantic refusal to have a prenup."

"I thought the divorce left you destitute."

"Another press fantasy. My parents were always dodging bill collectors, so I made sure I saved and invested."

Josh rocked back in his chair. "Obviously Colin's convinced you to give him another chance." He was still wearing his inscrutable cop face.

Abby snorted. "Not hardly. Colin's show is considering killing him off to save money and raise ratings. He wants me to pretend to go back to him because he thinks the good PR will help him net a new two-year contract. He heard about my stalker and threatened to sue for sole custody on the grounds I'm endangering Maddie unless I agree. Once he gets his contract, we need to wait a few months so our reconciliation doesn't seem staged. Then we can break up again, and this time he'll legally terminate his parental rights to Maddie. I'm sure the stalker's finished with me now that Samantha's dead. But since I can't prove that, Colin has a good case, according to my divorce lawyer."

"Can't you tell the press now about his affair with his TV daughter and why you didn't disclose it?"

She got to her feet and walked over to the coffeepot, her nerves too twitchy for her to stay seated. "As Colin pointed out, who'd believe me? For starters, you're talking Samantha the bitch versus Pastor Jim the saint, at least in most people's minds." She refilled her mug. "And as Colin also noted, even most of my friends wouldn't believe I'd agree to have my reputation trashed and my cheating husband deified for my daughter's sake, especially when I might have gotten sole custody anyway if I'd told the truth. I wanted to avoid a custody fight because I could lose, and because I didn't want to destroy Maddie's illusions about her dad."

Abby slammed her mug on the counter, overflowing coffee on the black granite. "But damn it, I should have. I should never have protected that slime whose only decent act was giving Maddie a little DNA." She grabbed a dishcloth and wiped up the spilled coffee, then rinsed the cloth and spread it meticulously over the edge of the sink before she turned toward Josh. "So now besides Colin, our lawyers, my therapist, and Laura and her parents, you're the only person who knows the truth about my divorce."

Josh righted his chair. "Why did you tell me?"

From his lack of expression, she'd tossed the dice and gotten a three. Abby slumped against the counter, disappointment like a hand shoving hard against her chest. "I wanted to tell you before, but I didn't feel I could violate my agreement with Colin until he pulled this. I told you now because I trust you won't tell the tabloids. I also didn't want you hating me for using you, because I wasn't. And I thought you might care, but obviously I was wrong. Or maybe you think I'm lying." She waved a dispirited hand. "Why should you believe it any more than anyone else would?"

Josh got to his feet and walked over to her, resting his hands on her shoulders. "Why wouldn't I believe you? Your reasons for going along with Colin make perfect sense to me, knowing how you grew up and what a terrific mom you are." His eyes were dark velvet, his voice steady. "Actually, what never made sense was that the woman I think I know, the one who doesn't lie and hated that her dad cheated, would have ever cheated herself."

She stared up at him, the sudden lump in her throat making a response impossible.

"Of course you have to go along with him now. You can't risk having Maddie living even part-time with a dad who's willing to give up his parental rights for a damn two-year contract."

"Thank you." Knowing Josh didn't hate her made things much easier.

"This gives me one more reason to work like hell to identify your stalker, so I can shorten the time until I can see you again. Since once Colin loses his leverage, I assume you can leave California."

Abby's jaw dropped. "You'll want to see me after I've been with Colin? I mean living in the same house. I'd never really be with him."

For the first time since she'd known him, Josh looked uncertain. "I know we don't have a serious relationship, but I'm not ready for it to end. Although maybe you are." He released her shoulders. "You wouldn't be in this mess if I'd treated the letter writer seriously after the lipstick incident and arrested him before he shot at you."

"I don't blame you at all for this. And I definitely want to see you."

He let out an audible breath. "Good. I know you have to go home, but could I kiss you first?"

When she nodded, he pulled her into his arms and kissed her, stroking her bare back below her sports bra. "God, I can't believe how good you feel," he murmured between kisses. "How good I feel holding you. How much I want to make love to you."

"Maddie and Colin won't be up for a couple of hours." She barely got the words out before he picked her up and carried her upstairs to his bedroom.

— — —

Josh had driven Abby home, but he'd reluctantly agreed to drop her off at the path along the river two blocks from her house, after first having her call her guard to be on the lookout for her. When she got to her house she was glad she'd insisted—a few reporters were already parked out front. However, she managed to slip in the back door unnoticed. Then she grabbed the caffeinated beans she kept in the freezer for guests, started a pot of coffee, and headed upstairs to take a shower—and rehearse.

She'd come up with a plan. Actually, Josh had inspired it. His belief she'd sacrifice for her daughter had reminded her that someone else knew for a fact she would. Namely, Colin.

This had to work. That Josh believed her and planned to wait for her made her love him even more, and she didn't want to give him up for six months. Not because she couldn't handle delayed gratification, but because she was afraid Josh would meet someone else while she was in California. Long-distance romances were always hard, and this one would be markedly harder with her pretending to be someone else's wife and unable to risk even a phone call to Josh. Besides, he could easily forget her—he didn't love her, and they hadn't made that many memories yet.

Abby went into the main bathroom, since using the shower right off her bedroom might wake Maddie, who'd slept with her last night. It would be best if Maddie stayed asleep until she'd gotten this resolved, one way or another.

Abby stripped off her running clothes and stepped under the shower. She'd soon find out just how good an actor she really was.

CHAPTER 16

Despite an even stronger motivation to identify Abby's stalker, Josh didn't have a clue what to do next. He hadn't unearthed anyone who hated Abby personally or because of her dad or who was known to be crazy enough to be a suspect. They hadn't found the phone or anything else that would help identify the caller. The only tangible evidence—the bullets—narrowed the suspects to one of the 873 handgun permit holders in Alma County, assuming the stalker was local and had a permit.

At a loss, Josh went to see Laura.

"I'm surprised you're working on this," she said as Josh followed her into a family room with enormous windows and sunlight reflecting off a terra-cotta tile floor. A golden retriever got up from a navy bed in the corner and ambled toward him.

"It's my job."

"You could have had someone else handle it." Her tone could have frozen mercury. "Obviously the news Abby's going back to Colin didn't upset you much."

"That's because Abby told me the truth about Colin's affairs, including with his TV daughter," he said, "and why she kept quiet about them."

Laura stopped beside the sofa. "Abby told you that? When?"

Josh leaned over and scratched the dog's neck. "She ran over to my place this morning, before Colin woke up. She also told me why she's going back to him."

"Sit down," Laura said, her voice markedly warmer. "No, Maggie." She shook her head at the dog nudging Josh's leg for more petting. Maggie immediately trotted back to her bed.

Josh sat down on the sofa. "She's very well behaved."

"Much better than my kids," Laura said, taking a seat beside him. "Why in God's name is Abby going back to Colin? You can tell me. She will, I promise."

Abby had asked him to keep it secret, but Laura would be more willing to help if she knew the stakes and was undoubtedly right that Abby would tell her. "If she doesn't, he's going to court and claiming Abby's stalker is endangering Maddie, so he should be granted sole custody."

Laura's forehead creased. "Why does he want Maddie? He couldn't care less if he even sees her."

"What Colin really wants is for Abby to come back to him temporarily," Josh said, then explained why.

"That bastard." Laura spit out the words, her features twisted with disgust. "Although I shouldn't be surprised. Colin's a minimally talented prick with an ego the size of California who's incapable of putting anyone else first."

"I take it you're not a fan." Josh could see why Laura had been Abby's best friend for so many years. Many things about her—including her fierce loyalty—reminded him of Kim.

"Not since the first day I met him. He was a little too smooth for me to trust him. But Abby thought she was so much in love, and I think Colin probably loved her at first, too." Laura picked a browning white flower out of the vase on the coffee table and set it on the dark wood. "Unfortunately, he developed an aversion to women over twenty."

"He thinks sleeping with younger women proves he isn't becoming old and inadequate," Josh said.

"That sounds like something Abby would say," Laura said. "I thought she was crazy to stay with him after his first affair, let alone his sixth, but she was so determined to give Maddie a happy home with two parents that she ignored her own needs."

"Parents do that," Josh said, remembering sacrifices he hadn't even realized his own had made for their kids until he'd reached adulthood.

"Especially when they want to protect their child from something they've experienced firsthand." Laura plucked off a couple of fading peach flowers and set them beside the white one. "Personally, I don't think Maddie needs as much protecting as Abby thinks. She's been raised in a much more liberal time and place than Abby was, and I'll bet she's already figured out Colin isn't dad-of-the-year material. Abby's past has made her a little irrational about the issue."

"Although I can understand why she doesn't want Maddie living with Colin."

Laura rolled her eyes. "That would be an absolute disaster. So Abby's planning on staying with him until he gets a contract?"

"Unless I arrest her stalker first, since without that factor, no court would ever consider Harrington more dangerous than LA."

"Then Abby gets paroled."

"Precisely. Don't bother pointing out that Abby probably wouldn't have this problem if I'd taken her seriously from the start, since I'm well aware of that." Josh dug a legal pad and pen out of his briefcase. "I know I asked before, but now I'm willing to grab at straws. Can you think of anyone, no matter how far-fetched, who might hate Abby? Even some guy from high school who resented that she wouldn't date him or some girl who was jealous. Anything." Josh's lips twisted wryly. "My next idea is subpoenaing everyone in the county with a hand-gun permit."

"I've got a question for you first." Laura's green eyes were fixed on his. "What are you going to do while Abby's in California?"

"Work like hell to identify the stalker. Call you annoyingly often to find out if you've heard from her and know the status of Colin's contract negotiations." He smiled grimly. "Take a lot of cold showers." He might not be in the market for a long-term re-lationship, but thinking he'd lost Abby last night made him realize he wanted more time with her. He wasn't about to jeopardize his chances of getting it by doing anything that might upset her, like being with another woman.

"Good answer," Laura said. "Because Abby's one of the best people I know, and hardly anyone knows about Colin's affairs and their agreement."

"Just you and your parents, the attorneys, and her therapist," Abby said. And Colin, of course."

"Not even my parents know." Laura smiled faintly, shaking her head. "I didn't realize it before now, but Abby probably fig-ures otherwise they'd have disowned her after all those horrible tabloid stories. Between her parents and Colin, she's got a few trust issues. But she asked me not to mention it to anyone, and I didn't see any reason to violate her confidence. I knew my parents would love and support her anyway."

"Which is what families do. She's very lucky to have yours."

"Thanks." Laura rested her hand on Josh's arm. "My point is that if she told you the truth about this, she obviously cares for you. I'd appreciate it if you wouldn't hurt her."

"I'll do my best, and not just because otherwise your mother will have my ass," Josh said, setting his legal pad on his thigh. "Let's get going on that list."

– – –

Colin was still sound asleep when Abby walked into Maddie's room. He lay on his side, his tousled curls and guileless expression making him look almost angelic. She smiled ruefully. Too bad he was such a devil when he was awake.

She jostled his shoulder. "We need to talk, Colin."

He opened one eye. "Maybe we should practice being married instead." He snaked an arm around her shoulders and tried to pull her to him. "You remember how good we were together."

She moved free of his arm. "We have some things to discuss before Maddie wakes up. I'll be in the kitchen."

Abby was leaning against the counter drinking coffee when Colin came downstairs. He was dressed in jeans and a black T-shirt, his face covered with stubble and his hair sticking up.

"I hope you plan on cleaning up before you address your adoring public again," she said, pouring him some coffee.

Colin took the cup from her and sat down at the glitter-topped table. "Are they here this morning?"

"After the bait you threw out last night? Of course they are."

"They'll assume I had more important things to do than shower and shave," he said, his smirk making Abby long to dump the contents of the coffeepot over his head. But she couldn't let anything interfere with her much more important agenda.

Colin took a swig of coffee, then set down his cup. "When can you be ready to move? Good thing I kept our house, although the taxes are killing me."

"I'm not moving to California," Abby said.

"You're going to desert your daughter?"

"Maddie's not moving back, either."

"Then I'll see you in court," Colin said, his blue eyes narrowing. "You know I've got a case—I overheard you talking to your lawyer. Maddie will also have to testify. Do you want to subject her to that?"

"Neither of us is going to California with you, Colin."

Colin obviously decided to try a different approach, because his expression suddenly softened. "Look, all we're talking is six months. Maybe even less, although once you're there, I assume you won't want Maddie to have to change schools midyear."

"It will take you six months to negotiate a new contract?"

"I'll probably get one after a week of publicity, but we should keep this going longer." A smile ruffled his mouth. "I wouldn't want anyone to think it was a publicity stunt."

Abby refilled her cup, then sat down across from him. "You agreed to give me custody of Maddie because you didn't want me to tell the media about your affairs, remember? Especially the last one?"

"You think threatening to tell all will make me drop this? We already covered this. No one will believe you, and you know it. Not now." He got up and walked over to the coffeepot.

"Oh, they'll believe me, Colin, for one reason. I've got pictures. Very explicit pictures, taken by one of the most reputable private investigators in LA, showing Pastor Jim banging his teenage daughter and doing a few other things illegal in numerous states, even if you ignore the adultery issue. The photos are dated, so it's clear they were taken before our separation."

The glass pot clanged down on the counter, and Colin whirled toward her. "You had a PI following me? I don't believe it. You're not that kind of person."

Abby gave him a condescending look. "You didn't really think my timely arrival that day was coincidental, did you? I honestly never intended to use the pictures, but you're forcing my hand. If you don't drop this, they'll be all over the Internet by tonight. Your fans will love that."

"I don't believe you."

"Let's go down to the bank, and I'll show them to you. And don't think you'll be able to charm your way into my safe-deposit box and destroy the only copy. My lawyer also has a copy, although she doesn't have a clue what's inside that sealed envelope I gave her." Abby got to her feet. "You want to go to the bank with me? I'm sure the reporters outside would be fascinated to know where we're going and why."

"I can't believe you'd stoop to blackmail."

"That's precisely what you're doing."

He was silent for a moment. She could see his mind shift gears—good thing Colin didn't have a weakness for poker. "You obviously haven't thought through how this will hurt Madeline," he said, his expression now the concerned father he'd clearly decided would play best. "The minute those pictures are made public, the negative publicity's going to make the tabloid articles about you look like promo pieces. Maddie will resent you for subjecting her to that, not to mention hiring a PI to follow her father. What the hell kind of mother does that?"

Abby sat back down in her chair. She'd have laughed at his righteous indignation if the situation hadn't been so serious and her stomach dangerously close to expelling her last cup of coffee. "I think my relationship with Maddie is strong enough to handle that."

She rested her palms on the table and leaned toward him, flashing the determined look she credited for at least two of her Emmys. "Don't doubt for one second that I'll do it. My concern about protecting Maddie's opinion of her father disappeared when that father proposed trading his parental rights for a two-year contract." She picked up her cup and took another sip of coffee, delighted her hand was steady. "So what do you say? Do you agree I'm not a suitable wife for Pastor Jim?"

Colin walked over to the table and sat down, silently staring into his coffee cup. Weighing his options to figure out what would be best for him, no doubt, which was the closest he ever got to deep thinking. After a moment, he met her eyes. "As long as you keep custody of Maddie, the photos stay buried?"

Abby nodded, her gaze unwavering. "When she's eighteen, I'll destroy them. I promise."

"You've got a deal." His look switched to grudging admiration. "People never realize how tough you are."

"I've had to be," Abby said, keeping triumph—and a major dose of relief—out of her voice and expression. "You don't need to keep out of Maddie's life. She loves you. The reason I let you stay last night and carry out this charade was because she was so happy. That's also why I don't want you to terminate your parental rights."

Colin drained his coffee cup, then got to his feet. "I'd better go. It'll be easier for Maddie if I leave while she's asleep."

"Easier for you, you mean."

"You're so much better at explaining these things than I am. Tell her I love her, and I'll call her soon."

Abby raised an eyebrow. "Will you actually call her?"

"She's my daughter."

"I'll tell her you love her."

When Colin went upstairs to dress and pack, Abby collapsed in her chair, totally drained. She couldn't believe he was actually going, wouldn't believe it until he told the press.

She'd recovered when Colin came downstairs, showered, shaved, and carrying his suitcase. He told her he'd advise the press he was going now, with Abby and Maddie following as soon as they could make arrangements to put the house on the market. When they decided to stay in Minnesota after all, he could play the heartbroken husband and father. Trust Colin to figure out a way to spin this to his advantage.

Colin's taxi had just pulled away when Maddie came downstairs. "Where's Daddy?"

"He had to go back to California to work," Abby said. "He didn't want to wake you to say good-bye, but he said to tell you that he loves you."

Maddie furrowed her forehead. "I thought he was going to be here longer."

"He wanted to, but he had to go back because he's really busy with *Heavenly Days*," Abby said. "He made time to come out here because he was worried about you because of my stalker."

The furrows deepened. "Why? The stalker isn't after me. He isn't even after you now that Samantha's dead."

"I know," Abby said, which wasn't exactly a lie. He wasn't after Maddie, and Abby had her fingers crossed about the other. "Your dad didn't know any of that, just what a reporter for the *Enquirer* had told him. You know how they exaggerate."

Maddie nodded.

"Your dad even told the press that he wanted to take you back to California, where you'd be safe."

Maddie rolled her eyes. "Like it's safer there. I couldn't go swimming without a babysitter or walk to Dairy Queen with my friends or even Rollerblade on the front sidewalk like I can here."

"Your dad knows that now that he's visited," Abby said.

"Does that mean I can sleep over at Rachel's tonight?" Maddie asked. "Since I didn't get to last night?"

The remaining tension in Abby's body evaporated. Her only concern about Colin's quick departure was that Maddie might be upset, but she didn't seem to be. "Why don't you call Rachel and ask her?"

– – –

Josh rang Abby's doorbell at ten to four that afternoon. "I heard Colin left and you're going later, then got your message to stop by when I could," he said the instant she opened the door. He was still wearing his uniform. "What do you need?"

"To tell you I'm not going to California."

Josh looked at her blankly. "You're letting Colin take Maddie?"

"Of course not. He decided to leave her custody arrangements the way they are."

"Colin finally considered what was best for his daughter," Josh said, stepping into the foyer.

"You're giving Colin *way* too much credit in the paternal instincts department," Abby said. "He only decided to drop his threat because I told him I'd hired a PI and had pictures of him with his TV daughter. I said I didn't want to use them and didn't have to when we divorced since we'd reached an agreement. But

I'm concerned enough about Maddie now that I will. I said the instant he tries to change Maddie's custody, the pictures are on the Internet."

Josh's eyes widened with obvious surprise. "You hired a private investigator to take pictures of Colin?"

"Actually, I didn't. I bluffed. But after I left you, I realized that if I could convince Colin I had photos, he might see reason." She looked down at the stained carpet, her cheeks heating. "Are you terribly disillusioned with me? Since now I lied about something more important than rocket science?"

He grabbed her chin and raised it. He was grinning. "I'm in awe of your acting ability, being able to fool someone who knows you as well as your ex-husband. This lie was justified, considering what he was trying to pull." His grin faded. "How did Maddie take it?"

Trust Josh to worry about Maddie. "After I told her he'd left, she asked if that meant she could sleep over at Rachel's tonight since she missed last night. So I guess she took it OK."

Josh let out a breath, slumping back against the wall. "Jesus, that seems like weeks ago, not just last night. Do you want to go out to dinner?"

"Is that your best offer?"

He straightened. "What did you have in mind?"

"I've got some cheese and crackers and leftover pizza if you're really starving." Abby began tracing random patterns with her fingertips on his bare arm below his short shirtsleeve. "What I'd really like is a massage. It's been a stressful day."

Josh's eyes darkened. "I've always been good with my hands."

"I'll vouch for that." She moved her fingertips to his neck, slipping them under his collar. "A long, relaxing bath would also help. The main bathroom upstairs has a giant old tub, more than big enough for two people."

"Like the one Evan and Samantha used in the hotel room?"

His features had tightened and she could feel drops of sweat on his collarbone. She gave him a slow smile. "Just as good." Then she put her lips to his. "I'll even throw in some moves that would never have made it past the network censors."

CHAPTER 17

The knife was in the air, pointing downward at an angle. Fresh blood stained the tip, halfway up the steel blade. A fisted hand clenched the brown walnut handle—a man's hand, she could tell that even though she could only see his hand and wrist.

The man thrust the knife down through the air and out of view, raised it, thrust again. More and more blood coated the blade, dripping into the air below and sending rivulets toward the handle, as the knife rose and plunged, over and over. The knife disappeared. Instead she saw a window, built-in bookshelves, a light wood floor. Narrow planks with an oval pool of bright-red blood seeping onto some pale-blue fabric beside it. A pool that was getting bigger...

Then she saw the man. Probably in his thirties, he was clean-shaven with brown hair hanging over his collar, medium height, and skinny in faded jeans and a Minnesota Vikings T-shirt. He no longer held the knife, but was squatting beside a body. A woman, lying on her side, her peroxide-blonde big hair obscuring her face. She was wearing only a blue bra and matching panties. The pale-blue lump Abby had seen before, the one beside the pool of blood.

The focus shifted to the woman's front torso and face. Sharp features, big lips with lipstick even redder than the blood. Her eyes were open, not blinking, just staring blindly as blood flowed from gashes on her neck and chest. So much blood...

"Abby, are you all right? Did you have the nightmare again?"

Abby opened her eyes. She was shaking, but she was all right because Josh was beside her, holding her, his warmth heating her chilled body. "This time I saw the murderer. And the victim's face," she whispered. "I saw her face and the rest of her body, where she'd been stabbed. She'd been stabbed so many times."

"You still didn't recognize her?"

"I've never seen her before in my life. I don't know the murderer, either."

"What did the victim look like?"

Abby took a shaky deep breath, then closed her eyes and forced herself to remember. "She was pretty, in her twenties, I think, with big platinum hair, a heart-shaped face, and great lips, like in collagen ads. Her eyes were blue, lighter than Maddie's, but wide open, even though she was dead. At least I think she was dead." Her voice trembled. "With all that blood, she had to be."

Josh tightened his arms around her. "She isn't dead because she isn't real. You just imagined her, probably because of the stress of dealing with Colin."

"But she could be real." Seeing the victim's face and wounds had changed things, had made the entire dream seem less likely to be the product of imagination. "I've always been sensitive to the moods of people and even places. What if something happened here, something no one knows about but I've sensed because I'm psychic?"

"I thought you didn't believe in psychics."

"Maybe I was wrong."

Josh was silent for a moment. "What did the murderer look like?" he finally asked.

It was easier to picture him. "He's probably in his thirties, the kind of guy you'd never remember or even really notice. Average size and features, with brown hair just a little too long. He was wearing jeans and a Vikings T-shirt, one with number nine and Kramer on it. Everybody had that shirt when I was growing up, even my dad, because Tommy Kramer was the quarterback."

Josh released her and rested his hands on her shoulders. "I think we're both too tried to consider this logically," he said, kneading her tight flesh. "Let's go back to sleep and discuss it in the morning."

Abby wrapped her arms around her bare midriff. "I'll never get back to sleep." The way her brain was racing, she knew once she closed her eyes, the scene would replay over and over again.

"Then I'd better do something to help relieve your stress." Josh moved his hands off her shoulders and unfolded her arms, then stroked her breasts with his fingertips. "As police chief, I'm responsible for the well-being of the community." He kissed her neck.

Josh's talented hands and mouth soon banished all thoughts of the dream. "Do you do this often?" Abby got out between gasps. "For other stressed women in the community?"

"This is just a pilot program. So far you're the only participant." His mouth closed on her nipple.

"You're planning on expanding it?"

He raised his head and grinned. "I don't think that's feasible. Just keeping you relaxed completely exhausts me."

– – –

It might be overcast, but the whole world seems brighter today, Abby thought as she walked to the garage at just before ten that morning, on her way to pick up Maddie. Josh had believed her about her agreement with Colin. He might not love her, but the way he'd treated her last night showed he cared about her. Now that she'd gotten rid of Colin, she had time to convince Josh to move from caring to love.

The only thing getting her down was her dream, that she didn't recognize either of the actors. They certainly didn't seem like characters she'd ever imagine putting in a book, either. Why would she be dreaming about two people she didn't know unless she was dreaming about something real?

Except that would mean she was psychic, and she didn't believe in psychics except when she was half awake.

A few feet from the garage, she stopped. Goose bumps prickled on her neck and shoulders and down her arms. She had the same feeling she'd had at the school, that something was off, maybe someone was watching her.

She looked around the yard. Nothing.

Of course there was nothing. She was being paranoid.

Abby walked the rest of the way to the garage. She stuck her key in the lock of the entrance door, turned it, and grabbed the door handle. The door wouldn't open.

She automatically turned the key again. Then she froze, her blood turning to slush.

She'd locked the door when she'd first turned the key. That meant the door had been unlocked. But she always locked the garage door, just like she always set the car alarm even when the car was in the locked garage.

Someone had been in the garage. Someone who might still be there.

Abby turned and took off running.

She didn't dare slow down long enough to look behind her. She couldn't hear anyone, but then again all she could hear was her heart pounding in her ears. Someone could be following her, someone who could attack her in the secluded backyard before she got the back door unlocked. She'd go in through the front. At least it was on the street.

She flipped through her keys as she raced past the garden on the side of the house, finally locating the key to the front door. She ran up the front steps two at a time, then aimed the key at the lock. Her hand was shaking so hard she missed. She tried again—

"What's wrong?"

She opened her mouth to scream, closing it before more than a screech escaped. Her guard was standing behind her. She'd been so panicked she'd forgotten all about him.

"Someone's been in the garage," she puffed out. "He might still be there."

He drew his gun. "Did you see or hear something?"

"No, but the garage door was unlocked, and I know I locked it last night."

"Give me your keys, then go inside," the guard said. "Call nine-one-one. I'll keep an eye on the garage and make sure no one leaves."

While Abby waited for the cops to arrive, she paced between the dining and living rooms. A blaring siren announced the arrival of a police car, followed almost immediately by a second. Both parked at the front curb, then three uniformed cops ran along the side of the house to the garage. Abby went into the family room and watched the garage through the window, gripping the sill with both hands and bracing herself.

Nothing happened, no shots, not even yelling loud enough for her to hear. No intruder exiting with his hands up. Her car alarm went off, then her neighbors' security system alarm, but both were soon silenced.

After a few minutes, Ben knocked on the back door.

"The chief's in a meeting, so you're stuck with me," he said. "Are you positive you locked the door last night? It was unlocked when we tried it."

Abby joined him on the back stoop. "That's because I unlocked it again when it wouldn't open, before I realized it had been unlocked at first. I assume no one was inside."

"Abby? Are you OK?" Bill Tate was coming around from the front of the house, half jogging even though he was wearing a suit and tie.

"I'm fine," Abby said. "What are you doing here?"

"The mayor was at the police station for some reason when you called about a possible break-in here. He called Mary," Bill said. "I was driving to a meeting when she demanded I make a detour to check things out. What happened?"

"Abby found the garage door unlocked, and she always locks it," Ben said, then he returned his attention to Abby. "We haven't found any evidence anyone was inside. The locks are too old and beat-up to tell if they've been messed with. How long was it between when you tried the door and when the guard went to the backyard?"

"Probably a minute," Abby said.

"I doubt anyone could have gotten over the fence on the south side that fast, if at all," Ben said. "It's ten feet high. And your neighbors' motion detectors would have caught anyone who went through their backyards. We actually set them off. So no one was waiting for you in the garage and got away."

"Did you check Abby's car?" Bill asked. "Someone could have tampered with it."

"We didn't because the alarm was still armed—we set it off, too," Ben said. "We shut off the alarm, then left the car. We can have a mechanic check it if you'd like, Abby."

"Don't bother," Abby said. "That alarm's so sensitive it would have gone off if anyone even brushed against the car, let alone tampered with it, and you can only deactivate it with a key. I must have forgotten to lock the door after all. I'm probably not as careful as I was in California because around here people don't always lock doors."

"You're always neurotic about locking up," Bill said. "Do you honestly believe you'd have been any less careful with a stalker possibly after you?"

"Maybe stress made me forget." She usually *was* careful, but she obviously hadn't been this time. And she was starting to feel a little foolish over panicking. "I'm sorry I wasted everyone's time."

"You did the right thing to call me," Ben said. "That phone call could mean the stalker's been watching you, and he still could be."

Bill's head pivoted toward Abby. "What phone call?"

"I got an anonymous call on Friday," she admitted. "The good news is it confirmed that my stalker hates Samantha, not me. He's got to be satisfied now that she's dead."

"Why do you think he was watching you?" Bill asked.

"Might have been watching me," Abby said. "He called right after I finished a run and said I looked good in blue. I was wearing a blue T-shirt. But Samantha was wearing blue on Friday when she was killed, so I think it's more likely that's what he meant."

"Even if nothing happened now, I'd recommend changing the locks on the garage," Ben said. "The ones you've got are pretty worthless."

"I should have had that done when I changed the locks on the house," Abby said. "I'll call the locksmith today. Thanks for checking this out."

"Much as we hate to have you leave, Mary and I will sleep easier when you're back in California," Bill said as Ben walked away.

"Actually, I'm not going," Abby said. "Colin and I decided we shouldn't get back together and that Maddie will have a better life in Minnesota." Mary and Bill deserved to know that she and Maddie were staying, but she wasn't about to burden them with news of Colin's newest threat. Not when she'd hopefully defused it for good.

"Colin said you'd be following."

Abby shrugged. "He was just saving face. He didn't want the press to realize he'd panicked and come out here for nothing."

"It wasn't for nothing," Bill said firmly. "It was because of the stalker."

"Who's finished with me," Abby said. "He hasn't contacted me since Friday, which is longer than he's ever been silent before. The timing corresponds with Samantha's death, which is further evidence he's done." The more she repeated that, the more convinced she was that it was true. "Call Mary and tell her not to worry, that nothing happened here today."

Bill studied her silently for a moment. "I'm not so convinced it's nothing."

"Nothing did happen," Abby said, managing to keep her tone nonchalant despite the concern still pricking at her nerves. "You heard the cops. Why would someone break into my garage and do nothing? It doesn't make sense."

Bill was right that she was neurotic about locking doors, but she wasn't perfect. She must have forgotten. Nothing else made sense.

CHAPTER 18

Josh digested the message Ben had just left on his cell phone as he pretended to listen to one of the members of the task force on Harrington's nonexistent school violence problem ramble on. The good news was that Abby was still taking the stalker seriously, despite her claim to be convinced he hated Samantha and would now leave her alone. To be honest, Josh wasn't so sure.

The bad news was that the stalker had Abby stressed out. The fact she'd forgotten to lock the garage door when she was apparently neurotic about doing that confirmed it. That she'd had an even more detailed and disturbing version of her dream last night was further evidence of just how on edge she was. And the dream had disturbed her—although this morning she'd claimed she'd overreacted, that she certainly wasn't psychic and the victim and murderer must be figments of her imagination, Josh could tell she was only pretending so he wouldn't worry.

Unfortunately, he had no idea what more he could do to identify the stalker until he made another move. But maybe he could relieve Abby's mind about her nightmare by convincing her she wasn't dreaming about anything real. Proving a negative was always tough, but if he checked the Harrington police records himself and could assure Abby that no one matching the victim's description had disappeared or been assaulted or killed, she'd hopefully be satisfied her dream was totally imaginary. It was worth a try. How long could it take to look through the records in a peaceful place like Harrington?

When he finally got back to the station, Josh Googled Tommy Kramer and discovered he'd been the Vikings' quarterback for ten years, beginning with the 1979 season. The murderer's T-shirt could have been around long after Tommy's tenure ended, but at least he had a starting point. He headed for the basement where the precomputerized records were kept.

Josh flicked a light switch, illuminating the dreary, cabinet-filled basement, then located the gray metal cabinet that included 1979. He jerked the top drawer open, and the odor of musty paper bombarded him. The files in the drawer were all traffic offenses; the folders were jammed in so tightly that years and humidity had cemented them into a solid mass. Good thing he didn't care about traffic offenses.

He closed the drawer and opened the one below it. It was much emptier, holding fairly thick files labeled "Assault and Battery" and "Domestic Disturbances," along with thinner ones for "Homicides" and "Missing Persons." He removed the drawer and carried it to a table the same gray metal as the cabinets. Planting himself on a wooden chair as uncomfortable as it looked, he pulled out the "Homicides" file.

– – –

Three and a half hours later, Josh hadn't found a potential victim. However, he had learned more than he'd wanted to know about Abby's parents, mostly domestic disturbances, although a few bar fights had landed her dad in the assault-and-battery category. No wonder she'd been so anxious to escape.

He pulled out the first folder in the Missing Persons file for the year he was currently working his way through. A seventy-seven-year-old man had wandered off, according to his grand-kids. He checked the note stapled to the bottom of the report. Apparently Grandpa had been found in Arizona with the woman he'd wandered off with. No photo, but since the girlfriend was sixty-nine, he doubted she was Abby's woman, even if she'd been a plastic surgery addict.

Josh grabbed the next folder. Probably a runaway of either the teenage or senior citizen variety. The only missing persons he'd found so far were either under seventeen or over seventy, and all had shown up alive and well.

He skimmed the report. Someone different this time. A secretary named Deborah Springer had been reported missing after she'd skipped two days of work at the Ken Parks Allstate Insurance Agency. Attached to the report was a Christmas greeting from the agency, a photo of the employees huddled together with a silver "Seasons Greetings" over their heads. Deborah was the second from the left.

A woman in her twenties with big platinum hair, sharp features, blue eyes, and red lips.

Shit.

– – –

She'd certainly gotten her wish that Maddie have a social life, Abby thought as she pulled into one of the few empty spots in the Harrington Pool parking lot. She was starting to feel like she was running a taxi service. But Maddie was so much happier than she'd been a couple of weeks ago that she wasn't complaining.

The Harrington Pool, located beside the City Park, was enormous, featuring a water slide, three diving boards, a kiddie pool, and a concession stand. Abby had dropped Maddie and a bottle of waterproof SPF 45 lotion off there almost four hours ago. Rachel was busy with a doctor's appointment, but Maddie had been sure she'd run into other friends, promising to call if she didn't. She hadn't called.

Abby looked toward the pool entrance, where Maddie had promised to meet her. She wasn't waiting, but Abby was a couple of minutes early. Maddie would be there soon. She was compulsively prompt, something she'd inherited from her mother. Abby smiled faintly. It was ironic, since she herself was compulsively prompt to counter her own mother, who hadn't been on time to anything besides her own funeral.

The sky was a deep sapphire blue decorated with a few puffy clouds, the temperature in the eighties with low humidity and a hint of breeze. Weather far too nice to enjoy through glass, even with Rachmaninoff's Second playing on public radio. Abby shut off the car, got out, and leaned against the Volvo. The sun baking her bare arms and neck, the scent of chlorine, and the sounds of splashing, giggling, and shrieking resurrected memories of innumerable afternoons spent with Laura in this pool's predecessor. The same kind of childhood memories she wanted Maddie to have. Thank God they didn't have to leave with Colin.

After a few minutes, Abby checked her watch. It was 4:35 and Maddie still hadn't come out. She strode to the high chain-link fence that surrounded the pool and looked for Maddie and her red swimsuit in the water, on one of the diving boards or the water slide, or waiting in the long lines to each. She walked along the fence, circling the entire pool as she searched the crowd. No Maddie.

Abby's stomach tightened reflexively, and she told herself to relax. This was Minnesota, not LA, and it was broad daylight. Both Laura and Kim left their older kids here unattended all the time. Maddie would be out in a minute. She was probably changing.

Two tall blond teenagers, Kari and Dylan according to their name tags, both wearing green T-shirts with HARRINGTON POOL STAFF in white letters, manned the pool's admission counter.

"I'm looking for my daughter," Abby said as Dylan stamped the hands of a couple of smiling teenage girls and waved them into the changing area. "She's a little late. Is it OK if I check the locker room?"

"You're Abby Langford, aren't you?" Kari said. "I loved you on *Private Affairs*." She opened the swinging half door on the right side of the counter. "Go on in."

Abby went through another full-size door into the girls' locker room. The room was quiet, an open changing area with long blue vinyl benches and four rows of lockers. The bikini-clad girls who'd entered before Abby were rinsing off in the shower and discussing how hot Dylan was.

Abby called Maddie's name a couple of times as she walked around the dozen changing booths, opening doors and looking underneath the two occupied booths for Maddie's bright-red toenails. She wasn't there.

As she left the changing area, Abby pulled out her phone and dialed Maddie's number. The phone went over to voice mail on the first ring. Maddie never shut off her phone, so she must be talking to someone. She'd somehow missed her and would find her outside, talking on the phone.

But Maddie wasn't outside, not at the designated meeting place or by their Volvo, even though it was four forty. Abby's stomach clenched again, and her pulse accelerated.

Calm down. She was doing it again, being neurotic and panicking unnecessarily, the way she'd done this morning when she'd found the garage unlocked. She needed to relax.

Unfortunately her stomach and pulse refused to comply, probably because she was neurotic by nature. She was no doubt overreacting, but Abby went over to the counter, fished her wallet out of her purse, and flipped it open to Maddie's photo. "Have you seen her?" she asked the kids behind the counter.

"I remember her coming in," Kari said. "I knew she was your daughter because I saw you all on TV when your husband was here. She's really cute."

"Did you see her leave?"

Kari shook her head. "What about you, Dylan?"

Dylan leaned over for a closer look at the photo. "I didn't notice her. We've been real busy since the weather's so nice."

The girls' locker room door opened. Abby glanced toward it as a couple of dripping, towel-wrapped girls exited. Neither was Maddie.

"She's probably still in the pool," Kari said. "Kids lose track of time when they're having fun."

Abby nodded, then dialed Maddie's number again. It rolled over on the first ring.

She walked back to the pool, trying to reason away the cold knot in her stomach. Maybe Kari was right. Maybe Maddie was having so much fun she'd lost track of time. She was a kid, after all. Abby circled the pool again.

No Maddie.

The knot in Abby's stomach tightened like an icy tourniquet. She wasn't worried about drowning—Maddie was a strong swimmer and the pool had six lifeguards, all of whom looked alert.

But someone could have taken her.

Abby strode along the chain-link fence as she frantically looked around the pool for Maddie. She should never have let Maddie go anywhere alone, not while there was any possibility her stalker wasn't finished. Like Kari had mentioned, Maddie had been in the television coverage of Colin's visit so the stalker now knew what she looked like, if he hadn't before. He could have taken Maddie. Or someone else might have decided to kidnap Maddie after learning she had famous and presumably wealthy parents. Not everyone in Minnesota was law-abiding.

Abby tried Maddie's phone again. It again rolled over on the first ring.

She was pacing faster, breathing harder, chewing her bottom lip so forcibly she tasted blood. She needed to think, to calm down, to be logical. If Maddie was still swimming, she wouldn't be talking on her phone because she wouldn't bring her phone by the water. If Maddie was talking on her phone, she'd be in the locker room or out here, but she wasn't. The only other reason her phone would immediately go to voice mail was if she'd shut it off, and Maddie never shut off her phone.

The only logical conclusion was someone had shut it off for her.

– – –

Josh read through Deborah Springer's file. The company had withdrawn the report a couple of days later, so she must have turned up. He needed to confirm that and hopefully find someone who knew Deborah was alive and well. If he was lucky, the agency was still around. He called the number on the report.

The agency existed, but closed at four thirty and it was four forty-five. Josh left a message asking someone to call him—he couldn't justify bothering anyone at home over this, especially since that person would have to come back into the office and check personnel records. Abby's dreams were annoying, but not dangerous, and could certainly wait until tomorrow.

His phone rang.

"I can't find her," Abby said. Her voice sounded even shakier than when someone had been shooting at her car.

Josh tensed. "Can't find who?"

"Maddie. She's disappeared."

CHAPTER 19

"I came to pick her up after swimming, and she isn't here," Abby said. "I've looked everywhere. I should never—"

"Calm down, Abby. Where are you?"

She tried to take a couple of deep breaths, but her lungs would barely inflate, and the shallow inhalations brought her even closer to hyperventilating. "At the Harrington Pool. I was supposed to pick Maddie up at four thirty but I can't find her. And her cell phone is off."

"Is she with Rachel?"

"Rachel has a doctor's appointment. I don't know who Maddie was with. She wasn't meeting anyone, though she's made friends she says are here every day. Laura and Kim said it was safe to leave her here. But what if my stalker or someone else saw her on TV and decided to go after her? Either to hurt me or for ransom." Abby's voice was high and shrill, her words running together. She sounded hysterical, but she couldn't help it. Not when Maddie could be in danger.

"You looked around the pool and in the changing area, I assume," Josh said.

"I've looked everywhere."

"I'll come over, although I'm sure nothing's happened," Josh said. "Maddie probably left with a friend and is a little late getting back. I'll bet she's somewhere in the park."

"Maddie would never leave the pool," Abby said, trying to replicate Josh's slower cadence. "I've drilled it into her head since she was little that it isn't safe to wander around without an adult. It's one of our rules. And she's never late." Despite her efforts, Abby's voice was racing uphill again. "I know her phone was on when I dropped her off, and she leaves it on so I can always get a hold of her if I need to, except when she's in school. It's another rule. Someone must have—"

"Call Kim and see if she knows who Maddie might have met there," Josh interrupted. "Her friends' mothers might know something. I'll be there in ten minutes."

Kim's phone was off, too, probably because she was in a doctor's office, so Abby left a message. She redialed Maddie's number as she strode back to the fence surrounding the pool. Maddie's phone immediately went to voice mail. Gripping her phone with one hand and the chain-link fence with the other, Abby checked the pool again. No luck.

Maybe someone had taken Maddie to the park. She wouldn't go willingly with a stranger, but she'd go with someone she thought she knew, the dad of one of her new friends or someone else. Or maybe she'd been drugged. The lifeguards and kids at the counter might not have noticed, not when it was so busy. Or Maddie could have gone into the park on her own, thinking it would be OK because it was connected to the pool and she'd be back before four thirty. Someone could have followed and attacked her there.

Abby was clutching the fence so hard her hand cramped, the chain ridges digging painfully into her palm. The chlorine smell was choking her, each shriek, giggle, and splash shocking her already-sparking nerves. She couldn't stand here waiting for Josh, doing nothing while someone could be hurting Maddie. She raced across the blacktopped parking lot to the park.

The park covered four city blocks and had a large playground on the far side. Maybe Maddie had gone there.

Abby jogged along a dirt path, heading for the playground. She passed through a thick grove of trees, raced by a sparklingly quiet pond, over a hill, through more trees. Her feet ached as she stumbled over the roots and rocks on the path, slowing her pace. Why wasn't she wearing tennis shoes instead of sandals with two-inch heels, no matter how cute they were? Someone could kill Maddie all because her mother was so damn vain.

She couldn't think that, couldn't panic. Maddie had to be safe. So where was she?

Abby eased to a walk and dialed Maddie's number again, wiping her sweaty neck and forehead with the palm of her free hand. Maddie's voice mail message had just started when she spotted it—a flash of red on the ground, in the trees off to the right.

Abby's entire body felt as if it had been flash frozen, but she made herself resume jogging, ignoring her sore feet and the branches that scratched her bare arms and cheeks. The trees and grass concealed most of the red, but it could be a person.

A person wearing a red swimsuit and lying motionless on the ground.

"Maddie!"

Abby called her name, but she was so winded it came out as a loud whisper. The red didn't move. Keeping her eyes on it, Abby sprinted the last steps.

A beat-up Macy's shopping bag was lying in the grass.

It wasn't Maddie, thank God. Abby doubled over, puffing.

Her relief lasted only a moment. Because Maddie might not be lying here hurt or even dead, but she was still missing, could have been missing for up to four hours. Abby's eyes filled, the ache inside her turning her breaths into painful gasps. Colin was right.

She'd endangered Maddie by insisting on staying in Harrington when there was a possibility her stalker wasn't finished with her. The person she loved more than anything in the world could be hurt, even dead, because she'd—

Her cell phone rang. Her heart lurched to her throat, choking off her air. Her hand was shaking so much she fumbled before she finally hit the answer button.

"She's here and she's fine," Josh said. "We're both in the parking lot."

Abby's knees buckled, and she leaned back against a tree trunk for support, slithering down the bark until she was squatting.

"Abby? Are you OK?" Josh asked when she didn't respond.

Her mouth was too dry for saliva, but she swallowed anyway. The movement of her muscles cleared her throat so she could speak. "I'm fine. I'm in the park, but I'm on my way back."

An adrenaline spurt enabled Abby to stand and hurry through grass and trees toward the path she thought she'd taken. Even though she logically knew Josh wouldn't lie about this, she needed to see Maddie for herself. She passed the pond again, then turned onto the path, the increasing volume of swimming pool sounds confirming she was heading in the right direction.

She finally spotted Maddie, dressed in her red oversize T-shirt cover-up and standing beside Josh and his police car. She sprinted across the parking lot, grabbed her daughter, and hugged her fiercely, Maddie's chlorine-scented damp warmth proved she really was all right. "Where were you?"

"Hannah and I walked to Dairy Queen," Maddie said. "It's only a block away, and I thought I'd be back before you got here. Why were you so early?"

"You were supposed to be here at four thirty."

"You said five. You're squishing me," she said, wriggling in Abby's arms.

Abby released her hold and took a step back. "I said four thirty. And you're never supposed to turn off your phone."

"I didn't," Maddie said. "The battery ran out. I think I need a new one since I just charged it last night."

Abby fought the urge to shake her. Maddie was acting nonchalant when she could have been killed. But she wasn't going to make a scene in public. That was the kind of thing her mother had done—on those rare occasions she'd bothered to show up. "Thanks for coming, Josh," Abby said.

He touched her arm. "I'm glad things turned out OK. I'll see you both later."

Abby drove with the radio on so she wouldn't start talking until she got home. Now that her fear had passed, she was furious.

"I didn't say you could go to Dairy Queen," Abby said the instant she and Maddie stepped into the house.

"I only had a little cone," Maddie said, walking through the kitchen. "I didn't ruin my appetite for dinner or anything."

"That's not what I'm upset about." Abby grabbed her daughter's arm, stopping her. "I told you that you could go to the pool. I didn't give you permission to go anywhere else. It could have been dangerous."

Maddie gave her a parents-are-so-useless look. "We didn't even have to cross a street. It's not dangerous."

"It could have been," Abby said, fastening her hands on Maddie's shoulders. "You know our rules. You go somewhere and you stay put." Abby shook her, then abruptly released her when she realized what she'd done. She'd never shaken her daughter in her life.

"I thought that's why we moved to Minnesota, so I didn't have to keep following rules like that," Maddie said. "So I could do things like walk one block without worrying it was dangerous." She was gesturing as expansively as her dad during a sermon scene. "We even talked about it yesterday, that here I could walk to Dairy Queen. What other Dairy Queen would I be able to walk to?"

"Don't use that tone with me."

Maddie held her hands out, palms up, looking confused and angry. "What tone?"

"Go to your room."

Maddie stared at her a moment, then walked over and picked the phone off the counter.

"What are you doing?" Abby asked sharply. "I told you to go to your room."

"I'm supposed to call Rachel about tomorrow. Since my phone doesn't work, I need to use the phone down here before I go upstairs."

Abby grabbed the phone out of Maddie's hand. "There is no tomorrow. You're grounded for the next week."

Maddie's eyes widened. "That isn't fair. I didn't do anything wrong."

"I'm the mom. I don't have to be fair. Now go to your room."

– – –

Josh sat behind his desk, raking his fingers through his hair. Abby was even closer to losing it than he'd imagined. The way she'd reacted when she couldn't find Maddie showed that.

Sure, the stalker could conceivably have discovered Abby had a daughter and decided to go after Maddie. But Maddie had at most been a few minutes late, and no one was going to risk doing anything at a crowded public pool during the day. Even if someone was stupid enough to try, it wouldn't work. Maddie wasn't some sheltered small-town kid, she was a city girl used to being careful, as Abby's rules made clear. She wouldn't fall for someone claiming to need help finding a dog or to be a friend of her mother's sent to get her. She also would never have willingly gone with a stranger, and if anyone had tried to take her, she'd have raised bloody hell.

Abby knew all that, but she'd still been nearly hysterical. If things didn't change fast, she could be heading for a nervous breakdown.

The good news was that while he'd been at the swimming pool, he'd gotten a call from Karen King, the office manager of Ken Parks Agency, who planned to be at work until six thirty. Hopefully, the woman still traded Christmas cards with Deborah Springer.

– – –

Abby sat on the living room couch, hugging one of the cobalt pillows and chewing her lip with the intensity of a beaver working a tree branch. She'd spent the past ten minutes like this, reliving the fear and fury of the past hour. She'd been coldly terrified, and the whole time Maddie had been at the damn Dairy Queen eating an ice-cream cone. She couldn't believe Maddie would be so careless when a stalker might be out there. Clearly she needed not only this grounding, but also a review of their house rules.

Except Maddie didn't think the stalker was anything to worry about because her mother had gone out of her way to convince her it wasn't.

Abby started, dropping the pillow, the words so distinct she was half convinced she'd heard rather than thought them. What was she doing, auditioning for the part of the unreasonable mother in a made-for-preteens movie? She'd been intent on keeping Maddie from worrying, and she'd succeeded. Why the hell was she punishing Maddie for that?

Maddie was usually good about time, so making one mistake wasn't that big of a deal, assuming the mistake had been Maddie's and not her stressed-out mother's. It certainly wasn't Maddie's fault her phone had chosen today to malfunction.

No wonder Maddie had claimed it wasn't fair. It wasn't even close.

Abby raced up the stairs two at a time, then strode down the hallway and knocked on Maddie's door.

"Go away."

Since it was her house and she was the mother, Abby ignored her daughter's command and opened the door. The shag carpet in here was Pepto-Bismol pink, the walls only a slightly more muted bubblegum shade, although fortunately Maddie liked pink. She was hunched over her computer at the maple desk that was part of the bedroom set Abby had bought right after they'd moved in.

"I said go away," Maddie said, sliding and clicking the mouse, her eyes on the monitor.

"I will just as soon as I apologize," Abby said, walking up behind her. She rested her hands on Maddie's shoulders. "I'm sorry. I shouldn't have blown up at you like that. Maybe I was wrong about the time. Even if I wasn't, you're right—I've been telling you that we moved here so you can do things you couldn't in California."

Maddie finally turned to look at her. "Then why did you get so mad at me?"

"Because I thought you'd disobeyed me."

"I really didn't think I had." Maddie's expression was so earnest she had to be telling the truth—she wasn't a good enough actor yet to fool her mother. "You don't usually get that mad even when I do things I know are wrong."

After the abuse she'd experienced growing up, Abby had done her best to be lenient with Maddie, who was by nature a good kid and anxious enough to please that a disappointed look was enough to change unacceptable behavior. She smiled ruefully. "Parents do that sometimes when they're relieved. Get mad."

Maddie gave her the condescending useless-parents look again. "That's dumb."

"I guess it is," Abby said. "I'm sorry. I promise I won't do it again. At least I'll try not to."

"Am I still grounded?"

"No, you're not grounded."

Maddie smiled—her dad's beautiful smile but without Colin's inevitable ulterior motives. "Good. Can I call Rachel?"

Abby hugged her daughter. "Go ahead. When you're done, I think we should go to Ruby's for dinner. After we buy you a new cell phone battery."

– – –

Karen had been the agency's office manager for twenty-six years and remembered Deborah without even checking the records. "She was real specific that her name was Deborah, not Debbie or Deb," Karen said. "Corrected people all the time. What's the problem?"

"Probably nothing." Josh tapped his pen on his legal pad. "Hennepin County asked us to check on blondes reported missing during the eighties and nineties, and I ran across the report your agency filed when she didn't show up at work." He'd learned you could blame anything, no matter how absurd, on some bureaucrat in Minneapolis, and no one around here would blink. "Do you know where she is now?"

"Sorry, we didn't keep in touch. Actually, she never came back to work."

He stopped tapping. "I assumed the report was withdrawn because she did."

"No, because we found out where she was. We got a note explaining she'd broken up with her boyfriend and been so upset that she couldn't live in Harrington anymore. She moved in with a girlfriend in the Twin Cities."

Josh's fingers tightened around his pen, the hairs on the back of his neck snapping to attention. "She left town on the spur of moment? Wasn't that unusual?"

"Not for Deborah," Karen said, her tone dry. "She was one of those drama queen types. She moved here in the first place because some romance in Duluth went sour. She hadn't even been here a year when she left."

"Did she collect her last paycheck?"

"Her note said she felt so bad leaving us in a lurch that we should keep it. I remember that because it was a little unusual giving up money, but it was only for a couple of days, and I figured she thought she'd get a better reference from us if she did that." Karen sniffed. "Like that made up for leaving us understaffed."

"Did you give her a reference?"

"Lucky for her, no one asked."

Josh resumed tapping. "Do you remember the name of her friend in the Twin Cities?"

"Sorry, no. I do remember Deborah spent a few weekends there while she was working for us, and she probably mentioned her friend's name, but I missed it. A lot of the time I didn't listen real close to her. Deborah was kind of a motormouth."

"Do you still have the note?"

"No. We were in the Canton Building when it burned down eleven years ago. We lost everything, including our files." Karen chuckled. "At least we had good insurance."

He'd heard about the Canton Building fire. Arson, but no one had ever been arrested. Although he doubted there was a connection, Josh wrote it down. "Do you remember anything about the note? Was it handwritten?"

Karen was silent for a moment. "I assume it was typed. Being a secretary she could type faster than she could write. But I'm not positive. Sorry."

"Don't apologize. You've got an excellent memory," Josh said.

"You've gotta to work in insurance around here. If you forget a client's third cousin who he introduced you to once fifteen years ago, he's likely to get offended enough to switch to Frank Brown's agency."

Josh glanced at his ink-dotted notes. "Who was Deborah's boyfriend?"

"I remember being surprised when her note mentioned him since I didn't know she had one," Karen said. "Deborah hung out at O'Gara's and at a dance club called Oz and talked about men she met at those places. But she'd never mentioned anyone being special. Knowing Deborah, I figured that meant her boyfriend was married."

Josh hung up, then lowered his chin to his chest and massaged neck muscles his conversation with Karen had ratcheted tight. He wouldn't let himself jump to conclusions. Deborah might not be the woman in Abby's dreams. And disappearing—even leaving a note that could have been typed by anyone and forfeiting a paycheck—didn't prove something had happened to her. Deborah could be alive and well today. He just had to find her.

For Abby's sake, he hoped to God he could.

CHAPTER 20

Josh arrived at work the next morning determined to find Deborah Springer before he went to Abby's for dinner that night. Unfortunately, she appeared to have vanished.

The woman listed as Deborah's emergency contact in the police report had been a casual friend from Duluth who hadn't talked to Deborah after she'd moved to Harrington. She did remember Deborah was originally from Iowa and didn't have any family. She also remembered the boyfriend whose rejection had caused Deborah to leave Duluth, an engineer at 3M who'd married a local girl a few months after he and Deborah had broken up. Josh called him. He was still married to the same woman, had four kids, and still worked for 3M. He hadn't been in contact with Deborah since their breakup.

Josh had even gone to Ben, an admitted computer nerd, explaining his interest with a variation of the Minneapolis excuse he'd used with Karen. Despite spending hours looking, Ben also had no luck. Using methods Josh didn't want to know, Ben even verified that unless Deborah had gotten a new Social Security number, she hadn't paid any federal or Minnesota taxes after she'd left her job at the insurance agency.

So Josh headed over to O'Gara's—the dance club was long out of business. He should probably wait until Abby had identified Deborah's picture, but her hair and lips were distinctive enough that his gut said she was the woman in Abby's dream. His lips twisted ruefully. Or maybe his brain had convinced his gut of that because he felt like getting out of the office. He had to admit he missed the investigative part of his old job. Maybe he wasn't cut out to be an administrative stiff after all.

O'Gara's was located in a part of Harrington filled with well-kept but small bungalow-style houses with even smaller yards. Josh turned right onto Marshall Avenue, the major commercial street in the area. He passed a body shop, a tattoo parlor, a machine shop, and the Curl Up and Dye beauty shop before reaching O'Gara's, a brick building decorated with signs advertising several varieties of American beer. He pulled into a large dirt lot with a half dozen rusty sedans and one pickup parked in it, then got out of his car and headed for the bar.

The place was clean, but a little run-down around the edges, and it smelled of cigarette smoke despite Minnesota's no-smoking laws. Even at four in the afternoon, several middle-aged men were already parked at the bar, all drinking beers. The bartender, a guy about Josh's age, identified himself as the current owner, who'd bought the place from his dad and worked there since his late teens. His name wasn't O'Gara, but Pete Petersen—the place had apparently been started in the forties by Pete's grandfather Ole, who'd figured an Irish-sounding bar would attract more customers than a Norwegian one.

Pete stopped drying glasses and took the holiday photo card from Josh. "She used to hang out here," he said. "I had a crush on her, but I was only in high school, so she wouldn't give me the time of day. Her name was Deborah, right?"

"Deborah Springer," Josh said. "Was she ever with a man here?"

"She was usually talking to some man," Pete said, returning the card to Josh, then picking a beer glass from beside the sink and drying it. "I think she came here to meet men, since she usually came alone. Most women come with a girlfriend, even if they plan on leaving with a man. But Deborah was always real self-confident. Or maybe she didn't have any girlfriends." He set the glass on the counter behind him, then picked up another.

"Do you remember any specific man she talked to more than others?"

"No, but I didn't work all that often back then. I'll ask Ed. He's been coming here forever." Pete turned his head. "Hey, Ed? Do you remember Deborah Springer? From probably twenty, twenty-five years ago?"

"That her picture?" asked a beefy guy with a gray crew cut and a Budweiser two stools down from Josh, his gaze on the photo card.

Josh handed him the card. "She's the blonde."

Ed looked at it, then handed it back. His fingers were cigarette stained. "Yeah, I remember her."

"Do you remember any specific guy she was with?" Josh asked.

"Can't help you there. I do remember she flirted with every guy in here. Came on to me a few times, even though I was married."

"That don't matter to a lot of guys," Pete said. "But Ed's never stepped out on Ruthann. Right, Ed?"

"Damn straight." Ed's gravelly chuckle held a hint of resignation. "She'd boot my ass from here to Denver if I did."

On a hunch, Josh pulled out another photo, one he'd gotten from Laura. "How about him? Was he ever a customer?"

Ed took the photo and frowned. "Speaking of guys who ignore their wedding vows. Dan Langford came here for years, up until he killed himself driving drunk. I think this was one of the few places he hadn't gotten kicked out of. He must have been around when Deborah was."

Pete leaned over the counter and looked at the photo Ed held. "His daughter looks a lot like him, except her hair's blonde, not brown. Abby Langford, the actress who just moved back here. Have you heard about her?"

Josh nodded.

"That's right, she has some crazy guy after her, so of course she called the police," Pete said. "She was a few years behind me in school and always real friendly. I felt sorry for her, having such a shit for a dad. Her mom wasn't much better."

"Do you remember if Dan Langford was ever with Deborah?" Josh asked.

"I don't remember seeing them together," Ed said, returning the photo to Josh. "But from what I heard, Langford slept with every halfway-decent-looking woman who'd have him, and his being married wouldn't have stopped Deborah. I'd say it was damn near certain he was."

– – –

Abby grabbed the papers spread over the kitchen counter and stuffed them into an Erickson's bag, then headed for the family room. Much as she hated it, she was going to have to add cleaning to her to-do list. Real cleaning, not the kind she was doing now, stuffing things into a grocery bag she planned to hide at the back of a closet. She could get a cleaning service, but she felt guilty doing that when she wasn't working long hours at a paying job anymore.

Abby added a Minnesota guidebook, a stress-relief squeeze ball, and a Pilates DVD case to the bag, then retrieved three playing cards sticking halfway out from beneath one of the recliners. She didn't own a deck of cards, so she assumed these were from a former occupant and had fallen out of the recliner. At least he hadn't left another knife.

She examined the yellowed cards. A queen of spades, a two of hearts, and a ten of diamonds. Maybe that combination meant something.

She snorted, tossing the cards into the bag. Yeah, it meant the owner of the deck would have a heck of a time winning at solitaire. That dream was getting to her.

"We must be having company," Maddie said, waltzing into the family room from the kitchen. "Otherwise you'd never be cleaning."

"You're right. Josh is coming for dinner tonight."

"Do you want me to go over to Rachel's? Or Laura's?"

Abby removed a T-shirt she'd draped over the treadmill and carried it to the basement door between the family room and kitchen. "Why would I want that?" She opened the door and tossed the T-shirt to the left of the basement stairs, into the general vicinity of the washing machine.

"Mom, I'm not a little kid," Maddie said. "I know you like Josh more than just because he's Rachel's uncle."

Abby's fingers tightened around the grocery bag handle as she returned to the family room. "Is that a problem?" she asked, her eyes on Maddie's face.

Maddie shook her head, her swinging braids adding emphasis. "I think it's cool. If you marry him, then Rachel and I will be related."

Abby's taut muscles relaxed. "I'm not planning on marrying anyone."

"You should marry Josh so he can have kids."

Marriage and kids—Maddie definitely wasn't upset. Abby smiled faintly. "Don't you think I'm a little old to have another kid?"

"Lindsay Perkins's mom did because she got a new husband, and she's way older than you." Maddie tilted her head. "Josh really wants kids, you know. That's why he got a divorce, because his wife didn't want to have kids. And because she had an affair like Daddy did."

Maddie's last three words slammed Abby's stomach like well-aimed punches, and she grabbed the back of one of the recliners. "Why do you think that?" she got out, her eyes on Maddie's face.

"Rachel told me about Josh. I heard you talking on the phone to Laura about Daddy once before we moved here, when you didn't know I was there." Maddie shrugged. "Lots of people have affairs. Especially actors."

A half nod was all Abby could manage.

"But not you," Maddie said. "Because that would be like lying, and you don't lie, right?"

"Right." Abby nodded again.

Maddie tilted her head, her expression considering. "I don't think Josh would ever have an affair, either. He's not the type."

"What do you know about types?"

Maddie raised an eyebrow. "I watch TV, you know." Then she headed back into the kitchen.

Abby's stomach relaxed, and she let go of the recliner. Laura and Olivia had both been absolutely right. News of her dad's infidelity wasn't anywhere near as devastating to Maddie as the same news had been to Abby. Of course, Maddie had learned about it after she'd adapted to her parents' divorce, but it was more than that. Maddie had been raised in a world where happy, intact families were more the exception than the rule and where divorce and infidelity were so common they might warrant a little gossip but not the pity and condemnation Abby had encountered growing up in Harrington.

She dug last week's *TV Guide* out from between the seat and arm of the recliner. Although as a *Heavenly Days* fan, Maddie would probably still have a tough time if her dad's fling with his TV daughter became common knowledge.

Maddie was right about something, too—Josh was far too honest and decent to ever have an affair. Abby raised her eyes to the peeling ceiling as she cruised toward the living room. *Thank you, God.* She wasn't destined to end up on some afternoon talk show focusing on smart, successful women who continually fall for lying scums just like their fathers.

– – –

When Josh got back to his office, the report on the stain on Abby's floor was on his desk. He skimmed it, read it closer, then leaned back in his chair, thinking. After a moment, he flipped through his old Rolodex until he found the number of a psychiatrist he'd worked with on several cases in Chicago. Surprisingly, Jeremy was in his office and available.

After a brief conversation, Josh hung up the phone and glanced at his watch. Twenty after five. He'd better leave now if he intended to shower and shave and still get to Abby's by six.

Although he wasn't at all certain she'd be happy to see him once he told her what he'd learned. He had a feeling he knew why she was having those disturbing dreams, and she wasn't going to like it.

CHAPTER 21

"I'll go up to my room for a while," Maddie said after she'd greeted Josh. "In case you want to kiss or something."

"She's figured out we're not just friends because of Rachel," Abby said as Maddie raced upstairs.

Josh's forehead creased. "Is it a problem?"

"She thinks it's cool." Abby wasn't about to mention Maddie's other supportive comments.

Josh wrapped his arms around her. "Good. Much as I'd like to do the 'or something' part, I guess I'll have to be satisfied kissing you." He kissed her thoroughly, then released her and picked up his briefcase. "I need to talk to you before Maddie comes back down. Let's go into the living room."

His sudden seriousness had Abby's stomach churning like a whirlpool on overdrive by the time they were both seated on the couch. "What did you find out?" she asked.

Josh pulled a manila envelope from his briefcase. "First, you're not psychic."

"I'm not?" Of all the things Abby had expected him to say, that hadn't even made the list.

"I suppose you still might be, but it's unlikely the murder you're imagining actually happened in your house."

"Because the stain on the floor was a different blood type than the stuff on the knife?"

"Because the stain on the floor was paint."

Abby's spinning stomach screeched to a stop. "Paint?" Although she'd considered it a possibility at first, discovering that the victim and murderer were both strangers had convinced her she was seeing a real murder, no matter what she'd claimed. But if it wasn't even blood—

"That doesn't mean your dream is simply a product of your imagination." Josh removed a card from the envelope, a photo of several people with SEASON'S GREETINGS in silver script over their heads. He pointed to the woman just left of center. "Do you recognize her?"

Abby took the photo. The blood left her head, pooling in a stomach that had resumed spinning. "She's the woman in my dream. How did you find her?"

"In the department's old missing persons' reports. She worked as a secretary at the Ken Parks Insurance Agency when you were in seventh grade. When she didn't show up for work, the agency reported her missing. They withdrew the report a couple of days later after she sent a note explaining she'd broken up with her boyfriend and had impulsively moved to Minneapolis to get away."

Abby let out a relieved breath. "She's still alive? Thank God."

"Actually, I haven't found any evidence she is. I also haven't found anything proving she isn't."

"What about her boyfriend?"

Josh set the manila envelope on the cushion beside him. "No one knows who he was. Deborah liked men, but never mentioned anyone special until after she left town. That made my contact suspect he was married."

Josh turned toward Abby and rested his hands on her shoulders. "Is it possible you saw her with your dad?"

Abby studied the photo again, chewing her bottom lip. "I really don't remember ever seeing her before my dream. And why would I imagine some man killing her if..."

She stopped, feeling as if she'd belly flopped into a wintry Lake Superior. "You think I might have seen my dad kill her and blocked it out." She forced out the unwelcome words. "I'm remembering the crime, but setting it somewhere else and replacing the murderer with someone else. Some imaginary man who coincidentally is wearing my dad's favorite T-shirt. And has hair the exact same color as my dad's, I just realized."

Josh kneaded her stiff shoulders. "I called a psychiatrist friend in Chicago who said that's a possible explanation for your dream, given your other repressed memories about your parents. Finding an unrelated knife could have made you finally start remembering, but you're having trouble facing it because the memory's even more painful than your others. Although you should check with your own therapist."

Abby closed her eyes for a moment, the glacier filling her chest making it hard to breathe. She didn't want to think about this, let alone seriously consider it. But she was done blocking things out. She opened her eyes. "I don't need to check with Teresa." Her voice trembled. "I called her about my dream the afternoon after you took a sample from the floor. She agreed it was probably the product of stress and my imagination. But she said if I discovered I was dreaming about real people, I might be psychic, which I'm not. Or it might be a repressed memory that somehow involved my parents."

She cleared her throat. "Your explanation about it being harder for me to remember this particular thing my dad did makes sense. I could have set the murder here because that's where I found the knife, but I think it's more likely I set it in my current home because I saw him kill her in the trailer that was my home back then. I remember walking in on him with women there a couple of times when my mom was at work, although I don't remember Deborah or a murder. We had a fake wood floor in all of the rooms except the bathroom."

"Like the wood in your dream?"

"Darker, but that isn't why I mentioned it. What I meant was that the floor was some kind of plastic-feeling material or something that you could spill anything on and it would never stain, so my dad wouldn't have had trouble cleaning up the blood."

Pain was stabbing her forehead, like a brain freeze that wouldn't subside. She tried to massage it away with her fingertips. "God, I knew he was a son of a bitch, but I didn't think he was capable of murder."

Josh moved his hands from her shoulders and gripped her forearms. "We don't know he was. Even if he did kill her, it was probably a heat of passion thing. Your father apparently had quite a temper, especially when he was drinking."

"You obviously ran into him during your record check. And into my mother, I'd imagine." Abby smiled bitterly. "Hell of a gene pool I got, didn't I?"

He squeezed her forearms. "It makes what you've made of yourself all the more impressive."

"With Bill and Mary's help." She was silent for a moment. "You know, they might remember if I had any connection with Deborah, something I've forgotten. Or even whether Deborah and my dad had an affair, something they didn't bother mentioning to you since Deborah's long gone from Harrington." Her lips twisted. "Eleanor Blake would be even more likely to know, but she'd also want to know why I care and then tell everyone who'll listen."

"I'll check with the Tates tomorrow," Josh said, taking the card from Abby and returning it to the envelope.

"Can we do it tonight, after dinner?" Abby asked. "Mary and Bill are eating at Laura's."

"They probably won't know anything about Deborah," Josh said.

"But they might, and I want to get it over with."

Even if they didn't know anything, talking to them might help her recall something she'd blocked out, either because what they mentioned triggered the memory or simply because being with people who loved her would give her the courage to remember. Because the more times she had the dream, the more she felt like it was something she'd really seen happen. If she wasn't psychic then it made sense that it had involved her dad. Much as Abby didn't want to find out her dad was a murderer, she needed to know.

– – –

After dousing Maddie with bug spray, Laura sent her outside to play with the kids and dog in the backyard. Then she led Josh and Abby into the family room, where her husband and parents were watching a baseball game on a large flat-screen TV.

"Abby told Laura you wanted to ask us about someone," Mary said. "Who?"

Josh removed Deborah's photo from the manila envelope. "Do you know the blonde woman in this picture?"

Laura squinted at the photo. "I'm sure I've never seen her before. Who is she?"

"Her name is Deborah Springer, and she worked for the Ken Parks Allstate Insurance Agency more than twenty years ago, when they were in the Canton Building." Josh walked over and held the photo out to Mary, who was seated in a deep blue chair to the left of the matching couch.

"We've always gotten our insurance from State Farm," Mary said, "although I've been on a couple of committees with Ken. I honestly don't ever remember seeing her." She raised her eyes to Josh. "Why are you asking about her?"

"Because she's the victim in my dream," Abby admitted.

"You saw the victim's face?" Laura asked.

Abby nodded. "And the murderer. I didn't recognize either of them and assumed they weren't real people. Until Josh found her."

Mary handed the photo back to Josh. "Is she dead?"

"That's what I'm trying to find out," Josh said. "All I know for sure is that she left Harrington suddenly, supposedly to move to the Twin Cities."

"When did she leave?" Laura asked.

Josh gave her the date, then handed the photo to Bill.

Bill studied the picture through gray-rimmed reading glasses. "I don't remember her, either."

"Are you sure, Dad?" Laura asked. "You got that look for a second."

Bill shifted his attention from the photo to Laura. "What look?"

"The one that means you know more than you're saying." Laura wrinkled her nose. "You usually got it when I was finishing some lie you were pretending to believe about why I'd gotten home three hours after curfew or a C in biology. Right before you revealed what gave me away."

Bill chuckled. "I think this means my family knows me too well." He examined the photo again, then shook his head, removing his glasses. "Something about her seems familiar, but I can't think of why. It's been more than twenty years, and my memory isn't what it used to be. Probably I just passed her on the street and remember her hair."

"Did you see her with my dad?" Abby's voice was quiet, but Josh could hear the strain in it. "Or hear someone mention she'd been with him?"

"Why would you think that?" Bill asked.

With her ramrod-straight posture and expressionless face, Abby could have been guarding Buckingham Palace. "Because I'm afraid I saw my dad kill her and blocked it out, just like I did all those other bad things about him. Now I'm ready to remember the crime, but I can't face my dad being the murderer so I'm replacing him with some imaginary man."

"But you'd never been in the house before—" Laura began.

"I'm sure your dad was never in that house—" Mary said simultaneously.

Abby interrupted them. "It wouldn't have happened in my house, since as you said, I'd never been inside it until a few months ago. Josh had the stain on the floor analyzed, and it was paint, so I'm not psychic, either. Maybe I saw the murder someplace else, maybe even in our trailer, and transferred it to my new house. My dad apparently spent a lot of time at O'Gara's, and so did this woman."

Although Abby's voice had been steady throughout her explanation, she'd clenched her hands together in front of her and was now wringing them furiously. Josh reached down and took hold of them, stopping her assault.

"If you know something, please tell me," she continued. "I need to know the truth so I can face it and go on. So I'll stop having those awful nightmares."

Bill met Abby's eyes. "I'm sorry, but I don't remember where I saw her."

"Now that we've finished with that, I'll get dessert," Mary said. "Would you two like to join us?"

CHAPTER 22

She'd seen her dad murder Deborah Springer.

Abby sat at the kitchen table the next morning, staring into her steaming coffee mug. She'd spent much of last night too agitated over that possibility to sleep, finally breaking down and taking one of the sleeping pills left over from her divorce. Unfortunately, falling asleep had triggered the dream again. This time the man kneeling over the woman's bloody body had been her dad.

She still couldn't force herself to remember this particular incident when she was awake. But the more she thought about it, the more convinced she was that she'd not only witnessed a murder, but her dad committing it. From what she knew of her dad, if he'd met Deborah at a bar, he'd have tried to seduce her. She also knew her dad had been violent—his bar fights and physical abuse of her mother established that. Maybe the reason she'd felt so compelled to return to Harrington was because her subconscious knew otherwise she'd never face this last, horrible memory—that she was the daughter of a murderer.

A murderer's daughter who'd witnessed the crime and hadn't even tried to save the victim.

A half hour later, Abby was still sitting at the table, staring into her now-cool coffee, when Laura called.

"Get yourself and Maddie dressed," Laura said in the authoritative tone she used when her kids misbehaved. "I'll be there in an hour."

"What are we doing?" Abby asked.

"Bethany is taking the kids swimming, then out for pizza. You and I are spending adult time together. We'll see *Lost Dreams* at eleven, then have lunch at Zelda's Bistro. My treat."

"I really should work."

"You know you're not going to get a bit of writing done today," Laura said. "You'll spend the entire time staring at the monitor and agonizing over whether your dad could actually have hurt that woman. The same thing you've been doing since I saw you last night."

"How did you know that's what I've been doing?"

"Because I've been your best friend for nearly thirty years." Laura's voice was full of warm concern. "You need something to take your mind off it for a while."

"I don't know what's wrong with me," Abby said. "I've always known my dad was horrible, even when I didn't remember all the specifics. Learning one more bad thing about him shouldn't surprise me, let alone upset me."

"Of course it should. You loved him, whether he deserved it or not."

Laura was right. "What makes it worse is knowing I probably witnessed it and didn't do a thing about it," Abby admitted. "I didn't try to help the woman or report it or anything."

"You were only twelve, and it was your dad, for God's sake. You couldn't have done anything to stop him, and if there was that much blood, you couldn't have helped the woman." Laura cleared her throat. "Obsessing about it today won't do you any

251

good. The only thing that will help is a trashy romantic comedy and a large serving of Zelda's Death by Chocolate."

– – –

Josh spent Saturday morning doing yard work at his town house and thinking about Abby. He wanted to call her, but he wouldn't, not yet. She needed time to digest what she'd learned. He'd just finished mowing the lawn when his cell phone rang.

It was Bill Tate. "Mary and I agonized most of last night over whether to tell you this, but we've decided to trust you've got Abby's best interests at heart," he said. "That you don't want her hurt."

"Did you remember something?" Josh walked over and plopped down on the cement back steps.

"Where I'd seen that woman before."

"Where did you see Deborah?" Josh prompted when Bill didn't continue.

"At O'Gara's. It's a bar over on Marshall Avenue."

"I'm familiar with it." Sweat was dripping from Josh's forehead into his eyes. He pulled off his T-shirt and used it to wipe his face.

"I never stopped at bars, wasn't the type," Bill went on. "But I had this client. Walt Simpson—he's dead, so I guess it isn't violating attorney-client privilege to tell you I did his legal work. Not that it was a secret in town, anyway."

Bill sounded flustered. "What does he have to do with Deborah?" Josh asked to get him back on track.

"Nothing. Walt's plant was near O'Gara's, and he asked me to meet him there once. I'm sure the year was the one you're concerned with because I was a state senator and the governor called a special session that year that went on for a couple of months. I was in Saint Paul so much I ended up having a lot of night meetings to fit in all my clients. Otherwise, I avoided working at night, especially when Laura was young. So I went to O'Gara's to meet Walt."

"And?"

"I stepped inside the door, spotted Abby's dad at the bar, and left."

"Why?"

"Dan Langford wasn't too fond of me—I don't know if Abby mentioned it, but he used to hit her," Bill said. "When Laura told us, Mary and I tried to have Abby removed from her home. When that didn't work, I went over to Dan's trailer and told him if he ever touched Abby again, he was going to prison until he was a very old man. He'd never come after me, but I didn't want to risk a confrontation when he'd been drinking."

Josh leaned forward, resting his elbows on his bare thighs just below his gym shorts. "From what I know about him, that was a good call."

"I decided to tell Walt I hadn't been able to make it and went to my car," Bill said. "I'd just started the engine when a woman came out of the bar. I assumed she was walking to her car, so I waited to be sure she made it safely. The parking lot was dark, and that's not the best part of town." He paused, then let out an audible breath. "Instead of going to her car, she stopped by the doorway. A few seconds later Dan Langford came out, kissed her, and they both headed to his car."

"The woman was Deborah?"

"I'm sure she was. The doorway was well lit, and I was parked close enough I got a good look at her face and hair. Of course, that doesn't mean Dan killed her. They looked pretty friendly to me."

"It doesn't," Josh said. But it provided the first concrete connection between them.

"You don't have to mention this to Abby, do you?"

"She made me promise to tell her everything I found out," Josh said.

"All I saw was her dad with this woman, nothing else. Maybe you should make sure there's more to it before you give her more reason to worry."

"I'll think about it," Josh said. "I appreciate you told me."

"Mary's the one who convinced me to do it. I didn't want to risk having you tell Abby, but even if you do, Mary's sure she can handle it. She's probably right, but..." Bill cleared his throat. "Do you have kids?"

"Not yet."

"If you ever do, you'll know how I feel. You want to protect your kids, and Mary and I consider Abby to be our daughter even if she isn't by blood. Use your own judgment about what you tell her. We trust you to do the right thing."

After he'd hung up, Josh sat staring at the petunias beside the steps. Bill trusted him to do the right thing.

Whatever the hell the right thing was.

– – –

When she finally returned home at three thirty, Abby realized that thanks to Laura—who'd talked things through with her over a long lunch—she felt a lot better. Even if her dad was guilty, it must have been a heat of passion thing. He certainly wouldn't have planned to kill someone in his own trailer, especially when there was a chance his daughter would walk in. Laura was also right that she couldn't have expected herself to remember it, not when she'd become so adept at blocking things out by then. Maybe she hadn't even seen it happen, just enough of the aftermath to fill in the blanks.

She'd wasted too many hours moping around, feeling sorry for herself. It was time to take control of herself and her life. She'd give this memory a few more days to come on its own, but if it didn't, she was going to call her therapist and revisit the hypnosis option. Even if her subconscious wasn't ready to face the truth, she had a feeling her conscious self would be going crazy by then.

In the meantime, she'd keep busy with her writing, with Maddie and Josh, and with her house. She'd start by cleaning the kitchen.

Twenty-eight minutes later, Abby surveyed her work, then shook her head. She really couldn't understand the high some people got from an immaculate kitchen, assuming anyone like that actually existed outside of TV commercials. It would just get dirty again. Or maybe part of the problem was that even immaculate, this kitchen was still hideous.

After that much cleaning, she deserved a break. As soon as she emptied the trash, she was going to call Josh and see if he wanted to go with Maddie and her to Ruby's for dinner. Being somewhere filled with good memories and happy people would definitely help her mood.

She tossed some Windex-soaked paper towels into the garbage under the sink, tied and removed the trash bag, and carried it out the back door, heading for the cans behind the garage.

She never made it.

CHAPTER 23

In Chicago, he'd have summoned the bomb squad, but Harrington didn't have one. Not that Josh was convinced the wrapped box the mail carrier had left on Abby's back steps contained a bomb, but it might. With a typed label and no return address, it could have been sent by her stalker, and thanks to the Internet, almost anyone could make a bomb. The postage indicated the package was light enough to have been dropped into a postal box instead of left with a clerk, but some letter bombs weighed far less than the thirteen-ounce limit. And the biggest reason Josh couldn't rule out an explosive device—Abby had informed him that nine years ago on *Private Affairs*, someone had left a similar package in Samantha's car. That package had turned out to contain a bomb.

Josh had spoken with the Minneapolis bomb squad, who'd given him a lot of information, including the cheery news about letter bomb weights. They were more than two hours away, and he didn't want to waste their time and money coming here until he'd checked out the package himself. But all it was getting was a perfunctory examination. If it looked the least bit suspicious up close, he was evacuating the neighborhood, calling in Minneapolis, and getting the hell out of there.

Josh pulled his Prius up beside Ben's squad car, which was parked in Abby's alley. He planned to slip through the bushes beside the garage, which was the most direct route to the back steps, as well as the path least likely to attract her neighbors' attention.

"Everything's in the trunk," Ben said, getting out of the squad car. "I'll check the package. The chief shouldn't be doing that."

"I'm checking it." Josh appreciated Ben's offer, but to his mind, the chief was the precise person who should be taking a risk like this, no matter what official protocol might dictate. "Thanks for bringing the gear. I'll use it, even though my gut says it's nothing dangerous."

"Better safe than sorry, my mom always said."

Ben's words prompted a faint smile, despite Josh's concern that in this instance his gut could end up splattered with the rest of his body over Abby's back steps. That proverb must be printed in some official motherhood manual. "Keep an eye out for anyone in the vicinity," he said. "And don't use your cell phone. I think any radio remote to detonate a bomb would be on a different frequency, but I'm not betting my life on it."

Once all the gear was in Abby's backyard, Josh donned a fire-resistant suit that was marginally better than nothing; since the department didn't have a trained bomb squad, it also didn't have a bomb suit. Just as well—between today's heat and humidity, even this lighter, looser suit instantaneously turned him into a steam iron. Josh wiped his exposed forehead with his hand, then put on the hood and goggles.

He was not looking forward to this. His gut might not think this was a bomb, but from the way his heart was hammering, his brain disagreed. At the moment, Josh truly wished he'd never dropped out of law school.

He put on his gloves, picked up the portable X-ray machine the Masters Clinic had donated to the department, then started toward Abby's steps. He seemed to remember the guys in the bomb squad—the maniacs who defused things by choice—called this the long walk, heading by yourself to an explosive device. This walk was less than fifty feet, but it seemed damn long to him. And hot. Eighty-five humid degrees plus this suit were bad enough, but his jackhammering heart must have shot his body temperature up even higher.

Josh reached the peeling forest-green staircase and set the X-ray machine on the grass so he could examine the package. It was on the top step where Abby had found it, shirt box size, wrapped in brown paper, and secured with masking tape. Nothing overtly suspicious—no oil stains, protruding wires, or leaking white powder. The address label had been printed on a computer and taped onto the package with four more strips of masking tape.

Josh moved his ear toward the box, but his pounding heart made it impossible to hear anything other than the blood throbbing in his ears. He took a few heavy, moist breaths and focused on relaxing. When his heart had slowed enough that the throbs stayed in his chest, Josh leaned toward the box again, this time cupping his hand around his ear. He couldn't hear anything, no ticking, occasional click, or other mechanical sound. Of course, it could still be an explosive device, one triggered by a silent timer or radioactivated by someone secretly watching.

Rivulets of moisture flowed from Josh's sweating forehead, around the sides of his goggles, and down onto his chin. He wiped the drops off with his sleeve, then turned his head and sniffed the box, being careful not to touch it. It smelled like an empty grocery bag, with no worrisome odor of gasoline or gunpowder.

Josh picked up the X-ray machine. All he had to do now was position the damn thing so it would show the contents without accidentally brushing it against the package and possibly setting off an explosion. According to Minneapolis, that the package had been tossed around by the postal service without incident before it had ended up on the steps didn't necessarily mean it was safe to move or even touch now. The X-ray machine was heavy, clumsy, and Josh had never been near it before today, but otherwise, this was a piece of cake.

He really should have become a lawyer.

– – –

Maddie was watching TV in the police station break room while Abby paced back and forth in the reception area, her arms crossed, nodding and pretending to listen to Gina, a plump, grandmotherly woman with improbably red hair who worked as the weekend receptionist. The room felt freezing, the way places got on days so warm the air-conditioning never kicked off.

When she'd spotted the package, Abby had immediately thought of Samantha's bomb. So she'd run the trash back into the house, grabbed her cell phone, and hauled Maddie out the front door and around the corner and through the alley to the garage, avoiding the backyard. Then she'd driven to the police station, calling 911 on the way.

According to Gina, Josh was checking things out before deciding whether to call in the Minneapolis bomb squad, which made this whole situation even scarier. It probably wasn't a bomb, she told herself, hugging herself even tighter. She was overreacting because on *Private Affairs* suspicious packages always ended up being something way bad. She had to keep remembering real life wasn't like TV.

In real life, bombs really killed people.

She kept pacing.

– – –

Josh moved the X-ray machine into position. His consultant had said it was unlikely—but not impossible—that turning on the machine would trigger the bomb. He really hadn't needed to hear that. Holding his breath, he flipped on the machine.

A click, then a low whir. Once he was positive the only sound was coming from the machine, he carefully moved it so he could see inside the box.

He squinted, studying the image for a moment. Then he expelled a long, relieved breath.

"It's not a bomb," Josh yelled to Ben, stripping off his goggles and hood. "Bring me an evidence kit." Sweat streamed from his hair onto his face. He wiped it with his sleeve again.

As Ben approached, Josh carefully unwrapped the brown paper, exposing a generic collapsible shirt box. He handed Ben the wrapping, then lifted the cover off the box.

The single sheet of white paper inside the box contained ten words:

LEAVE OR THIS WILL BE YOU. FROM YOUR BIGGEST FAN

Josh picked up the paper by one corner and looked underneath.

– – –

Abby grabbed the phone from Gina. "Josh?"

"It was just another threat," he said.

Abby rested her free hand on Gina's desk for support. Josh wasn't hurt, and she could handle threats. "Tell me what it said."

He recited the short message.

"What was with it? What will be me?"

"A dead mouse, caught in a trap."

Abby closed her eyes and doubled over, bile filling her throat.

"Abby, are you OK?" Josh asked after a moment. "I know the mouse makes the warning more graphic, but it was still only a warning. Not anything that would have hurt you. It didn't even stink because it was inside one of those odor barrier baggies that campers use."

She forced her eyelids open and swallowed hard, trying to get rid of the burning in her stomach, the acid in her mouth. "I'm fine. I just have a problem with mice." Her self-deprecating laugh sounded tinny. "Actually, I'm terrified of them, although I have no idea why. My therapist thinks it's one of those irrational fears. Before I moved in, I had an exterminator go through my house twice to make sure it was mouse-proof."

"Who knows about that fear?"

"Several articles have reported it over the years. I get dozens of mice from fans every birthday, cute stuffed ones or Mickey and Minnie figures."

"Where's Maddie?" Josh asked.

"In the break room watching TV. Gina put us in there, along with the best chocolate chip cookies I've ever tasted." Abby managed to give Gina a small smile. "She's promised to trade the recipe for an autographed picture of Patrick Dane. Can I come home now?"

"A unit will be outside in a few minutes to follow you home," Josh said. "I'll wait for you here. We can order pizza for dinner tonight, then I'm spending the night. On the couch, since Maddie will be here. And don't bother arguing."

"I wasn't planning on it," Abby said.

"I'll have Ben take the note and mousetrap away before you get here, in case you don't want to tell Maddie everything."

"I don't want Laura, Bill, or Mary to know, either," Abby said. "They're already worried enough about me."

"They strike me as the type of people who'd want to know everything that's going on so they can help, or at least offer moral support," Josh said. "But it's up to you. I'll make sure no one in my office breathes a word to anyone. Now let me talk to Gina."

After Abby handed Gina the phone, she walked over to the coffeepot, filled a Styrofoam cup, and took a sip. The coffee was as bitter and overheated as she'd expected, but she needed something to get the awful taste out of her mouth. The taste of terror.

She now knew for sure her letter writer hadn't gotten his hatred out of his system. And he'd left a dead mouse.

Samantha Cartwright didn't give a damn about mice, had never encountered a mouse on the show as far as Abby could remember, and she would have remembered. Abby Langford was the one with the mouse phobia.

The stalker hadn't come after her because she'd played Samantha, and he wasn't going to leave her alone now that Samantha was dead.

The stalker hated her.

CHAPTER 24

Lightning flashed in the black sky outside the picture window. A perfect metaphor for the way Abby felt—dark depression, interrupted by an occasional slash of pain.

Maddie was asleep upstairs, and Abby and Josh were sitting on the living room couch. They'd raised the venetian blinds so they could watch the storm, but Josh had insisted on moving the couch perpendicular to the picture window so she would be out of sight.

"Did you learn anything more about Deborah Springer?" Abby hadn't wanted to ask while Maddie was around. So far Maddie didn't have a clue about her dreams—assuming she hadn't overheard another telephone conversation—and Abby intended to keep it that way.

Josh was silent for a moment. "Bill called this afternoon," he finally said. "He apparently was meeting a client at O'Gara's years ago. When he walked into the bar, he spotted your dad, so he left. Before he drove off, he saw your dad come out with a woman he's sure was Deborah. Your dad kissed her, then they headed to his car."

Abby hugged her knees, resting her heels on the couch. She took a long breath that made her lungs feel raw. "I had a feeling Bill knew something he didn't want to tell me. Laura was right about the look he got."

"Bill didn't want me to tell you about it, but I said I'd promised to."

"I need to know."

"That doesn't mean your dad killed her."

Abby nodded, her eyes fixed on the bare wall directly in front of her. "I dreamed he did. Last night he was in my dream, instead of the other man. But that doesn't mean anything, either."

She moved out from under Josh's arm and walked over to the window. She stood off to one side, where she could safely watch the streaks of lightning, followed by low rumbles of thunder. Weather as turbulent as her life had become.

"I moved to Minnesota because I thought it would be good for Maddie," she said, her words edged with pain. "Instead of harmless reporters, I've got a stalker. I can't pretend he's upset with Samantha, not after today. He hates me, presumably because of the lies the tabloids printed about my affairs. That's what he was talking about in his call, that he thinks my cheating and divorce hurt my daughter."

She folded her arms, then leaned her shoulder and head against the wall beside the window, staring at the sky. "I'm not only endangering my daughter, but I'm worrying the people I care about. Maybe I should move back to California after all."

Josh came up behind her and rested his hands on her shoulders. "You don't want to move back, do you?"

"I don't know what I want anymore, besides for all of this to go away." She pressed her arms into her midriff, trying to squeeze out the burning there. "I feel like I'm on the verge of falling apart. I'll probably end up in a psych ward, rocking, humming, and watching reruns of *Green Acres* and the *Beverly Hillbillies*."

Josh massaged her shoulders. "If you were going to fall apart, you already would have," he said, his voice as firm as his kneading fingers. "You also can't be sure returning to California would solve your problems. This guy could decide to follow you to California. Or another crazy fan could pop up there."

"And there are more crazy people in California than in Minnesota."

"If only because there are more people in California," Josh said. "You wouldn't have had such a compulsion to move to Harrington unless you subconsciously knew you were strong enough to face all your memories and move on. It goes along with why you wanted to live in this house, to prove to everyone and yourself you've overcome your past and are different from your parents. Like you told Kim."

She'd told Kim that the night Josh had brought them to introduce Maddie to Rachel. Abby grabbed his hands, removed them from her shoulders, and turned to face him. "You heard me say that? I thought you were ignoring me."

"I was having a lot of trouble ignoring you, since I thought you were the hottest woman I'd ever seen," he said, a touch of humor in his voice. "Which pissed the hell out of me, since I also didn't think I liked you much." He kissed her forehead. "One of my bigger mistakes."

She stroked his sandpaper cheek. "That's OK. Back then I didn't think I liked you much, either." Her hand fell. "I'm sorry you got stuck in the middle of everything that's going on with me now."

He gave her a slow smile, one that even in her current emotional state made her stomach flip. "That's what I get for wanting those notches on my bedpost."

− − −

Josh had planned to stay for brunch on Sunday, but ended up being called into work to supervise yet another fatal car accident. Abby had told him not to bother coming back because she needed to spend most of Sunday writing and with Maddie. She did plan to do that. But the primary reason she'd wanted him gone was so she could think about what she'd been fixated on since she'd awakened at five this morning.

Maybe she should move back to California after all.

When she'd mentioned that possibility last night, the idea had been the product of stress and desperation, not anything she was honestly considering. Much as she hated running away, though, sometimes it was the only way, like when she'd left Harrington for California to escape her parents and her fear she'd turn into them. This time she'd be leaving to keep her daughter safe, both from a stalker and from living with a mother on the edge of a breakdown, constantly afraid she was about to be attacked either physically or by the horrifying memory of her father murdering his lover.

She could move somewhere else, of course, but in California Maddie would be back with her old friends and occasionally get to see her dad. Abby also could go back to her show, which was important. She had a feeling she'd once again need acting to distract her from how miserable she was. Because by moving, she'd also end up losing the only man she'd ever truly loved.

Abby's eyes filled, that reality stomping on her heart. She'd been so anxious for a happy family that she'd fooled herself about Colin and her feelings for him, something she'd figured out long before his affairs had shown just how foolish she'd been. She wasn't fooling herself about Josh or about how she felt about him. Josh didn't just play a good man on TV; he was a good man. Being with him made her happier than she could ever remember being with Colin.

Abby carried her mug to the coffeepot on the counter, refilled it, and took a sip, the liquid burning her aching chest. If she left Harrington, any chance of a relationship with Josh was over. Her move to California would be for good, or at least until Maddie went to college. She wouldn't uproot her again, not when they were leaving Minnesota for their safety as opposed to because of Colin's blackmail. Josh wouldn't move anywhere for her, not when he didn't love her or even want anything serious, and their relationship was too new for a long-distance one to work. If she said good-bye to Harrington, she'd be saying good-bye forever to Josh. She didn't have a choice, though. For Maddie's sake, she had to return to California.

But damn it, it wasn't fair!

Abby kicked the cupboard with her bare foot, frustrated, agitated, and depressed. Why did she have to leave now, when she'd finally met the man she'd swear she'd been looking for her entire life? She kicked the cupboard again, even harder, but partially missed her target. Pain shot from the three smallest toes, the ones that had connected with wood. Her mug thumped down on the gold-flecked counter.

Jesus, now she'd probably broken her toe. She hobbled to the refrigerator on one foot and one heel, the initial cracking pain now a worse throbbing pain. She needed to ice it. She opened the freezer and pulled out one ice cube tray, then the other tray, then swore. Both were empty because Maddie was forever taking a few cubes at a time and never refilling the empty tray with water. The only other thing in the freezer was the last frozen Dove bar. She grabbed it, then sat down on the floor, crossing her legs so her foot was slightly elevated. Her little toe and the one beside it were already turning purple, and each throb felt like a stab with a hot needle. She stuck the Dove bar over them.

All she wanted was one good relationship with one decent man and a chance at a happy family. Was that too much to ask? Clearly it was. And fate wasn't satisfied just keeping her from finding true love. No, it had to torture her more by letting her find it, then deciding this show would play better as a tragedy. It was as if the prince had finally found Cinderella and they were about to head to the palace. Then a lawyer arrived and informed Cinderella that glass slipper or not, she contractually couldn't leave her wicked stepmother and sisters in the lurch and had to go back to sweeping cinders.

The Dove bar wrapper was muffling the cold, so Abby unwrapped it and stuck the chocolate coating directly on her toes. Of course, she wasn't Cinderella, not by a long shot. She wasn't sweet enough and hated mice, for two things. And even if she found a glass slipper, it probably wouldn't fit with a swollen broken toe. She couldn't get happily-ever-after because she wasn't a fairy-tale princess. She was a thirtysomething woman sitting on gold linoleum in a kitchen that belonged in Disco Barbie's Dreamhouse, holding a Dove bar on toes she'd broken kicking a cupboard like a cranky two-year-old.

"Mommy, what's the matter?" Maddie asked, walking into the kitchen.

Abby suddenly realized she was crying. She wiped away her tears with the back of her hand. "I ran into the counter and broke my toe, I think. And somebody used up all the ice cubes."

Maddie looked stricken. "Sorry."

Abby forced out a wan smile. "I'll bet you are, since you're not going to get to eat this last Dove bar." She moved the Dove bar and checked her toe. Chocolate meshed with the purplish red that had engulfed two swollen toes and was spreading along the top of her foot. Lovely.

"Do you want me to get you some Tylenol from upstairs?" Maddie asked.

"I'd appreciate it."

She couldn't let her feelings for Josh keep her from doing the right thing, Abby thought as she watched Maddie race out of the kitchen. If something happened to Maddie because she'd been selfish, she'd never forgive herself. Never.

She was moving back to California.

– – –

On Monday morning, Abby looked at the clock, then threw off the duvet and got out of bed. Almost eight, which was six o'clock California time and too early for *Private Affairs*'s head producer to be at the studio. She'd call Susan in a couple of hours to discuss coming back, then call her former agent to work out a deal. She and Maddie needed to leave as soon as possible, preferably tomorrow. Right after she talked to Susan, she'd tell Maddie about it and have her start packing.

Tonight she'd tell Josh. She had to have everything in place first because even if he didn't try to talk her out of leaving, seeing him would make her consider it. And she had to leave.

Abby yawned. She was skipping the treadmill this morning—she hadn't fallen asleep until after four and was exhausted. She probably shouldn't run with a freshly broken toe anyway. A broken toe, a broken heart, a broken life. A little melodramatic maybe, but that's how she felt.

She went down to the kitchen and started coffee, then retrieved the *Harrington Herald* from the front porch, dropped it onto the kitchen table, and headed for the coffeepot. She'd finished filling a mug when her phone rang.

"Are you OK?" Laura asked. "I was worried when you didn't call me back yesterday, but I figured you were with Josh."

"Actually I spent the day with Maddie. I needed to think some things through." Abby sat down by the kitchen table, then took a deep breath and let it out. Saying the words would make it real and help her get used to it. "I'm moving back to—oh my God."

The air went out of her lungs and she dropped her mug, spilling coffee over the newspaper.

"What's wrong?" Laura asked.

"Do you know a man named Ron Murphy?"

"He did yard work for nearly everyone on our block back when I was a kid," Laura said. "I saw in today's paper that he was killed driving drunk at Red Bluff. I was worried you'd see the article, and it would trigger another memory of your parents. Did it?"

"I just now saw the article." Abby couldn't look away from the paper. "There's a photo of him."

"So?"

"He's the man in my dream."

CHAPTER 25

"The murderer in your dream was Ron Murphy?" Josh asked. "Are you sure?"

Abby looked again at the coffee-stained newspaper on the table in front of her, although she didn't need to—the black-and-white photo had been etched into her brain. "He looks younger in my dream, but I'm positive it's him. His picture's on the front page of the *Herald*, along with a story about him being killed in a car accident."

"That's why I had to leave yesterday, because some kids discovered the car and his body. He'd been dead a couple of days. Did you know him?"

"He did yard work for everyone on Bill and Mary's block back when Laura and I were in junior high." Abby had called Mary to check the dates.

"You saw him back then, which is why he looks younger," Josh said.

"The problem is I swear I never saw him back then," Abby said. "Mary said I probably wouldn't have because she remembered he always worked weekday mornings on their block. I was either in school or working at Ruby's then."

"I assume you haven't seen him since you moved back," Josh said.

Abby shook her head, confusion furrowing her forehead. "I know I haven't. He also died driving drunk at Red Bluff. That's the same place my parents were killed." It was freaky enough that he was in her dream, but the last part made it even worse. "Why would I dream about someone I've never met who happened to die the same way my parents did?"

Josh didn't answer. "I don't know," he said after a long moment. "I've got to go. I've got a meeting with the mayor. I'll call you back when I'm done."

"You don't have to bother, not when you're so busy," Abby said. "I'll see you tonight."

"Right," he said. "Try not to worry."

Abby flipped off the phone and set it on the table. Josh had sounded anxious to get off the phone, maybe because he did have a meeting or maybe because he'd spent too much time on her dream already. Or maybe he was tired of her and her neuroses. No matter how nice he'd been about it, he couldn't be happy being caught up in a personal crisis with a woman he was casually dating. She'd bet Saturday night's pity party had triggered the urge to stay far away from her, even before she'd called today and given him evidence she could be psychic, a medium, a pathological liar, or outright nuts. He'd no doubt be relieved she was leaving.

But she was going to take Josh's advice and try not to worry, not about him or about why her dream starred a recently deceased man who'd died in the same place and manner as her parents had. She needed to stay upbeat today. Abby folded the newspaper and deposited it in the recycling bin in the closet, then went to the bottom of the spiral staircase. "Maddie, it's time to get up," she yelled. "We're making pancakes."

– – –

Josh grabbed his briefcase and keys and headed for his car. Usually he'd walk the four blocks to the mayor's office, but today he was driving, and not just because he was already late. It was because he had a theory about why Ron had shown up in Abby's dream. Namely, that Ron and Dan Langford had been drinking buddies, and Abby had seen them together, even though she didn't consciously remember. That's why she was using Ron as a stand-in for her dad in her dream. That both Ron and her dad had died at Red Bluff was simply a coincidence—last night the coroner had told him that had been the site of six fatal car accidents in the past twenty years, all involving too much alcohol.

The bad news was that his theory provided more evidence Abby had seen her dad kill Deborah. That's why he wasn't going to mention it until he'd checked it out, which he planned to do the instant he could escape the mayor.

It was after eleven thirty when Josh finally got to O'Gara's. Since Dan Langford had frequented the place, maybe someone there would know about his relationship with Ron. At the very least, Josh hoped someone could point him to other bars he could check.

Pete was tending bar and talking to Ed. Two other men Josh didn't recognize were at a back table, but the place was otherwise deserted. "I've got another photo for you to look at," Josh told Pete, handing him the picture of Ron Murphy from the paper. "Did he ever come in here?"

Pete glanced at the picture and nodded. "Ron Murphy's been coming here off and on for longer than I've been working here. He wasn't here the night he died, if that's why you're asking. I was relieved to realize that because I always worry about dramshop issues. We try to be careful, but sometimes it's hard to tell with heavy drinkers like Ron."

"Was Ron a friend of Dan Langford's?" Josh asked, retrieving the picture.

"I don't remember ever seeing them together," Pete said.

"I doubt Ron and Dan were buddies since they didn't have much in common," Ed said. "Dan's hobby was hooking up with women. Ron hated women."

"How do you know that?" Josh asked.

"He never had nothing to do with them, for one thing," Ed said, waving his beer bottle. "Never even had a date, far as I know. And a couple of times when he was drunker than usual he started going on and on about how women seduce men and take advantage of them and break up their marriages."

Pete snorted. "Like the men don't have anything to do with it."

"Was Ron divorced?" Josh asked.

"Never married." Ed set down his bottle. "I think Ron's issues were because of his mom. He said she was a slut and cheated so much that his dad divorced her. Ron got stuck living with her, and she moved him from Minnesota to Mississippi. He hated it there, even ended up in prison, which is why he never got to be a navy SEAL the way he'd always wanted." Ed's lips twisted wryly. "To be honest, I couldn't picture Ron as a SEAL, but he claimed he would have been if his mother hadn't ruined his life."

"Do you know why he was in prison?" Josh had no idea if that was relevant to Abby's dream, but it paid to be thorough.

"He never said, and I never asked," Ed said. "Didn't figure it was any of my business."

"I never heard about that," Pete said.

"He only mentioned the prison thing one time to me." Ed took a long swig of beer, then tapped his bottle on the bar. "You know, Chief, I don't think he was a friend of Dan's, might not have even known him other than to look at. But he knew that other person you asked about before. Deborah."

Josh blinked. "Ron and Deborah were friends?"

"I don't think they were exactly friends," Ed said. "I'm not sure how he knew her since I never saw them together, not here or anywhere else. One night I asked everyone if they knew what had happened to her since she'd stopped coming in." He grinned, showing a gold tooth. "Not that I'd ever have anything to do with her, but we don't get enough eye candy around here. Ron said he'd heard she'd left town. He said it was good riddance because she was as big a slut as his mother had been, then he left. Didn't even finish his drink. I thought maybe Ron had a thing for Deborah, and she'd turned him down."

– – –

When Josh got back to his office, he checked Ron's criminal record. He only had a single conviction, in Mississippi when he was seventeen, although he'd been tried as an adult. He'd served seven years of a ten-year sentence for manslaughter, for killing one of his mother's boyfriends. He'd claimed it was self-defense, but the jury hadn't bought it.

Probably because he'd stabbed his victim a dozen times.

Josh told himself to slow down. He couldn't get too excited. The idea percolating in his brain could easily be so far off base it had landed in a neighboring stadium. This was real life, not some novel where two seemingly unrelated issues ended up connected after all, leading to a satisfying conclusion.

He dug through the piles on his desktop until he located the report on Ron's accident. He skimmed it, then picked up the phone and called First State Bank.

He was transferred to Ellen Carlson, the head of Human Resources. "Ron worked here as a custodian for eleven years this September," she said after Josh told her what he wanted. "His hours were four to midnight, Monday to Friday."

"Did he work an earlier shift anytime during the last two weeks?"

"No, just his regular shift," she said after a moment.

Josh gave Ellen the date of the *Private Affairs* event, which had been on a Tuesday. "Was he working then?"

"He should have been," the woman said. "Actually, he called in sick that day."

Josh's pulse accelerated. "He didn't work the Sunday before then, either, right?"

"He didn't," she said.

Yes. "Thanks for checking," Josh said, making notes.

"No problem," Ellen said. "Is he suspected of a crime?"

"Would that surprise you?" Something in her voice made Josh ask that, despite his eagerness to end the call and check out something else.

"I don't know anything illegal he might have done," Ellen said. "The only complaints we got were from some of the female custodians who said he was condescending and ordered them around, that he didn't seem to like or respect women much. But no harassment or anything like that." She paused. "Although there was that other thing."

"What other thing?" Josh asked.

"I probably shouldn't mention it since we couldn't prove it. Though with him being dead..."

"I won't publicize it," Josh said. "What did he do?"

"A few years ago we got some anonymous notes about one of our accountants, a woman just a few years out of college. The notes said she was having an affair with a man who also worked in our building, though not for us. She wasn't married, but the man was and also had a couple of little kids. We ignored the first notes, but after the third one we thought we'd better talk to her. That last one claimed she'd been hooking up with her boyfriend in her office after hours, which is against company policy. So we talked to her, and she admitted the affair. She also told us that her boyfriend was getting a divorce, and they were both moving to Omaha, that she already had another job lined up."

"What's that got to do with Ron?" Josh asked.

"I'm getting to that," Ellen said. "The notes were kind of nasty, said she was going to rot in hell for breaking up a marriage and hurting the guy's kids, called her a slut and whore and said she was evil, stuff like that. We strongly suspected the notes came from Ron."

Josh's hand tightened around his pen. "Why do you think that?"

"He was the one who cleaned the offices on the woman's floor and would have most likely been the one to see her and her boyfriend together. The notes had typos and also were slipped under my door sometime after I left for the day, which means they were probably from someone who worked nights and wasn't a secretary, which narrowed it down. And like I said, we already knew Ron didn't seem to like women."

"What did you do about it?"

"We talked to our lawyer, who pointed out we couldn't prove it was Ron, especially since the notes were all typed," Ellen said. "A few days after we confronted the woman, she sent an e-mail to everyone in the office announcing she was leaving, and we never got another note about her or anyone else. So we didn't do anything."

"Have you had any contact with the woman since she moved?"

"Just to send her last paycheck," Ellen said. "But my friend's husband was a friend of her boyfriend's, and they exchange Christmas cards. She told me they got married and last year had a little girl."

So it wasn't at all like Deborah's exit from Harrington. "Do you still have the notes?" Josh asked.

"I assume our lawyers do," Ellen said. "Are they important?"

"Possibly," Josh said.

After he'd gotten the lawyer's name and phone number, Josh sat for a moment, thinking. Maybe he was jumping to conclusions because he was too close to this situation, wanted to resolve it too much. He picked up the phone and called Ben.

"I haven't had any luck tracking down who bought the special baggies the mouse was in," Ben said as he walked into Josh's office. Fortunately he'd been at the station when Josh had called. "REI in the Cities sells them and checked their mail orders, but didn't find any customers from Harrington. They also sell them in their stores, but—"

"I think I've identified Abby's stalker," Josh said, interrupting him.

"Who?"

"Ron Murphy. The drunk driving victim."

Ben sat down in one of the chairs facing Josh's desk. "What makes you think that?"

"Several reasons." Josh looked down at his notes. "Ron worked the four to midnight shift as a janitor at the First State Bank building. He was off the night of the lipstick incident, called in sick the day of the shooting, and hadn't clocked in yet when Abby got her threatening call, so he had opportunity. He also drove a white Buick, and Abby said her shooter drove a light-colored American car."

"So do millions of other people," Ben said. "What about the mouse? That package was postmarked Friday, and the coroner said Ron died Thursday night sometime after he got off work."

"He must have left it in a mailbox Thursday after the day's last pickup," Josh said. "Ron also fits a stalker profile—a loner who had problems with women. First State Bank's Human Resources department head fielded several complaints from his female co-workers over the years. A few years ago his employer suspected he sent letters similar to the ones Abby got." Josh filled him in on the letters.

"Those earlier letters weren't threats or even sent to the woman," Ben pointed out. "They were sent to her boss."

"True," Josh said. "It also was never proven that Ron sent them. But a drinking buddy at O'Gara's confirmed that Ron especially hated women who cheated the way the tabloids claim Abby did." Josh doubted that had been Ron's actual motive, but he needed to give Ben something. "Ron also was convicted of manslaughter. It was years ago, but it shows he was prone to violence." With a knife, although Josh couldn't point out the significance of that to Ben without disclosing Abby's dream.

"He's certainly not the only guy like that in Harrington," Ben said, his gray eyes narrowing. "What turned you on to him in the first place?"

Ben's inquiring mind and willingness to challenge his boss were a couple of things Josh appreciated about him. However, he wasn't about to admit the truth. "A woman called about him. She hadn't realized the importance of what she'd seen until she spotted his picture in today's paper."

"What did she see?"

"Nothing that would hold up in court," he hedged. "My gut tells me it's worth checking out Ron's place for anything linking him to Abby. Am I onto something or confusing heartburn with inspiration?"

Ben thought for a moment. "It's not as if we have to worry about a defense attorney screaming illegal search," he said, getting to his feet. "Should I drive, or do you want to?"

– – –

Ron Murphy's apartment was in a three-story brick building that appeared to have been built in the forties and last maintained in the sixties. A single window air conditioner blasted in a first-floor window. Most of the other windows were wide open, a couple holding whirring fans.

The manager, a stereotype named Stan with a straggly gray ponytail, a beer gut beneath his Harley T-shirt, and enough tattoos to qualify as an art exhibit, met them at the door.

"Ron Murphy lived here for nine years," he said in answer to Josh's question as he led them through a shabby but clean entryway, then up a flight of creaky wooden stairs. "Kept to himself, never fighting or having loud parties or wild women like some of the guys here. Hell, he never had any kind of woman here, far as I know."

"Have you been inside the apartment since he died?" Josh asked.

"I went in yesterday after the cops told me he'd been found dead. I wanted to make sure everything was locked up and unplugged, and I threw out any food that might spoil. I also took out the kitchen trash—in this heat, it was already starting to stink."

"Has it been hauled away?" Josh asked.

"Garbage pickup was this morning. What, you think old Ron might have hidden something valuable in the trash?" Stan chuckled, the sound a cross between a wheeze and rattle. "He was a strange one, but I doubt that."

Stan stopped in front of unit 31, then unlocked and opened the battered door. "I'll leave you here. Guess I can trust you since you're cops." He repeated that asthmatic chuckle. "Although lots of places you couldn't say that. Stop by my apartment when you're finished so I can lock up."

Josh stepped into the stifling apartment and looked around. The living room's stained beige carpet had come loose in several spots and the oatmeal-colored walls were peeling, revealing several spots of the puke-green the room had previously been painted. The only furnishings were a lumpy multicolored sofa as stained as the carpet, a floor lamp minus the shade, a TV on a wire stand, and a coffee table holding an overflowing ashtray and an empty Budweiser can. The kitchen and bathroom were to the left, the bedroom straight ahead.

Josh wiped the back of his hand over his sweaty forehead, then grabbed a pair of gloves from the evidence kit. His heart was pounding, his nerves as edgy as if he were about to interview his prime murder suspect. He hadn't realized before he'd gotten here just how much he was counting on his convoluted theory panning out.

"We're looking for anything connecting Ron to the stalking or letters," he said, keeping his tone level despite his apprehension. "A gun or a draft of a letter to Abby would be nice, but we're more likely to find something less obvious, like a receipt evidencing he was in Minneapolis that day or a few articles about Abby. Check everywhere, behind furniture, under cushions, in the wastebaskets. Everywhere."

"Too bad Stan threw out the kitchen trash," Ben said, slipping on gloves.

"If he hadn't, we might have needed gas masks to come in here," Josh said. Even without rotting food, the place stank of dirty socks, sweat, and stale cigarette smoke. "Check out the kitchen. I'll do the bedroom."

Ron's bedroom walls were bare—no taped-up photos of Abby, although Josh hadn't expected any. Things were never that easy in real life. After glancing beneath the bed, he checked under the mattress, pillow, and bedding, then rummaged through the dresser drawers. The bottom drawer held T-shirts sporting a variety of logos, although no Vikings shirt. He removed each drawer and examined every inch of exposed plywood, pulled the dresser from the wall so he could look behind it, and finally used a flashlight to search underneath. Nothing.

The bedroom closet was small, simplifying inspection. Unfortunately, Josh didn't find a smoking gun or even circumstantial evidence stuck in the pockets of the four hanging shirts, stashed in the pile of dirty underwear and socks, or hidden inside the Nikes or boots.

He let out a breath, exhaling his disappointment. He'd thought the bedroom would be the most logical place to find evidence. He lay down on his stomach on the scratched wood floor and scooted as far under the bed as he could, managing to get his head and both arms under the bed. He moved his flashlight around. All he could see were dust bunnies that appeared to have been multiplying for years.

"Chief?"

Josh started, bashing his head on the metal bed frame, then slid out from under it. Ben was standing in the doorway, his smug expression triggering a surge of adrenaline that revved Josh's pulse. "You found something?"

"It was behind the empty kitchen trash can," Ben said. "Ron must have intended to throw it out, but we lucked out and he missed." He held out a black tube of lipstick. "Lancôme Hot Nights."

CHAPTER 26

Abby grabbed the kitchen phone, not bothering to check caller ID. The only call she was expecting was from the *Private Affairs* head producer. "You finished early," she said, setting the water bottle on the counter. When Abby had called, she'd been informed that Susan would be in meetings until three, and it was just before two California time.

"Here I was going to apologize for taking so long to get back to you."

"Josh?"

"Who did you think it was?" he asked.

"Nothing important," she said. That was a lie, but she wanted to tell him about California in person.

"Well, my call is important," he said. "We've identified your stalker."

Abby gripped the counter with her free hand.

"Did you hear me? We've identified your stalker."

"I heard you." Abby closed her eyes for a moment. "Thank God. Who is it?"

"Ron Murphy."

The blood drained from her head, leaving a whirling dizziness. She doubled over to keep from fainting, gripping the counter with her free hand. "The man in my dreams? Are you sure?"

She was dreaming about a man she'd never seen in her life who just happened to be stalking her?

"I'm sure," Josh said. "After you told me he was in your dream, I checked him out. Several things about him fit, so we searched his apartment. Ron lived alone and apparently never had female company, but Ben found a tube of lipstick under the kitchen sink, just behind the trash can. Lancôme Hot Nights."

"That's what was used on my mirror," Abby said, slowly straightening up. The rush of blood when she'd bent over had started her head throbbing, but at least she didn't feel like passing out anymore.

"We also found a gun in his coat closet," Josh said. "A Glock automatic, with six shots fired. I've sent it to the crime lab in Saint Paul, and I'm hoping they'll have an easy time confirming the bullets we found in your fender and on the highway came from that gun. When we searched Ron's car, we found a receipt from a Burger King in Minneapolis, issued the day of the *Private Affairs* event at the Mall of America. Plus we also found a folder under the front seat with several magazine articles about your cheating and divorce and the *Harrington Herald* articles about the lipstick message and the shooting."

Abby walked over to the table and plopped down on a glittery chair. Why would she be dreaming about her stalker?

"The bottom line is we're convinced Ron Murphy was the person who shot at you and was responsible for all the threats against you," Josh said when she didn't respond. "And he isn't a threat to you anymore."

Josh's message finally penetrated the fog engulfing Abby's brain. So what if she'd dreamed about her stalker? She was losing track of the most important thing—*he was dead, and he couldn't hurt Maddie or her anymore. She and Maddie were safe.*

The throbbing in her head was replaced by a warm glow that spread through her entire body. Now she knew how Dorothy felt waking up and, after a moment's confusion, realizing she was back in her own bed and surrounded by farmhands, not a tin man and a scarecrow.

"Why did he hate me so much?" Abby asked.

"The official story is because the tabloids claimed you cheated on your husband until he divorced you, and then you moved your daughter away from her home," Josh said. "Ron's mom did that, and for a number of reasons, he thought it ruined his life. It's possible that actually was his motive. But I think it's more likely he wanted you gone because you saw him do something to Deborah, something you blocked out. He was afraid you were going to remember it now that you're back in Harrington. That's why you've been having those dreams."

Abby's forehead creased. "What did he do?" She really couldn't remember him.

"I don't know, but I do know he hated Deborah. He was also violent, stabbed one of his mom's boyfriends to death when he was seventeen."

The creases in her forehead deepened. "Why did he leave me alone back when he did whatever he did? He couldn't have known I'd make myself forget."

"Maybe he didn't dare do anything to you because of your connection to the Tates, or maybe he tried and failed," Josh said. "He might not have even been sure you'd seen him, and when you didn't report the incident, he felt safe that you hadn't. Until he read about your planned move to Harrington and that you'd been recalling painful memories you'd repressed. Kim said a recent article mentioned that."

"The May fourteenth issue of *Soap Opera Digest*." Abby nodded, her forehead relaxing. "The memory thing slipped out when

I was talking about moving back to face my past. I've always been up front about my lousy childhood, so I didn't see any reason to ask Sarah to keep it confidential." Another memory prompted a grimace. "Although the next week it showed up in the *Enquirer* as part of a story about how I was on the verge of a nervous breakdown."

"Reading one of those articles made Ron worry," Josh said. "Once you were here, he sent threatening letters and did other things hoping to at least scare you back to California and maybe even kill you. He was desperate to do it before you remembered what he'd done and also realized he was a real person living in Harrington."

That made sense. So not only was her stalker dead, she had a logical reason for dreaming about him.

Abby abruptly realized something else. "If he was the murderer, then he wasn't a stand-in for my dad in my dreams. From what Bill said, my dad probably had an affair with that woman, but he wasn't the person I saw kill her. I blocked out this memory because it was so horrible to remember, even though it didn't involve my parents."

"That's my conclusion."

Her dad wasn't a murderer. She'd not only returned to Kansas, she got to keep the ruby slippers as a souvenir.

"You still haven't remembered it all since it didn't happen in your upstairs bedroom," Josh continued. "It's possible the incident wasn't a murder or didn't even involve a knife, since those parts of your dream could be wrong, too. The particular knife you found obviously wasn't involved in what you witnessed, it just triggered your memories of the incident."

"Did Ron ever work at a school?" Abby asked.

"He was a convicted felon, so I doubt it. Why?"

"Because I got agitated when I visited my old school. I wasn't sure why, but maybe I saw Ron do whatever he did there and was trying to remember."

"That Ron didn't work there doesn't mean he wasn't there," Josh said. "Maybe Deborah was there for some reason and he met her. I'll look into it. What's the name of the school?"

"I can't believe you thought to check into Ron Murphy just because he was in my dreams," Abby said after she gave Josh the information.

He snorted. "I should have considered from the start that your dream might be related to the stalker instead of coming up with my theory about your dad. I never even asked if you'd told the press about your recovered memories, and I must have missed those articles."

"It made sense that the stalker was related to my career considering all the other hate mail I've gotten," she said, trying to assuage his apparent—and to her mind undeserved—self-condemnation. "It was equally logical the dream involved my dad, since I've only blocked out memories of my parents."

"If I'd had a police artist compose a picture of the murderer in your dream, I probably could have identified Ron sooner and saved you a lot of worry."

"Nothing changes that you pursued a hunch that led you to my stalker. I can't tell you how grateful I am for that." Abby cleared her throat and adopted what her director had christened Samantha's CEO-bitch tone. "So no more recriminations. We're spending tonight celebrating. If you want to kick yourself some more, wait until tomorrow, preferably when I'm not around."

Josh chuckled. "It's a deal. This is definitely worth celebrating. Although we should keep it quiet until we're ready to have it announced in the *Herald*. Except for telling Maddie, Laura, and the Tates, of course."

"Is that all right?" Abby said. "I don't want to screw up official police procedure, but I hate for them to worry longer than necessary."

"Go ahead. I'd also better tell Kim, or she'll have my ass." He lowered his voice to a seductive rumble. "But tonight's celebration is for just the two of us. I'll get the champagne."

"Let me do that. When do you want me?"

"Five minutes ago, but unfortunately I've got a pile of paperwork to finish first," he said. "Come over at seven."

"I'm looking forward to it."

"So am I. What do you need?"

Abby heard the murmur of voices, then Josh came back on the phone. "Sorry, but I've got to go. Tiffany informs me the mayor's waiting on line two."

Abby grinned. "At least for once he's not calling about me."

She hung up the phone, then hugged herself. She couldn't stop smiling, couldn't believe how terrific she felt. The kitchen seemed brighter, as if the sun had upped its wattage while she'd been talking on the phone, making the glittery kitchen set sparkle like a golden version of Dorothy's slippers. Her dad wasn't a murderer, her stalker was dead, and she didn't have to move back to California. She could stay here with her family. And with Josh, who she'd be seeing tonight.

Abby called Laura, who promised to relay the information to her parents, and Kim, who by then had talked to Josh and was more than happy to take Maddie now instead of later that afternoon. Abby told her guard the news and sent him back to Minneapolis.

Then she sat down to write a to-do list for a goal she was determined to achieve—convincing Josh he was ready for another serious relationship. The last time she'd been this resolute was back in high school, when her goal had been to get out of Harrington. And although she'd never use Samantha Cartwright as a role model, Samantha had definitely taught her a few more things about determination—and men. Abby's lips curved. Josh wouldn't know what hit him.

Item one was calling Bridget at *Private Affairs* and asking her to send out the black underwear Samantha had worn in the scene with Evan, the stuff Josh had liked so much. Then she was going shopping.

– – –

Josh stuck cartons of Chinese food into the refrigerator and headed upstairs. He really would cook for Abby sometime, but not tonight. Tonight he wanted to spend every second focused on her. He couldn't believe how much he connected with someone so different from him, how well she understood him.

That was because deep down, she wasn't that different at all. She'd just lived a different sort of life, and he was damn lucky to have her in his now.

He grabbed his shaver from the bathroom counter and flipped it on. He was also damn lucky he'd finally identified her stalker. And he definitely had—right before he'd left the station, he'd gotten a call confirming the bullets were from Ron Murphy's gun. Even if he blamed himself for not having figured things out sooner and considered Abby's gratitude misplaced, he wasn't above taking advantage of it. He grinned at his reflection in the mirror. He was looking forward to tonight's celebration.

He'd just finished dressing when the doorbell rang. He glanced at his watch. A quarter after six. When he'd finished sooner than expected at work, he'd been tempted to call Abby and ask her to come early, but he hadn't wanted to seem too anxious. She must be as impatient for tonight as he was. He ran downstairs, smoothing his damp hair with his fingers.

Heather was standing on his front steps, dressed in a short black skirt and turquoise T-shirt with a low V-neck. "Josh, we need to talk."

"It'll have to be some other time," he said. "I'm busy tonight."

"We need to talk now," she said, then breezed by him and into the house. "We've got a problem, Josh. I'm pregnant."

CHAPTER 27

Abby was ready by six fifteen, wearing a navy cotton tank dress and jacket. Underneath were the lacy red bra and matching panties she'd rushed out and bought that afternoon at the Victoria's Secret at Spring Place Mall, which actually didn't look half bad considering she was way too close to forty. Besides, Josh didn't care that she wasn't perfect. Shallow, insecure men like Colin cared about those things; she'd been right when she'd told Josh that. She'd just been wrong about Josh, thank God.

She got a mineral water from the harvest-gold refrigerator, took it into the family room, and sat down in the recliner that still reclined. After putting up the footrest, she turned on the TV. The local news was on three channels, but she didn't really care about any of the fishing stories they were all reporting, even though she now resided in a state with more than ten thousand lakes. She was actually—heaven forbid—channel surfing when her cell phone rang. She grabbed it off the coffee table.

"Abby? This is Colin. We need to talk."

Her stomach plummeted into the murky cold at the bottom of the deepest of those ten thousand lakes. Colin had finally used his brain for something other than memorizing lines and realized she'd never have hired a private investigator. Josh was convinced the stalker was Ron Murphy, but she wasn't positive what he had would satisfy a court.

Abby nonetheless forced herself to speak with brisk confidence. "I think we've talked quite enough, Colin. We have an agreement."

Colin laughed. "God, I've always loved your high-and-mighty act."

He sounded amiable, not like he was about to threaten her, but you never knew with Colin. "What do you want?" she asked.

"To thank you."

She leaned back in the recliner, her death grip on the phone loosening slightly. "For not publishing the pictures? I didn't do that for you, Colin."

"No, for your part in getting me the biggest contract of my career. Four years, more money than you can imagine."

Abby's eyebrows rose. "*Heavenly Days* gave you a four-year contract?"

"Just inked it. You wouldn't believe the good press I've gotten for being willing to forgive and forget for my daughter's sake. Everyone's convinced I'm as big a saint as that damn Pastor Jim. The producers begged me to sign on the dotted line."

"Congratulations," Abby said dryly. Colin truly was the king of PR.

"You're going to be portrayed as a bitch, since I told everyone you aren't coming back to me because you've already got a new boyfriend in Harrington," Colin said. "I hope you don't mind."

"I don't." It was a small price to pay. "But Josh might."

"Is that the police chief's name? Don't worry, I didn't identify him. Considering he's a cop and older than you, my publicist thought it would make you look less reprehensible."

Abby rolled her eyes. "Thanks for the warning. I'll brace myself for calls from the tabloids."

"You don't need to answer them. I told everyone you probably wouldn't, since you considered them bloodsucking vultures and had left California primarily to escape them."

"Just in case they weren't entirely convinced I was the villain in this story."

"It's what you deserve for hiring a PI, Abby darling." Colin sniffed. "Really."

"I assume this means you plan on leaving me alone."

"We made a deal," Colin said. "Besides, I owe you big-time. You and Bill."

"Bill who?"

"Bill Tate. Who do you think told me about the stalker?"

Abby lowered the footrest with a thud. She couldn't have heard Colin right. "Bill told you?"

"I wasn't supposed to tell you, but I think I've had a little too much champagne," Colin said. "Bill thought I'd be worried enough that we'd get back together. Like that would ever happen. But his call was a gift from God. I told David about it, and we cooked up the whole 'forgive for my daughter's sake and safety' crap to rev up my fans."

"You said you found out about the stalker from the *Enquirer*," she said, now pacing in front of the recliner.

"I lied. Actually, I told the *Enquirer* about it."

"I can't believe Bill did that." The calmness of Abby's voice surprised her nearly as much as that the receiver hadn't cracked in her grip.

"Calm down, Abby," Colin said—obviously she didn't sound as calm as she thought. "He wanted you to leave Harrington and go back where stalkers don't have your home address. He said it was for your own good."

"My own good."

In the background, she heard a female voice, then a giggle. "I've got to go, Abby. Give Maddie my love."

The instant Colin hung up, Abby called Bill's office. His voice mail answered, so she left a message. Then she resumed pacing, this time marching back and forth between the window and recliner, her arms and the phone swinging madly.

Bill was lucky he hadn't answered since she wasn't just hurt, she was furious. No matter how worried he was about her, how could he have wanted her to get back together with a man who'd cheated on her over and over again? How could he possibly have thought she deserved that?

After a moment, she stopped her ferocious pacing. It was only making her more agitated and her broken toe hurt. She needed to do something to calm herself down, something like talk to Josh. He'd understand why she was so upset about Bill's betrayal and wouldn't mind if she showed up a little early.

She stuck her phone in her jacket pocket, grabbed the champagne and her purse, and headed for the garage.

– – –

Josh stared at Heather, momentarily speechless. "Are you sure?" he finally got out.

"Of course I'm sure," she said, walking toward the living room.

Josh shut the door and followed her. Jesus, he hadn't felt like this since he was seventeen and stupid and Katie Martin had been ten days late. As if he'd taken a sucker punch to the gut, and now the walls were closing in on him.

But he wasn't seventeen and stupid. Josh stopped just inside the living room, crossing his arms and regarding Heather suspiciously. "How could this happen? We were always careful. Hell, we were more than careful. You were on the Pill, and I've always used a condom."

"I guess when it's meant to be, that doesn't matter." Heather wrinkled her pert nose. "Besides, I quit the Pill—it was making me fat. I almost had to buy size two at Gap."

OK, so the condom had lived up to its less-than-perfect success rate. Josh cleared his throat, trying to dislodge the lump clogging it. "I assume you want to take care of it. Will your insurance cover it?"

Heather's forehead furrowed. "Take care of it?"

"Have an abortion. Like your sister did last month." Something Heather had mentioned as casually as if Tanya had simply gotten rid of an ingrown toenail.

Heather's eyes widened. "Kill your baby? I could never do that. I love it." She pressed her hand protectively over her flat stomach. "I'm happy to be having this baby because it's yours. Aren't you excited?"

"Excited." That wasn't one of the emotions Josh was experiencing.

"I know how much you've wanted a baby, and now we'll have one," Heather said, patting her stomach. "I'll bet it's a boy, and he'll be just like you. If it isn't, maybe our next one will be."

"Our next one?"

"We can have as many as you want." Heather started dancing around the room. "I love kids as much as you do, and I'm young. Although I won't let myself get fat like some women do. I'll make sure I always look good even if we decide to have a dozen kids."

"A dozen?" Josh choked out.

Heather giggled and plopped down on the black leather couch. "I don't really want a dozen. Not unless you do. I'm just so happy." She hugged herself. "To know I have your baby inside me, to know we'll be together for the rest of our lives."

Josh slowly approached the couch. "Look, I think we've got a slight misunderstanding." He sat down, taking care to stay a couple of feet from Heather. "I'll pay child support and be involved in the child's life if DNA testing proves it's mine."

"Of course he's yours. I'd never cheat on you. And you'll have a lot of involvement in his life." She scooted beside him and took his arm, her fingers like a handcuff. "You'll be his daddy, after all."

That unwelcome reality was making it hard for Josh to think straight. He forced himself to focus. "Do you have health insurance?"

"Through work." She wrinkled her nose again. "I guess we won't be able to have a big wedding, since we should get married right away. People will talk about how we had to get married, but that won't matter, will it? Once they see how happy we are, they'll stop talking."

Josh extricated his arm from her grip. "I'm not marrying you."

"Of course you are. You're the kind of man who'll do the right thing." Heather rested her hand on her stomach and smiled wistfully. "The right thing for our baby."

"You think getting married out of necessity is the right thing?"

"It's not out of necessity. It's because we love our baby and each other."

"I don't love you, Heather," Josh said firmly. "And I'm not marrying you."

She tilted her head, confusion clouding her eyes and wrinkling her smooth forehead. "But you've always wanted to have a baby, and now you are. That's why you divorced Jennifer, because she wouldn't have your baby."

Josh's eyes narrowed. "Who told you that?"

"Tiffany overheard you say something to your sister when she didn't realize you were using the phone."

Tiffany was getting a lecture about eavesdropping. He doubted her phone light indicating his line was in use had conveniently malfunctioned during that particular conversation with Kim.

"That's not exactly why I divorced Jennifer," Josh said, getting to his feet. "I did divorce her, and after making one mistake in the marriage department, I'm not making another by marrying you. That wouldn't be fair to either of us."

Heather's full lower lip quivered. "You'd let your child grow up as a bastard? Without a name or two parents who love him?"

"If he's mine, you can give him my name if you want," Josh said, holding out his hands, palms up. "He'll have two parents, but they're not going to be living together."

She got to her feet and wrapped both hands around his arm. "You love kids. And this one will be yours. Not one of your nieces and nephews, but yours." Her voice was shaking, her dark eyes glistening.

Steeling himself against his instinctive inclination to comfort a distraught female, Josh dislodged his arm. "It doesn't mean I'm going to marry you."

"Is this because of Abby Langford?" Heather asked, every hint of emotion gone. She flipped her hair over one shoulder and pushed out her bust in a familiar gesture he'd found a turn-on what seemed like years ago. "She's going to leave here, you know, and she'll leave you, too. Pretty soon she'll want to go back to acting and her fancy life in California. She'll never have your baby. She's already got a daughter, and she's probably too old to have another one, anyway."

"This isn't because of Abby," Josh said. "It's because you and I aren't right together, the same reason we broke up." He hooked his thumbs over his jeans pockets. "The last thing I want is to raise a child in an unhappy marriage. If you're sure you want to have the baby, I'll pay whatever your insurance doesn't cover until it's born. If it turns out to be my baby, I'll pay child support. But I'm not marrying you."

Heather planted her hands on her hips. "People will think you're horrible to desert me. You'll probably lose your job, since no one wants a police chief who'd do something like that."

Josh struggled to hold on to his temper, which always flared instantaneously at any threat. This was a serious situation, and Heather was understandably agitated. "I doubt people will see it that way," he said, managing to keep his voice level. "If they do, I'll go back to my old job in Chicago, where they don't give a damn what I do in my personal life, as long as it's legal."

Heather spun around and stormed toward the door.

Josh raked his fingers through his still damp hair. Jesus, what a fuckarama. He wanted kids, but not like this, not with a woman he didn't love, a woman so immature he wasn't even sure he trusted her to take care of a baby. To be fair, Heather might settle down and be a terrific mother, but he'd need to stay in close contact with her to make sure.

Why the hell had she gone off the Pill? He raked his hair again. Although he'd trusted condoms alone in other cases and thought he was safe, despite knowing statistically it wasn't guaranteed. Surprise. Those damn statistics were about to mess up his life.

And his relationship with Abby.

Josh's hand dropped from his disheveled hair. He hadn't even known Abby when this had happened, but would she be willing to put up with the knowledge his child—and his child's mother—were going to play a big part in his life? She could very well end things immediately, especially since Heather's presence would be an irritating reminder of the older-man–much-younger-woman scenario that had destroyed her marriage. Maybe she'd even think he should try being married to Heather for their child's sake. She'd spent years trying to make her marriage work for Maddie's sake, after all.

He closed his eyes, the choking claustrophobia returning.

– – –

By the time Abby reached Josh's house, she was much less upset. Bill loved her, and he must have thought he'd had a good reason for calling Colin. She shouldn't have left such a hysterical message on his machine. Never act in emotion—unless you're in front of a camera, of course. She'd put her phone on vibrate so she could ignore it, then wait to call Bill back until some time with Josh had calmed her down enough to discuss it rationally. Heck, after time with Josh, she'd probably have forgotten why she'd called Bill in the first place.

She was smiling when she pulled up to the curb.

– – –

"I'm not sure you've thought this through," Heather said, turning and walking back toward Josh. She'd opened the door, and he'd assumed she was leaving, but with the naive optimism of youth, she'd clearly decided to try again.

"I've definitely thought it through."

She stopped directly in front of him, looking at him from under her long lashes. "I think you've forgotten how good we were together."

"I haven't forgotten anything—what the hell are you doing?"

She'd yanked her tight T-shirt over her head and dropped it onto the floor.

"I think you've forgotten lots of things." She circled her arms around his neck, hooking her fingers together. "Like how hot you used to get for me." She rubbed her bare breasts against his cotton shirt.

"Heather, stop it." Josh took hold of her arms, trying to remove them without hurting her.

"Because you can't resist me, right?" She kissed his neck.

"Because I—"

Abby walked through the open front door, carrying a champagne bottle.

Josh froze.

The shocked hurt and anger on Abby's face sliced his chest and gut, ending his momentary paralysis. He reached behind his neck and strong-armed Heather's hands apart, then took a step back. "This isn't what it seems."

Abby's face had gone expressionless, her eyes shuttered. "I've heard that one before. I'm sorry I interrupted, but I seem to make a habit of that, along with choosing the wrong man." She glanced at Heather's bare breasts, then back at Josh, a withering look replacing her impassiveness. "Although considering I was expected shortly, you probably take the cake, if you'll excuse the cliché." She spun away.

"Don't leave, Abby. I can explain."

She looked at him over her shoulder. "I've heard that one, too. Go to hell, Josh." Then she strode out of the house.

"Heather, it's time for you to leave," Josh said as Abby raced to her car.

"Now there's no one standing between us." Heather took hold of his arm, shaking her head. "I can't believe the way Abby talked to you, telling you to go to hell. I'd never do that."

He yanked his arm free. "Heather, get out of here." He was nearly yelling.

"But Abby…"

He forced his volume down. "Abby is not the reason I broke up with you. As I've told you, I don't love you." Through the open front door he saw Abby's car take off with a made-for-TV squeal. "Hell, I don't even like you anymore, not after what you just pulled." Since he had no doubt she'd decided to pull it when she'd seen Abby's car drive up.

"You should be happy I proved Abby doesn't trust you. She wouldn't even let you explain. It's a good thing you found that out before you married her."

He turned his gaze from Abby's lingering exhaust to Heather. "What are you talking about?"

"Tiffany heard you talking to Abby about how you were going to have champagne tonight to celebrate getting engaged. You should thank me for helping you see what she's really like before you announced it in the *Herald*."

Tiffany was going to be job hunting tomorrow. Josh grabbed Heather's turquoise T-shirt off the floor and shoved it at her. "I want you out of here. Let me know how soon you can get a DNA test on the baby."

She took her T-shirt and pulled it on. "There's no baby. Which is a good thing, since you're not decent enough to marry me."

No baby. She'd not only staged the last part; she'd faked the entire thing. "Get out of here," Josh said through clenched teeth, barely able to resist shaking her.

"I'd never treat you like Abby just did," Heather said. "Remember that."

Josh slammed the door behind her and locked it, then went into the kitchen for a beer. Heather was right about one thing.

Abby obviously didn't trust him if she wouldn't let him explain. He'd not only listened, but trusted her enough to believe every damn thing she'd told him about her dream and her marriage and her agreement with Colin. But would she give him the same courtesy? No, she'd assumed he was just like Colin, was cheating just like Colin had. If she'd cared about him at all, she'd have stuck around for his explanation.

He pulled a beer from the refrigerator, slammed it down on the counter, then dug in the drawer for an opener. Maybe she'd been using him so he'd find the stalker. Now that he had, she didn't need to be nice to him anymore. When she'd seen Heather, she might have also seen a prime opportunity to break things off with him.

Even if she'd honestly been upset, too damn bad. He opened the bottle with a force that sent the cap clattering across the granite counter. He wasn't wasting any more time on a woman who considered him on the same level as her slimy ex-husband, who didn't care enough to give him the benefit of even ten seconds of doubt. Heather had done him a favor showing him Abby's true feelings.

Of course, Heather had lied about being pregnant to get him to marry her. He took a long swig of beer. Women were definitely not worth the trouble. He carried the beer to the living room, picked up the remote, and switched on ESPN.

CHAPTER 28

Abby had managed to hold off crying until she pulled into her garage, but she'd been making up for it ever since. She'd spent the past half hour curled up on her bed, sobbing and hugging her pillow. Wasn't she ever going to learn? Even though Josh had dated a much younger woman, she'd convinced herself he was different from Colin and didn't prefer them because she'd wanted him to be different. Just like women who keep marrying alcoholics or abusers, ignoring all the signs with each new guy and ending up brokenhearted over and over again.

The doorbell rang. Her stomach clenched, and she dropped the pillow and ran to the open window. The street was empty, dashing her momentary hope she'd see Josh's car.

Of course it wasn't Josh. Josh was too busy with Heather to have even called and canceled their date. At least Colin had thought she was working; he couldn't have known the power would go out at the studio and everyone would be sent home early.

The doorbell rang again. Probably some kid selling or collecting for something. She sank back onto the bed and retrieved the pillow, resting her chin on its edge. She wasn't in the mood to deal with that tonight.

The unwelcome visitor pounded on the door. "Abby? Are you home? Abby?"

Bill. "I'll be down in a minute," Abby yelled, then she hurried into the bathroom. Bill would worry if he knew she was upset, but between eyedrops and a little fresh makeup, she should be able to get away with claiming she had a cold. She picked her jacket off the chair where she'd dropped it and slipped it on to hide the wrinkles in her tank dress. Then she headed downstairs, taking deep breaths and struggling to collect herself. Samantha had gotten married for the ninth time the day after Abby had found Colin in their bed with Tara, and she'd pulled off the happy act on camera. She could do it now.

After a last deep breath, she opened the door. "Sorry. I was lying down. I think I'm getting a cold." She dabbed at her nose with a Kleenex, a prop she'd brought from the bathroom.

"I apologize for waking you." Bill was carrying his briefcase and wearing a suit and tie, although he'd loosened the tie and had the jacket draped over one arm. "Where's Maddie?"

"At Rachel's for the night. Where's your car?"

"Believe it or not, I walked over from my office," he said. "It's such a beautiful evening I thought I'd take the opportunity to fulfill my promise to Mary about getting more exercise. Ever since her heart acted up, she's been worried about mine."

"So she's mentioned," Abby said. "Why are you here?"

"I got your message. You sounded so upset I thought I should talk to you in person. What's wrong?"

She couldn't believe she'd actually forgotten that phone call. Her fist tightened around the Kleenex. "Colin said you told him about the stalker. How could you do that to me?"

"Damn." Bill closed his eyes for a moment. "He promised not to tell you. Can I please come in and explain?"

When she nodded, Bill stepped into the foyer, closing the door behind him. He set his briefcase against the wall. "As you know, Mary and I were worried about your stalker, especially after he shot at you," he said. "In LA, people who threaten you don't know where you live. Much as we love having you living in Harrington, we'd rather have you back in California and safe."

"What does that have to do with Colin?"

"Mary and I thought he should know what was going on. We hoped if he knew you were in danger, he'd realize how much he still loved you and forgive you."

"Forgive me?"

Bill took hold of her shoulders. "You know we've never held your affairs against you, Abby. People make mistakes, but you don't stop loving them. We assumed Colin would realize that, too, and take you back."

Abby's jaw dropped, and she stared at him openmouthed for a moment. "I thought you knew," she said. "I never cheated on Colin, not once. Colin, however, has cheated on me more times than I can count. Including with his oldest TV daughter."

Bill's forehead creased. "You never said a thing about Colin's behavior. Or ever denied any of the rumors about you."

"Colin and I made a deal. He was concerned news of our divorce and his cheating would cost him his job. I agreed to refuse to comment on anything related to men or money. In return, I got full custody of Maddie." She pursed her lips. "The only reason Colin came now was because *Heavenly Days* was considering killing him off. He wanted us to pretend to reconcile, assuming the good publicity would motivate his show to give him a new contract. He threatened to use the stalker as a reason to change our custody arrangement unless I went along with his charade."

"Oh my God, Abby. I had no idea Colin was unfaithful." Bill's features twisted with obvious pain, his hands tightening on her shoulders. "Mary and I thought we were doing you a favor by calling him."

"When I was planning on staying married, I made Laura promise not to tell you about his affairs because I didn't want to upset you," she said. "Once I decided to divorce him, I assumed she told you everything."

"She obviously knew we'd love you anyway and didn't think she needed to break her word," Bill said, releasing her shoulders. "I only wish she had. We didn't believe most of the stories, of course, but we thought you'd cheated at least once and that had led to your divorce." He massaged his temples with his fingers. "Here Mary and I thought we were helping, but instead we caused a disaster. What can I do to fix it?"

"It's been fixed," she said. "Colin managed to manipulate his PR so he got a big contract. I'm going to be the bad guy again, but in return he's agreed to leave us alone permanently."

Bill tilted his head, scrutinizing her face. "You still look upset."

Clearly her happy act wasn't camera ready today. "That's not why." To her embarrassment, hot tears welled up in her eyes, then overflowed onto her cheeks.

"What's the matter, Abby?" Bill asked, wrapping his arms around her.

"I'm so stupid when it comes to men. You'd have thought I'd have learned after Colin, but I did it again." She rested her head on Bill's chest, choking the words out between sobs she couldn't stop.

"Did what again?"

"Fell for a man who cheated on me."

"Josh?"

Abby raised her head. "I caught him with Heather Casey, who he claimed he'd broken up with." She dabbed her eyes with the damp, crumpled Kleenex. "He cheated on me with a much younger woman. Just like Colin."

Bill's blue-gray eyes narrowed. "I'll punch him out."

"Josh or Colin?"

He waved one hand. "Both. Anyone who ever hurt you."

"Don't bother. Neither is worth it." She dabbed at her eyes again.

His expression softened. "Can I at least make you some tea, if that would help? I used to do that for Laura."

Abby managed a teary half smile. "It would help a lot." Even if she'd lost Josh, she still had her family.

"You know, this is the first time you've ever been in my house," she said, drying her face with the soggy Kleenex as they walked into the kitchen.

"Except when Laura and I checked it out and I advised you against buying it."

"And I ignored you. You were right that it needs a lot of work, especially the kitchen." Abby looked around. "Other than a couple of appliances, this room's the same as when Mrs. Henson lived here. Even the kitchen table and gold chairs."

Bill set his briefcase by a chair, then draped his suit coat over the chair back. "I warned you it would be a money pit." His faint smile robbed his words of any malice.

"The mugs are on that shelf," she said, glancing toward it, then quickly away. "Above the champagne bottle." She should have tossed the damn thing—preferably at Josh. "The tea's in the corner."

"Where's your teakettle?"

"Use the microwave. It's easier."

Bill opened one dark-wood cupboard door and pulled out a mug. "Laura always made me use a kettle. She claimed the water tastes bad if you heat it in the microwave."

"That sounds like Laura," Abby said. "I can't tell the difference." He closed the cupboard door and turned back to Abby, holding a mug. "You always were a good kid, Abby." He pursed his lips, his features tightening. "Do you honestly think you'll ever be able to forgive Mary and me?"

"For worrying about me and trying to help? What's to forgive?"

He exhaled audibly. "Like I said, you've always been a good kid."

– – –

"Sorry to bug you, but could you ask Abby if she cares if I take the girls to see *Dreamworld* tonight?" Kim asked. "It's PG-13, and Maddie said that doesn't usually bother her mom, but I thought I should check."

Josh shifted the phone to his left hand so he could raise his beer bottle with his right. "Abby isn't here." He took a long drink.

"It's twenty after seven. When's she coming?"

"Ask her."

"You're my brother, so I'm asking you."

Josh raised the bottle to his lips, but set it back on the end table without taking another sip. Even beer and sports weren't helping tonight. "She was already here. Unfortunately, so was Heather."

"What was Heather doing there?" Kim asked.

"She stopped by to tell me she's pregnant. She isn't, so don't freak out," he quickly added. "But she claimed she was and expected me to marry her. I told her I'd support the kid, but marriage wasn't in the cards. She was trying to convince me otherwise when Abby showed up."

"So?"

He picked at the edge of the bottle label with his fingernails, slumping deeper into the leather couch. "Heather's way of convincing me was to take off her shirt, then grab me. She was topless and kissing my neck when Abby walked in. I told Abby I could explain, but she assumed the worst and left."

"After Colin, what do you expect?" Kim asked.

Her words caused an ache in Josh's chest, one he tried to banish with anger. "Abby knows I'm nothing like him. At least I thought she did and would care enough to listen to my explanation." He pulled off a strip of label and dropped it onto the table. "Obviously I was wrong on both counts."

"God, Josh, give her a break. You weren't in bed, were you?"

"Of course not," he said, scraping loose more of the label edge. "We were in the living room."

"So it wasn't complete déjà vu for Abby."

Josh halted his assault on the label. "What the hell are you talking about?"

"About how Abby came home from work early one afternoon and walked in on Colin and his TV daughter, doing it in their bed. This wasn't her own house or bedroom, but walking in on you and a half-dressed Heather was probably too similar for her to think straight."

"Abby found them in bed?" Josh asked, sitting up. "She just told me she found out about Colin's last affair and decided she couldn't keep forgiving him."

"Because Colin had a woman in their house, even though Maddie and her babysitter were likely to come home at any time. Abby finally realized Colin wasn't going to change, and she couldn't shield Maddie from his indiscretions when he didn't seem to care if she found out."

"How do you know this?"

"Laura told me in confidence," Kim said. "Right after Abby told you the truth about Colin. Laura said that meant Abby must really care about you. She didn't want me to think Abby would treat a man the way the tabloids said she'd treated her husband just because she didn't bother denying their lies."

"Abby never told me she found them in bed." Josh massaged the bridge of his nose with his free hand. "Jesus, I got so mad she didn't trust me I didn't even go after her. I've got to call her."

"She'll hang up on you. At least I would."

"Then I'll go over and apologize." Josh raked his fingers through his hair. "Although she might not open the door, either. What do I tell her to convince her to talk to me?"

"Tell her the truth," Kim said quietly. "That when she assumed you were like Colin, it hurt you so badly you overreacted. Because you're in love with her."

– – –

Bill stuck the mug into the microwave and hit a couple of buttons. "A minute and a half and it'll be ready. The tea's in the corner cupboard, you said?"

"Uh-huh." Abby gripped the edge of the kitchen table, transfixed by Bill's suit coat. But she wasn't seeing the charcoal pinstripe. She was seeing Bill's blue-and-white plaid sport coat, the one Mary had hated, draped over the same chair.

She'd been skipping and twirling her way home from school, too excited to simply walk. She almost hadn't tried out for the play, but her English teacher had convinced her to, and she'd gotten the lead. Her parents wouldn't care, but Bill and Mary would be as proud and happy as if Laura had gotten the part. She'd call Mary the instant she got home, although Laura would probably have already told her. She'd been pretty excited, too.

Mrs. Henson's house looked even more majestic than usual. Someday when she was a famous actress she was going to live in that house. The garden reminded her of a stage, the way it stretched along one side of the house, the colorful flowers glowing in the sunlight like actors under a spotlight. She loved the flowers that bloomed in the fall even more than the ones that filled it during the summer. She should pick a few flowers to celebrate. No one would care—the house had been deserted since Mrs. Henson died, and even though it was only late September, it could snow tomorrow and kill them all, anyway.

Abby walked through the yard and was about to select a bouquet when she spotted Bill's car, parked in back beside the garage. She knew it was his black Cadillac because of the red and white KENNEDY MAGNET SCHOOL bumper sticker. He must be helping Mrs. Henson's family with the house since he was a lawyer and knew Mrs. Henson from church. It would be fun to tell him in person, before Laura spoiled the surprise.

The back door was unlocked. Abby opened it and stepped into the entryway. She could smell the perfume Mary always wore. She must be here, too.

"Are you coming, Bill?" The woman's voice was unfamiliar and came from upstairs. Bill must be meeting with her about the house, maybe trying to sell it to her. She shouldn't bother him now.

As Abby turned to leave the entryway, she spotted Bill in the kitchen. His hair was thick and black; his blue plaid sports coat was draped over a sparkly gold chair beside the kitchen table. He didn't look toward her as he picked something off the counter. A kitchen knife, with a gleaming blade and a wood handle.

"I'll be right there, sweetheart," Bill yelled.

Who was Bill calling sweetheart? Abby stood frozen as she listened to him walk upstairs, then to him and the woman talking, their voices loud but their words unintelligible. Then the woman screamed over and over, horrifying sounds that sent chills down Abby's spine, as if that kitchen knife's blade was scraping down her neck. She dove into the entryway closet, crouching behind the wool coats and rubber boots.

The closet was hot. After only a couple of minutes inside, Abby could barely breathe, her nose itched, and sweat was dripping from her forehead into her eyes and mouth. The screaming had stopped, but she stayed inside as she heard Bill cross the kitchen linoleum, then open the back door. A lawn mower was buzzing now, back behind the house. Bill yelled something and the lawn mower stopped. "You're early," Bill said a moment later.

"I finished my other job, so I thought I'd get an early start here." She didn't recognize the man's voice.

"I have another project for you to do first," Bill said. "Come inside."

Abby heard the door close, then Bill spoke again. "There's a dead woman upstairs. I want you to get rid of the body. And of the bloody knife."

"You killed her?"

"You don't need details. Just get rid of the damn body."

"Why the hell would I want to get involved with a murder?" the man asked.

"Because otherwise I'll swear you're the one who killed her," Bill said.

"I'll tell them you did it." The man was talking louder, faster. "You can't frame me for this."

"You're here, and the family gave you a key to the place so you can check on it. Who do you think the police will believe, a reputable lawyer and state senator or a guy who's killed once before?"

"How do you know about that?"

"I checked you out when Mary wanted to hire you to do our yard work," Bill said. "I had to make sure you weren't a thief."

"It was self-defense."

Bill's laugh sounded harsh, not like him at all. "That's what they all say. The jury didn't agree. But I know you'll be taking a risk doing this, so I'm willing to pay you well for your help."

"Who is she?"

"Her name's Deborah Springer, and she was going to ruin my life."

"I know her," the man said. "She's a slut."

"A slut who won't be missed. I promise," Bill said. "Are you going to do it? Or should I call the police and tell them what I walked in on?"

The man was silent for a moment. "What do you want me to do?"

"Drive around the block a few times while I leave, then pull your car up in back. Put the body in your trunk and dump it somewhere it'll never be found. The painters left a plastic drop cloth in the garage. You can wrap the body in that before you bring it out. The hedge will keep anyone from seeing you from the street."

The man grunted.

"Wipe up as much of the blood as you can, and dump the cloth with the body," Bill said. "Clean the knife and get rid of it, somewhere far away from the body."

Abby's heart was pounding so hard she was surprised no one heard it. This couldn't be real, not the screaming, not the things Bill had said. This was just her imagination. She'd always had a vivid imagination.

Abby waited until she'd heard both men walk out the back and the door close. Then she cautiously opened the closet door a couple of inches, shivering as cooler air bombarded her damp skin. She waited until she heard the familiar hum of Bill's car, then stepped out of the closet. She knew the screams couldn't have been real, but she needed to check to be sure. When she didn't find anything, she'd stop worrying. She ran upstairs.

The woman was all too real, lying on the wood floor of one of the smaller bedrooms. She was a platinum blonde with big hair and big blue eyes that were open even though she wasn't moving. She had big lips, too, and they were red, almost the same color as the blood flowing out of the cuts on her neck and chest and onto her powder-blue bra and bikini panties, the blood pooling on the wood beside her, the blood covering the blade of the kitchen knife.

Abby folded her arms over her stomach and doubled over, retching. Bill had killed this woman. She could see his hand holding the knife, then plunging it into the woman, again and again, each time drawing more and more blood. She hadn't seen him do it, but she'd heard him, and her mind was recreating the scene.

Abby couldn't walk, couldn't breathe, couldn't even close her eyes. All she could do was stand in the doorway, staring at the motionless woman, watching the bloody pool expand on the light wood floor beneath her.

Then she heard it. A sound, footsteps coming up the stairs, footsteps that sounded different from Bill's. A spurt of adrenaline sent her racing across the bedroom and into the closet, pulling the door shut behind her. The door was warped and stayed open a little, enough to see a mirror reflecting the woman and all the blood.

A man Abby didn't know appeared in the mirror. He was about her dad's age, clean-shaven with brown hair hanging over his collar, medium height, and skinny in faded jeans and the same Minnesota Vikings T-shirt as her dad had. The man squatted down and spread a big plastic sheet on the floor, then moved the body out of sight. For a while Abby couldn't see what was happening, could only hear crackling plastic and an occasional thud. Then the man stood up, now with the plastic-wrapped body slung over his shoulder, and walked out of the room.

She'd count to a thousand before she left the closet. Then the man would absolutely be gone.

Abby had reached 861 when she heard him walking up the stairs again, then come into the room. He wiped the blood off the floor, picked up the knife, and left. She'd count to two thousand this time.

At two thousand and one, Abby opened the closet door, then took two steps out and listened. All she could hear was her heartbeat drumming against her eardrums. She tiptoed along the hallway and down the stairs, her Keds soundless on the thick carpet. When she reached the bottom step, she froze. The man was still there, the knife on the floor by his shoe. He was using a screwdriver to fiddle with the board above the opening between the living and family rooms. He pulled one of the sliding doors out way too far into the middle of the opening, then grabbed the knife off the floor. Abby hurried back upstairs and slipped into the closet in the first bedroom. It was full of clothes that smelled like soapy roses. She held her breath, praying the man hadn't heard her.

After what seemed forever, she heard a car start behind the house. She tiptoed to the back bedroom, separated a couple of closed venetian blinds with her fingers, and peered out, watching until a big white car pulled away from behind the house. Then she crept down the stairs and to the back door. The dead bolt wasn't locked, just the night lock, so it was easy to get out.

She peeked around the corner of the house. No one was around, not even any cars in the street. She grabbed a handful of flowers when she passed the garden in case someone asked what she'd been doing. Then she hurried to the sidewalk and made herself think about the play. It was going to be so exciting being on stage in front of the whole school, getting to be Pippi

Longstocking, who'd had all those adventures, having everyone clap for her and tell her what a good job she'd done. Not her parents, of course—they probably wouldn't even come. But Bill and Mary would come. They'd be so excited to hear she'd gotten the lead. She'd call Mary as soon as she got home, although Laura had probably already told her. She needed to start studying her lines. Right after she called Mary.

Abby felt like someone had stabbed that knife into her own gut. She'd witnessed Bill killing a woman, and she'd blocked the whole thing out, just like she'd done with her parents. She'd had a harder time remembering this, though, because she loved Bill and his family more than she'd loved her parents.

"Abby, what's the matter?"

That's why she'd gotten upset at the school, because she'd been looking at that photo of herself as Pippi Longstocking. That's also why she'd obsessed about the knife and bloodstain, why she'd felt compelled to buy this house, probably why she'd needed to move back to Harrington in the first place. She wasn't at all sure she had the acting ability to fool someone who knew her as well as Bill did, wasn't even sure she could speak. She picked up the mug he'd just set on the table in front of her and took a sip before she answered. Maybe the hot beverage would melt the slush that had replaced her blood.

Bill rested his hand on the back of a chair, studying her face as if he were trying to see into her brain. "Did you dream about me, Abby? I was afraid that's why you called me and what had you so upset."

She met his intense eyes without blinking. "I don't think I've ever dreamed about you."

"You might, if you haven't already," Bill said. "I've never believed in psychics, but Mary does and she's a smart woman. So when I heard about your dream, I read up on them. I'm afraid they might exist. Sensitive as you've always been, you just might be one."

Abby took a sip of tea, then lowered the mug to the table. "I only pick up feelings from people. I've never been psychic."

"Then how did you know about the knife? And about Ron and Deborah?"

"I found the knife by accident and imagined everything else." She wrapped her chilled hands around the mug for warmth. "You know how I'm always imagining things. None of it was real. The blood I imagined and found on the floor turned out to be paint."

"You also said the kitchen set was left over from when Mrs. Henson owned the house," Bill went on. "How did you know she had these gold chairs unless you're psychic? You were never inside this house back then."

She had said that, Abby realized, releasing her mug as its heat nearly burned her palms. "My Realtor must have mentioned it," she improvised, although the Realtor hadn't, and until today, she'd assumed the Stanfords had furnished everything.

Bill walked over and picked his suit coat off the chair, then slipped it on. "We're going for a drive now, Abby." He pulled a gun from his briefcase.

Her heart lodged in her throat. "What are you doing?" she choked out.

He raised the gun until it was aimed at Abby's head. "We'll take your car."

CHAPTER 29

The world had taken on a glaze of unreality, as if Abby were watching herself playing a scene she could never imagine occurring in real life. She couldn't fathom that what Bill was doing now was real or that what she'd just remembered was true. "Why do I have to go with you?" Her voice sounded unnaturally high and breathy.

"Because if you don't, I'll kill you here and make sure Maddie finds your body," he said. He pulled some driving gloves out of the briefcase and slipped them on, still managing to keep the gun aimed at her. "I'll tell Kim you asked me to bring Maddie home, that after your breakup with Josh, you wanted her with you but didn't want to face Kim. Then Maddie and I will come in here and discover you shot yourself. Even your lousy parents didn't burden you with a memory like that."

Abby's hands tightened around the mug again, her palms now too frozen and numb to feel the heat. "Why would you kill me? I don't understand any of this." Appearing agitated and confused was easy because that's exactly how she felt. This couldn't be happening.

Bill picked her car keys off the counter. "Head for the car, Abby, or I'll shoot you here. Your choice."

She couldn't risk having Maddie find her, even though she couldn't believe Bill would carry out that threat. But she couldn't believe Bill would hold a gun on her, either. She stood up, bracing her hands on the table to support her shaky body. Then she forced herself to walk to the back door, down the steps, and along the cracked sidewalk. Bill followed directly behind her, the gun occasionally brushing the back of her jacket.

"It's nice your Volvo has those tinted windows so no one will know it isn't you driving," Bill said once they were in the garage. He deactivated the car alarm and opened the passenger door, then pulled off his tie. "Give me your hands." He looped the tie through the leather door handle, then tied Abby's hands together in front of her.

"Sit down," Bill said. "Remember, if you try to escape or attract attention, I'll shoot you and make sure Maddie finds you."

Abby sat down on the leather seat, then Bill closed the door. The car's interior was warm, a blessing since she was freezing.

Bill got into the car and pushed the button to open the garage door. He shifted the gun to his left hand, still aiming it at her. "Remember how I'd never let you and Laura go anywhere without putting your seat belts on first?" he asked as he clicked his seat belt shut. "You both always complained that it wrinkled your clothes, but I wasn't about to let you endanger yourselves." He started the car, put it into reverse, then moved the gun back to his right hand. "Today I'll give you a pass."

— — —

Josh made it to Abby's in half the usual time, primarily because he'd sped there with his flashing lights on and made sure he hadn't hit any red lights. He'd been such an idiot. So he'd been hurt that Abby thought he was like Colin. What did he expect, even if she hadn't been suffering déjà vu? After years with her dad and Colin, of course she'd overreact to a scene like Heather had staged.

Then he'd overreacted, and he had no excuse other than the lousy one of hurt pride. He needed to apologize for that and do whatever it took to convince Abby to let him explain. Not because he was in love with her; Kim was wrong about that. He wasn't ready to risk falling in love with anyone, let alone a woman so far out of his league that getting dumped was a given. He did care about Abby, and seeing him with Heather had clearly hurt her, if only because it brought back memories of Colin. He didn't want her hurt. And to be honest, he'd like a little more time with her. He'd lose her eventually, but not over a stupid misunderstanding like this.

He pulled up to the curb in front of her house, exited as quickly as possible from a car that wasn't a convertible, and sprinted to the front door. He hit the doorbell twice. No answer. She was probably ignoring him, but he wasn't leaving. He pounded on the door with one hand while ringing the bell with the other. Still no answer, even after a full minute of that annoying behavior.

Too bad he'd made her get good locks and a security system, or he'd break in. But he could look in the windows. God willing no one would see him—as the police chief, being arrested as a Peeping Tom would be more than a little embarrassing.

After he'd checked all the first-floor windows, he headed for the garage. The window was so filthy he couldn't see inside, but the side door was unlocked. He opened it.

Abby's Volvo was gone. Maybe she was at Laura's. He pulled out his phone.

– – –

Abby stared straight ahead, shock and terror paralyzing her. To actually remember witnessing the man she loved like a father killing someone was overwhelming. To realize he now must intend to kill her—her brain couldn't take that in.

It was true, though, all of it, and she needed to deal with it. She couldn't see any way to escape. She'd never be able to untie herself—Bill was an expert when it came to knots, as he'd demonstrated on several much more pleasant occasions. She had enough slack to reach the lock release and metal door handle so she could open her door, but then what? She'd still be attached to the door. A passerby might notice, but Bill also might notice first and shoot her before she got the door open.

Her best hope—her only hope—of getting out of this alive was convincing Bill he didn't want or need to kill her. She could do that—she'd won nine daytime Emmys, for God's sake. Of course, she'd always had scriptwriters, but she was an aspiring writer herself. More important, she knew Bill.

"When you decided to move back to Harrington with Maddie, I was thrilled," Bill said. "Until you told me you wanted to buy that house. I tried so hard to convince you not to. I didn't want you living where something so horrible had happened, even if you didn't know about it. I didn't want to relive it whenever I visited you. I still do, every time I can't avoid driving by the damn place."

"Bill, I don't know what you're talking about. Whatever you think I know, you're wrong." Abby had to over-enunciate to form intelligible words with her icy lips.

Bill continued as if she hadn't spoken. "It was bad enough having you living there, but then you found that knife. I didn't even know it was in the house. How did you find it, Abby?"

"The door came out, and I found it by accident. I didn't dream at all until after I found the knife." Although she now realized she'd seen Ron Murphy stash it there and had probably subconsciously been looking for it when she'd yanked the door past its stop. Just like she'd felt compelled to buy the house because she subconsciously needed to remember what had happened there.

"Those blasted dreams of yours." Bill signaled a left turn.

"Where are we going?"

"You'll find out soon enough. I thought I'd be able to get you out of that house before you dreamed everything. Now that I know you'll never go back to Colin, I also know you'll stay in that house and keep dreaming until you see me killing Deborah. You've already dreamed most of it, even the kitchen where I got the knife. It's just a matter of time."

Abby could counter being psychic much easier than the truth, that she'd been a witness. "I've never been psychic in my life. Why would I believe anything bad I dreamed about you, let alone mention something that absurd to anyone?" She gave Bill an incredulous look. "Your family is my family. I wouldn't hurt any of you any more than I'd hurt Maddie. Especially not because of a dream."

"You'll worry the dream might be true and tell Josh about it, the same as you reported the knife." He sounded tired. "You're too ethical to let anyone get away with murder."

"I let Colin get away with screwing his TV daughter."

"That wasn't murder. It wasn't even illegal, other than adultery, and no one bothers to enforce those laws. This is different."

"Who'd believe me? Josh certainly won't. He was only looking into my dream to humor me, and he won't bother doing that anymore." She didn't even have to fake the slight quiver that made her last sentence convincing.

"You're wrong." Bill's posture was a little rigid, but otherwise he looked perfectly normal—except for the gun he held on her. "Josh is too good a cop to let this go without checking into it, regardless of your personal relationship. As long as he's just looking into Deborah, I'm safe. I was very careful. But if you give him a reason to look into me, he'll learn that when Deborah disappeared, I was the attorney for the Henson estate and the house was unoccupied. Maybe someone will even remember I bought the carpet in that bedroom. It was hideous, but all they had in stock, and I needed to cover the blood."

"There wasn't blood, just paint. Josh checked it."

"Even after I came back and cleaned up the blood myself, I could still see a shadow. So I dumped some paint I found in the basement on it before I put down the carpet," Bill said. "Josh might find a trace of blood if he takes a bigger sample. Hell, maybe someone saw Deborah coming out of that house or at the Holiday Inn when she came to Saint Paul a couple of times to visit during the legislative session. Things that appear harmless, unless you're looking at me as a possible suspect.

"Someone might even remember Deborah and I were both at O'Gara's that night I went there to meet Walt. Your dad wasn't there—I didn't even know he hung out there until Josh mentioned it. But Walt was late, and when I went to call him, I met Deborah. She'd just come out of the restroom and talked to me by the pay phone. I told her I was married, but she gave me her number anyway, and I couldn't resist calling her." He let out a breath so sharp Abby felt it scrape her cheek. "I wish to God I'd never set foot in that place."

"I promise I won't tell anyone," Abby said. Now that Bill had admitted everything, convincing him she wasn't psychic was a waste of time. "Why would I? I care a lot more about you than I do about some woman I never met."

"You might think that now," Bill said slowly. "But I can't risk that you'll have an attack of conscience and decide you can't keep this quiet. Not for myself, but for Mary, Laura, and my grandkids. I can't let them face the humiliation of having me convicted of murder."

"So you're going to kill me instead? You always said you loved me like a daughter." Abby's heart was hammering so hard the vibrations made her voice shake.

"I do. I'm so proud of you, Abby. Mary recorded your show every day so we could watch it together."

"Then how can you do this to me?"

"Because more members of my family will suffer if I let you live. I also have to think of Mary first. She's my wife, and she could never handle the strain. Her heart isn't good."

"You know Mary's strong enough to handle anything. And what about Maddie?" Abby's words came out in a shrill vibrato. "You love her, too. What's going to happen to her if I'm dead? You certainly can't want her to live with Colin now that you know the truth about him."

"Laura will raise Maddie like her own daughter, you know that." In contrast to Abby's agitation, Bill's voice was calm and reassuring. "Maddie will be fine. She's a terrific kid, as tough as you were at that age."

Her ace in the hole had been appealing to his love for her and Maddie, but it hadn't worked. Abby chewed her lower lip, trying to keep from breaking down. Bill had been driving along deserted streets, no car or person anywhere, even if Abby dared to try to attract attention. But she couldn't give up. As long as she was alive, she had a chance to convince Bill they could forget all this and go back to the way things were before today. He didn't want to kill her. She just needed to—

Her right hip buzzed. Abby bit her lip, tasting blood. Her phone. She'd forgotten she'd stuck it in her jacket pocket when she'd headed over to Josh's. If she could answer it, maybe she could telegraph to the caller that she was in trouble. It was probably Maddie, but she'd give it to Kim when she realized something weird was going on, wouldn't she? She wouldn't just hang up; she was a savvy kid.

The phone buzzed once more. The tie had enough slack that Abby could move her hand to her pocket, could get her index finger on the phone. She pushed and poked around, trying to unlock the phone and hit the answer button. When the phone stopped mid-buzz, she coughed to cover Maddie's voice as she jerked her finger back out of her pocket.

"Are you OK?" Bill asked.

"I swallowed wrong," she coughed out. "I'm really nervous."

Don't let me down, Maddie. Please don't let me down.

CHAPTER 30

"Hello? Abby?" Josh heard coughing in the background, then a man's voice. He must have called the wrong number. Which was a sign phoning Abby was a dumb idea—like Kim said, she'd just hang up on him. He moved his finger to the disconnect button.

"I swallowed wrong," he heard, then more coughing. "I'm really nervous."

He froze with his finger on the button. That sounded like Abby, but why hadn't she answered? Why was she nervous?

The woman cleared her throat a couple of times. "Where are we going, Bill?"

That was definitely Abby. Was she with Bill Tate? That made sense, but why would he be taking her somewhere that made her so nervous?

"Won't you please tell me? Since it will be the last place I'll ever see."

The last place she'd ever see? What the hell was going on?

– – –

"You always liked the anticipation almost as much as the event, didn't you, Abby?" Bill said. "I remember that time we—"

"Sorry, but I'm not in the mood to reminisce," Abby said. They were leaving Harrington city limits now, and she had to find out where they were going so Maddie would know where to send help. "Can't you tell me where I'm going to die?"

"I guess it won't hurt. We're going to Granddad's Bluff. You're going to have another encounter with your stalker, but this one will be fatal."

– – –

The blood drained from Josh's head and pooled in his stomach. For a moment, he stood paralyzed beside Abby's garage, then adrenaline kicked in. In a matter of seconds, he was sitting in his car and removing his loaded gun from the glove compartment. He caught the phone between his ear and shoulder so he could cover the mouthpiece with one hand as he started the car.

"Ron Murphy was my stalker, and he's dead," Abby said as Josh called the dispatcher. Granddad's Bluff was ten miles away— God willing, someone else was closer.

"He had the gun and lipstick, but he could have found those things anywhere," Bill said. "The police will realize they were wrong about Ron when they get a letter from the stalker describing how he killed you. Although this letter won't include a mouse."

Abby gave him a startled sideways glance. "How do you know about the mouse?" She hadn't mentioned it even to Laura.

"Because I sent it to you. I sent all the letters." Bill chuckled. "I've always been your biggest fan, you know."

"Why?" Under other circumstances learning Bill had sent the letters would have been shocking. All she could manage now was mild curiosity.

"I thought the letters might scare you back to California, but they didn't faze you," Bill said. "After Laura told me you'd found the knife, I knew I had to step up my campaign. I took your key from Laura's and made a copy, then had Ron Murphy write on your mirror while we were all at Brandon's birthday dinner."

– – –

Bill was behind those letters to Abby?

"Sorry, Chief. Mrs. Fletcher had a problem with her cats," the dispatcher finally said. "What do you need?"

"Have everyone available head for Granddad's Bluff, looking for a black Volvo with Minnesota plates. Send an ambulance, too. No sirens."

– – –

"I was desperate to get you out of that house before you dreamed what I'd done there," Bill went on. "That's also why I called Colin, hoping he'd convince you to move back to LA. But that didn't work, and I discovered you thought the stalker was only upset with Samantha. I had to let you know you were the problem."

He tapped the barrel of the gun on his thigh. "We've been having problems with mice, and I came up with the idea of sending you one. Knowing how much you hate mice, I honestly thought that package would scare you back to California. I'm very sorry it didn't." He shook his head. "I never wanted you hurt, just to leave town before you knew the truth. I even killed a man to protect you."

"You killed someone?" Abby asked. Her body felt numb, as if she were already dead as they sped along the deserted highway. The trees and bluffs she usually found so beautiful passed by in such a blur she couldn't distinguish rock from vegetation.

"Ron Murphy disposed of Deborah's body, which gave him an interest in keeping you from figuring out the truth. I also pay well. So he agreed to help scare you away."

"By shooting at my car?"

"Not by shooting at your car," Bill said vehemently, shaking his head. "He wrote the lipstick message. I told him you'd be at the Mall of America to see Olivia, and he should paint a message on your back door since I didn't have your new key. Instead he went to the mall, then followed you back from Minneapolis and shot out your tire. I told him to stop it, that I'd handle things after that. When I heard about the threatening phone call and that you'd found your garage unlocked, I got worried. I knew you wouldn't have forgotten to lock up. I called Ron, and he admitted he'd been spying on you and had also been in the garage planning to kill you until you noticed he'd forgotten to relock the door. Your neighbor who was on vacation works in the building Ron cleans and keeps an extra house key and his security system code in his unlocked desk. Ron used those to escape without anyone realizing he'd been waiting in your garage."

Bill glanced at her, grimacing. "Ron was talking crazy, said he'd read about how you'd cheated on your husband and that when he'd divorced you, you'd taken his daughter away from him. He said you had to die because you were just like his mother and otherwise would ruin your daughter's life, that God wanted him to save your daughter as penance for all the bad things he'd done.

"I didn't want you hurt, just gone. I pretended I agreed you should die and told Ron we should meet to discuss it. I brought some expensive Scotch along. He was already drunk when he showed up, and after a few belts of the good stuff, he passed out. I stuck him behind the wheel of his car, started the engine, and pushed him over the bluff. I killed Ron to protect you."

"And now you're going to kill me?"

Bill's sigh was a half groan. "Because I have to protect the rest of my family, especially Mary," he said. "That's why I killed Deborah in the first place. I should never have gotten involved with her, but Mary and I were having problems, and I made a mistake. After a few months, I realized how stupid I'd been and told Deborah I was breaking things off. She threatened to tell Mary. I panicked and killed her."

"Mary would have forgiven you," Abby said. "She loves you."

"I couldn't risk losing her. I was terrified she'd divorce me and take Laura, maybe move to Connecticut to be near her family.

"And to be honest, back then I also needed Mary's money," he continued, waving the gun. "I liked being a state senator, but it paid shit. We'd just finished a long special session, and because of it I couldn't take on enough legal work to cover my expenses. If Mary had left me, I'd probably have been bankrupt. I'd have lost everything, including my family and my position in Harrington. I couldn't let that bitch Deborah ruin my life and destroy my family. So I killed her."

– – –

Jesus.

Josh's speedometer was nearing a hundred, but the car seemed to be slogging underwater. He couldn't believe what he was hearing, that Bill intended to kill Abby because he was afraid she'd dream he'd killed Deborah Springer. And that he'd already killed Ron Murphy to protect Abby.

Maybe he should say something so Bill would realize he'd been overheard and let Abby go. Except having the cops on his tail could make Bill kill her immediately. Being a lawyer himself,

Bill would know that a good defense attorney could discredit testimony someone overheard on a cell phone while driving a hundred miles an hour much easier than a live witness.

"This is it, Abby," Bill said. "Appropriate place for your last scene, isn't it? Kind of like *Thelma and Louise*, although Granddad's Bluff isn't exactly the Grand Canyon."

Josh heard the car engine stop. He was still at least five miles away—hopefully someone else was closer.

"I've never been especially fond of that movie's ending," Abby said.

"At least I'm not drowning you like poor Samantha. Or sending you over Red Bluff like I did Ron." Bill's chuckle was brittle enough to snap. "I thought it was fitting he died at the same place as another bastard who attacked you did. Although I just talked to your dad to make him quit hitting you. I had nothing to do with his death."

"You're really going to do this? You're really going to kill me at Granddad's Bluff?"

Abby had sounded amazingly calm until now, but even she wasn't a good enough actress to hide her terror. She sounded close to hysterical.

Exactly how Josh was beginning to feel.

– – –

"First I'll shoot you, then I'll send your car over the bluff. Since I'm assuming you won't agree to drive full speed ahead like they did in the movie."

Abby looked at Bill, trying to keep her focus on his face, not on the gun. God, she hoped Maddie had given the phone to Kim by now, and not just because Kim would have called for help. She didn't want Maddie hearing this, especially if it ended badly.

She had to delay, to keep him talking in case help was on the way. "How are you going to get home without a car?"

"I'll walk back to my office and get my car." Bill gestured idly with the gun. "It's only about four miles, and I'm not in a hurry since no one's going to be looking for you." He shook his head. "You know, it's ironic how my cheating on Mary caused this whole mess, but Josh's cheating on you solved my problem. Maddie thinks you're with him, so no one's going to realize you're missing until tomorrow. Heather Casey will tell the world you walked in on them, and people might assume you were so upset that you drove off a cliff and killed yourself."

"Until they find the bullet."

"If your car explodes, they might not. Then I'll be able to let everyone keep on thinking Ron was your stalker. If I can't, I'll send Josh a letter with enough specifics that he'll be forced to conclude your stalker killed you. He'll feel damn guilty he was satisfied Ron Murphy was the stalker and didn't suspect you were still in danger." Bill's mouth twisted into a bitter smile. "He'll feel even worse when I ask if you were upset about anything, since you tend to get distracted when you're upset and that would have made it easier for the stalker to get you. Josh will know exactly what upset you."

"If Josh feels guilty, he'll be even more determined to find my killer."

"Josh will never find the stalker. I was very careful," Bill said. "He also won't have long to do it. I predict our police chief will soon be leaving town over his part in your death, either on his own or because Mary, Laura, and I will drive him out. Which serves him right for hurting you the way he did."

Bill was speaking like he was rational. But he wasn't. This man she'd viewed as a father planned to kill her. She couldn't talk him out of it, doubted she could keep him talking long enough for anyone to find her.

For Maddie's sake, she had to try. "You keep mentioning family," she said, the tears she'd held in check finally beginning to fall. "You've always considered me part of your family. How can you do this to me?"

"I've told you how much I regret it, Abby," Bill said.

"You're still going to kill me." Tears were streaming down her face, choking her.

"There's no other way," Bill said, sounding sadder than she'd ever heard him. He pushed the button to unlock the car doors. "I wish there was, but there isn't." He shifted the gun to his left hand, then reached over and easily unknotted his tie with his right hand, releasing her. "I can't leave this tie here, though I'll never be able to bear to wear it again."

"I won't tell anyone what you did. I promise I won't." Abby needed to stop sobbing. Her tears weren't changing Bill's mind, and crying was making it harder to think. But she couldn't stop. She was going to die, leaving Maddie without a mother, and Josh feeling guilty about her when she should have let him explain, should have trusted him the way he'd trusted her.

"You won't be able to keep this a secret. You're too blasted honest." His eyes were red and watery. "I'm sorry, Abby. I've always loved you like a daughter."

"Then you can't kill me. Bill, please don't do this. Please."

He paused. Abby held her breath as he studied her face for a moment.

He raised the gun. "It's over, honey. I'm very sorry."

She was no longer tied to the door handle. She should open the car door, get out, run. But trying to escape would be futile.

Bill was right. It was over, and the knowledge had her legs para-lyzed. She closed her eyes tightly and braced herself, clutching the leather door handle with both hands.

Let Maddie have a good life.

That was Abby's last thought before the gun exploded.

CHAPTER 31

"No!"

Josh had been screaming into the phone since it had become clear Bill was about to kill Abby, hoping he'd realize he'd been overheard. Either Bill hadn't heard him or didn't care, since his response was a shot that pierced Josh's heart and gut, the pain so excruciating he could barely breathe. He forced himself to ignore it, to blink away the tears stinging his eyes, to keep driving. "Tell the ambulance to put on its sirens and get there fast," he ordered the dispatcher. "Abby Langford's been shot."

"What's her condition?"

"I don't know. She's in bad shape." If she wasn't already dead, but he couldn't think that. She had to survive.

Josh raced along the blessedly empty highway, clutching the phone to his ear, hoping to hear a sound from Abby, a moan or whimper, anything evidencing she was still breathing. After a moment, he dropped the phone onto the passenger seat. He'd heard nothing, and he couldn't listen to that echoing silence anymore.

He'd also been hoping to hear a second shot when Bill realized what he'd done and ended his own life out of remorse, but no such luck. At this moment, the bastard was probably figuring out how to get Abby's car over the bluff. And it was all his fault. If he'd gone after Abby and made her listen, she'd have known the thing with Heather was a setup. If he'd gone after her, she wouldn't be with Bill.

It seemed hours until he spotted Abby's car parked on the side of the road. Josh pulled up beside it, his front bumper even with the Volvo's rear one, grabbed his gun, and jumped out of his car. He couldn't see Bill and hadn't heard the door slam, so he must still be inside the Volvo, hidden by that damn tinted glass. He hoped Bill was suffering like hell over what he'd done to Abby.

Josh circled behind his own car, then made his way to Abby's, shielded by the rear fender on the passenger side. "Get out of the car with your hands up," he shouted.

Nothing happened.

Josh pounded the fender. "I said get out of the car. Now."

Still nothing. He couldn't afford to sit here, waiting for Bill to come out. If Abby was alive, the faster someone got in and tried to stop the bleeding, the better.

Since Bill was presumably still in the driver's seat, going in through the back on the passenger side was his best bet. He could use the door to shield him, and he could get off a shot at Bill, if necessary. Not as good as if he opened the front door, but seeing Abby's motionless body, maybe having it fall on him, would distract him too much. God willing, the back door was unlocked.

Josh crept along the side of the Volvo, leading with his gun and trying to stay out of view from the outside mirror. Finger on the trigger, he yanked the back door open and lunged into the car, shoving a briefcase out of the way. "Drop your gun."

No one moved. Not the body slumped over the steering wheel. Not Abby, who was sitting upright in the passenger seat, clutching the door handle.

"Bill's dead," she said, her hoarse voice the sweetest sound Josh had ever heard. "He killed himself."

Josh got the passenger door open and Abby out of the car and into his arms. She didn't move and felt cold and stiff. Shock. But she hadn't been shot.

He carried her to his car and got into the backseat, situating her on his lap. "Abby. Jesus, Abby," he repeated as he stroked her back and rubbed her arms, trying to warm her.

After a few moments, she spoke again, her voice accompanied by the wail of an ambulance. "I thought he was going to kill me, but he didn't. He killed himself."

"I know."

"He killed Deborah Springer."

"He was afraid you'd dream he had, and I'd look into him. I heard you on the phone."

She sank against him. "Bill was right."

"You did dream about it?"

"Not dream. I was there when he killed her," she said. "I made myself forget, like with my parents. When I saw him in my kitchen tonight I remembered." Her voice ran out.

"You were there?"

She cleared her throat. "I passed that house every day on my way home from school. The day I got my first lead in a school play, I saw Bill's car parked out back. I was so excited to tell him about my part that I went into the house to find him. But he was there with Deborah, so I hid in the closet. I heard him kill her, then saw Ron Murphy take the body out of the house and stick the knife behind the pocket door. After Ron left, I ran out of the house and made myself forget everything. Until I found the knife and started to remember."

"Is Abby OK?" It was Ben, running to the car's open door.

"She's fine," Josh said. "Bill Tate shot himself, and I presume he's dead. He's in the driver's seat of the Volvo."

"That must be why I had the compulsion to buy my house." Abby's voice was barely above a whisper. "Not because owning it meant I was successful, but because I was ready to remember what Bill did, just like I'd already remembered about my parents." She covered her face with her hands, and her words turned to sobs. "Why did I buy it? Why did I even come back here? If I hadn't, everything would be OK." Tears escaped from beneath her fingertips.

Josh resumed rubbing her back. "It wasn't your fault. You didn't do anything wrong."

She rested her hands and face on his chest. "Bill wasn't a bad man." Her tears dampened Josh's shirt. "He made a mistake having an affair, then panicked and killed Deborah to protect his family. He still felt horrible about it. He killed Ron Murphy to protect me." Her voice was louder, but choked with tears and pain.

"You don't have to talk about it. I heard everything."

She lifted her head and looked at him, wiping her eyes with the back of her hand. Her face was red, mascara smeared, and heart-achingly beautiful. "Were you at Kim's? Is that how you got the phone?"

"I was the one who called your phone, to apologize. I swear Heather set the whole thing up. I'd never do something like that to you."

"I know. Every other man I've loved lied to me, so I panicked, thought I'd messed up again. Then I realized you're not my dad or Colin. I finally love someone who's worth it. I was afraid I'd die and never be able to tell you I believed you."

"Bill's definitely dead," Ben said. "Do you want to have the ambulance take Abby in?"

Josh shook his head. "If you'll supervise here, I'll drive her to the ER. She isn't physically hurt, but she's had quite a shock."

"What happened?"

"I'm not sure, and I don't think Abby's in any condition to tell us yet. I'll handle her. You handle the scene. Try to keep the press away until we release a statement."

"Will do."

"Do I have to tell what happened?" Abby asked after Ben had left.

"That's up to you. As far as I'm concerned, Bill's paid for his crime, and there's no reason for his family to suffer more than they already will."

"I have to tell Laura and Mary the truth." Abby swiped at her face with her hand as the tears started again. "I can't lie to them."

"That's up to you, too."

"I need to call them. But what can I tell them?"

Josh put his fingers under her chin and lifted it so her watery eyes met his. "You can tell them that even in the end, Bill's first concern was for his family. That he loved his family and did what he thought best for all of them. Including you."

CHAPTER 32

Abby looked out the window behind her computer monitor, watching as a police car pulled up to the curb and Josh got out. Presumably some unfinished police business, since he was still in uniform.

She hadn't been alone with him since she'd given her statement six days ago. A lifetime ago, it seemed.

She'd ended up telling Laura and Mary the truth, except about Bill having also killed Ron Murphy. The surprise was that Mary had strongly suspected Bill had had an affair back then, but she'd loved him enough to forgive him. She'd probably have even forgiven him for impulsively killing Deborah Springer. Killing himself was proving a lot harder for her to forgive.

With Josh's approval, the official story was that Bill had just been diagnosed with pancreatic cancer and given only a few months to live. He'd told Abby, then suggested they take a walk along Granddad's Bluff to discuss how to break the news to Laura and Mary. However, the instant Abby got out of the car, Bill shot himself. Since he normally didn't carry a gun, he'd presumably intended to commit suicide all along and had wanted Abby to explain to his family, instead of simply leaving them a note.

With news still in the summer slows, the tabloid press had descended in droves on the assumption Bill had killed himself because of an affair with Abby or something similarly slimy.

However, Colin, as well as everyone in Harrington, had confirmed Bill's feelings for Abby were strictly paternal. More important, Mary, with one of her family's Wall Street lawyers by her side, had informed the press that anyone tarnishing the memory of her beloved husband and slandering Abby—who she loved like a daughter—would be sued. Mary's millions backing up her threat, plus an inability to find anything remotely scandalous, had convinced the press to leave.

The funeral had been three days ago. Mary had insisted that Abby and Maddie sit with the family. The following morning, Bill's lawyer had informed Abby that Bill had set up a trust for Maddie's education—just as he'd done for Laura's kids—and Abby had completely lost it. He really had considered her a daughter, as if killing himself instead of her hadn't already established that.

Josh had suggested they not see each other for several days, both to give her time with Bill's family and to avoid speculation about her relationship with the chief of police and a possible cover-up. Although since he hadn't called, either, Abby had a feeling neither of those was his primary reason. She was afraid what was really keeping him away was her declaration of love. Being the decent, considerate guy he was, Josh no doubt didn't want to hurt her by reiterating that he didn't want anything serious when she was already so upset. He probably hoped that if he avoided her for a while she wouldn't bring it up again.

Which she wouldn't. The words had slipped out, but now that she was thinking straight, she wouldn't put him on the spot again. Not that it mattered anyway, not after what she'd decided.

She opened the door. She couldn't believe it had been less than three weeks since the first time she'd seen Josh standing there, responding to her call about the knife.

"Do I have to sign something else?" she asked. "Or has someone asked potentially awkward questions?"

"Neither. I took the afternoon off." A corner of his mouth quirked. "I was planning to go home, but somehow ended up here. Can I come in?"

She moved aside, and he stepped through the door. In the past six days she'd forced herself to forget how good he looked, how much she liked being with him. How much she loved him. This was going to be harder than she'd thought. But she had no choice. She had to do what was best for her family.

"Let's go into the living room," she said. "Can I get you something to drink?"

"Nothing, thanks. How's the writing going?"

"I'm having a few problems concentrating." She sat down on the couch. "How's your work?"

"Too much paperwork, as usual." Josh had followed her but stayed standing, resting one hand on the back of the couch. "Were you in the middle of something? If so, I can leave…"

"Maddie's at the pool with Rachel, and I wasn't doing a thing besides staring at a blank computer monitor."

"Are you sure?"

"I'm sure. Sit down. I want to tell you something." Abby's fingers were playing nervous arpeggios on her thighs. She forced herself to still them as Josh sat down beside her, then took a deep breath, let it out. "I'm moving."

"To another house?"

"Another city. Laura and Mary have been wonderful. As I told you, even knowing the truth, they don't blame me."

"It wasn't your fault."

Abby stared out the picture window onto a glistening summer day. "I blame myself, at least a little, and I'm clearly the reason

Bill killed himself. That makes it hard for all of us. We need some time and distance." A woman ran by, pushing an infant in a Baby Jogger. Her life had been so much easier when Maddie was that age.

"Where will you go?" Josh asked in a conversational tone. He hadn't seemed surprised, let alone upset, by her announcement.

"I haven't figured that part out yet. Somewhere I can do some acting in addition to writing. I really need that escape mechanism." She met his eyes, her lips twisting with pain as she fought the ever-present urge to cry. "Since I can't seem to block out the last week."

"I think that's a good idea."

"You do?" Even though he didn't love her, she'd hoped he'd at least be a little sorry to see her go.

"Absolutely. Not only because you need it, but because you're a hell of an actress. Are you going back to your soap?"

"Not now. I considered it, and Maddie would love to be back with her friends, but for a lot of reasons California and *Private Affairs* trigger too many memories of the Tates. I need somewhere completely different." Her fingers had resumed moving, so she laced them together on her lap. "*Private Affairs* also takes time and energy I'd rather spend on Maddie right now, and I'd still like to write. I was thinking of shorter-term commitments, local theater, maybe guesting on a few TV shows." She tilted her head. "I'm lucky I don't need the money, but I do need to live in a bigger city."

"You're doing the right thing. It's a crime to waste talent like yours."

"Thanks." She felt as if she were talking to a fan. Maybe she should offer him an autographed head shot to remember her by.

"I also think you're right about needing time away from Mary and Laura. But time heals, and close as you all are, I'll bet it heals fast. Have you told Maddie you're leaving?"

Abby nodded. "Even though she doesn't know all the facts, she understands I have to go somewhere that doesn't remind me of Bill. She'll miss Rachel and a few other friends, but she'll be OK. She's a great kid."

"She's the best. When are you moving?"

"As soon as I figure out where to go." She wanted to research her short list of cities thoroughly before she made a decision. "I'll let you know."

"I'd appreciate it," he said.

God, her instincts about men really had gone to hell. Josh didn't care in the least that she was leaving. All he needed to do now to guarantee this would forever remain the undisputed worst week of her life was to tell her Heather really was pregnant, they were getting married, and he'd only pretended she'd walked in on a staged scene because she was so upset by Bill's suicide. Abby got to her feet. "You know, I should spend a few hours writing this afternoon. It's a discipline thing, writing even when I don't want to. Sorry."

"I understand." He didn't stand up.

"So if you don't need anything else..." She stared at him pointedly.

He remained seated. Had he come over here to break things off, but since she'd mentioned moving was waiting for her to broach the topic? She wasn't leaving for at least a couple of weeks, hadn't even picked a place. If he wanted things to end sooner rather than later, damn it, he was going to have to be the one to do it.

He still didn't say anything, and she wasn't in the mood for a stare down. He could let himself out. She turned and headed across the room.

She'd reached the base of the staircase when he spoke. "What do you think of Chicago?"

She stopped and turned toward him. "Chicago?"

He was still seated, still looking nonchalant. "Big city but midwestern mind-set. Lousy winters, but a great place for kids to grow up, as Kim and I will confirm."

She took two steps toward him, trying to read his face. She couldn't pick up even a punctuation mark. "I've always liked Chicago," she said. "Good theater. I'll certainly consider it."

"Good air connections to everywhere. And Rachel's grand-parents, a couple of uncles and aunts, and a bunch of cousins live there, so she visits a lot."

Abby managed to conceal her disappointment. She'd hoped he'd wanted her in Chicago because then he could see her when he visited his family. But clearly Maddie and Rachel were his priorities, and how could she resent that? One of the things she loved about him was his concern for kids. "Maddie would love to be able to see Rachel."

"I'll bet Rachel would visit even more often if her favorite uncle Josh lived there."

Abby started, her eyes widening. "Are you considering moving back to Chicago?"

He shrugged. "I miss my old job. I moved away to get my head on straight, and I've done it. Although I doubt I'd have any problem getting a job in another city." He smiled faintly. "You probably couldn't tell, but I'm usually almost as good at my job as you are at yours."

"I believe it. I think that's a good plan for you. You're wasting your talents here, too."

"Thanks." He paused, his fingers tightening on the arm of the couch, the first indication he wasn't as nonchalant as he seemed. "I've even been thinking about getting married again."

"Really." Abby's heartbeat accelerated.

"I guess once you've been married, it's easier to contemplate doing it again. If you find the right woman, that is, but I think you know that a lot faster the second time, too." He was gripping the couch arm so tightly his knuckles were white. "What about you? Would you ever consider another marriage?"

Abby was having trouble breathing. She walked over so she was standing right in front of Josh, her eyes glued to his. "I liked being married, at least until Colin started cheating. And for some reason, my biological clock has started ticking again."

Josh released the couch arm and took her hand, his fingers warm around hers. "Getting you and Maddie would be more than enough for any man, even if you don't want more kids." His gaze never flickered, his eyes confirming he meant every word.

Which only made her love him more. "Actually, I always wanted two kids, maybe three," she said. "Colin didn't, and after a few years, I didn't want to have them with him. But I'm not that old compared to a lot of new moms. Maddie would love a baby brother or sister, and if I happened to fall in love with a guy who'd make a terrific father…"

His smile made her heart stop. He pulled her down on his lap, wrapping his arms around her. "Although a guy could never just come out and ask a woman like you to marry him without first setting the scene. Roses, a romantic dinner, champagne, that sort of thing."

"I don't need that sort of thing."

"You deserve that sort of thing, and not the champagne you bought that awful day."

"I threw it out."

"Good."

She stroked his hair. "You know another thing that might be a good idea? Besides the dinner and champagne and roses?"

"A ring." He waved his hand. "I know. But that will take a little longer."

She shook her head. "I only want a plain gold band. I had a gorgeous diamond last time, but a lousy marriage. I think once you've been divorced, you get superstitious."

Josh wrinkled his forehead, pressing it against hers. "So if it isn't the ring, what have I forgotten?"

"Now I've spent a lot of time in the soap opera world, so maybe my mind-set's a little warped," she said. "But it usually seems important for the man to tell the woman he loves her at least once before he proposes."

Josh lifted his forehead from hers and chuckled. "I thought that was a given. We're talking a small-town police chief's salary here. You think I'd spring for roses, champagne, and dinner for just anyone?"

"I love you, too, Josh." She leaned toward him, but before she could kiss him, he stood up, depositing her onto the couch.

"I'd better get going."

She grabbed his arm and tried to pull him back down. "Don't go. I've changed my mind. Writing definitely isn't what I'm in the mood for."

"I'll be back. I stopped by because I couldn't wait another minute to see you, but suddenly I've got other priorities. Like locating a restaurant that serves decent champagne and has an open reservation for dinner tonight. And buying out Johnson Floral's entire stock of roses."

She got to her feet and kissed him, a kiss he returned with both passion and a reverence that made her realize that despite the last week, she was one of the luckiest women alive.

When Josh withdrew his lips from hers, he was breathing hard. "Hell, would just roses and champagne work? No dinner?"

"How about if we skip the champagne and roses, too?" She moved her lips to his ear. "I called a friend at *Private Affairs* last week. She sent me Samantha's black underwear."

ABOUT THE AUTHOR

Photograph by Steve Rouch, 2008

When she was eight, Diana Miller decided she wanted to be Nancy Drew. But no matter how many garbage cans she dug through, conversations she "accidentally" overheard, and attics she searched, she never found a single cryptic letter, hidden staircase, or anything else even remotely mysterious. She worked as a lawyer, a soda jerk, a stay-at-home mom, a hospital admitting clerk, and a conference host before deciding that the best way to inject suspense into her otherwise satisfying life was by writing about it.

Diana is a five-time nominee for the Romance Writers of America Golden Heart Award and winner of a Golden Heart for *Dangerous Affairs*—a romantic suspense novel that shows not everyone in her home state is Minnesota Nice. She lives in the Twin Cities with her family.